THUNDER MOUNTAIN

BY
UNCLE RIVER

for Betty and Howard,
who did so much to
enable me to believe
the life by which to
do the creative work
can be legitimate.
with greatest love
and appreciation,

Stephen Kaufman
Uncle River

April 24, 1996
Blue River, Arizona

Mother Bird Books
PO Box 2766
Silver City N.M.
88062

Cover Design By Paul Malécot

Library of Congress # 95-082041

ISBN # 1-883821-10-X

CHAPTER ONE

"You a cowboy?"

Harry Upton looked up at the sound of the booming voice. "Uh, no," he said to the ample belly in front of him.

"Then why you wearin' that hat?"

Above the belly was a large chest, covered by a blue checked flannel shirt. Harry's eyes continued upward to a bushy grey beard, topped by a pair of mean little pig eyes.

The big man laughed. The eyes stopped looking mean. Harry wondered why on Earth he had been so frightened. "Gotta hold my head on somehow, ya old fart."

"Watch your tongue, Boy." The eyes sent another lightning flash of panic through Harry's midsection. Then the older man laughed again and stuck out his right hand. "Howdy, Boy. I'm Chuck Randell."

Harry shook the hand. "I'm Harry Upton. Pleased to meet you, Mr. Randell."

"You sure about that? Looked like you was gettin' ready to shit your pants."

Harry was not sure what to reply, but his disconcerting new acquaintance saved him having to think of anything by continuing.

"My friends call me Chuck. – And everyone else gets the hell out of my way if they've got any smarts. What are you doin' in Elk Stuck?"

The eyes narrowed for just an instant, then waited cool and neutral.

"I came up here because it's cool." Chuck grunted. "And to find out where the name came from."

"Came from a Hebe."

"You mean you know?"

"Course I know. What's it worth to you?"

Harry was nonplussed once again. His mouth went up and down, but all that came out was a sound sort of like: "Aah; buh."

"You don't need to recite the alphabet to me. I'm no school-teacher. Now why don't you just wag your ass down to the house. We'll have us a cup of coffee. And, if I don't decide to wring your scrawny neck, maybe I'll tell you what you want to know – and see if Louella's got any more pancake batter before you die of starvation right in the middle of the street."

Harry did not think of himself as skinny. He thought of himself as slim and sexy. Numerous young women had confirmed his opinion. Coffee and pancakes certainly did not sound like a bad idea though. – Nor did a chance to learn how Elk Stuck got its name.

Louella Randell was built on the same scale as her husband: Big. Big hands. Big bosom. Big voice. And a lot of greying hair piled up out of the way on top of her head. "You been out intimidatin' the tourists again?" she hollered.

"Tourists, my ass. I got you some bait for the mousetrap."

Harry had the most peculiar sensation that this was not altogether a joke. However, when he looked up, he saw that though Chuck Randell was looking at him a bit pointedly, he was also chuckling.

Louella introduced herself to Harry, noisily, and invited him in. Then she turned to her husband again. "Just don't be scarin' off money."

Harry did not want to be caught between these two in a domestic dispute. A quick glance convinced him there was nothing serious amiss. Just ornery on general principle, he concluded.

Louella did have some pancake batter. She also had real butter, a big jar of homemade elderberry jam, bacon, and excellent coffee.

"You ain't workin' for LemTron, are you?"

"Who?" Harry's fork froze in mid-air as he looked up at Chuck's coffee mug.

Chuck drank, then set the mug down. "That's the right answer. Now how did you get here?"

"Hitched. Got a ride up the hill with a Forest Circus clown."

Chuck and Louella both laughed. "And why'd you come?"

"Like I said, I heard it was cool."

"Who from?"

Harry considered briefly, then decided to tell the truth. "A guy I met in jail."

"What were you in jail for?" This was Louella.

"Stealing from the government on my last job."

"Stealing what?"

"Tools mostly. A little plumbing."

Chuck grunted. "Where?"

"Alamogordo."

"How long were you in the poky?"

"Ninety-six days."

"Pretty warm down there this time of year."

"Hotter'n hell."

"So who was this guy told you about Elk Stuck?" Chuck began filling a curved-stem pipe with tobacco. "I got papers if you want to roll one."

"No thanks. I'm saving my lungs for pot. An etymologist."

Chuck roared with laughter. Louella did the same. "Ballsy little shit. What's an entomog...Whatever the hell it was?"

"Guy that studies words."

"What was he doing in jail?"

"Busted for selling four ounces of cocaine to a cop in a bar."

"Whooee." Harry suspected Louella would use that sound to call a severely hard-of-hearing hog. "Bet they'll put him away for a long time."

"Naw. What he gave the cop was just a bag of soy flour. They had to let him go."

Chuck lit his pipe and pondered briefly. "So what'd he tell you about Elk Stuck?"

"Said it had the southernmost post office in the United States located at over eight thousand feet. And said..."

"Well?"

Those eyes again! Harry felt like a fly looking at the wrong end of a fly swatter.

"Said he'd pay me fifty bucks if I could find out how Elk Stuck got its name," said Harry in a tiny voice.

Chuck grinned. "Don't worry. I ain't gonna squeeze you for the fifty. Though I may or may not decide to tell you."

"If he won't I will." Louella was draining the bacon grease into an empty jalapeño can.

"I *might* offer you a job....Course, I catch anyone stealin' *my* tools, I just hang 'im."

Harry still held the same forkfull of pancake.

"Eat your breakfast, Boy. It's on the house, and it's gettin' cold. You'll insult Louella."

"After living with you? Not likely."

"See what I have to put up with?"

Harry looked at each of them a little dubiously. They were both smiling, so he grinned too. "Don't worry," Harry said. "You're not the government."

"We got us a philosopher, Louella."

Louella chortled.

"What did you have in mind?"

"Mostly a water line. I want it underground before fall so we can have indoor plumbing this winter."

"I told him twenty-two years of hauling water on the ice was long enough."

"She thought twelve years was long enough too, but I like to take my time with big decisions."

"You like to shoot the shit, insult everybody's ancestors, and do as little work as you can get away with."

"And that is why I am in perfect health at the advanced age of fifty-three."

Harry finished his pancakes and another cup of coffee while Chuck smoked and Louella cleaned up the kitchen. Then Chuck took Harry out and showed him around.

"I'm not real ambitious. Probably won't work you over eighty hours a week."

Harry blanched.

"No, make that more like two hours a week. Hell, I don't know. I don't carry no watch. I do need a hand with the water line though. You can sleep in the shed. And Louella'll do what she can to put a little meat on your bones. You got any stuff?"

"Sure. I stashed my pack under a tree to look around."

"Well, let's go git it. Then I'll give you the deluxe guided tour of Elk Stuck. Stay a week, I imagine we can spring for twenty bucks."

Harry had the distinct impression that what Chuck Randell wanted far more than help on the water line was just someone to talk to. He had certainly seen worse deals in his twenty-five years.

They got Harry's pack, but they did not get very far on the guided tour. They also did not get much done on the water line, though they did look at the places Chuck had in mind to put it and find a pick, a pulaski, two spades with handles (plus four without) and a heavy pry bar.

3

"Set the pump and casing eight years ago. Before that we used a bucket on a rope."

Harry looked into the well: old, hand-dug, lined with logs of all things. The water appeared to be twelve or fifteen feet down. In the middle was a ten inch steel pipe with the water line and the wire to a submersible pump inside that.

"I figure four feet down should do the trick, 'specially seein' as I plan to let it drain clear when the pump shuts off. Then we got the tank to build." Chuck pointed what looked to Harry about a quarter of a mile up the hill behind the house. Elk Stuck lay in a canyon, bluffs steep on both sides.

"Build?"

"You bet. Concrete. Set in the ground. Five hundred gallon capacity. Gravity feed to the house. And the garden. No point having two systems."

Harry looked where Chuck waved his hand. He saw a tank made of two fifty-five gallon drums welded together and black plastic water line that ran up from the well and back down to a T. From the T, one side went to the house; the other connected to a garden hose which, in turn, led to a series of drip hoses. As Harry watched, Louella came out and stuck her finger in the ground. Then she unscrewed the hose from where it was watering the second planting of lettuce and mustard and moved it to a row of winter squash and pumpkins, just starting to vine.

"You don't plan to do all that in one week?"

"Shit, no. Just before snow flies so Louella don't run off to San Antonio or someplace on me. You can stay on too, if we get along."

"Oh. Uh, how do you plan on getting the concrete up the hill?"

"I don't. I plan to run a hose up there and mix it on the spot."

Harry looked up the hill again.

"Come on," said Chuck.

Chuck started up the side of the bluff at a pace that soon had Harry huffing and puffing. When they got to the water tank site, he stopped only long enough to refill his pipe and light it, while Harry caught his breath.

"When'd you say you got out of jail?"

"Day before yesterday."

"How'd you keep your tan?"

"They let me out to work."

"Doing what?"

"Feeding a cement mixer."

Chuck thought that was hilariously funny. After a moment of anger, Harry found himself laughing too.

"They were building a dog pound."

Chuck laughed so hard the tears were rolling down his broad cheeks. "A doggy jail!" He bellowed some more, then sobered. "How's your back?"

"Fine."

"Young. That's how it is. Don't use it up. You only get one. You might as well stay long enough to get used to the altitude. Then I'll take you up on Thunder Peak and show you a view."

4

Just then, Louella came out again. "You boys preparin' to die of overwork? Or is starvation going to carry you off first?"

"That means it's lunch time."

Harry had already eaten as much for breakfast as he often ate in a whole day. "But..."

"Now you wouldn't want to insult Louella."

Harry followed Chuck, who fairly danced down the rocky slope despite his build, back to the house. Louella greeted them at the door.

"Coffee or beer?"

"Shit, he's only been out of jail two days. Give 'im a beer. And I'll have one too."

"Or three if I know you."

"Don't ever marry a lippy woman, Harry."

"Unless you need one that can carry you home when you pass out at forty below."

Lunch was tunafish salad, garden salad with homemade Russian dressing or store-bought thousand island, and homemade oatmeal cookies with raisins. After lunch, Chuck went in the bedroom and lay down. Harry offered to help Louella clean up, but she shooed him away. So he found a *National Geographic*. When Louella was done, she went in the bedroom too. After a while, Harry began hearing noises which, if he had not known better, he would have bet money were two bears making love. He quietly took the *National Geographic* outside, read a while, and then went to check out the shed he had been in so far only long enough to set his pack down there.

CHAPTER TWO

"Shit, Boy. Why are you workin' so hard?"

A little over a week later, Harry was swinging a pick with all his strength in the morning sunshine. "Gotta stay in shape for sex." He grinned up at Chuck.

"Ah, youth!"

"And you're not paying me enough to buy bigger pants. I gotta burn off all that wonderful food somehow."

Harry was used to the roar by now, the usual sign that Chuck found something funny. "You gotta tell Louella that. She'll love you forever."

Harry climbed out of the trench, picked up the faded turquoise T shirt he had earlier tossed on a rock, and wiped the sweat off his face. The T shirt had a picture of a bear and an arrow and read: "Turquoise Trail Treasures." It was eleven o'clock on a Friday morning and getting pretty warm, but clouds were already starting to build over Thunder Peak.

Weather classic for mid-July in the Southwest, every morning was brilliantly sunny. Most days thunderheads built up by mid-afternoon. There had been several spectacular storms and two rainbows. Once it rained at night. Other than that, it usually cleared in time for a sunset.

"You got a letter." Chuck handed it to Harry.

"From my old boss," Harry said as he slit it open with a twig.

"He gonna try to get you to pay back on your loot?"

"Not likely. He's the one tipped me off the company was gettin' ready to belly up and to get what I could while I had the chance."

Harry looked briefly at the letter, then laughed.

"What's up?"

"He says, 'Cover your ass better the next time, you dumb shit.'"

"Now there's a true patriot."

"He also wants to know if he should send my stuff."

"Up to you. Far as me and Louella's concerned, you're welcome. But twenty a week is all we can spare."

"I was wondering about that, Chuck. Maybe it's none of my business. But that tourist trap of yours can't be making enough to support you and Louella – let alone me."

The Randells had a trinket, shlock Western art, and snack shop across the road from their house. Friday afternoon through Sunday they took turns running the store. The rest of the week, a neighbor, Meridell Devore, tended the customers while working on her weaving – an attraction in itself, for a percentage of the till.

Meridell's work was by far the best-quality item in the store. Harry thought it was beautiful and had already spent several hours watching Meridell at her loom. Of course, Harry thought Meridell was beautiful too, even if she was thirty-one and had two kids.

It had taken Harry all of seven minutes to find out that Meridell was, indeed, happily divorced and unattached. He still could not tell, though, if she found him attractive. He was beginning to wonder if he was losing his touch.

"It isn't any of your business. But I'll tell you anyhow. I got lucky fourteen years back."

"Won the sweepstakes?"

"No. I got hurt when the transmission froze on a government dump truck I was driving on a road project at the army base by El Paso. I could hardly walk for two years. They gave me a hundred percent disability."

"Not a bad deal."

"No, it's not. But you don't see me humping sacks of cement up the hill either."

"And I thought you were just lazy."

"Boy, you sure do like to live dangerously."

Harry grinned.

Chuck looked at the trench where Harry had been digging by the well. "That's gettin' close. Looks like we might could drill through in the morning."

"Long as I don't hit any more boulders."

Harry was already used to Chuck's version of the work ethic and approved completely. Harry believed a little hard work was a lot better way to keep in shape than pushups. More than three or four hours a day, he considered a bore. Chuck considered even that much a lot. Harry had plenty of time to watch both the thunderheads and Meridell, as well as bullshitting with Chuck and Louella.

"We get the line set, maybe we'll go down the hill and celebrate. Hank's Longhorns'r playin'. They're pretty good even if they are Texans."

The Randells' Elk Stuck Emporium and the post office were the only two public establishments in Elk Stuck, New Mexico. The nearest town was Lariat, fourteen miles away — and most of a mile lower. A nice place in winter. At this time of year, it was fit for human habitation only at night.

Lariat had an overpriced gas station and general store — with another post office inside — and two bars. The State Line had a cafe. The Chiricahua had a dance floor. It also had a big sign over the door that read: "Closest place to celebrate Geronimo's surrender."

Some Indians had picketed once, protesting the sign. Snakeye Swisher, the proprietor, invited them in for drinks on the house. They agreed to quit as soon as the reporters left. Snakeye got his picture in three newspapers and eighteen seconds on the tube out of Tucson. He figured that picket line netted him at least three thousand dollars, and he didn't even have to pay for advertising. The sign stayed right where it was.

The Thunder Range, mostly in New Mexico, extended across the state line to Arizona on the west and south just past the border into Mexico. Apex, the Coyote County seat, was about three times the size of Lariat. For any serious shopping, people in Elk Stuck or Lariat drove to Lordsburg in the next county or to Douglas, Arizona.

Chuck measured the depth of the trench where Harry had dug it up to the edge of the well. Then he measured down the water line inside the well. The water line now came out over the top to an L that rested on two logs, drooped to the ground, then rose to the tank up on the hillside. Even in summer this surface system was not the greatest as the sun eventually caused the black plastic pipe to go brittle and crack. In freezing weather it was unuseable. The Randells would disconnect the water line four feet from the well, where it would drain back down the hole when the pump was shut off. Every couple days they had to hook up a hose they kept indoors where it wouldn't freeze to fill the little tank in the house. In nasty weather, they washed in an old fashioned galvanized tub on a tarp by the stove.

They also had a solar shower which, with New Mexico's bright sunshine, they could use most of the year. They'd set a flat gas tank connected to the water line and a shower head in the sun above a nauseous blue tarp strung up for a curtain over a wooden pallet behind the house. The gas tank had come out of a '59 Ford pickup, one of several dead vehicles in the yard.

Chuck headed across the street to see how things were going at the store. Harry finished cleaning out the rocks and clayey dirt that he had been loosening from the trench. By then Louella was hollering to him to get ready for lunch.

Since he did not expect to do any more work that day, Harry took a shower and put on a different pair of pants that were not all sweaty. The thunderheads had not overtaken the sun yet, so he did not put on a shirt at all. Besides, he wanted to ask Meridell if she liked to dance when he got Chuck for lunch. Harry figured if a man looks good to a woman a shirt will not improve him.

Meridell was not a bit like the Randells. She was slender and graceful, with hazel eyes and rich, wavy light brown hair that she kept styled and trimmed at shoulder length. Meridell had a good figure and a ready smile. She was also quiet, though Harry figured she must be pretty tough to raise two kids on her own as far out in the tulies as Elk Stuck. Harry thought Meridell was very beautiful.

Meridell thought Harry was pretty good-looking too. She kind of liked his manner, alternately brash and puppy-dog timid. His strutting around the store seemed ridiculous to her, but she was too kind to tell him so since he clearly intended it as a compliment. She told Harry she loved to dance – and invited him for dinner Sunday besides. She mostly left the store to Chuck and Louella weekends when they did their biggest business and there were too many interruptions from customers for her to get any weaving done.

"You better watch out," said Chuck. "She eats like a bird, and Chink food at that."

"I guess you don't want any more of my ginger chicken."

"I take it back! I take it back!"

"I don't know now. I think I'm going to be offended."

"I'll buy you a beer at the Chi tomorrow night."

"And give me a ride?"

"Hell, I always give you a ride."

"You always buy me a beer too." Meridell smiled radiantly.

Chuck looked amazed. "I do? Then I'll buy you two."

"You get me sloshed who'll drive you back up?"

"I thought Louella was the one gettin' me home."

"But you don't know, do you?" Meridell grinned. It was the first time Harry had seen Chuck at a loss for words. "Why don't you plan to come early Sunday, Harry, if you're not too hung over. I'll invite some other folks too and have a pot luck. We can play some volleyball if it doesn't rain."

"Okay."

Harry was a little disappointed not to get to be alone with Meridell, though there was not much chance of that at her house anyhow. Suzie was twelve. Jeff was eleven. Neither of them was shy, and they were used to spending a lot of time with grown-ups for lack of other kids their own age. Anyhow, Harry did want to meet more of the residents of Elk Stuck. There were fourteen of them, fifteen counting Harry. If Meridell threw a pot luck, most would probably be there, except Isaiah and Gertrude Overman who did not speak to Chuck and Louella, and old Burl Trent who did not speak to anyone if he could help it. For volleyball they might need to import some people from Lariat.

"We can head down the hill soon as the store closes tomorrow if Suzie'll put up the chickens."

"Sounds just fine to me. How about you, Harry?"

Meridell's eyes could have as powerful an effect on Harry as Chuck's, but the substance of the effect was quite different. Harry felt like his legs were made of butter. Warm butter. "Sure," he grinned.

Meridell suddenly stepped over and gave him a little peck on the cheek, then stepped back too quickly for Harry to respond. "See you then if not before."

Chuck herded the thoroughly bemused Harry out of the store and back to the house where Louella had yet another enormous meal ready. That afternoon Chuck helped Harry find some boards for shelves. Then Louella showed him where he could put the accumulated miscellany that had been stored in the shed.

The shed was about eight by twelve. There was a light fixture with a bare seventy-five watt bulb on one wall and a wooden table and chair sort of under it. Harry had been sleeping on a foam pad on the floor. Once they got things cleared out, he moved this to the loft. There was even a window up there for ventilation, as well as one off-center over the table and one in the middle of the wall opposite the door.

"We can put in a stove too." Louella pointed to the fourth wall, where a foil pie plate was tacked over a stovepipe hole. "It can be chilly sometimes when there's a lot of rain."

"You got a spare?"

"We've got three spares – and the best heater of the lot the least likely to make us any money 'cause it's ugly."

It was also heavy. Chuck was strong as a horse and had better wind than Harry, age, belly, and pipe notwithstanding, but his back really was touchy. Harry manhandled the stove onto the homemade bicycle-wheeled cart himself; Louella helped him get it in the door of the shed. This still left room for another chair and two more folding chairs that could be opened if there were that many people.

"Gosh. You'd think I was moving in to stay."

"You might as well be comfortable long as you're here," Louella replied.

"And," added Chuck, "if you run off with some señorita and leave us at the dance tomorrow, whoever comes next gets a set of shelves."

"If I finish them by then."

"Hell, there's only about an hour's work to it."

This was not true. However, it poured all afternoon. There were so few customers that Chuck and Louella decided to leave the store to Meridell. They then proceeded to devote the rest of the day to seismically detectable lovemaking. Harry, once begun on the shelves, just continued till they were done.

It stopped raining about seven but stayed cloudy. By the time Louella called Harry in for dinner, he discovered that she and Chuck were well into a big pitcher of margaritas. That evening was the first time Harry saw Louella really drunk. She got emotional, he learned:

"You mean it was the Fourth of July and they kept you in jail two more days? The slobs!"

"They did take us outside to see the fireworks."

For some reason, obscure to Harry, this inspired Louella to a surprisingly good rendition of "Ramblin' Rose," after which Chuck joined her for a rather raucus "Rose of San Antone." Harry did not mention that he had watched the Fourth of July fireworks handcuffed to a man who was on his way to the penitentiary for breaking two ribs and knocking three teeth out of the mouth of a sixty-seven year old convenience store operator during a bungled robbery.

Louella got out her guitar. The rest of the evening was devoted to music and more margaritas.

CHAPTER THREE

"Greasin' your hair with garlic oil again, Wop?"

"You ol' bear bait. You smell like you been dead three weeks."

"Chuck. Tony. Take it outside. We can't afford to replace the furniture."

Harry looked to Louella in amazement. The reddish-haired man looked as old as Chuck and was skinny as a rail. But sure enough, they did go outside, only to reappear ten minutes later covered with dust and laughing.

Tony Firenzie did not look Italian to Harry, but his grandfather (whose hair had been redder than Tony's) had, indeed, come from northern Italy to the copper mines of southern New Mexico and Arizona. Arturo Firenzie was not a sculptor in Florence, as he often had claimed. However, he felt Americans would not know enough to accord proper respect to an hereditary cobblestone layer.

It was ten minutes past last call and twenty minutes to closing. Lucille Firenzie saluted Louella with her long-necked Bud. "You'd think they'd outgrow it, but they don't feel like they been out without at least a little fight."

Harry turned back to Meridell, who shrugged and smiled. The smile and the way her breasts rose and fell with her shoulders brought a slightly delerious flash of pleasure to Harry's throat and mouth. His right hand unconsciously slid across the table, where Meridell briefly allowed it to find hers. Meridell's fingers were slim and graceful, but strong from working her loom.

Thanks to the margaritas and another wet afternoon, Harry and Chuck had not gotten a thing done on the water line. They'd all gone to the dance anyhow. Most of the people at the Chiricahua Bar were local. Meridell and the Randells introduced Harry to way more people than he could remember. Meridell danced more than half the dances with Harry. By the last set, Harry's best shirt was drenched with sweat, and he was far more drunk on Meridell than beer. Meridell's blouse, which she had embroidered herself, somehow still looked fresh and dry, though her face glistened.

Next day no one even mentioned the water line. Louella fixed a big potato salad. Harry somehow found himself in a frisbee game with Meridell's kids and a long-haired boy wearing buckskins who called himself Brownie McGee. Brownie claimed to be twenty-one. That seemed only slightly less improbable than his name. However, he knew how to take care of himself and had not done anyone in Elk Stuck any harm. Everyone accepted him on his own terms. He had a camp a few miles out of Elk Stuck in a canyon. No one pressed him too closely on where it was.

Brownie usually stayed with Jim Barnes when he came to town. This weekend, Brownie was taking care of the house while Jim was off visiting his ex and boy in Show Low. Jeff, Meridell's son, hoped Jim would bring Steve, who was just his own age, back for a while. Being summer and a weekend, Jim wanted someone in the house while he was gone to keep the tourists from just walking in out of stupidity.

"The book says it's a ghost town," explained Suzie in her best twelve-year-old-professorial manner. "It never enters their heads anyone lives here."

Harry never did get to be alone with Meridell; he had a good time anyhow. Other neighbors showed up: Wayne Hart, Jesus Lucero, and Cindy Stone. Wayne and Jesus stayed for the volleyball, but left soon after. Harry did not really even meet Cindy. The volleyball was fun, interrupted by only one sprinkle. Afterwards, Brownie had some smoke, which was not bad. Especially, Harry mused, considering it's almost certainly fresh trimmings. The food was excellent too, but Harry largely ignored it.

Monday, Harry and Chuck finally got around to the well. It was quite an operation: They hung a short section of aluminum ladder down the well, and Harry climbed in. Chuck drilled through from the outside while Harry held a cardboard box to catch as much of the dirt and wood chips as possible. When the hole was big enough, Chuck stuck a section of black plastic water line through at the angle he wanted. Harry marked the spot on the casing with chalk.

"Why didn't you set the casing lower to begin with, ya dumb old fart?"

"Want to go for a long swim in a short pond?"

"You want my carcass in your drinking water?"

Chuck laughed — his customary bellow. He passed Harry a slab of quarter inch steel eight inches wide and a foot and a half long, hung from a length of heavy fencing wire. Chuck secured the other end of the wire, then passed Harry a vice-grips on another wire. This Harry locked to the eight inch U of the casing he planned to cut away.

"Mind the water line," Chuck reminded. Then he passed down goggles and the torch with a cutting tip. There was not much room to work. Harry managed to make the cut without any serious burns, glad he was wearing a heavy, old, long-sleeved shirt. Chuck pulled up the torch and the piece of casing metal. "Oh shit. Forgot the other pipe."

Harry waited while Chuck went for it, a short piece to replace the top section of the steel water line at the right length. They had already pulled it up once and loosened the connection pulling against each other with two monster pipe wrenches.

Harry looked up at the sky over the top of the well opening above his head. It seemed so serene, with a little wisp of cloud floating across the deep blue. The dark blue. The dark, endless blue that...

Harry was flying, flying into that clean, immense blueness. It was so dark now he could see the stars, but he could still see blue color too. There was a humming noise, like a refrigerator or a vacuum cleaner motor at first.

Then it became musical.

A little smudge of light appeared in front of Harry, like a hint of dawn. This gradually grew. Then it seemed there was a face, a woman's face, breathtakingly beautiful, ageless, with sparkling blue-black hair....

"Harry! Harry! You all right?!"

Harry blinked and shook his head in confusion. Chuck was bent so far over the top of the well he looked ready to dive in.

"Huh? Oh. Yeah. I'm okay."

Chuck passed the short pipe down to check the length. The fit was perfect, within an inch of where it was now at the bottom. Chuck took the pipe back and pulled up the piece of metal protecting the electric wire. Harry climbed out and pulled the ladder out of the hole. The well was chilly, but the ten o'clock sun was bright and warm. Harry took off the old flannel shirt and faced the sun, arching his back and spreading his arms to drink it in.

"Ready for a cup of mud?"

Harry stretched luxuriantly in the warm sunshine.

"Sure."

They went back to the house and heated up the coffee. Louella was gone to Douglas for groceries. When the coffee was hot, they each filled a mug and went back outside. Chuck sat on an upturned white plastic five gallon bucket in the shade of an apple tree. Harry stood out in the sunshine. Harry loved the mountain sun. He felt it picked him up and filled him with its vitality.

"Thought you was about to pass out down there," said Chuck; he set his empty mug down on a juniper round. "What happened?"

Harry pondered a minute. "Chuck, you ever know anyone to have a...a vision?"

Harry half expected some crack about people that smoke locoweed. Instead, Chuck's eyes narrowed and got real sharp and clear. "Maybe."

Harry shivered. What was it about people here? So strong. Realer than real. "Well. Uh. It was like this face....A woman's face. God, she was beautiful. Deep..."

"Long black hair? Almost blue?"

"You know her?" Harry spoke so eagerly he almost spilled his coffee.

"Maybe." Chuck got out his pipe and filled it slowly. He tamped it in a deliberate, meditative manner. Then he lit up and puffed a while. "There's a story....You asked me once how Elk Stuck got its name."

A person listening to Chuck's usual way of talking who did not know him might have thought he was some sort of all-purpose bigot. He called black people niggers, he called Southeast Asians gooks, he called Germans krauts and the French frogs. He had at least a dozen offensive names for Indians and twice that many for Mexicans, though Louella had both Mexican and Apache in her ancestry. His only real prejudice, though, was the usual one of mountain people against flatlanders – especially if they came from Texas, California, or Phoenix.

Chuck did not know what his own ancestry was. His mother grew up in an orphanage in New Orleans. She came west just in time to get a job

12

in the first bar in Bisbee to open after repeal of prohibition. She was not sure, herself, who Chuck's father was, and might not have known his name anyhow. Because of Chuck's usual manner of talking, it struck Harry immediately that Chuck left out all the gratuitous slurs in the tale he now told:

"The Thunder Range was one of the last places Geronimo held out. One time, the army had him pinned down pretty tight, but they couldn't quite catch up with him. They hoped to starve him out, when a company of soldiers came into this little high valley."

Chuck pointed across Double Eagle Creek, which ran by a few yards below the well, to a wide area by the bluff on the other side of the road above the shop. "Right over there, they saw a beautiful young Indian woman, all by herself, gutting an elk. They took her prisoner, but their captain wouldn't let them abuse her. It was late in the day, so the soldiers made camp and made the Apache woman cook them up their fill of fresh elk steaks. Then they tied her to a tree and went to sleep.

"No one heard her get loose, but it must have been getting light by the time she did. When the guard saw she was gone he hollered out an alarm. The whole company jumped to, ready to fight Geronimo and the Chiricahuas. One of them spotted her. He shouted and pointed. They all looked, just in time to see that woman disappear over the top of the canyon with the whole rump of the elk on her shoulders. They knew they would never catch her, so they didn't even try. They called the place Elk's Ass.

"It was unexplored country, so the army had sent a cartographer along to draw maps. He was a Jew from Poland that could speak ten languages and write most of them. He used a lot of big words, but he was a dead shot and cool as they come. The rest of the company were glad to have him along.

"Folks Back East didn't think Elk's Ass was a proper name, so the mapmaker wrote it in Jewish. I don't know what he put down, but it came out Elk Stuck."

Harry was chuckling softly by now. He soon stopped as Chuck continued.

"The main thing the army was interested in about this valley was the creek. Soldiers came back for water – and to keep the Indians from getting any. A man named Leo Murphy, a lieutenant at the time, noticed the formations. He knew a little geology. A couple years later, he resigned his commission and came back. He made twenty thousand dollars on gold and silver in under a year, came down with a fever, and died without getting to spend a cent of it. There were a couple more rich strikes, but most of the ore was too thin to turn a profit with the refining methods of the time. – And anyone who did hit a rich pocket seemed prone to accidents.

"Population grew from one to over eight hundred in a year and a half. Five years later, it was under forty. When Louella and me moved in, there were only four people in Elk Stuck. Mrs. Martinez was already postmistress and already a widow. She was friendly enough, but she kept mostly to herself outside business hours. Still does. Isaiah and Gertrude Overman wouldn't have anything to do with us then, and they still won't.

13

Guess they thought they owned the place. Resented us moving in. That left Eleanor Fay, and she only lived five more years. There's enough people here now, but I'm glad for the newcomers. They're more tolerant. – We like people, just don't like 'em too thick. Guess there's folks believe Louella'n me'r too thick all by ourselves."

Chuck relit his pipe. "Eleanor was pretty much a recluse but she could be sociable. And she was grateful for a hand now and then. Her arthritis was already pretty bad when we met her. She always said she hoped to go before she got too crippled up, and she got her wish. Heart attack took her just like that one day.

"She told us some stories though, about people seeing a beautiful black-haired woman when there wasn't anyone there. I won't say I've exactly seen her face to face myself, but...Ask Louella. Or Meridell. Better yet, ask the kids. They probably see more than any of us."

Harry drained his mug. The coffee was cold, but he hardly noticed. "Wonder what she wants."

"Don't know as she exactly wants anything. Just checking you out, maybe. It's her valley, after all."

"Hunh," was all that Harry came up with in way of reply. After a while, though, he looked up and noticed how far the sun had moved across the canyon and that the clouds were beginning to build over the peak. "Let's get the water line done before Louella gets back so we can fill in the hole."

"My God, Boy. You are just the worst workaholic I have ever met. There's enough water in the tank to last a month."

This was not true. However, with almost daily rain to take care of the garden, there was certainly no need to hurry for water, even with showers and laundry. "I just thought it would be good to plug the hole before it rains and washes a bunch of mud into the well."

"Should'a known I'd get a picky perfectionist when I hired someone so skinny," Chuck grumbled. But he did get up and head back to the well, stuffing his pipe into a pocket as he went, still half full of tobacco.

They had used a block and tackle on a tripod to check the length of the water line section. They used it again to pull up the pipe to work on. This time they had to retie once to get it high enough. They replaced the full-length top section with the short piece and a new angle connector to meet the slope of the water line, screwed on the plastic connector, then lowered back the whole assembly.

"Don't be spacin' out on no Indian maidens down there now." The tone was jovial, but something drew Harry's attention back to Chuck's eyes. They were hard as diamonds. Not mean like he had thought the day they met. But cold. Objective.

Harry smiled a little wanly. "I'll be okay."

They lowered the ladder and secured it again. Harry climbed back down with the metal plate Chuck had prepared with a hole in the middle, a short piece of steel pipe just a size bigger than the water line welded to it and two bolts welded to the outside of the plate. Harry threaded the plate over the end of the plastic water line as Chuck slipped it through the hole. Once it was in place, Chuck slid the bolts through the holes he had drilled in a length of bar. Then he screwed on the nuts and washers, pulling the bar tight against the outside of the well and the plate on the inside.

After that, it was a straight-forward matter to wrestle the water line onto the connector, tighten the clamp, and tie everything in place.

Harry climbed out and pulled the ladder up after him. "Shall we fill the hole?"

"You can if you want. I'm ready for more coffee."

They both got another cup. Then Harry mixed up a tiny batch of concrete and closed the hole in the well wall. He was just done cleaning up when Louella got back with the groceries, including a defrosted frozen pizza which she popped right in the oven for lunch. There was also a fresh supply of beer.

As far as Chuck was concerned, they had done more than an adequate day's work. Harry was ready for something else too. So when Chuck and Louella disappeared into the bedroom after lunch, Harry went for a walk. It was still fairly sunny. He figured this would be a good opportunity to do a little exploring.

CHAPTER FOUR

Harry followed the road through town and up the ridge till he was looking almost straight across to the post office on the other side of the valley. The canyon was too narrow below town for a road, so the road came in over the opposite ridge. The post office was on top, almost a thousand feet above town, because the downslope into Elk Stuck was on the north side. In winter, anyone who really needed to be sure they could get in and out would park up by the post office in the sun and hike up the hill. Even at that, the road only got plowed the three days a week mail was due in. The plow came all the way through town, but that north slope was still often a solid sheet of ice.

In summer the road went all the way through the range and came out in Arizona. The post office was actually at the highest point of the road, but the ridge where Harry now stood was more open. He could see the Peloncillos to the east and the Chiricahuas to the west. To the north was Thunder Peak. At nearly eleven thousand feet, it was the highest point in a hundred miles.

Beyond the ridge where Harry stood, the road headed down and westward. Harry followed the ridge east. Coming up the slope there had been ponderosa pine and a patch here and there of oak. The upper half of the climb, the oak was replaced by aspen. There was some doug fir too. On top, where it was windiest, there was piñon. With all the rain, there were wild flowers and summer greenery everywhere. Occasionally, Harry would step on some low-growing sage. Every time this happened he found himself breathing deeply and sighing with pleasure at the pungent aroma.

The clouds seemed to be thinning rather than building today, so he kept on going. The ridge naturally curved around to the north, defining one side of the watershed of Double Eagle Creek. Harry passed a juniper with berries and picked a ripe one to keep his mouth moist. A saddle was all aspen. When he came out the other side he was in fir and spruce country. He must be at least two miles from town by now, he figured. The town of Elk Stuck was long since hidden from sight, though he still got an occasional glimpse of the post office to the south. He was sure he was into the Thunder Peak Wilderness by now too. That pleased him.

The ridge sloped just slightly up, with humps and hollows here and there. Then he came to a steep stretch for about a hundred yards, where you could not tell at all what was ahead. Just as he topped the rise, he heard a rock fall. He looked that way. What a thrill! A big, tawny mountain lion bounded over loose rocks at the bottom of a slope.

Harry looked down into the most beautiful little mountain valley he thought he had ever seen. Grass and wildflowers fairly pulsed with life, luxuriant with sunny summer mornings and afternoon rains. A tiny stream sparkled down the middle of the valley and even formed a little lake directly between where Harry stood and where the mountain lion disappeared around a rocky outcropping at the mouth of a high canyon.

Harry surveyed the valley joyfully and then made his way slowly down into it and over to the little lake. There were birds and colorful butterflies all around; a scolding squirrel in a lone fir tree only made Harry smile. He stopped when he came to the lake and stood silently for a timeless time, just drinking in the beauty. How peaceful it was. How tranquil.

Harry had no idea how long that feeling lasted, but he was sure it really did feel good, clean and benevolent for quite a while. Then, out of nowhere, he suddenly felt grimy. A chilly little breeze seemed to have struck his bare chest where the sweat of his climb had dried. Something was wrong. The pulsing air no longer seemed like the inhalation and exhalation of the breath of life. He looked around with a growing feeling of inexplicable panic.

Then it occurred to Harry to look up. He could not see anything yet, but as soon as he turned his attention to the sky he realized he was hearing a helicopter approaching. Just at that moment a voice spoke, seemingly out of the very rocky outcropping where the mountain lion had disappeared:

"Over here! Quick!"

A rush of adrenaline shot through Harry from the tips of his toes right through the top of his head. He looked. To his amazement, there was Brownie McGee, beckoning to him. Harry had no idea what was happening, but he ran like his life depended on it. Brownie laughed lightly as Harry came up to him. Then he led the way a little farther up the canyon and ducked behind some bushes. Harry followed and found himself standing in the entrance to a cave.

The cave was just high enough to stand up in and about ten feet across. It kept its height to about a depth of ten feet, then dropped off sharply to a hole, still big enough to crawl into, which disappeared into the dark. The floor of the cave was flat. Ancient stonework defined the outline of four very small rooms. There was plenty of light to see out, but they were completely hidden from view. Thanks to the bushes and the lay of the rock, it was almost impossible to tell the cave was there from outside even if you were looking right at it.

Brownie looked his name. Thinner than Harry, he was deeply tanned, his shoulders were almost as dark as his long, straight hair. His eyes were just a shade darker. Brownie wore leggings and a loin cloth made of smoked buckskin. Moccasins were elk hide. Brownie might have seemed displaced in time, but he belonged completely to the place.

Harry's heart slowly quit thundering as Brownie grinned at him like a leprechaun. Brownie frowned, however, as the sound of the helicopter came closer. At its nearest and loudest, Brownie's glower, combined with the, "Sput, sput," echoing off the walls, had Harry shivering. The helicopter flew on by without slowing. Brownie soon relaxed.

"You practicing kundalini yoga or gettin' ready to have a fit?"

"Huh?"

"Look at you."

Harry looked. He could feel the rhythmic pulses of energy ride through him, and he could see his hands and knees shake with each one. The image came to his mind of when he was a kid and used to put a ball card in the spokes of his bicycle. Harry smiled.

"That's it, Man."

"What happened?"

"Not a thing....And that's exac'l how we aim to keep it."

Brownie is just like everyone else around Elk Stuck, Harry thought. When he looks directly at you, you know it! Brownie was smiling again though, as he opened a small pouch on the left side of his belt. Harry smiled too when he saw Brownie pull out a little hand-carved green stone pipe and fill it. They smoked while Harry looked over the stonework. Then they went back out in the sunshine.

"What was that helicopter?"

"Border Patrol. Forest Fire Patrol. I don't know. Just as soon not be seen anyhow. Matter of principle."

Harry nodded sympathetically. Brownie led the way to the stream and drank. Harry did the same and splashed a little water on his face. They both looked around. The valley was peaceful again.

"Look over there."

Harry looked where Brownie pointed.

"Not everyplace you see deer out in the open in the middle of the afternoon."

They watched the deer, a doe and her fawn, not the least bit perturbed by the presence of the two young men. Another doe and a young buck in velvet eventually joined them. Harry and Brownie watched as they slowly browsed their way up a little slope and out of sight. Then Brownie turned back to Harry.

"You ever hear of Black Bear City?"

"I don't think so."

"It's not on the map. Whole place is illegal, in fact, 'cause it's in the Wilderness. Northern California."

"Oh, that's the place I read about. Center of the marijuana war."

"Just about. That's why I left. I was walking down the trail one day

17

about a year and a half ago when I came on a couple guys I knew. One of 'em was packin' a thirty-ought-six and a forty-five. The other one had a twelve gauge shotgun he had a professional gunsmith saw off to a certified legal eighteen and three eighths inches.

"Just as I came up I heard one say, 'They're giving out stiffer sentences for growing now than for murder. You're better off to shoot.' That's when I knew it was time to leave. There's a lot of cops this close to the border. But most of them are otherwise occupied. Even the ones that aren't, I'm small potatoes. Shit, they caught some jerk the other day tryin' to haul so much cocaine his truck was weavin' from the weight. No need to bother a peaceful little pot grower. No need a'tall."

Brownie led the way to where there were some nice flat rocks to sit on. Then he filled the pipe again, and they smoked another bowl. Harry wanted to ask how Brownie happened to be up here at all but had not figured out how to put his question when Brownie spoke up.

"I got to admit, agricultural pursuits are not my only reason for not wanting to be seen. I grow a lot lower anyhow."

"How's that?"

"Hotter. Longer growing season."

Harry was sure Brownie was mistaking his question intentionally, but he played along. "No. I mean..."

"Ohhhh." The leprechaun twinkle flashed across Brownie's face again. "Come on."

Brownie leapt up and dashed across the meadow and up a slope. Harry followed. They ran almost as fast as when they hid from the helicopter, but the feeling was now playful. The atmosphere was again clean and light. As they crested the little ridge and entered the woods, however, Harry felt a darkness which seemed not just to be coming from the shade of the trees.

They climbed a couple hundred yards up and down across the ridges. Harry very much hoped he would not have to find his way back on his own. They had not gone all that far, but he had no idea where he was. They had started down a steep slope densely covered in spruce when Brownie pointed:

"Look at that. The sons of bitches."

Harry looked, but did not see anything till Brownie led him right up to the survey stake.

Brownie pulled up the stake with an angry jerk, looked about purposively, and then strode diagonally across the slope. Soon they were each carrying over a dozen stakes, and Harry had a pocket full of plastic ribbons in various colors.

"Bastards!" said Brownie. "This is the fuckin' Wilderness."

Harry followed the line of Brownie's eyes to the cat tracks. Harry was amazed. Wilderness regulations were nearly fanatical. The Forest Service even made fire fighters walk out rather than allow a motor vehicle to sully the Wilderness. Yet someone had been way up here on a bulldozer. It was not long before Harry found out who.

"What'cha lookin' for?"

18

"Rock."

"What for?"

Brownie pointed. Harry looked to the tree Brownie had spotted thirty or forty yards up the slope.

"Read me what corner it is."

Harry went up and read the notice nailed to the tree.

"Northeast. Who's LemTron anyhow? Chuck asked me if I worked for them the day I got here."

Brownie climbed up too, with a rock, which he used to knock the piece of plywood that the notice was attached to out of the tree.

He recited the information on the notice to himself several times to commit it to memory, took his bearings south and west, then looked around. "Shit, we're gettin' too much stuff. Come on."

Harry thought it was amazing how Brownie always seemed to know how to find what he was looking for. This time they came to a place where big boulders jutted out of the slope. Under one of these was a broad hole almost impossible to see unless you were looking right at it from within a few feet.

"How'd you know that was there?"

Brownie looked at Harry kind of funny. "Hell, Man, there's a million holes like that."

Harry felt pretty silly, but Brownie did not seem to hold his ignorance against him. He just stuffed survey stakes and the notice, board and all, into the hole. It was plenty deep enough to push everything completely out of sight. Then they went back for more.

"Guys I met seemed okay. One crew even had bud good as mine. But I don't believe they knew, themselves, what's comin' down. They claim LemTron's in the minerals business. Copper. Silver. Gold. Lead. Uranium. I asked them what they were doing mining the Wilderness. They said they didn't think there would be any mining any time soon. Said companies just wanted to get their claims on file 'cause the government was liable to cut off new claims in the Wilderness. They may even have believed that story. I don't. LemTron's got a going operation down on BLM land; and if it's a mine, I'm a Martian."

Just about the time they had destroyed as much of the survey as Brownie figured to find, a big black cloud rolled over the ridge from the southwest. Brownie glanced at it. "Come on. Let's get out of here before it gets muddy. I don't want to leave no tracks."

Brownie led the way once again, unerringly, back to the high valley. The first drops were already falling. By the time they reached the cave it was really starting to come down. Brownie filled the pipe once again and lit up. It held about a toke and a half apiece. The air cooled rapidly. Harry put on the yellow pocket T shirt he had been carrying stuck in his belt and still felt chilly. Brownie seemed not to notice.

They watched it rain in silence for about half an hour. Then the rain got finer and the light changed. Brownie began to smile. "Come on." He was out of the cave, quick as a hummingbird. Harry did not ask why. He was not a bit surprised when he found himself looking at the materialization of a brilliant double rainbow.

The rain eventually stopped. The rainbow faded away, and the clouds began to break up. Harry realized they were colored and looked to the sun.

"Wow! It's late. I better get back."

"I got a spare blanket."

Harry thought a moment. It would probably be dark well before he could get down. He was sure he could find his way: Drop down and follow the creek if nothing else. Stumbling around in the dark did not seem real appealing though. "Chuck and Louella'll be worried."

"You're a big boy. They're probably too drunk by now to miss you anyhow."

Harry laughed. This was not true, but they probably were too drunk to worry. What the hell? "Where's that blanket?"

"Right in the cave."

Harry was amazed once again. He would not have believed there was any human artifact in that cave less than seven hundred years old. Brownie now showed him two neatly folded brown wool army blankets and a tightly-lidded plastic bucket painted black. In the bucket was a large bag of venison jerky, salt, a bag of home-dried apples, a box of kitchen matches, and a box of twenty-two bullets. Harry looked around for the rifle to go with the bullets but could not see it. Brownie smiled and picked it casually off a ledge Harry did not even realize was there.

"Full moon tonight. Maybe we'll go bear hunting."

"With that?" Harry pointed to the little rifle.

Brownie grinned mischievously. "Just git right up on 'im and shoot 'im through the eye."

Harry was not totally convinced Brownie would not do it. However, Brownie set the rifle back on its shelf and did not mention it again. They did go out in the moonlight, but did not see any bears...which was fine with Harry. They did see more deer. In the morning they saw a herd of elk, including a mature bull in velvet.

CHAPTER FIVE

"Is that Zuni?"

"No, Ma'am," said Harry without a moment's hesitation. "It's Quappeta."

"Oh my!"

The woman was highly impressed. Harry suppressed a grin. When he got back to town Tuesday, Chuck was out in the yard drinking coffee. His greeting was to turn back to the house and bellow: "Call off the snakebite squad, Lou. He's back."

Harry was not sure what Chuck and Louella's reaction would be to his disappearing overnight. They didn't really say either. Near as Harry could tell, they were both a little relieved he was showing some independence.

Chuck did not want to work on the water line. He wanted someone to talk to. Harry got a cup of coffee and joined Chuck in the morning sunshine.

"Kitchen's yours," Louella said while Harry was in the house.

"Thanks. I'll fix something in a little bit." But he didn't. He was feeling light and enjoying it. Only thing he did want, after about an hour, was to smoke. Brownie had given him a little stash. Now he really wanted to roll one. Finally, he asked Chuck:

"Chuck, would you and Louella mind if I smoke pot here?"

Chuck looked very serious. "Now, it you was dumb enough to get caught, we would be deeply shocked that there was a drug problem in a conservative little Western town like Elk Stuck."

Harry was not sure what to make of that. He kept his face neutral.

"I got papers if you're not too snooty for Buglers."

Harry must have frowned. Chuck laughed. Then he got out the papers, and Harry rolled a joint. Chuck rolled a cigarette. Chuck finished first and lit up. Harry figured he ought to offer Chuck a hit.

"No thanks. I got my own brand."

They both smoked. The pot was mild, but a third of a joint was plenty. Harry put the rest away for later.

"Here. I got more." Chuck handed Harry the pack of rolling papers. Then he launched into a long tirade about the government. "Takin' away all our freedom. They got no damn right!"

Harry agreed with everything Chuck was saying. Yet the government was supporting them both. Chuck's disability pension brought him and Louella twice as much as the store. That was really how they could afford for Harry to be there.

Chuck did not want to work on the water line at all that week, but Harry put in a couple hours Wednesday morning and a couple more Friday. Chuck seemed grateful, though he distracted Harry far more than he encouraged him to work. Then, Friday afternoon, Louella asked if Harry would mind the store next day so she and Chuck could go to town.

"Want to hit the bars early, huh?"

"Smart ass." Louella laughed. "Flea market today at the rodeo grounds. We're having a good summer. Need some more stock for the store."

So now Harry had on his newest levis and a clean Western shirt with little flowers on a light blue background. He had even polished up his ratty old Western boots for the part. He put on the cowboy hat that Chuck had razzed him about when they first met too, but by mid-morning, it was too hot, so he hung it on a nail to add to the atmosphere. One customer even asked him for a price on it. Harry had bought it out of season at the K-Mart in Las Cruces for $11.97. He named a price of $75.00. The customer did not offer to buy it but did not act shocked at the price either.

"You play poker?" Chuck had asked.

"A little," Harry replied noncommittally. − A wise friend had told Harry once that discretion is the better part of valor.

"Take your pick. Minimum wage or twenty percent of the gross."

Harry had gone for the twenty percent. By eleven-thirty, he figured he was making about sixty-five cents an hour. He was having fun though.

He had sold a couple thunder eggs right off. Then a pasty-looking couple came in who said they were from Dallas. They were as loud as Chuck and Louella – and as grating as Chuck and Louella were enjoyable. They wanted to know about real estate.

Harry shook his head dolefully. "Whole valley's in litigation."

A look of horror came over the man. "Christine, do you have my nitroglycerine?"

After they left, Harry went outside. Several loads of campers went by on up the mountain. Most of them waved. Harry waved back. Then the street was empty of all traffic for a while. Harry lit a joint. He took a few tokes, then put it away.

A couple deep blue Stellar's jays flew back and forth in some willows by the creek. There was a chipmunk at one end of Chuck and Louella's woodpile and a canyon wren at the other, each intent on its own business. One of Louella's cats started to stalk the bird, but the chimpmunk saw it and piped a warning and they both zipped off. Harry smiled and stretched. A new-looking gold station wagon came over the top of the hill by the post office.

Harry watched as the station wagon made its cautious way down the slope. Definitely not used to mountain roads, Harry concluded. The people inside looked in wonder as they pulled up. The parents appeared to be in their forties. The kids looked about the same age as Meridell's. The station wagon slowed to a stop.

"Do you have Indian jewelery?" the woman asked. Her voice was nasal; her manner was eager, but also a little on the arrogant side. Harry had had enough experience of people to recognize the type. These people expected service. They also expected the people who served them to know their business. Therein lay a great creative entrepreneurial opportunity.

"Of course, Ma'am."

"Where can we park?"

"Right up there." Harry pointed to the empty lot just above the store. Connecticut, he saw on the license plate as they pulled past. Harry told them a little of the history of the area. What he did not know, he improvised. They ate it up. Then they looked around the store. The woman wanted to see turquoise, but there was nothing big enough to interest her.

The kids wanted arrowheads. There were a few on display and a couple boxes full under the counter. Harry got ten dollars apiece for two he knew were priced at three. The man was looking at some old traps. Harry wondered if he had any idea what they were for. The woman asked about Meridell's weaving.

"Quappeta? Are they Puebloan?"

"Yes. Southern Pueblo. Related to the Mimbres."

"Oh, yes. I believe I've heard of them."

Harry hated to deprive Meridell of credit for her work, but what the hell? These people did appreciate it. Why not sell them something they would value as much as Harry valued Meridell? Besides, these people had money, and they wanted to spend it on things made by Indians.

When the family finally left, Harry could hardly believe his good fortune. Meridell had seven hundred dollars coming. That was twice as much as she had made yet in the two and a half weeks Harry had been in Elk Stuck. And he had two hundred, two-oh-four, counting the arrow heads. They had taken two blankets and a wall hanging. They had not batted an eye at the prices Harry quoted. The man just signed ten hundred dollar traveler's checks and pulled out his driver's license. Harry tried to keep his hand from shaking as he wrote the information from the driver's license down. Then it was smiles and thank yous all around.

That was Harry's biggest single sale. But it was July, peak season. By the time he closed up, Harry had over four hundred dollars for himself. The Quappeta tribe was a thousand dollars richer. Only one person all day had doubted their existence. – He had not acted likely to buy anything anyhow. Harry had also sold two pieces of Meridell's weaving on her own bonafides.

One woman from Santa Fe gushed over the growing crafts resurgence and acted like she knew something about weaving. A retired air force couple from Eldorado, Oklahoma gave Harry the impression they had been to Elk Stuck before – and might come back. Harry did not expect Chuck and Louella home till late. He put things away as Louella had told him, padlocked the door, and headed up to Meridell's to tell her the good news.

Meridell feigned shock when Harry told her about the Quappeta. "You're gonna get us in trouble, Harry."

"It'll probably be okay."

"But Chuck's been selling them as Wannabbee."

Harry did a double take. "Wannabbee?"

"You know," said Suzie, who had been listening. "Wannabbee an Indian."

Harry laughed. Meridell and Suzie did too.

"And your prices are outrageous."

"You just don't know how much your work is worth."

Jeff was over at Jim Barnes'. Jim had brought his son, Steve, home to stay for a month. The boys were inseparable. Harry stayed the evening and had a pleasant, quiet time, even if Meridell still was no more encouraging than a, "Thank you for the compliment," to his advances. She did agree to go for a hike with him tomorrow up to the high meadow, if the weather was good.

"Brownie's been promising to take me up there all summer and show me the ruin, but we haven't gotten to it."

CHAPTER SIX

Harry woke in the night from a dream. He was running. First it seemed he just ran for pleasure, full of exuberance and clear, fresh air. Then the feeling changed. There was something he needed. He had to reach it. He ran harder. Striving and hope propelled him. This was hard work, but if he could just reach his goal it would all be worth it. Only now there was something after him. Whatever he was running to, his immediate need was to escape the terrible something that was coming rapidly closer and...

Harry awoke with a start, his heart pounding.

It was a while before he got back to sleep. Once he did, he slept kind of late. By the time he got up and went down to the house for coffee in the morning, Chuck and Louella were already into their second or third cup. Chuck was puffing away on his pipe like a house afire.

"Listen to this," said Chuck pointing portentiously to yesterday's paper, which he was just now reading. "Thought they had a bomb on a plane. Made an emergency landing and evacuated all the passengers. Then the bomb squad took the suspicious object out in a field and set off a little charge of their own to blow it apart." Chuck paused for effect and looked up. Harry picked up where he had left off:

"And it made a crater half a mile across."

"Shit, Boy, you been watching too much TV."

"TV? Where?" There was not a television in Elk Stuck, as there was no reception; and satellite dishes were still too new and expensive for anyone there to have one. "It's the drugs....What was it?"

Chuck looked terribly serious. "Dirty diapers."

It took about three seconds for this to register on Harry. Then he laughed so hard he nearly fell down. When he recovered, he got himself a cup of coffee, to which he added a big dollop of Rodeo honey. As he was licking the spoon, Louella asked:

"Well, did you sell the store?"

"No, Ma'am," replied Harry soberly.

"Horsefeathers," Louella muttered under her breath, looking disgusted at the, "Ma'am."

"I traded it for an oil well."

"Shee-it, Boy. They let you out of jail much too soon."

Harry told about his day's business, including the immense popularity of Quappeta handicrafts.

"Damn, Lou, we've missed our calling."

"How's that, Sugarpants?"

"We ought to sell this boy to the government."

"I thought they abolished slavery."

"For propaganda. Show those Commies what a little incentive'll do."

"By God, you got somethin' there. There's even a romantic angle. Meridell made out like a bandit."

"Money and love. If the government won't buy it, we'll sell it to Hollywood."

"Honey," said Louella to Harry, "we have had that store open twelve seasons now. It has never before even come close to a two thousand dollar day. You are a wonder."

"Aw shucks." Harry realized he actually felt exactly like the stock line.

Louella already had sausage on, but Harry said he was having breakfast with Meridell. Louella sent a dozen eggs with him.

Jeff was already off with Steve. Suzie was not in the mood for a hike. That was just fine with Harry. He was pleased to see that it appeared

24

to suit Meridell too. Soon they were on their way.

Meridell was as strong a hiker as Harry, but they were in no hurry. The day was lovely, pine-needle fragrant in the morning sunshine. Heading up the slope, Harry spotted a little timber rattler sunning itself on a rock not ten feet from the road. "Wow! Look at that. First one I've seen."

"There aren't many this high."

Harry's response to the snake had been so spontaneous he had not stopped to think he might frighten Meridell. He had not though. They both stopped to take a good look at the rattlesnake. For all the interest it showed, the rattler might not have noticed their existence. It had not moved an inch when they continued on up toward the ridgetop, where they turned off the road.

The route Harry had happened on up the ridge was the most direct way to reach the mountain meadow. It could be approached up the creek, but that was a harder climb – and did not have the view either. There was no trail at all. So though the high valley was easy to find if you knew it was there, it got almost no human traffic. When they reached it, Harry could see that Meridell, too, immediately felt the vitality of such a pristine place.

Meridell did not say a word, but the little tension lines on her face smoothed away; she took a deep breath and then smiled. Harry did the same. Neither of them spoke. The only sounds were birds and a small whistling chorus of chipmunks.

They drank from the stream, then headed for the cave. Harry could see that their timing was perfect. It was somewhat before noon. The angle of the sun sent the most light into the cave through the bushes there would be all day. Meridell looked at the ancient stonework with wonder.

"What do you suppose they used this for?"

"I dunno," replied Harry. "Hunting camp, maybe. Place to meditate. Maybe a family or two just lived here."

"Look how tiny the rooms are."

"Yeah, would of been crowded to live in, I guess."

"We lived on the Navajo Reservation when the kids were little. Jeff was born there. Paul had a job."

"Science he teaches?"

"And math. We saw quite a lot of ruins there. People said the Old People were little, just four feet high."

"You believe it?"

Meridell shrugged.

There was not enough light to see into the deeper cave at the back of the large open one, just enough to tanatalize you into wanting to see more. Harry wished they had brought a flashlight, but he had not thought of it. He lit a match and saw the cave was clean and went back some distance. He crawled in a little way and lit another. The cave got wider. He looked up and saw the ceiling sloped up too.

"Meridell, there's another whole room. Come take a look."

"You sure there's no drop-offs?"

"Not yet anyhow."

He saw her block the light at the entrance as she started in. He lit another match to show her where he was. Then he held out his hand. It was only ten feet or so. It seemed to be taking an awfully long time. Suddenly Harry was aware of a humming noise. Was a plane passing by outside? It did not sound like a plane. It sounded like it was here in the cave and getting closer, but he was not sure where it was coming from. It seemed to come from all directions at once.

Meridell's hand touched Harry's. He clasped it and pulled them together.

"Harry, what's that noise?"

"I don't know." Harry tried to light another match without letting go of Meridell's hand but couldn't do it. "Put your hand on my leg." He guided it there, then tried again. The match still would not light. He tried another. Nothing.

Meridell gasped. Harry looked. The light at the entry was gone. They were in total darkness. Harry took Meridell's hand again. The humming intensified. They just held hands for a moment. Then their arms were around one another's shoulders, hanging on tight as they both shivered in terror.

Harry looked around, holding back panic. What had happened to the entrance? Where was the light? Which way was out? There it was now! How could he have lost it?

"Oh," said Meridell. "What on Earth?" They kept hold of each other as they crawled back out.

There was a woman in the outer cave. She was just laying down a bundle of kindling. She did not seem a bit surprised to see Harry and Meridell. Harry's first thought was that she must be a Wetback. She was dressed in plain cotton skirt and shirt and buckskin moccasins. Her long black hair was loose and a little dishevelled. Harry looked again and thought she must be an Indian. When she spoke, her slight accent did not sound at all Spanish:

"Are you hungry?"

Harry had intentionally skipped breakfast, preferring to climb on an empty stomach. Meridell had had toast and tea when she fed the kids, before Harry got there. They were about ready for something. They had a loaf of Meridell's homemade bread and half a dozen peaches in a little shoulder bag lying on one of the ancient stone walls. Meridell pointed to it.

"We've got something. Would you like to join us?"

Their new acquaintance smiled. "That's good." She then quickly built a little fire on the remains of an old one.

"Meridell," Harry said, very quietly, "was that there?" He nodded to the sign of fire.

"I didn't really notice. I don't think so," Meridell replied equally quietly.

The Indian woman either did not hear them or pretended not to out of politeness. Harry was certain there had been no trace of fire when he had been in the cave earlier in the week with Brownie. He could not swear there was none when they got there today, but he did not recall any fire remains. Surely he would have noticed.

Meridell got the bag. Their new companion finished building the fire. "Light?" said Harry. She stepped aside for him. His matches worked fine now. The fire caught well. The woman went outside. Harry and Meridell looked to one another. Neither knew what to think. The woman returned with a chunk of fresh meat and an old-fashioned lightweight frying pan. Harry now saw she wore a sheath knife. She set the pan down and brushed off a flat rock. She blew on it to get rid of any dust, set the meat down, and cut off a panfull of steaks.

She went out again. This time she was gone longer. Meridell stepped up to the fire in case the frying meat needed attention. Before it did, though, the woman came back with a coffeepot and a small bucket, both full of water. She set the coffeepot on the fire and then got out two little bags. One turned out to contain salt, the other ground chile. She sprinkled some of each on the meat. Then she flipped the steaks with her knife.

There had been not a word spoken in several minutes. Harry stepped outside. Everything looked just as it had a short while earlier, when he and Meridell arrived. He gathered up an armful of firewood and brought it in. The Indian woman had just handed Meridell her knife. Meridell cut three slices of bread and handed the knife back. Harry set down the wood and put another couple sticks on the fire. Soon the steaks were done. The strange woman speared them with her knife and set them on the three slices of bread. Then she cut three more pieces of meat and set the pan back on the fire. The water was boiling by now. She pulled it off to the edge of the fire using her skirt for a pot holder. Then she dumped in a handful of coffee from another little bag. And they all ate.

The woman went outside again and returned with three metal cups. Harry had not seen a pack when he went out. He shrugged. He had not seen Brownie's provisions either till Brownie pointed them out. The woman seasoned and turned the second pan of steaks, then gave Meridell the knife again to cut bread, while she poured coffee. Harry and the Indian woman had a second cup of coffee apiece. They each had a peach.

"That meat was delicious," said Harry. It was the first time any of them had spoken since they lit the fire. "What was it?"

"Elk."

Harry's eyebrows went up. He saw Meridell's do the same. No one said anything though. After a couple minutes, the Indian woman got up and stretched and walked outside. Harry and Meridell found themselves following her without thinking. They all walked silently around the rock outcropping where the cave was, into the main part of the high valley. The sun shined bright; it had to be about twelve-thirty or one, Harry figured. It was just delightfully warm, not hot. Indian paint brush, asters, yarrow and innumerable other flowers bloomed everywhere. Grass grew thick and luxuriant.

The woman led the way to the upper end of the little valley, where Harry had not been before. There, right at the edge of the woods, the stream which ran through the valley and eventually became part of Double Eagle Creek lower down, bubbled up out of the ground in a spring. Above it was a slope, densely wooded in spruce and some aspen. Beyond, out of sight through the woods, was Thunder Peak.

To the right of the spring, the land narrowed to head up in a little dry, rocky canyon. The Indian woman now turned that way. Harry and Meridell went with her. They walked just a short way around three little bends, when the woman stopped and raised her hand just enough to point. Harry and Meridell looked. Were they coyotes? There were four of them, two adults and two year-old adolescents. Harry had never seen coyotes so red before. They were almost salmon colored. Could they be wolves?

The animals approached a little closer before they noticed the humans. Then they stopped abruptly, but they did not run. The adults looked about. The young ones appeared mostly curious. The wolves and the human beings stood for some time, looking one another over. Then the four animals loped casually away up the steep bluff on the side of the canyon. Harry let out a breath he had not realized he was holding and turned to Meridell as she turned to look at him.

"God, how beautiful." Suddenly Meridell looked all around. "Where's she gone?"

Harry looked too. The Indian woman was nowhere in sight. They looked in every direction, but there was no sign of her. So they walked back down to the open valley. She was still nowhere to be seen. Slowly, they walked back to the cave. They did not really expect to find her now. She had gone as silently and mysteriously as she had come. Meridell slipped behind the bushes first.

"Harry! The fire!"

Harry stepped into the sheltered area at the mouth of the cave too. The fire was gone. It was not just out. There was no sign that there had been a fire there any time in the last hundred years. No ashes. No blackened rocks. Nothing. The coffeepot, the bucket of wash water, the firewood, all were gone. The only thing left as it had been when they saw the cave a few minutes ago was the shoulder bag, right where Meridell had left it, with the half-eaten loaf of bread still out, sitting on its cut end on the bag on an ancient foundation stone.

CHAPTER SEVEN

Harry and Meridell decided, on their way down the mountain, that they wanted to discuss what had happened with Brownie before they even mentioned it to anyone else, but he was nowhere to be found. Not particularly unusual, but the result was that Harry and Meridell kept the Indian woman to themselves while attending to other matters.

Meridell's weaving was having an excellent summer, and the tourist season was generally doing well by the shop. So she kept it open long hours, which probably increased sales slightly...and gave her a lot of time at the loom. On Saturday, a letter came from Santa Fe. The woman Harry had charged such a fancy price a week earlier turned out to be a buyer for a boutique. Thanks to Harry, she was offering Meridell more wholesale for her weaving than Meridell usually charged retail in the Elk Stuck Emporium.

There was a number for Meridell to call, collect. Naturally, the first four times Meridell tried, she reached a machine. The phone was in the shop, one of only four in Elk Stuck. Chuck and Louella had a jack in the house on the same line, but they kept it unplugged a lot. Meridell did not like to use the phone. She did not like to impose on Chuck and Louella, and she could not afford to get in the habit of making long distance calls. – And everything was long distance except Lariat.

Finally, Tuesday morning, when she still could not get through to a person, she dialed direct and left a message. The message was rather curt, as Meridell had about figured she was wasting her time and the price of a phone call. This turned out to be just the right tone. The buyer from Santa Fe believed Meridell must be too successful to bother with her. She practically groveled for some of Meridell's work when she called back at eight-thirty on Wednesday morning.

Meridell jumped when the phone rang. She had been peacefully weaving for an hour and expected things to stay peaceful at least another hour. The woman wanted to come down Saturday and look at everything Meridell had. She wanted as much as she could get right away for what was left of the summer season. And she made it a point to remind Meridell that Santa Fe was a year-round market – and one with a world clientele. Meridell could hardly believe this was happening.

Meridell spent the next three evenings and Saturday morning going over and over everything she had. She packed and repacked boxes with each re-evaluation. She wanted to be able to get at everything of professional quality readily without exposing anything amateurish. She also wanted the very best items out on display, but she kept changing her mind as to what was the best.

"You're gonna get too uptown for us home folks," Chuck said with a ferocious look. Louella threatened to slit his throat if he scared off Meridell's big break. Meridell kissed him, which melted him completely.

Two o'clock Saturday afternoon, Aspasia Suny of Santa Fe, Sarasota, and Paris gushed in. Aspasia seemed to Meridell to have the soul of a lizard and the style of a six year old. She oozed through Meridell's work, making a mess Meridell would never have tolerated from her kids. But she actually did like Meridell's weaving. She compared it to several people who, from the tone of Aspasia's voice, Meridell figured must be big shots in the weaving world, though Meridell had never heard of any of them. And Aspasia Suny bought. When she left, Meridell had a check for fourteen hundred dollars, which was more money than she had ever been paid before in one lump in her life.

"I had to insist to hold back something for the shop here. She's even talking about a contract to agent me for custom work."

"You tell her you keep banker's hours?" asked Chuck.

"No, but she brought it up herself. She knows how long it takes to do a good piece of work. That's what makes it valuable. 'Sweetheart,' she said, 'you won't even have to change your name. Meridell Devore is marketable.'"

Louella gave Meridell a big hug. "How does it feel to be discovered?"

"Let's celebrate."

So Sunday morning Meridell drove her little blue Toyota pickup over to Douglas for some fancy groceries. Harry rode along. He was ready for a break too.

Harry had worked pretty hard the last two weeks himself. A couple times he actually went at it from dawn to dark. In early August that was still a lot of hours. The hole for the water tank turned out to be a major operation. Twice he even had to dig under a rock and winch it out with the come-a-long. Both Chuck and Louella told Harry to relax, that there was no need to work so hard; but he could not relax. He was just all keyed up. Besides, they were obviously pleased that the water system was really moving along. So why not, he thought. Eventually the hole was all done. Forms were built. On Friday of the second week, they fired up the cement mixer, and Harry and Chuck both put in a fifteen hour day.

Saturday, Chuck announced he was dead. Even Harry did not do much besides spray the concrete a couple times. The rains had thinned out considerably the last two weeks. The sun was bright and hot. They did not want the concrete setting up too fast and cracking. Sunday, Chuck declared himself resurrected, and Harry was certainly ready for a party. As Harry and Meridell left for town, Chuck and Louella were arguing amiably about who was going to do what.

"You won't spray the concrete right."

"You won't water the garden at all."

"All right," grumbled Chuck, as if any other outcome was ever possible. "I'll go open up the store."

It was after three by the time Harry and Meridell got back. Jim Barnes' Harley was parked at Meridell's. As they pulled up, Harry and Meridell saw Jim and Brownie playing frisbee with Jeff and Steve in the yard. Steve flipped the frisbee to Jim, who tried a fancy catch over his shoulder and missed. Then he turned to the truck, followed by Brownie and the boys.

"Need a hand?" Jim called out.

"Sure," Harry replied.

Meridell did not get to town very often. Town was seventy miles either way. Some success at her craft might make the cost of a trip less of a consideration than it always had been, but Meridell still did not have any desire to make the drive very often. She had stocked up while they were in town. There was something for everyone to carry.

"How's the world out there?" Jim asked, picking up a twenty pound sack of potatoes.

"Hot," Meridell replied.

"Big Burro Gulch washed the road two days ago," Harry added. "But it didn't feel like it's rained down there in fifty years. You could forget up here we're living in a desert."

"Ignorance is bliss," said Jim.

"Thank God for mountains," said Meridell.

"Where you been, Brownie?" Harry asked.

"Snooping. Also, it got dry. I had to water."

"Who were you snooping on, the constabulary?"

"Only local law we've got's the deputy at Lariat. Pete Wiggins is okay. He's of the old school."

"How's that?"

"He believes a peace officer's job is to stop trouble, not to cause it."

"Amen to that," Jim interjected.

Brownie continued. "I was conducting a little investigation of the LemTron Metals and Refining Corporation."

"Kid don't value his hide." Jim, at thirty-nine, was old enough to be Brownie's father. He was also a veteran of the war in Vietnam. "At least you got sense enough to listen to reconnaissance lessons from a pro."

Harry was impressed. "Didn't know you were in reconnaissance."

"Long range reconnaissance. Scouting way behind enemy lines."

"He must of done something right, too." Brownie had his leprechaun smile on again.

Harry looked to Brownie and Jim, who was smiling wryly to himself. They obviously were waiting for Harry to ask something further. "Okay, I'll bite. What's the secret of your survival, oh great warrior?"

Jim adopted a sagacious demeanor and raised his right index finger significantly. "Stay stoned."

Meridell did not want to light the oven in the house. It was warm even in Elk Stuck. So Brownie made a fire in the outdoor fireplace and roasted green chiles for the guacamole. Harry helped Meridell peel avocados and cut veggies. Jim gave the boys rides on the Harley.

"Why can't I drive it myself?" Steve had been begging since he could talk.

"When you're big enough to start it, you're big enough to drive it."

Steve thought that was most unfair. "I drive the truck okay, don't I"

"That's different. Weight don't count with the truck."

Steve accepted this, but everyone knew he would disbelieve it again by tomorrow. He was at an age where wishful thinking is the mother of invention. No one worried about it though. If he outgrew it before he got old enough to do any significant damage he would be doing better than most people.

About the time the guacamole was ready, Chuck and Louella showed up with a cooler of beer. The boys headed out on their bicycles. Meridell brought out a big platter of chicken and a bowl of barbeque sauce. They all sat in the shade with guacamole and chips and beer while the chicken cooked slowly on the coals.

"Well," asked Louella. "What did you learn?"

"Not enough," Brownie replied, "but enough to know somethin's fishier'n hell."

"Could just be some new kind of refining plant," Chuck said, playing Devil's advocate. He was actually the most paranoid person in Elk Stuck.

"Could be. But nearly all the air traffic's military."

"So what do you make of it?" Meridell turned to Harry, "You've got guacamole in your beard."

Harry's beard was just long enough to flip up and suck the

31

guacamole out. "Survival reserve," he said with a grin.

"I don't," Brownie answered Meridell. "Don't know what to make of it. But I sure would like to find out."

Speculation continued the rest of the afternoon. The LemTron employees any of them had met seemed ordinary enough, if a little credulous. They seemed genuinely to believe LemTron was just in the minerals business. One of the surveyors had even pointed out the various formations in the rock across the road from the Randells'. Everyone knew there was gold and silver in recoverable – though probably not profitable – concentrations. None of the little group assembled that afternoon wanted another mine.

The small-scale operation below Post Office Ridge, mostly rerefining the largest of the old tailings piles at the Dead Man, kept a few people employed. That was plenty. Even a good-sized operation would not overrun them. Gold just does not create that many jobs. No one was exactly enthused though. Elk Stuck was quiet. Everyone there liked it that way. Jobs, environment...No one was seriously concerned one way or another about small scale mining. LemTron was something else. None of them had any real clues to what, but none of them trusted it.

After a while, the conversation drifted to other topics. The chicken got done. The boys and Suzie showed up, and they all had dinner. Then Meridell put on a pot of coffee while Louella and Suzie took a little walk over to the Randells' to gather the eggs before dark. When they got back, everyone was delighted to find they had two fresh pies with them: pecan and cherry. Jeff and Steve were eager to crank the ice cream maker; everyone else let them.

As purple bluffs faded to gentle summer evening, Jim produced a bottle of whiskey, and Brownie got out his pipe. Chuck made several cracks to Louella about keeping company with outlaws. Jim silenced him by pointing out, "Outlaws make the best music." Jim, Brownie, and Louella all played guitar, and Meridell played fiddle. Suzie played guitar some too and was getting good on mandolin. Chuck played spoons, badly; but no one said anything. Harry played his thigh. Everyone sang.

Chuck and Jim cleaned up most of the whiskey. Louella helped. Harry and Brownie both had a nip – as did Jeff and Steve. Jim smoked at every pass of the pipe too – and rolled Buglers in between. Meridell had a few tokes of the pot, which she did rather seldom. Brownie and Harry drank most of the coffee. Eventually Chuck said he figured they'd better put the chickens to bed, "Before the Susquach get 'em."

"You mean while you can still find the chicken house."

"Why Lou, I wouldn't get any drunker if I stayed."

She took the bait. "Like hell."

"S'gospel." Jim held up the empty whiskey bottle. "Meridell, the bike's yours. I think I'll walk."

"Or crawl. You want to sleep here?"

"I'll make it."

"We'll roll him out of the road if he doesn't," said Steve. He and Jeff had a tent behind Jim's.

Suzie was ready for bed too. Before long, everyone was gone but Brownie and Harry. They were both still drinking coffee and smoking pot and offered to help Meridell put everything away. They mouseproofed the food and put the leftover chicken in the refrigerator. (There wasn't any guacamole left. There never is.) Then they brought in the dishes and stacked them by the sink. Brownie turned on the water and started to get out the plastic bottle of Crystal White detergent.

"That can wait." Meridell waved at the dishes.

"I don't mind. — 'Less you want me to clear out so you can go to bed."

"I want to talk."

"Something wrong?"

"No."

"Just...Meridell and I saw something strange while you were gone. If anyone knows what to make of it, maybe you will."

They sat down in the living room, still warm enough to have the door and windows open. Meridell told Brownie about the Indian woman, while Brownie and Harry smoked another bowl. Meridell concluded the story: "Any idea? You ever see her?"

Brownie considered for a while. Finally he replied. "Well...yes. I have....She fed me some of that elk once too. And she was the first one showed me the survey in the Wilderness. Then she left me. I got lost all day. But once I found my way out, I been able to find my way back every time."

"How did you know that cave was there at all?"

"Plane flew over one time. I ducked under some bushes, and there it was."

They all knew the story of the Apache woman and how Elk Stuck got its name. None of them really had any more explanation, but Brownie had more information.

"She don't like mining, I think. But she really don't like the army."

"How's that?"

"When did you say you met her?"

"Two weeks ago today. Maybe eleven o'clock in the morning."

Brownie thought. "Now that is weird. My camp is fifteen miles from here. Downhill and overland. Nearest road's eight miles the other way. It was that same day, a little before sunrise. I'd watered at dusk and been out that morning to make sure the wet didn't show. I was almost back at camp when I smelled juniper smoke. It had happened once before: Dentist from Tucson and his son home from college. They thought I was a mountain man. I had a hard time convincing them I really didn't want my picture took, even if they paid me. But you can bet my heart was pounding when I smelled that smoke.

"I tiptoed over the rocks and didn't believe I made a sound. But when I came in sight of her, she was looking right at me. Didn't act one bit surprised to see me either. Offered me coffee. — She had a fresh pot just ready and two tin cups. She even had a little bag of sugar. So I sat down and drank coffee with her. Made me nervous being out in the open around there in daylight, especially with a fire. But I didn't feel like I could say anything. Just kept my ears peeled.

"After a while I did hear a plane, but it didn't come close. It passed by way off to the southeast of us. She nodded toward it. 'Bad men,' she said.

"The only things over there were the LemTron compound about twelve miles away, and the road eight miles beyond that. 'A lot of white men are stupid. You can't eat gold. Those white men are worse than stupid. You stop them. I'll help.' It's about the most I ever heard her say.

"She put out the fire and disappeared it so good I couldn't tell it had ever been there. Then she packed up the coffee pot and cups in a cloth bag and headed off over the rocks toward higher country. I watched her appear on the next two ridges and then disappear on the flat of a mesa top. The sun was just clear of the Peloncillos. Where you saw her was eighteen miles away and almost six thousand feet higher."

Brownie shook his head, then shrugged. "Anyhow, that's why I decided to go scouting. All I really learned is that LemTron's doing something with the military. But I guess that's more than we knew before."

It was late. Meridell was ready for bed. Harry and Brownie were so coffeed up they decided to go for a walk. The moon was not much past new and was already set, but the stars were brilliant. Brownie led the way up the bluff behind the house. The open ponderosa-covered hillside let in a surprising amount of light. On the ridgetop they could see even more clearly and could easily avoid the occasional little prickly pear that managed to exist at this altitude.

They walked a couple of miles as the ridge headed up to define the east side of the Double Eagle Creek watershed. Harry had never been up this side before. The stars were beautiful, and there were a lot of meteors. Finally, they came to a little rocky open peak jutting up from the ridgetop. There Brownie indicated they should stop. They both found comfortable places to sit on the rock. Then Brownie loaded the pipe one more time, and they sat and watched the dawn come in.

There was a three hundred sixty degree view, including the first time Harry had yet seen Thunder Peak. It was about five miles away, about seven hundred feet higher than the peak they were on. Harry wondered, wishfully, if he could get Meridell to come back here with him sometime.

CHAPTER EIGHT

Harry was well aware that he had been up all night and had a lot of pot and coffee. He did not want to seem flakey, so he hesitated to say anything. They had only walked a few more steps before Brownie stopped them.

"Com'ere."

Brownie walked, slowly, back the way they had come twenty-five or thirty feet. Then he turned around and covered the same territory again in the opposite direction even more slowly. Harry followed. Brownie repeated the circuit several times, each time covering a shorter distance before turning around. Finally, he stopped, facing just a little west of south and almost perpendicular to the direction they had been walking along the open ridgetop. He spread his arms, closed his eyes, and stood very still. Harry stood a few feet behind Brownie and did the same. When Harry opened his eyes, Brownie was leaning and peering off to his right. Then he leaned the other way and looked back into the woods and sky in that direction. Then he turned around.

Harry jumped. The expression on Brownie's face was mostly a friendly, concerned query; but Brownie's eyes were full of power again. Harry thought they could burn right through solid rock. Harry did not think he would want to meet those eyes angry.

"What'd ya get?"

Harry knew exactly what Brownie was asking, but it was hard to articulate. "This side was sort of colors." Harry waved his left hand in the general direction they had been coming from. "Blue like a peacock's tail. Golden yellow like...like a sunflower made of light. It felt good too. Lifted me up. Like walking in the dark and suddenly smelling flowers."

Harry gestured to the right and frowned. "Over there....Man, I felt like I was gonna lose my supper."

"Now look." Brownie stepped a few feet to the right.

Harry did the same and peered out. Most of the view was the ridge on the other side of Double Eagle Creek. Harry spotted the cut in the trees where the road went over the top. Town was below, though it was not visible as the drop was too steep to see the bottom from there.

Brownie brought Harry a few steps the other way and told him to look again. Harry immediately noticed the birds singing their morning songs to the newly risen sun. Mostly the line of sight was just trees. A little bit of what might be two separate ridges some distance off was visible too.

"Turn around."

Harry did. The view was changed. The ridge with the road crossing it was not visible. There was no way to tell there was a valley there at all. The next sight to meet the eyes was a higher ridge farther north – and much farther away. "What do you make of it?"

"I dunno. I think something's wrong in town."

They went the rest of the way down the hill very cautiously. Everything looked peaceful. The only person in sight was Louella moving a hose in the garden. Then, as they approached, they heard something coming over the top of Post Office Ridge. Brownie stopped them in a thick stand of oak scrub near the road, where they could see but not be seen.

There was a whole caravan. There were two Forest Service trucks and three other pickups. Each of these had a load, covered by a big green tarp. There was also a funny looking four wheeler – not the kind that is fixed up for a toy, the kind that can go anywhere. The last truck was bigger and had a canvas cover on the back. The truck was white, and the canvas cover was tan. The flap in back was open just enough to see there were men inside. Harry could not tell what they were wearing, but he would have bet money it was uniforms. The colors were not right; yet the truck was surely a troop carrier.

"Grunts get to eat dust, I see." Harry looked where Brownie nodded.

The caravan had just come to the end of the pavement. It had been mostly dry for two weeks now. The troop carrier at the rear was nearly hidden in the dust cloud.

"What do you make of it?"

Brownie shrugged. Then something caught his eye. "What the...?" Suddenly he burst out laughing. They crossed the road. Jim Barnes stared foggily at the line of trucks grinding slowly up the slope. He looked rather green and held his head.

"Here I was dreaming I was dead and buried and peacefully enjoying my eternal rest." He gestured to the rather lumpy piece of ground where he now sat and clearly had spent the night. "When a God damned herd of buffalo decides to stampede across my grave....Holy shit. Am I gonna have to live with this head?"

"All day."

Harry thought Brownie's cheeriness rather callous. Jim was in too much pain to notice. "How the hell'd I get here?"

"Guess that's as far as you got."

Jim shook his head — and then regretted it.

"Think you can make it home?" Harry asked.

Jim stood up, none too steadily. He looked up the street. His house was only about two hundred yards away, just out of sight around the next bend. "I think so." He climbed the short slope up to the road, carefully not jiggling his head any more than he had to. Harry and Brownie watched his slow, but steady progress out of sight.

Harry turned to Brownie and nodded up the road. "What do you think we should do?"

"He'll live."

"Quit jivin' me, Man."

Leprechaun grin. Harry was half inclined to be pissed. Lightning bolt. Harry shivered. Where was that? Up his spine? Brownie's eyes?

"I'm going scouting."

"Can I help?"

"I'll do a better job alone."

Harry felt a little jealous, a little left out, diminished. He also felt relieved. He was ready for a whole bag of Zs. But, damn it, where did Brownie get off being such a hot shit? He's just a kid too, Harry thought, resentfully. Then he remembered how tired and stoned he was. Quit being paranoid, he told himself silently.

Harry looked up. No telling how long Brownie had stood waiting for some response. Harry smiled sheepishly. "Sorry, Man. I'm spacin' out."

"Yeah. Get some shuteye. If there's anything to be done, you'll do it better after you sleep."

This made sense to Harry. It also made him feel better about his own competence. Brownie was a bro. "Okay." Harry smiled. "I'll see if anyone here in town knows anything later too."

"Good man." And Brownie was off like a swallow.

Harry watched Brownie disappear up the hill. Then he turned and headed down to the Randells'. Chuck was in front of the house, puffing away.

"Oho!" Chuck bellowed. "The prodigal returns. Boy, you're late for work."

"In a pig's eye."

Chuck broke up, as usual. Unfortunately, he swallowed a mouthful of smoke, which precipitated a lengthy and terminal-sounding coughing fit. Eventually, this subsided.

"You okay?"

The gasps slowed to something that approximated normal breathing. "I *may* live."

"Did you see all those trucks come through?"

"You bet I did"

Harry jumped. More lightning bolts. "Know who they are?"

"LemTron, the army, and the Forest Circus. No, I don't know what they're doing. Whatever it is, I bet I'll want to stop them when I find out."

The racket brought Louella out. "You look like you been dancin' with a bear."

This staying up all night was a trip. Had he ever seen eyes on a human being so wild? Louella looked like she was a bear herself. Harry wondered why he'd never noticed before.

"Want anything to eat before you hibernate?"

"Uh, piece of bread, maybe."

"How about some hash browns and a couple eggs?"

"Sounds great. Thank you. Maybe just one egg though."

"Wimp!"

Harry jumped again. Had Chuck deliberately snuck up behind him?

Harry foolishly drank two cups of coffee – with Rodeo honey. He also drowned his egg and potatoes in salsa. Naturally, when he went to bed, he found himself hopelessly wide awake. So he thought he might as well read a while. Unfortunately, he picked up a story about a place where the worms got hit by a cosmic ray. The ray made them grow bigger, and bigger. After a while they were eating everything: gardens, houses, people.

"Lordy, I don't need this!" Harry said aloud. He flipped to another story. It turned out to consist largely of a blow-by-blow description of a battle fought with swords. Harry kicked off his shoes and lay down. Next thing he knew, it was three, and he was thirsty. He had forgotten to open a window. Now the shed was hot enough to melt a man's brain.

Harry guzzled down a jar of tepid water on his way out the door. Blech, he thought. He had slept in his clothes too. Harry took off his shirt before he even went back in for clean clothes and a towel. The shirt had been clean yesterday afternoon. A dressy western shirt he had put on for the party, it was sixty-five percent polyester. Harry held the shirt at arm's length. Three goats, he decided – on a scale of four that is.

Harry actually had to let the water in the surface cold water line they were still using run out before it cooled enough to let him take a shower. However, when he got the temperature right, he rapidly concluded that the reason the resurrection had been so long postponed was to allow time for completion of the heavenly plumbing. Harry sang to himself as he dried off and combed his hair:

New Jerusalem's got showers,
New Jerusalem's got rain.

There was a mirror on a nail on the back of the house by the shower. Harry thought he could use a trim. He was pretty sure both Louella and Meridell cut hair. He wondered which one he wanted to ask. He knew he wanted Meridell to do it, but he did not want to get too brother-and-sister with a woman he wanted to be lovers with.

Louella was in the shade of the porch, reading *People Magazine* and listening to a Willie Nelson tape of old crooner tunes. There was no more radio reception in the canyon Elk Stuck was in than TV — except at Jim's. Jim had an antenna up the bluff that got him tolerably good radio reception. Chuck and Louella listened to tapes and got their news from popular magazines and conversations.

Chuck was across the street in front of the store looking at the sky. Harry looked too. The clouds were beginning to build more substantially than they had in a week. "Looks like we might get a little action."

Louella looked up. "Couple'a days. Yeah. We need it, before some damned Texan burns the place down with a butt."

"Louella, you cut hair, don't you?"

"Thought you were gonna go native like Brownie."

"Not my style."

"I use it for spells, you know."

"Huh?"

"Hair. How do you think I keep my reprobate husband in line? — I witch 'im with his own hair. Fingernail clippings work too."

"Why, Louella, you don't need to cast any spells on me." Harry threw back his arms in an expansive gesture. "My body is yours any time."

"Mmm. Now you're talkin'. Mind if Chuck takes pictures?"

"Pervert."

Louella's laugh could hit the same magnitude as Chuck's. Harry clutched his straw hat on his head and hunkered down against the hurricane. Louella laughed so hard at this that Chuck came up to investigate.

"We're gonna found a new church," Harry grinned. "Tickling'll be the main sacrament."

"Been done."

"Yer shittin' me."

"Russia. Sometimes they tickled 'em to death."

Louella was gasping for breath.

Harry looked at her. "Maybe she'll have a vision."

"I dunno," replied Chuck laconically. "Heart attack looks more likely."

Just then the sound of approaching vehicles became audible. They all looked up. Three more Forest Service pickups came over the top of Post

38

Office Ridge. All three of them were pulling full four-horse trailers.

"Holy Moses," said Chuck. "They've called in the cavalry. However, we've got the Apaches." Chuck gestured and looked to Louella, who made a face designed to scare the whiskers off of Bluebeard.

The latest caravan passed slowly through town. Several people in the trucks waved. Chuck and Louella and Harry all waved back.

"Why that's Ray Morse," said Louella. We'll just have to kidnap him and pry some information out of him under torture."

"She's been wanting to get into his pants for years. Only thing stopping her is Mrs. Ray Morse."

"He isn't even married."

"Senior."

"Why don't you distract her for me?"

"Honey, don't you value my huevos?"

"You're right. I wouldn't want you to go the way of Ray, Senior." She turned to Harry and shook her head dolorously. "Mountain oysters simmered to mush." Then she turned back to Chuck. "I like my men barbequed. Besides, it would be cradle robbing."

"You're gonna insult Harry."

"Harry's a man. He's just skinny."

Chuck looked stern. "Louella, I will not have you molesting the help."

"Scuse me." Harry spoke up. "Am I gettin' anywhere near the Muskogee turnoff?"

Eventually, Chuck wandered off, packing his pipe. Louella went back to her magazine, after scheduling Harry for a haircut tomorrow afternoon.

Harry climbed up to the water tank. The concrete was looking good. Now all there was left to do was the large, but straight-forward job of digging the water line trench from the well to the tank and from there back to the house. Harry wondered if he would have to go around any boulders. He was sure tomorrow was plenty soon enough to find out.

Then what, Harry wondered. There was quite a bit more work to do on the water system, but it would be done eventually. He had just come up here to get out of the summer heat in Alamogordo. The water line was Chuck and Louella's reason to feed him. He never really decided to stay, yet he had landed in Elk Stuck pretty solidly. It was time to think about what he wanted to do and how to do it.

Harry mused briefly and inconclusively on his future. Then he headed across the street to say hi to Meridell.

CHAPTER NINE

The next few days were weird. Harry worked hard on the trench. Mind blank with exhaustion was the only time he felt relaxed. Otherwise, just craziness.

Meridell was distracted. She was pushing herself at her weaving and not liking the results. Louella was morose. Chuck was mean.

Harry had about forgotten the nasty little pig eyes he had seen on Chuck when they first met. Now they were back. Chuck ordered Harry and Louella around arbitrarily, found fault constantly, and was generally extremely unpleasant to live with. He drank even more than usual, but he did not enjoy it. He bitched constantly. Harry was thankful most of the venom was, at least, directed at the government rather than at him. Chuck's language also became far more foul than usual.

"Fuckers!" Chuck was finishing off a sixpack of Bud. It was Chuck's fifth can. Harry and Louella had split one. "You know what this ought to cost? Fuckin' taxes. Tax the farmer. Tax the brewer. Tax the trucker. Tax the storekeeper. And then the bastards tax the fuckin' sixpack again when you go to buy it. Lookit this."

It was a questionnaire from the local congressman about tax reform. Harry had glanced at it. Nothing on it affected him. He had never made enough on the record to pay taxes. He would have last year, but Jason Sanders, his old boss, showed him how to deduct his legal expenses. The only thing he had not figured out how to get back was his Social Security. That was a pisser though. The President had said in so many words on TV that guys his age were not going to see jack shit of it.

"Think I'll go check the mail."

"Better take a life jacket," Louella responded, with a half-hearted smile.

It had rained pretty good Tuesday night — which only seemed to make the flies worse. At least the garden was happy. Now it was three-thirty Thursday afternoon. The clouds were thick on Thunder Peak, and it was rumbling all around. Harry shrugged and headed up the hill. Chilly little gusts billowed the loose T shirt he was wearing. The air felt good, a relief from the choked-up pressure cooker Chuck had become.

Harry knew it was those people he and Brownie saw going up the mountain that had set Chuck off, but he did not know why. Chuck didn't know either. All he really knew was that he did not trust them. He did not like them. He did not know who they really were, and he did not know how to find out. Harry wished Brownie would get back.

Jesus Lucero's green '58 Chevy pickup was parked outside the post office. Wayne Hart was reading his junk mail while Jesus talked with Mrs. Martinez, the postmistress.

"I ain't gonna use it for work no more."

Harry did not know Jesus or Wayne as well as some of the other people in town, but he did know Jesus was always *going to* fix up his old truck and sell it for a lot of money. Jesus never did a thing about it. It was a standing joke.

Jesus and Wayne worked at the mine. It was unusual to see them in the middle of the afternoon. Wayne looked up as Harry approached.

"Win the sweepstakes?"

"No, Man. We're shut down."

"Oh yeah?" The mine was steady work when operating, but that was not all the time. This was the first shutdown since Harry had been in Elk Stuck. "So now you're a man of leisure."

"I don't know, Man."

"How's that?"

"Izzy's talkin' about selling out."

"You're kidding."

Isaiah Overman had reopened the Deadman Mine when deregulation of the price of gold made it worth mining again for the first time in forty years. Everyone called it a gold mine too, though the price of silver usually determined whether or not it was profitable enough to work.

"No, Man. He's talking about retiring to Tucson."

That was quite amazing. Isaiah was an institution in Elk Stuck. Harry did not know him at all. He would not even respond when Harry said hello. Harry had no idea what his prejudice was against the Randells, but it apparently extended to anyone associated with them. Gertrude Overman would say hello to Harry and even smile but they had never said anything more.

Harry knew Isaiah had come to Elk Stuck as a kid. His father had left Missouri in the depression and found a job at the mine. When the mine shut down, he drove truck, did carpentry, and stayed on. Isaiah had done the same. When the mine got cheap enough, they bought it. The old man was now dead. Isaiah's mom was in a nursing home.

Gertrude was from Apex. She had met Isaiah at the cafe where she worked thirty years ago. It was a late marriage for both of them, but they had one daughter, who now lived in Phoenix. They had lived in Elk Stuck their entire married life.

"How old is he?"

"Sixty-two. But I guess he's got an offer on the mine so good he can afford to quit working completely even before he gets his Social Security."

"I'll be damned. How much is the mine worth?"

"Depends on how bad you want it," said Jesus.

"I guess."

"Missile silos are top dollar."

"What!?"

Jesus shrugged. "That ain't no mining outfit."

"Who?"

"LemTron. Claim they are. But I don't believe it. That's the army."

"Really?"

Jesus shrugged again. "Shit, Man. I don't know."

"What're you guys gonna do?"

"I'm gonna work on my truck. See what happens. Maybe I'll go work for my uncle for a while. He's got a wrecker on the Interstate. It'd be better money than I been gettin' here anyway."

Harry looked to Wayne. Wayne shrugged. "Jim's got a thinning contract coming up. The mine don't reopen, maybe I'll work in the woods a while. You ought to check it out too. Lay up a little stash before winter."

Thinning contracts were part of the way the National Forest was managed. National Forests were administered by the United States Department of Agriculture. Except for congressionally designated Wilderness, the land was largely classified for "Multiple Use" management.

41

This included trails for hikers and hunters, grazing permits (throughout the National Forest, including the Wilderness) and timber.

Except for Wilderness areas, most of the National Forest capable of producing timber was treated as a vast tree farm. Very little of the forest was virgin any more. Trees reseed themselves, but the commercially preferred species were also planted on contract. As well, in order to encourage optimum growth, the Forest Service let out thinning contracts through competitive bidding. Tree planting and thinning, along with the actual logging, were significant sources of employment in any forested area in the Southwest.

"I don't have a saw," said Harry.

"Somebody's got to stack the brush. You don't need a saw for that."

"Hmh. When's he start?"

"Right after Labor Day."

There was a letter for Louella. Otherwise nothing but junk mail. It was starting to sprinkle. Harry headed down the hill. Jesus and Wayne were inside talking with Mrs. Martinez.

Harry was only about a third of the way down when it started raining harder. Dumb shit, he thought, I knew this was going to happen. Should have waited.

He took off his T shirt, wrapped the mail in it, and started to run. Soon it was not only pouring, but hailing. Harry looked for shelter. The ruin of an old stone shed stood near the road, so he ran to it. It did not really keep him dry, but it at least got him out of the direct battering of the hail.

The rain lasted a long time. After the hail stopped, Jesus and Wayne came by. They didn't know Harry was there, so they did not stop. By now he was shivering. Harry figured he was already wet and he would be warmer moving, so he ran on down the hill.

"Didn't your mama teach you to come in out of the rain, Boy?" Chuck was smiling, but his eyes still looked mean.

Harry stayed in the house just long enough to heat up a cup of coffee. Then he headed up to the shed, with the coffee, to change into something dry.

By then, the rain had about stopped, but he was still cold. He thought about lighting up the stove. Instead, he went out and started digging on the water line trench. This was as aggravating as productive because the wet, clayey dirt stuck to the pick and shovel. Harry was soon cursing and muddy, but he was warm.

That evening, he went over to talk with Jim about the thinning contract. He wondered why Jim had not mentioned it. Harry saw Jim far more often than Wayne did. However, he decided not to get paranoid.

It was just as well Harry made that decision before he got to Jim's. Jim was in a foul frame of mind. Worse, he was just looking for someone to talk to about it.

"Steve wants to stay this fall. Jennifer doesn't want him to." Harry kept his mouth shut. He had never had any kids (though he had been married briefly) and he had never met Jim's ex. He knew enough to keep away from the subject. He wished Jim would do the same.

42

Jim wouldn't though. He was as intent on ranting and raving about Jennifer as Chuck was on vilifying the government. He was also drinking whiskey. Harry hoped Jim would still be coherent by the time they got to talking about the thinning contract.

He was, though Harry figured it might be well to reconfirm things later.

"Five bucks an hour. And expect to bust ass."

That sounded just fine to Harry. September days would still be reasonably long. He stood to put away some money. He would have to bust ass between now and then too, though. Otherwise he'd be leaving Chuck and Louella hanging on the water line.

Jim finally ran out of things to say about Jennifer. Unfortunately, the discussion of the thinning contract got him onto the subject of the government. Bugshit, Harry thought: I'm surrounded. He resigned himself to the topic, and gave Jim a hand with the whiskey.

"Fuckin' Freddies'll hang you up half a day.* *You're* paid for production. *They* get a salary. -- And if you miss their fuckin' deadline, the bastards'll default you, and you don't get paid at all. I just hope we get Pete on this one."

"Who's he?"

"Pete Padilla. Forest Service inspector. Cousin of Jesus'. He's okay. You do your contract. He goes over it. You get your check. That Harold Simms, now, he's an asshole. Comes up with a fuckin' tape measure. He decides you've left them too close together, he'll make you cut more. Then he'll come back and claim the trees are too far apart and fuckin' dock you. Asshole ought to be strung up by the balls."

Harry was getting into the spirit of the conversation. The whiskey helped. "Or have to work for a living for a boss like him."

Jim thought that was funny. His laugh lightened the mood. But not very much.

Harry was relieved to go to bed, but he tossed and turned a long time before getting to sleep. Worse, he had drunk more whiskey than he realized and hadn't drunk any water. He woke the next day with a hangover.

He decided to sweat it out, so he set to work, somewhat grimly, on the trench. The ground was a good consistency today anyhow. Moist enough to be loose. Not so wet as to stick to everything.

"Hey, Harry."

Harry looked up, startled. He had been pouring himself into his work. He was dripping and feeling good. His mind had been blissfully blank for some time till Louella called.

"I know you didn't have anything but coffee this morning. Your agent just called to say you're the wrong color for the Ethiopian relief poster. You might as well come have some lunch."

* - Freddy: Government employee, especially a Forest Service Employee. Disparaging term used regionally, especially by other people who work in the woods.

It sounded like she was in a better mood. He hoped Chuck was too. He wanted to talk with them about the future.

"Don't you know skinny men are sexy?" Harry struck a pose.

"Lecher."

Chuck appeared at the door. "I warn you, Boy, she's insatiable. You better eat first, or you'll flat out die when she comes."

It sounded like Chuck and Louella were back to normal. Harry was relieved. He put the tools up in case it rained before he got back to them. – Lunch with Chuck and Louella could eat up most of the afternoon. – Then he headed into the house with a smile.

Louella pinched Harry's butt when he got a cup of coffee. Chuck was already on beer. He laughed when Harry jumped. Harry figured that was a good sign.

CHAPTER TEN

"Shit, Boy, stay as long as you can put up with us."

"Fact is, Harry, he feels quilty we're not paying you more."

"Shush, Woman. You want to give him ideas?...Whatever it is you run on, Boy, you ought to patent it."

"Coffee and pot. Jet fuel." Harry grinned.

"Have some more potato salad." Louella urged the bowl on Harry. He was about stuffed, but he took a little more. It was good. "Fact is, Harry, we were both kind of hoping you'd stay on long enough to help with firewood. Chuck's back shouldn't do all that lifting. And I was dreading it."

"Shit, Boy, stay all winter. We'll will you the place in case we drive off the road."

Serious subjects settled, Harry replied to the banter in kind. "What about Jerry?"

"That shyster?" Jerry, Chuck and Louella's son, was an insurance agent in Gallup. "He could pave his driveway in turquoise and silver now. He don't need this place."

Harry had not met Jerry. Chuck and Louella had had dinner in Lariat with him once since Harry had been with them, but Jerry would not come up the hill to Elk Stuck.

Chuck and Louella also had a daughter, Deliah. Deliah was a stewardess for Continental Airlines. She regarded her parents as an embarrassment. They did not hear from her much.

Eventually, Chuck and Louella stopped urging more food on Harry and retired to the bedroom. Harry went on out with a smile. It sure felt good to know he didn't have to think about where he was going to live unless he wanted to.

Harry did not feel much like swinging a pick on a full stomach. He wandered over to the shop. All the kids were there.

"Mom, he's got to stay." Jeff looked very earnest. "The Lady wants him to."

"If the Lady wants him here, can't she arrange it?"

"Mama!" Suzie looked professorial. "The Lady's not God. She's a good Spirit. But she needs our help."

"It's really not up to us, dear. It's between Jim and Jennifer."

"Maybe we could pray." Suzie held out her hand.

"Okay." Meridell took it. "Want to join?" Harry did. The boys took places too. The five of them stood in a silent circle.

After a few minutes, Suzie spoke again: "Lady, please show Jennifer that Steve's got to stay. They've gotta decide soon 'cause school's gonna start."

There were a few more minutes of silence.

Rumble. Boom! Rumble. Thunder spoke on the mountain. A hand squeeze rounded the circle. Then everyone opened their eyes. All were smiling. Suzie looked confident and determined. After a bit, the boys took off on their bikes.

"How's it going?"

"Harry, I just don't know."

"That rich bitch doesn't own you, Meridell."

"I know it. I'm not even trying to give her everything she wants. But I keep thinking: I'm a recognized professional now. Then I step back from what I'm working on, and it just looks tacky."

"So don't think."

Meridell smiled a bit wanly. "That's easy for you to say."

Harry put a comforting arm around Meridell's shoulder. Her response told Harry this was welcome.

"What happened to your weekend?"

"Louella said she'd be here by three."

"When she gets here, let's go for a walk. Then don't even look at your loom before Monday."

"That sounds just right."

A carload of Texans pulled up. Harry and Meridell both waited on them. They bought a few small items. Soon after they left, Louella arrived. It was getting about mail time. Meridell and Harry headed up Post Office Ridge.

They took their time. When they got there, Wayne and Jesus were just pulling in, coming up the hill the other way from the highway. They were in Wayne's truck today, a ten year old blue and white Chevy.

Wayne and Jesus were both built stocky, with bigger muscles than Harry, but less defined. Jesus was the same height as Harry's five eleven. He was dark skinned, his black hair was trimmed short, and he was clean shaven. Wayne was fair complected but deeply tanned where his customary T shirt didn't cover. His straw colored hair came down around his ears. His thick full beard was trimmed short like Harry's, and he was slightly taller than Harry. Wayne, at twenty-four, was a year younger than Harry. Jesus was a couple years older. They both had a bit of a beer gut.

Meridell smiled and waved as the two men got out of the truck. "Hi Jesus. Wayne."

"Hi. How's it going," Jesus replied.

"Okay," said Harry. "How 'bout you?"

"I'm okay. Ol' Wayne's been seeing ghosts though."

"Oh?" Harry perked up. Meridell was interested too.

"It was just a dream. Snow everywhere. Then this Indian lady started to walk up to me. But she couldn't get to me. And when she talked, I couldn't hear her. Scared the piss out of me."

They all got their mail. Meridell had a check from Santa Fe and a note from Paul. He wanted to take the kids camping Labor Day weekend. Said he'd call at the store Tuesday, a little after five when the rates went down. That was fine with Meridell. She and Paul had managed to dissolve their marriage three years earlier with a minimum of rancor. Now they were pretty good friends.

Harry had a letter, somewhat to his surprise, from the etymologist. There was actually a check in it for fifty dollars too. He said he might come up and see Harry sometime and invited him to stop in if he ever got over to Tucson.

The only other mail was something for Chuck that looked like a bill.

There were some apple trees by the creek half a mile below town. Most of the ones in town had lost out to a hard freeze in May, but there was fruit on the ones down the canyon. Meridell suggested they go see how it was coming along. They walked out the ridge and down the bluff on an old trail.

The apples were doing okay. They found some late raspberries too and each got a mouthful. Then they climbed up the other side of the bluff and walked across the top of the ridge. It was a couple of fairly level miles to the road on the far side of town. They took their time. Several places, views were magnificent. There was a dense mass of cloud to the west.

"Must be a hell of a storm in the Chiricahuas," Harry said. "Wonder if we'll get any."

The clouds were headed their way, but they also seemed to be breaking up as they came. Except on Thunder Peak, where they were black and roiling. Thunder rumbled, and they could see lightning flashes on the mountain.

Suddenly there was a terrific crash to the east. They both jumped and then looked up just in time to see two jet fighters roar over.

"Sons of bitches." Looking to the east, Harry now saw the clouds were thick on the Peloncillos. It was storming to the south too. Only directly overhead was there a brilliant bowl of clear blue. Harry took a deep breath. "Wanta smoke?"

"I don't think so. But you go ahead if you like."

Harry got a joint in a little piece of a plastic bag and a Bic lighter out of his left pocket and lit up. He offered it to Meridell, who took it.

"Just a toke maybe." She took one. Harry took several more, then put out the joint, a little more than half gone, and wrapped it back in the plastic.

Then they talked about the Indian lady and whatever was going on. Meridell told Harry the kids all saw the Indian woman often. They were friends. The kids said she was the Spirit of the mountain and wanted them to help her protect it.

"From what?"

Meridell didn't know. She did not think the children did either. Just that it was evil and that it was threatening Thunder Mountain.

Harry was impressed that Meridell would not be afraid for her children to live in a place where such things went on. Meridell saw it differently.

"There's no less evil in Douglas or Silver City. Last time Paul and I met in Albuquerque, someone stole the battery out of his car. Woman next door said they'd taken hers twice in the last month. Here, if there's evil, we can see it. Here we have allies too."

Harry thought about that for quite a while. It raised his already-high opinion of Meridell further. It also made him feel more serious about the situation here. He was not altogether sure he wanted to be serious. He had been serious enough last spring in jail. He had been terrified they were going to send him to prison for a long, long time when they set his bail at forty thousand dollars.

He could not even run away. Who could he ask for four thousand dollars for a bondsman? No way he could pay that back. The lawyer ate up all he had saved. Harry had been grateful to that lawyer though, and to his boss, Mr. Sanders. Between them they convinced the judge Harry was a good kid who had just made a dumb mistake. The judge let him plead guilty to a misdemeanor and let him off for time served. It all happened so fast — and the jail in Alamogordo was so hot — he was still half punchy when he got to Elk Stuck.

Harry liked feeling serious about Meridell though. And he liked it here. He was not sure about winter. He bet it would be long and cold. But if things worked out with Meridell, maybe he just would stay.

They had been sitting up near the ridgetop for some time. The sun had been behind the clouds to the west for a while. Now it shown through. Meridell got up to stretch. "Oh look."

Harry did. Arcking across the entire sky was a magnificent double rainbow. They watched it with their arms around one another till the sun dipped behind the clouds again and it faded out. Then they walked the rest of the way to the road and back down the hill to town.

When they passed Jim's house, he and Steve were packing the truck, but they looked happy. Jeff was there too.

"Mom, can I go with them?"

"What's up?"

"Steve's mom said he could stay. They're going to visit her and get his school clothes."

"I don't know. What's Jim say?"

"It's all right with him."

"Jim, have these little conspirators consulted you?"

"It's fine. We'll be back Monday."

"School starts Tuesday....I guess so."

"Oh boy!" Jeff ran off to pack.

"Be sure you take enough socks."

"My mom's going to have a party for me tomorrow."

"Sounds great. Jim, you need us to feed the dogs?"

Jim had two fairly useless dogs: part hound, part shepherd, part who knows: Speed Bump, named for his habit of sleeping in the middle of the road; and Imogene.

Boing! Harry lit up inside. Meridell said, "Us."

"Thanks. No. Brownie's back."

"Oh good," said Harry. "I was wanting to see him."

"Stash low?" Jim grinned.

"That too."

"He's got some leaf. Kind of mediocre. But there's plenty of it."

"Beggars can't be fussy."

"He's saying howdy to Petunia." Petunia was Jim's jenny. She was a pet, but she was a good little packer too. She and Brownie were fast friends.

"I'm going to go make sure Jeff takes something fit to wear in town. Why don't you and Brownie both come to supper. Jim, you want to eat too before you go?"

"I promised the boys tacos at the State Line."

"Okay." Meridell headed down the street. Jim went back to his packing. Harry went around the house.

There was sort of a field back there fenced: some grass in the creek bottom and a piece of hillside. A washtub was full of water. Brownie and Petunia were racing. The burro kicked up her heels playfully. Brownie saw Harry and ran over. Petunia followed like a puppy. The dogs looked on from a prone position.

Harry slapped Brownie on the shoulder. "Good to see you back."

"Yep." Leprechaun twinkle.

"Learn anything?"

"Yep."

"Gonna tell me?"

"Where's Meridell? I'll tell you both at once."

"Home. We're both invited to supper."

"Sounds good. I'll bring the drugs."

"How's it doing?"

"Males'll be ready to harvest soon. Then we'll see what we got. I sure wouldn't want to be into it for money."

"Oh?"

"My few little plants are pretty easy to hide. Guy with a field full's playing Russian roulette. Lot of planes out. They're not just looking for Wets either."

"You got more balls than me growing at all this close to the border."

Brownie shrugged. "Best place if you're not greedy. Cops are busy lookin' for big time coke smugglers. They don't need to work up a sweat over a little fish like me to fill their quota. Let's do a number with Jim before he goes."

They did. Jim also rolled a dozen joints to take with him. About then, Jeff got back with his pack, and Harry and Brownie headed down the hill. Jim was letting the boys ride in back as far as Lariat. They were already having a party.

Harry and Brownie stopped by the shop, where Louella was just getting ready to close, to tell her Harry was eating with Meridell. Louella had them come by the house for a dozen eggs. Harry liked Louella's cooking, but there was always too much. Meridell's was just right – like everything else about her. Harry did not know how it had slipped up on him. But he realized he was in love.

He was also raring to hear what Brownie had learned as they walked up the street in the dusk. A pasty-looking family rolled past in a new Toyota. They waved, drunk on the mountains. Harry and Brownie waved back. Harry looked at the license plates as they went by. New Mexico. Bernalillo County.

"You could tell 'em about this place in Albuquerque." Harry nodded at the car starting up Post Office Ridge. "They'd think you were making it up."

"Try telling them in Dayton."

"That where you're from?"

"My dad lives north of there, on a farm. Can't make a living on three hundred acres though. He has to work outside jobs. It was plenty big enough for me to grow my first crop."

Brownie's face took on a faraway gaze, as of pleasure remembered from the distant past. Harry thought it looked funny on someone so young.

"Lived with my mom more. Sonoma County. Moved to Humboldt on my own when I was fifteen. How 'bout you? Where are you from?"

Harry shrugged. "Noplace. I was an army brat. Lived in Germany and Hawaii. Never lived anyplace very long. I called Eastern Oklahoma home for a while, but I haven't been there in over a year. I'm not sure where my folks are now."

"You ought to look them up. I bet they'd like to hear from you."

"I know it. I sort of get embarrassed when I get prepared: 'Dear Ma and Pa, hi. I've been in jail.' Couldn't do it. They'd think they raised a thief."

"Thought military types stole from the government all the time."

"My dad's a master sergeant. Real straight arrow. Believes in his country."

"So do I. But I don't believe a government that makes war on me is my government."

"He doesn't see it that way."

"Mmh."

"They would like to hear from me though. I guess I don't have to tell them about jail. I'll just say I been on the road."

CHAPTER ELEVEN

Supper was stir fried garden veggies with tofu and homemade bread. Satisfying, but light. Suzie said she would do the dishes. Brownie and Harry helped Meridell clear the table and clean up the kitchen. Then the three of them retired to the living room, Brownie and Harry with coffee, Meridell with a cup of 'Cinnamon Rose' tea.

"...So I gave the plants a little water. Then I headed for the road cross country. I came out just west of the LemTron operation and lucked out on my first ride: Fort Bliss. And he told me the guys' favorite bar."

"Man, what do you eat out there. That's a long walk."

"I carry a little jerky and dried fruit. If I run out, there's plenty of cactus. Makes you shit green, but it'll keep you going. Has water in it too. Soon the tunas'll be ripe. They're so rich I won't even want anything else."

That was one of the things Harry liked about this country. If it came to it, survival was so simple. That was why it was where the Apaches held out so long. That and the fact it was so rugged they were real hard to catch.

Brownie continued. "After a while, I found someone on the project. So I bought him a beer. Told him I'd just come in from Bisbee. He turned me on in the parking lot and asked if I knew where he could get any 'shrooms. After a while, he mentioned LemTron.

"'Isn't that a mineral outfit? I passed their operation,' I said.

"'Yeah. They're into minerals. But that ain't the whole story.'

"'Oh yes?'

"'I ain't supposed to tell anyone about this. Whole project is classified.'

"'Maybe you better not then.' So of course he did.

"He says there's going to be a big war to the south. Mexico's economy's going over the edge. The Commies'll take advantage of the situation. And the boys in Washington want a war anyhow to bring the country together.

"Right now, copper costs more to mine in this country than it brings. We're buying more from South America than we're mining. In wartime, who knows about foreign suppliers. So the army's working with mineral companies like LemTron to set up secure operations."

"So that's what it is."

Harry had been a kid during Vietnam. He was just about to go past draft age, but a war on the United States' own border might be different.

"No, Man. That's what he believes it is. That's not even what they're telling him. The official version is just, 'Training exercises on multiple use-designated Public Lands.' Who knows how much more of the picture he hasn't figured out? It's more than we knew before though. And we have an inside contact now: Pfc Johnny Higgins. He'll be back here soon too. I'll introduce you."

"Thought you told him you came up from Bisbee."

"He told me how beautiful it is in the Thunders and how nice and cool. I said I might check it out. You just got to remember, when you meet him, I haven't been here long." Brownie's expresion reminded Harry of a time in fourth grade when he had won an ice cream cone.

"He even got me a ride to the Interstate turnoff with some buddies of his coming through from Corpus. And how's this for a turn on?" Brownie now got out a piece of an old towel and carefully unwrapped it.

Neatly rolled in the towel in layers were fourteen fleshy dull turquoise segmented disks. They ranged in diameter from about three quarters of an inch to about three inches. There were an equal number of gnarly yellowish chunks.

"Wow! They're even fresh!"

"That's peyote, isn't it?" said Meridell.

"Sure is. Ever done it before?"

"Tea a couple times. I've never seen it fresh though."

"This is just three days from the South Texas desert."

"Bet it's hot down there."

"Crazy too. Prickly pear trees. Rattlesnakes that weigh more than you do. And baby factories."

"What!" Meridell was shocked.

"Mexican women come over to have their babies in America so they'll be citizens."

"Oh yeah. I read about that."

"Shall we do up some?" Brownie indicated the peyote, lying on its towel in the middle of the living room floor. To Harry, it seemed to pulse quietly.

"You guys go ahead if you want," Meridell said. "I don't think I want to stay up that late."

"I'd just as soon wait too and do it with you," Harry said to Meridell, "if that's okay with you, Brownie. And won't Jim want to get in on it too?"

"Nah. He says his stomach can't handle peyote."

"With the rotgut whiskey he drinks? Man!"

Brownie shrugged. "I like daytime tripping anyhow. You get out and see more."

"Oh yes." Meridell looked enthusiastic now. "I'd really love it if we all went up to the valley with the cave."

Suzie had finished the dishes and come in quietly. "Can I come too?"

"Won't you be bored with a bunch of tripping grownups?"

"You do get kind of silly. But you see the Spirits better."

"'And a little child shall lead them.'"

Suzie knew the quote. The expression she turned to Harry registered both compliment and insult. Whew, he thought. Kids are really sensitive. If he was going to get serious about Meridell, he would have to be serious about her children too.

"How about tomorrow. I promised Harry I wouldn't go near the shop. And I want Suzie to spend Monday making sure she has everything ready for school."

"Mom. That won't take all day."

"You could have fooled me."

"In a pig's eye."

Harry broke up.

Suzie exchanged a warm kiss with her mother. Then she gave Harry and Brownie each a quick little hug and retired to her room to read a Stephen King novel. – A lot of her reading was on an adult level.

Brownie rolled another fat joint. He was rolling them big because the trimmings they were smoking were not very strong.

Harry got up to refill the coffee cups. "Want more tea while I'm at it?"

"Yeah. I'll have another. – If you're going to drink coffee all night, you might as well do the peyote now."

"You're right. Maybe I'll switch to tea too. How 'bout you, Brownie?"

"Sounds nice to me. Got any 'Emperor's Choice?'"

Harry and Brownie smoked the joint. And they all had their tea. Suzie's light eventually went out. After a while, Brownie said good night and headed up to Jim's.

Meridell put on a tape: a homemade recording of a clear-voiced woman singing ballads with a sort of bluegrass backup. She and Harry sat quietly, listening to the music.

Eventually they took hands. By the time the tape was done, Meridell's head was in Harry's lap, and he was alternately carressing her cheeks and massaging her shoulders where they were stiff from tension and weaving.

They did not say anything as they walked to Meridell's bedroom and undressed. It was the first time Harry had slept with a woman in six months – since before jail. It was very different. That had been balling. This was making love.

They made love again when they woke. Harry told Meridell how much he cared about her. Meridell told Harry she cared about him a lot too.

"But I don't want to rush into anything. When a good marriage falls apart, it leaves you with doubts for a long time."

Harry was divorced too, but his marriage had been a joke. Thank God they had not had any kids. He could hardly believe someone was telling him not to get too serious too fast. Till now, what he had been into by way of relationship was friends and flings.

After a while, the smell of coffee and bacon began wafting into their awareness. "That Suzie," said Meridell.

"What a sweetheart." Harry gave Meridell a big kiss.

After a little bit, they got dressed, minimally. Meridell just wrapped on a cotton robe, and Harry pulled on his pants. Then they went on into the kitchen. Suzie had a pot of coffee steaming and pancake batter ready to go.

"Brownie said fasting before a trip's bullshit. You should eat a good breakfast. Then you'll have the strength to do something."

"Yes, Ma'am." Harry saluted.

"Has Brownie already been by?" Meridell asked.

"Him and the dogs got lively about dawn. I heard them run down the street. So I said hi when they came back. He'll be over soon. Chuck came by too."

"Oh?"

"He didn't even know you were still here, Harry. Mom, he wanted you to run the shop again this afternoon. I said no."

"Thank you." Meridell gave her a hug.

"I think he felt a little ashamed asking."

"He should." Harry was at least half serious.

"I also told him you probably wouldn't be there all day. He said you're a wise man. Louella's on the rag. Thinks it may be her last time, and plans to make it a doozie."

Harry and Meridell both laughed. Meridell squeezed Suzie's shoulder. "My Suzie Sunshine."

Suzie began cooking pancakes. There wasn't any syrup, but there was sorghum. And Meridell got out a jar of homemade apricot preserves. – Last year had been a bumper season for fruit.

About the time they had all had a round of pancakes, Brownie showed up with his towel of peyote.

"I like them fresh, but I'll make tea if you'd rather."

"Either way's fine with me. How about you, Meridell?"

"I'm game."

"Half of what's wrong with dry ones is people don't do it right. They grow in an intense desert. They lose water real slow. People let them sit in something damp, and they rot before they get dry. Fresh I even kind of like the taste."

Harry washed the dishes while Meridell and Suzie watched Brownie clean the buttons.

Neither Harry nor Meridell could quite see how anyone would like the taste of peyote. But they were not too bad, especially after the first one.

Brownie and Harry each had four. Meridell had three. That left three buttons and the stems for a batch of tea later. Brownie and Harry had one more cup of coffee apiece too. Then Harry and Meridell washed up and got dressed. And they were ready to go.

Meridell asked Suzie if she wanted to bring any lunch. Brownie said there was jerky and raisins up there. Suzie took a little bag of crackers. Then they all headed up the ridge. The sky was mostly blue, but there were a few clouds already over Thunder Peak.

CHAPTER TWELVE

Meridell and Suzie walked springily but sedately. Harry and Brownie frisked like puppies.

Meridell laughed. "You look like a panther taking running lessons from an antelope."

"That wouldn't work." Suzie had a very practical bent. "The pupil would eat his teacher."

Everyone laughed at that.

It had not rained at town, but there was enough moisture around that the ground was damp in the morning sunshine. The fragrance struck Harry powerfully as they stepped off the road at the top of the ridge. His stomach did little flip-flops too. Must be the peyote coming on, he thought.

It was. Everything was just that much more vibrant as they walked through the ponderosas of the ridgetop. After a while, Harry found a little mantra floating through his mind that had come to him once before on acid: LSDisease. LSDelightful. LSDemonic. LSDevine.

That was how it felt. The air was thick with Spirits. Friendly and nasty. He was nervous for a moment. Then Mescalito was there.

That was the nice thing about peyote. It had its own Spirit guardian. Harry wondered if Mescalito was real or just something conjured up because of the Don Juan books.

Castenada did some good giving the world Mescalito, Harry thought, even if he did spend most of his time shuffling bullshit.

As Harry's body relaxed from the first peyote rushes and the climb up to the ridgetop, he had to excuse himself to go visit the bushes.

"How come I always have to shit so much going up on psychedelics?" he asked when he rejoined the others.

"STP for the Kundalini," said Brownie. "Clears out the passages for take-off."

"Wasn't there a drug called STP once?"

"Yeah. My old man knew some people that did a bunch of it."

"Was it any good?"

"I don't know. Most of the guys that were into it are dead."

"Hey, did your old man know about that first crop?"

"He never found it. Scared the shit out of him when I told him after harvest."

"What did he say?"

"'Don't get caught.' What was he gonna say? Only reason he didn't start smoking, himself, till he was eighteen is 'cause he didn't know about it any sooner."

A world where people did not know about drugs seemed very foreign to Harry, though his own parents had grown up in it. Still lived in it in a way.

The women were ignoring the male crudities in favor of the faces in tree bark and similar more aesthetically pleasing pursuits. Suzie, far from being bored, was enjoying her mother's company even more than usual.

Harry watched Meridell and Suzie. Her childhood was no less chaoic than his own had been, but she had adults to share her questions with. God, what a luxury, Harry thought.

Harry prided himself on being tough. That did not mean he had to like all of how he got that way.

"How quick the season is."

Harry looked up. Meridell was pointing to the leaves on the aspens they were walking through now. There was already some yellow. Sure different from Alamogordo – or Oklahoma.

Harry shivered at the thought of the coming mountain winter. Yet it was so beautiful. He had found Meridell here. He wanted to stay to be with her, but he wanted to stay anyhow. For the place itself.

Thunder rumbled, right on cue, over the peak. What was he doing living in a place that was such a movie?

"Clouding up early," said Meridell.

"I've got some wood dry at the cave if it gets cold."

They went back to enjoying their surroundings.

"People are a spiritual bottleneck," said Brownie, as they started up the last steep slope. They were all moving right along, and comfortable doing so. However, only Brownie had extra breath to talk.

"Look how much of Spirit has gotten into the world through us."

Brownie gestured around him. The immediate view did not contain a single man made object.

The realization brought Harry to a full halt just as they topped the rise and could see into the valley.

They all stopped to catch their breaths and take in the view.

There was the mountain lion again. This time it stood and looked right at them for several seconds before it took off.

"She comes here to drink and hunt. Den's over there." Brownie pointed. "I don't disturb the babies. They're out now though. She might even let us see them."

Suzie had seen them and told Meridell. Harry was the only one who did not know about them. He was full of wonder. They all were, surveying the high valley in the wake of the mountain lion.

"I don't go up there much either." Brownie pointed in another direction. "Elk calving ground. Mama lion'll take her share. I'll take one. Most of the rest'll be out of harm's way by the time the season opens."

"You'll take a calf?" Suzie clearly did not approve.

"No. I'll take a young bull that's not getting any. No trophy, but the best meat in the world. Best hide too, if it's tanned right. It's a crime how many of them end up in the dump. Shit, if they don't need the money they could give them away."

"Too complicated to make it legal. The dump's safer."

Harry's old man had taught him to hunt – by the book. Earl Upton did not approve of waste either. He always sold his hide, except one he had tanned himself as a teenager, which he kept on the wall.

"Sheeit," said Brownie.

Harry now realized Brownie was dressed completely in buckskins. Well used. Brownie dressed that way often. He did not have a lot else. Mostly just another set of clothes that would not get him arrested if he went to town. Brownie did not go to town much. Harry could hardly visualize him in a bar in El Paso talking with the soldiers.

The sun was warm and bright. All three adults had their shirts off. (Suzie was modest and kept hers on.) Thinking of El Paso made Harry thankful, once again, that he was up here where it was cool and the air smelled good.

Brownie glided at an exuberant run down into the valley, smooth as a cloud. The others followed almost as lightly.

Brownie took off all his clothes by the stream and splashed water on himself. Harry followed suit. What a rush! The water was about thirty-four degrees.

Harry was grateful to let Mescalito hold his hand for just a moment. Then it was like bursting through a geyser of every imaginable color of gems in the top of his head. "Wow!"

The others all looked at him. He was immediately embarrassed to have made such a loud noise. But they were all smiling. They knew exactly how he felt. Even Suzie. Especially Suzie.

Suzie was slightly disdainful of the drug use of her elders. She regarded it as a burdensome source of anxiety in her world due to the law. However, she was grateful for the occasional breakthroughs drugs produced in the wall of adult stupidity. She did not like pot. She said it made her sleepy and hurt her throat. She had never been inclined to try any of the others, but she had her preferences.

Peyote was the only one she actually liked being around. – She had even gone so far as to get a taste on her tongue – which was plenty to deter her from going further. Nonetheless, she claimed Mescalito for a personal friend. She had her own well-developed relationships with several Spirits she refered to casually by name. Someone who did not know her might find confusing her references to those of her friends not limited by bodies.

Suzie was one of those special people who retained the easy access of early childhood to the Spirit world as she grew. At the same time a thoroughly down-to-Earth person, she was more clear-headed than many adults about what was what.

Suzie knew the difference between Spirits and people and the difference between good Spirits and bad. It had come to her naturally. Luckily for her, she had parents who gave her a sense of value and encouraged her to learn rather than just teaching her an arbitrary code of fear. They had even managed their divorce decently.

Suzie was somewhat lonely. Aside from being the only girl anywhere near her age in Elk Stuck, she knew more than most of her contemporaries, whose horizons were more limited. It made her different. She had suffered for this at school. However, it gave her poise – and the respect of most of the adults she respected. She wore the position in the adult world she had already earned with grace, if not always with ease.

Brownie started to get a bag of pot and a pack of zig-zags out of his pouch. (Weak as the leaf was, the little pipe was more bother than it was worth.)

"You sure are in a hurry to wreck your lungs," said Suzie.

Brownie thought for a moment, then said, "Bad habit. It is sort of redundant now." He put the pot and papers away.

Harry put his pants and shoes back on and tucked his shirt into his belt. He and Meridell took hands. Then they all walked up to the cave.

The cave was still there, but not especially interesting, so they headed back to the meadow. Then they scattered, looking at a flower here, a bird there.

Harry and Meridell stayed together a while. Then Harry had to shit again and excused himself.

He went a little ways into the woods, found some thick bushes with leaves at a convenient height, and squatted.

When he turned around and stood up, so did the bear.

The bear had unwittingly approached Harry from upwind.

Harry was downwind of the bear but failed to notice due to what he was doing.

Ten seconds later, Harry and the bear were half a county apart. The only problem was, the bear was between Harry and the meadow.

Or might be. The bear also might be on either side parallel to the meadow.

What if it was a mama with cubs?

Harry had contemplated that prospect for some indeterminate but lengthy period of time when he realized he was still holding his pants up.

Harry fastened his pants and eventually decided maybe he was not going to have a heart attack. He had no idea where his shirt was. This did not seem very important. He was certainly warm enough.

He also had no idea what to do next. So he listened.

No noise. Presumably the bear had not blundered out into the meadow among the others. But all that told him was where the bear was not.

Harry's old man had once told him bears are built better for going uphill than down. — Just like cows. "If a bear's after you, run downhill. It's your best chance."

This bear was not after Harry though. He just did not want to get that close again by mistake.

Harry was sure he had run basically downhill and the bear basically uphill. That was why he was now farther from the meadow than when he started. He decided to circle on down and approach the valley again from below. When he crested the ridge, Suzie heard him. She held a finger to her lips, then pointed.

The panorama was idyllic. Summer grasses and brilliant wild-flowers: Vermillion paint brush. Purple asters. A dozen shapes in yellow. White lace yarrow.

Brownie was naked except his moccasins and a belt with a couple of pouches and a knife. His name seemed most apt.

Meridell would have to put her shirt back on soon or she was liable to burn. But she sure looked radiant now.

Suzie, the only one fully dressed, was the near point of a triangle about a hundred fifty yards across and an equal distance from him. Brownie and Meridell did not know Harry was there.

Harry looked where Suzie pointed and the others were also looking.

There, at the very farthest edge of the high meadow, was a bear. It had to be the same one. And sure enough, there were two cubs, wrestling. Mama cuffed them and sent them rolling. Then she led them back into the woods with more dignity than most generals Harry had seen.

They all converged, meditatively, on Suzie's position.

"Space your shirt?" Suzie had little use for adults who did not keep it together, and she always noticed.

Harry somewhat embarrassedly told what had happened. Suzie, on the evidence of the scratches Harry had acquired running through the branches, decided to believe him. They all went to the edge of the woods while Harry retrieved his shirt from where it had dropped the second he took off.

Harry was quite sure the bear was half a mile away as he retraced his steps the fifty feet into the woods. But his heart was still pounding by the time he got back.

The contrast in color between Harry's arm and Meridell's, as he took her hand, reminded Harry that Meridell needed to watch the sun. So they all migrated back to the middle of the meadow again, where Meridell's shirt was sitting on a rock by the creek.

The next few hours were calmer, at least partly because it was getting on toward noon. The only animals out and about were chipmunks.

Once a plane flew over. Brownie started to head for cover, but Suzie stopped him.

"Quit playing cops and robbers. We've got a right to walk in the National Forest, just like the tourists. Wave."

Meridell agreed. "I don't want to live with a bunch of outlaw energy."

Brownie sat down and covered himself with one of his leggings. They all waved. The plane came in and dipped its wings. It was the Forest Service fire patrol, pretty casual as wet as it had been lately.

When the plane tilted toward him, Harry recognized the same man on the passenger's side who Chuck and Louella had pointed out the day the caravan came through town. Ray Morse. That was the name. None of the others knew him.

After a while, Suzie got hungry and went up to the cave for crackers and raisins.

The clouds seemed undecided whether to build up or dissipate.

Brownie lay on his back in the lush grass. Harry and Meridell talked quietly. Suzie watched the birds and the woods.

Brownie eventually got up and stretched and put on his leggings and loincloth. "Let's get up on top of something."

So they did. It was another climb and the highest Harry had been yet. The ridge they came out on looked like the highest thing around short of Thunder Peak itself, to which it connected, perhaps four miles farther north. The view was breathtaking.

"Chuck said once he'd take me up on the Peak."

Meridell chuckled. "He hasn't walked that far in twenty years."

"I'll take you," said Brownie. "When it's drier and the tourists clear out....Have some bud by then too, maybe."

Thunder grumbled on the peak. It looked stormy over the Chiricahuas again. Still mostly blue over them. But the thunder was a reminder they had a long walk home.

They had everything with them except the last of Suzie's crackers. She had put them in Brownie's storage bucket and was content to leave them there. So Brownie led them back by a route farther east than Harry had yet been.

Harry had only the vaguest idea where they were going. He knew they would eventually come out in the canyon of Double Eagle Creek because that was where everything on the whole southern watershed of Thunder Mountain came out. But he had no idea where.

Brownie led the way with complete certainty till they came to a trail. "East Fork," he said. And it was. Before long they reached the road just above Mrs. Martinez's. She was out looking at her pansies. Harry had never seen her before anyplace but the post office.

Everyone called out a friendly hello. Then they continued on. Wayne's was the only other inhabited house on the East Fork Road. No one was home there. Below Wayne's house, the road cut off to the left to run on the level to the main road a hundred yards up toward Post Office Ridge.

They followed the creek around a sharp bend to the right and on down to where it met the Double Eagle Creek Canyon between Jim's house and Jesus', toward the upper end of town.

Jesus and Wayne were drinking beer by their trucks. "Come have a beer," Jesus called out.

"Thanks. We're ready to land," Meridell answered for all of them. They went on. Brownie stopped to check Petunia's water. Then he joined the others at Meridell's for supper.

"That sure was a beautiful hike," Harry commented. "But I was thinking maybe we'd see the Indian Lady."

"Didn't you see her?" Suzie was appalled. "She was on the same ridge where the bears were. Oh, that's right. You were in the woods."

"Harry saw her," said Brownie. "A little close too."

Harry considered this. "I thought she was an elk Spirit."

Brownie shrugged.

Suzie replied, "I call her the Spirit of Thunder Mountain. She's with all the animals."

CHAPTER THIRTEEN

Everyone was tired. Harry did not want to push Meridell. He went back to his shed to sleep. In the morning, he woke early, slipped into the house quietly for coffee, and was out digging on the water line trench long before the sun came over the edge of the canyon.

Harry worked on the trench a lot that week. He figured if he got it all dug and the water line in before going on the thinning contract, there would still be time to fill it back up when he got back. It looked like he would make it. Louella was delighted. She had never really expected the project to be done this year.

It pleased Harry to please Louella, so he worked all the harder. Besides he enjoyed swinging the pick. Some people would call that sort of work punishment. They would find some job that did not take any effort – and then lift weights to get in shape. Some people are nuts, Harry thought. – Of course, it helped a lot that he could always set his his own hours and quit when he felt like it.

Jim and the boys got back, and school started. One major bonus to Steve's presence was that it brought the school bus up the hill as far as the post office. For two families the county had to send it. This was a great relief to Meridell. Keeping a vehicle sufficiently together to make it up and down the hill twice a day last year had been quite a strain. Time consuming too.

Meridell was busy weaving, and happier about her work than she had been. "That break was good for me." It was Thursday afternoon. Harry had stopped in the shop to say hi. "Now I'm back in the rhythm. Aspasia Suny can take it or leave it. I'm weaving what I feel again."

Jim was having a little get-together that evening for Cindy Stone.

"I need nookie!" That was Harry's introduction to Cindy. She had been on a fire fighting crew all summer. She was at that first pot luck at Meridell's, but she left early, and Harry did not really meet her. Since then she had been fighting fires in Oregon and North Carolina. Cindy was very fit, with a good figure, a little chunky. She was five foot four and had shoulder-length brown hair.

Six months ago, Harry would have hopped right in the sack with Cindy. Now he just smiled. "'Fraid I'm spoke for."

"And I was hoping for some fresh meat. Guess I'll have to make do with Jim and the gruesome twosome."

Wayne and Jesus were already at Jim's when Harry and Meridell arrived. Cindy roared in with two cases of beer and a bottle of tequila a few minutes later.

Jim was in a good mood. (He was often morose.) This was partly because he was getting it on with Cindy, but he was mainly happy because he had a little welding job to fill the gap till the thinning contract. Jim liked welding better than any other work. However, in an area where everybody and his uncle was a welder it was not work a person could count on.

Six months ago, Harry would have disappeared into the boozy blur. Now he found himself growing bored, and noticed Meridell was too. They left together early, and Harry spent the night with her again.

Brownie was away. He was keeping fairly close to his crop to catch the male plants as they started to flower.

By ten o'clock Friday morning, Cindy was gone again. Meridell took the call at the shop. Three minutes and eighteen seconds later Cindy was roaring up Post Office Ridge. She did not even know where the fire was.

That afternoon Chuck and Louella went to town to pick up their chainsaw at the shop and do a few other errands. There was a dance again at the Chiricahua. Harry and Meridell met them there about nine.

"Hey, Boy," Chuck boomed. You could tell the locals. They were the ones who did not turn around and stare. "Howdy, Meridell. Sell the shop yet?"

Louella looked up and smiled. There was also another man at the table. Harry quickly recognized Ray Morse. Louella did the introductions.

"Didn't I see you up in a plane the other day?"

Ray winked. "Shush. I'll buy you a beer you don't tell no one. They could ground a pilot for unauthorized passengers."

And we were paranoid about them seeing us, Harry thought. He would have to tell Brownie that one.

The dance soon started up. Harry and Meridell danced three together. Chuck and Louella danced a little too. Then Harry danced one with Louella while Meridell danced with Ray and Chuck sat out. A few other people who knew various members of the group joined them at times. Harry danced twice with women whose names he didn't know. Mostly he danced with Meridell. He was not sure he danced best with her, but it sure felt best.

By the time the set was over, Harry was dripping. He was ready for a beer. Chuck bought, as usual. Everyone had one. Ray had joined them again, with an attractive, if slightly hard boiled looking girl named Sally Platt.

"Well Ray," Chuck held his customary bellow to a conspiratorial level, "what the hell's goin' on with those LemTron bastards and the army."

"Damned if I know. LemTron says they're exploring for minerals. Gold. Silver. Copper. The usual. Sell what's profitable. Stockpile the rest. Their geologists sound legit. And there's bound to be something worth mining in the Thunders. Army just plans training exercises. It's Public Land. They're talking to LemTron to get in some hazardous materials training. LemTron gets a fee. It's all out front."

"You don't believe it."

"Nope."

"Why not?"

"Every mineral company I've worked with's stingy with information. The army's worse. These geologists're blabbing their heads off. What they say they're doing's not worth that much talk. Know what I think?"

"What?"

"I think they're gonna build a hideout."

"For what?" asked Harry.

"For who?" Meridell said at the same time.

"Some big shot. Maybe even the president, in case the Soviets bomb Washington."

"Isn't this kind of close to the border for something like that?" Louella asked.

"I bet they've got a dozen of 'em. They'd use this one if the Soviets were winning. They could skedaddle down to Mexico and run a government in exile if they had to."

"Seen any evidence that's what they're doing?" Louella asked.

"No. I don't really know what they're up to. But it's not all they're saying. I'm sure of that. I'll let you know anything I learn though. You're close to it up on that hill. You tell me if you see anything too. Just don't get me in trouble."

"Your secrets are safe with Chuck," said Louella. "No one respectable will speak to him at all."

Sally giggled.

Saturday Chuck was hung over and asked Harry to tend the store for him for a few hours. Harry did not mind the chance to make a little money....If he did get together with Meridell, he wanted to carry his weight.

The rest of the weekend Harry and Meridell spent together.

The next week, Harry finished the trench. He and Chuck laid in the pipe and kicked enough dirt on top of it to hold it in place.

Labor Day Weekend, Paul arrived. He was sort of intellectual but easygoing. Harry liked him. His girlfriend, Pat, was along. Pat was classic Colorado wholesome, tanned and athletic. The hair was a little blond for Colorado – more California. She was easy company too. Suzie and Jeff went off with them and a carload of nylon tents and dehydrated food for the weekend.

Saturday, Harry and Meridell joined Jim and Chuck in an all-day woodcutting expedition. They took all three trucks down the hill a few miles. Jim and Chuck cut. – Harry spelled Chuck a couple times. Otherwise, he carried wood to the trucks, and Meridell packed it. When it accumulated Meridell and Jim would carry too. Steve worked right along with them. His specialty was lopping off the occasional little branch a cutter missed, with the ax. When Chuck was not cutting, he leaned on one of the trucks smoking his pipe and giving nonsense directions, which everyone else cheerfully ignored.

By the end of the day, all three houses had a load of oak and a load and a half of juniper. Everyone was tired.

Tuesday morning, Jim, Harry, and Wayne headed out on the thinning contract.

"We've got till November," Jim said. "But I want to get in and out before the place fills up with day-glo bozos with bazookas. It's prime elk country over there."

Jim was not going out for elk this year. He planned to get his deer in black powder season when the woods were less crowded.

Jim liked black powder. He said it was because the guns were not legally guns, so the government was more likely to leave them alone. Harry suspected what Jim really liked was the noise. The hand cannon Jim wore once in a while looked and sounded very intimidating. It could do a lot of damage too – if you could get a shot off without dropping the cap. Not the weapon for a quick draw man. Actually, Jim had a small arsenal. A lot of people did in the Southwest.

The thinning contract was only about twenty miles from Elk Stuck as the crow flies, on a spur of Thunder Mountain just outside the north edge of the Wilderness. However, it was over a hundred mile drive. So they made camp. The nearest town was Manzanita, Arizona, twenty-five miles away, twenty-two of them dirt.

The first weekend, Harry rode back with Jim to see Meridell while Jim checked in on Steve. Steve was taking care of the animals. Meridell was looking after him. – Not that he would allow as how he needed any looking after.

The second weekend, Meridell brought the kids up to camp.

Saturday, Steve and Jeff worked with Harry stacking brush. – Kept their hours too. Jim was paying them two dollars an hour if they really worked. Meridell and Suzie cooked up a feast

After a while, Wayne went to the bar in Manzanita.

Sunday morning, everyone relaxed. Wayne slept late. That afternoon, Harry and Meridell went for a little walk. The kids did the same. Jim and Wayne worked on their saws: A thorough cleaning and a more careful sharpening than they had taken time for during the week.

When Harry and Meridell got back, the kids were still out. Harry could hear them, just barely, by a creek. Jim was scowling blackly. Wayne was gone.

Jim looked to Harry. "Wanta run a saw?"

"What's happening?"

"I fired Wayne. I got a spare. Job'll take longer I don't hire no one

62

else. But you'll make more money."

"Suits me. But what...?"

"Stupid fuck. I don't know why he bothers to wear his name on the back of his belt. He wouldn't have the brains to read it if he *did* pull his head out of his asshole."

This was not a very informative explanation for Wayne's absence. Harry and Meridell waited.

"Dumb fuck brought some sleazebag he met at the bar up here wanting to buy pot. Crumbum wasn't a narc, he'd sell his grandmother to one. I told him to get lost. Wayne too. I don't think the slimeworm learned much. He does know we live in Elk Stuck though. Fucker. I oughta hang Wayne by his balls and leave him for the buzzards."

"You think Wayne told him about Brownie?"

"Wayne doesn't know about Brownie. Brownie had Wayne spotted for a jerk the day he got here."

Harry relaxed. None of the rest of them was doing anything the law would spend extra gas money on. He *would* keep things clean for a while. He habitually put his stash away anyhow. He would keep the roaches off the table now too. They would have to warn Brownie next time they saw him.

The following weekend Meridell came back, without the kids, and had Brownie with her. He had all his male plants harvested. He figured it would not hurt appearances for him to stack brush for a week. He could use the money too.

They finished up Thursday.

Friday morning, Pete Padilla did the inspection and okayed everything. By three o'clock, they had broken camp and headed out.

They took a detour to Lordsburg so Jim could do some errands. They had supper in a cafe. Then Jim wanted to stop at a few bars. It seemed strange to Harry to see Brownie in town in levis and a western shirt joking with storekeepers and cowboys. Only two of the bars questioned Brownie's age. He did not carry any I.D. One place he got in as Jim's son. The other place, they left. They did not quite close down the bars. By two-thirty in the morning they were home.

Harry slept late. When he came in the house for coffee, there was a letter that had come for him earlier in the week. It had taken a while getting there, by way of Alamogordo and Strawberry, Oklahoma. The original postmark was someplace he had never heard of in Massachusetts called Acton. The addresses were in his mother's handwriting:

> Dear Harry,
>
> I hope you are all right. It has been an awfully long time. I am writing because I thought you should know your father had a heart attack. It wasn't too severe. He is determined to finish out on active duty. The doctors are saying maybe. Call collect if you need to.
>
> We love you,

There was no date. The first postmark was a month old. Harry looked at the return address once more. His father had been transferred again since he last was in touch. Now he had had a heart attack.

Harry's father was only fifty-two years old, just twice Harry's age. He had spent twenty-nine and a half of those years in the United States Army. He would retire in six months.

It was definitely time to call the folks.

CHAPTER FOURTEEN

"Draw pardner."

"What's happening?"

"Pick a card." Chuck was holding the spread deck, face down, for Harry.

Harry pulled out a card. It was the jack of clubs. Chuck turned to Louella. Then he drew one himself. Chuck turned the seven of diamonds up on the table. "What'cha got?"

Louella laid down the nine of spades. Harry put his jack next to it.

"High card gets the pick. First season, middle or late? License is on me."

Harry thought about it. The early season was shortest, but the deer were least spooky. – Of course, Brownie could probably show him someplace no one else knew about where the deer were not spooky at all. It sure would be nice to bring Meridell some venison. She even had a little freezer. Of course, he was sure they would all get some of any deer any of them took. "Shit, I don't know."

"All right, ya slob. Draw again. High card's first."

This time Louella pulled the king of spades. Chuck drew the six of hearts. Harry got the three of clubs.

"Lucky you. You get to freeze your feet off in the snow."

There might well be snow by late season, especially if he hunted high. Snow was good for tracking though.

It was Wednesday. Harry had been dividing his time about equally between Chuck and Louella's and Meridell's. He was still working his way up to calling his parents. Brownie had disappeared before Harry was up Sunday. Jim said Brownie was promising some good smoke next time he got back. Harry thought maybe he would wait to call till then. His folks might not approve, but it would make it easier to tune in. And he wanted to. He was fond of them even if they did live in another world.

Cindy was back. She and Jim were spending a lot of time together, mainly devoted to drinking and sex.

Jesus was mostly gone, working with his uncle on the wrecker.

Wayne was not doing too well. Jim was speaking to him again – enough to say, "Hi, Shithead." The mine was still shut down and looked to stay that way. Wayne's truck had eaten up most of the money he made on the thinning contract. He had not found any more work within a reasonable distance of Elk Stuck. He had payments to make on both the truck and his house.

Besides, Wayne was scared. He smoked pot. What if that guy did narc on him? What if he was under surveillance? How would he know? What could he do about it? And his neighbors were treating him like a leper. – Except Mrs. Martinez. All she knew about was his being out of work and having bills, so she was sympathetic.

Rita Martinez was fifty-nine and widowed. She had been post-mistress at Elk Stuck when Coronado was a boy. She was Wayne's closest neighbor, and he was grateful she was friendly. But he needed a job.

Harry was thinking about a job too. Business at the shop had dropped off sharply after Labor Day, which meant Chuck and Louella's income did the same. He had about filled in the water line trench. His help would be welcome getting in firewood, but he and Meridell were talking about Harry moving in. If he did, he wanted to pay his way. He wanted a vehicle too – and maybe a chainsaw. Meridell didn't have one.

What was happening with Meridell's business was not altogether clear either. Aspasia Suny had been back once for more of Meridell's weaving, but she wasn't buying it outright now. Summer season was over in Santa Fe too. Aspasia was taking Meridell's work on commission. There had been one more check, but it was only for two hundred dollars.

Meridell and Aspasia had signed a contract. All it really said was that Aspasia got X percent wholesale, X percent retail, and Meridell got the rest. For all Meridell knew, her weavings could be sitting in Aspasia's closet waiting for a good deal. It did not cost Aspasia anything to wait. In the meantime, Meridell was left hanging. She couldn't even go to the craft fairs because she didn't have enough to show.

Thursday, a lot happened. The first frost hit, and Louella harvested all the tomatoes. Harry borrowed Chuck's saw and truck and went on a firewood run with Meridell. She brought her truck too. They were out quite a while.

When they got back, there was a moving van in front of the Overmans'. How it got up the hill was beyond Harry. The hairpins were tight even for a horse trailer. Presumably, if it got up, it could get back down. Harry was glad he was not driving. Four men were loading the Overmans' belongings. Isaiah and Gertrude were coming and going. Isaiah looked determined, maybe even triumphant. Gertrude looked like she had been crying.

Harry spotted Wayne. Isaiah and Gertrude had given him several things. Now he stood by his truck watching. "What about the house?" Harry asked.

"Part of the deal. Izzy says LemTron's gonna buy the whole town."

"Whole town's not for sale."

Wayne shrugged. "I know I'll talk to 'em. For a job or to buy me out, one. I got no choice."

It was Harry's turn to shrug.

That evening, Brownie got back. He had the first buds, and they were beauties. He also had news. He had talked to a contact of his who worked for the Forest Service. The army was coming back for more "training exercises" next week.

"You been wanting to check out Thunder Peak."

Harry looked to Meridell.

"We'll go scout a base camp. Then we'll come back for you." Brownie turned to Meridell. "The kids can come too. We'll take Petunia and some supplies. Kids are the best cover in the world."

Meridell looked a little doubtful.

"Nothing illegal about going for a walk in the woods. This is still the United States, isn't it?

Meridell considered. "It sounds like fun. The leaves will be beautiful."

They were, aspens at peak of gold. Brownie was ready to go right away while there was still a couple good hours of daylight, so they did. Harry thought he was in shape. He was certainly more muscular in the arms and shoulders than Brownie. However, he had to push himself hard to keep up. He was just as glad the kids would be along the second round. Once was plenty at Brownie's pace.

They did not go to the summit the first trip. What they did that evening was find a route the burro could take that led right through the LemTron survey and from there on up to the West Trail.

Weather was crispy and clear. They camped under the stars. Friday they looked for caves. What Brownie wanted was several places to take shelter – or hide – just above the area he believed the "training exercises" were going to be in. They found three.

They slept out again Friday night, but Brownie had them back in town by the time the sun made it to the bottom of the canyon. The kids were packed and excited. Steve was coming too. Jim had Petunia ready. Meridell had packed four new plastic buckets with the supplies Brownie had asked for, all painted black like his other one.

Brownie did not want anything he had to build a fire for. There were raisins, sunflower seeds and peanuts, crackers and corn nuts. There was also garlic and salt. He had most of the things already at Jim's. Louella contributed the peanuts and crackers. Brownie seemed a little weird to her and Chuck, but they liked him. If he could find out what LemTron and the army were up to, he was doing them a favor too.

"No one I'd sooner trust than an honest outlaw," was Chuck's pronouncement.

Going up, they took the East Fork trail. The army was due tomorrow. Brownie wanted to let the soldiers get there first and stumble on them coming down. They would not bring Petunia within half a mile of any of the caves. The kids knew what was happening and were ready to help any way they could – whether it was carrying a bucket through the woods or keeping their ears open if they met any soldiers.

"Just like Apaches," said Jeff.

Suzie thought the Indian Lady would approve.

The weather was perfect. – October is often the nicest month of the year. It was brilliantly clear and invigorating. Warm but not hot. The aspens were spectacular. Harry did not even mind his aching legs. Birds and squirrels were everywhere, as well as lots of tracks of larger animals.

By noon, they were well up the ridge of the peyote hike. They stopped at one of the many picture-book-spectacular vistas for lunch. They carried the food they planned to eat in their packs. They also all carried water, which they would share, sparingly with Petunia. They were above the last spring, and would be till they got well down tomorrow.

By four o'clock, they were climbing the last slope. Harry was used to the altitude by now, but he could still feel it, especially his legs. Thunder Peak was ten thousand nine hundred six feet. They had climbed nearly four thousand feet – not counting ups and downs. Harry had covered a lot of ups and downs the past two days.

The view was worth it. Thunder Mountain was the highest thing for a long long way around. To the east, they could see right over the Peloncillos to Animas Peak in the next range. Farther north were the Burros and the vague outline of the Gila beyond. On the Arizona side, the Chiricahuas stood out bold, straight to the west. To the north lay the White Mountains. South, they could see way into Mexico.

"See that?" Brownie pointed to a dim hump somewhat west of north. "That's Baldy. On the Res. It's over eleven thou. Over a hundred fifty miles away too."

Harry was impressed. The playas between the ranges were a long way down. It was still summer down there, could easily be another month till it even frosted. The Peak had already gotten a dusting of snow in the last storm the day they got home from the thinning contract. (It just sprinkled in Elk Stuck.)

They made camp a little below the summit on the east side in case it got windy and to be in line for the sunrise. Then they went back to the Peak for sunset. Brownie and Harry smoked some bud. Meridell took a couple hits too. The bud was delightful: fragrant, light but potent, a fine high. Harry was just as glad he did not have any more mountain to climb after smoking though.

As the sky faded, they went back to camp and lit a fire. The moon was near new, and there was no reason not to. They had pork and beans, corn chips and slightly mashed fresh plums for supper. Then the kids roasted marshmallows, and they all had s'mores.

The night was clear. Stars sparkled magnificent – three times as many as in thick air of the flatlands.

Harry dreamt the Indian Woman was singing. When he woke, there was the most extraordinary sound he had ever heard. It was just barely first light. Brownie was already sitting up listening. So was Suzie. Harry could see their outlines. Soon the others woke too. Harry had never heard the sound before, but he did not have to be told it was bull elk bugling.

There were at least four or five of them. When it got a little lighter, they found they could actually see one in an open spot several hundred yards across the slope. He swaggered back and forth, his little harem sticking close. The others were in the woods.

By the time the elk were done, the sun was rising, the coffee was steaming, and Jeff, Steve and Harry were slightly gooey with pancake syrup.

The walk down would be a lot easier than the walk up had been, but it would be a good deal more complicated. Brownie wanted to scout ahead to make sure they did not run into anyone before they had the buckets off Petunia and their packs on her in their place. They left fairly early.

As it turned out, there was neither sign nor sound of anyone when they got to the the spot where Brownie wanted to cut off with the supplies. That was just fine. They took all the buckets off Petunia and hid them in some bushes. Then they made a camp that looked like lunch.

Someone needed to stay with Petunia. Suzie volunteered. Meridell said she would stay too.

"Anyone asks, we're looking for water," Brownie said. They had all taken a drink, including Petunia, and poured most of the rest they had left into one plastic gallon milk jug, which stayed in camp.

Brownie took two buckets. Harry carried one. Jeff and Steve had the last between them.

All three caves were on the same side of the trail, the first half a mile away, the farthest nearly two miles.

"Man, I don't feel so hot." They were about to leave the first cave after secreting a bucket there. Harry had been feeling a little nauseous for a while. Standing up to go, he suddenly got dizzy and clammy all over.

Brownie looked him up and down. "Better lie down. We'll pick you up on the way back."

"I don't want to flake out on you."

"No problem. Take 'er easy."

Brownie did not leave Harry any time to argue. Jeff and Steve followed right after him.

Harry lay down in the shade of the cave. He was wringing with sweat. Lying down felt better. He closed his eyes.

Where was he?!

He was looking into a black whirlpool, a black hole. Harry had never been so scared in his life.

Then he heard the singing again, like in his dream last night. Like the elk.

A hand touched Harry's shoulder. He looked around. It was the Indian Woman. She smiled, a calming smile. Harry's fear receded.

"He's asleep."

Harry blinked, confused.

Steve peered down at him. Brownie and Jeff stood at the entrance to the cave.

Harry sat up slowly. He felt better, but light-headed.

"Make it back to camp okay?" Brownie asked.

Harry stood up, a little tentatively. "Yeah. I'm okay." He was. He felt more himself as they walked back across the slope. Just a little spacy. Brownie had found water too. They now carried two full half gallon water bottles as they approached camp. Harry was not sure how far it was.

Harry heard Meridell's voice. A male voice replied. Brownie had them halt so he could take a look before they let themselves be seen.

CHAPTER FIFTEEN

"Get your hands off me!" Meridell shouted.

Zip! Zoom! Jeff and Steve were off like lightning. Harry was about a tenth of a second behind them.

There was a crash, and a man roared in pain.

Harry burst onto the trail. Meridell stood to one side, apparently unhurt. Suzie stood to the other side, very straight, eyes closed. An M.P. was backing away from Jeff and Steve. The boys were both on him like wildcats. Another soldier, a major Harry saw, was on the ground. Petunia stood over him, screeching. Harry had never seen Petunia excited before, except playfully with Brownie or the boys. There was a pistol on the ground near the M.P.

"Murderer!" Jeff yelled.

Steve bit the M.P. on the right wrist. The M.P. leapt back, flinging both boys clear. They started for him again.

"Jeff! Steve!" Brownie was not in sight, but his voice stopped them.

Harry now heard someone running up the trail. There were two more M.P.s with rifles ready, a colonel, and a civilian. Harry flashed that none of them were used to the altitude. If they all ran, he bet they could all get away. How to get everyone's attention before anyone was caught?....

"What the hell do you think you're doing?"

If Harry did not hear it, he would never have believed it. A skinny, long-haired kid in levis and moccasins spoke with enough authority to stop two M.P.s and a colonel in their tracks.

Brownie was all thunderbolts. Thanks to the altitude, none of the men he was staring down on could speak. No one moved. The only sound for several seconds was gasping breath.

The colonel looked to be in good shape for his age. – Reminded Harry of his father last he had seen him. – But he was still puffing as he said, "This is a restricted area, young man."

"There's no signs. It's National Forest. In fact, it's Wilderness." Vehicles and road were not visible or audible from where they stood, so Brownie did not mention them. "Who do you think you are pulling guns on unarmed civilians?

"He tried to shoot my mom!" Jeff pointed to the first M.P., who had not retrieved his pistol.

"Kid, your animal attacked the major. That's a dangerous animal."

"Buddy, I saw your major grab the lady. That's my idea of a dangerous animal," said Brownie.

The major was still on the ground. Harry could not tell how badly he was hurt. The face he turned to Harry showed as much fear as pain.

The colonel and the civilian whispered to one another. When the colonel spoke again, his tone was conciliatory. "I'm sorry for this misunderstanding. Apparently some of the trails haven't been properly marked yet. If you'll just show us your I.D.s..."

"Stuff it, buddy. You show us your I.D.s. We've got every right to be here."

The colonel had heard about all he was going to take from Brownie. But before he could speak, the civilian tapped him on the upper arm. "This is a closed sector. Where are you going?" The tone was mild again, if strained.

"Double Eagle Creek Canyon." This was Suzie, her eyes open now, cool as can be. Harry would have said, "Elk Stuck."

The civilian and the colonel whispered a bit more. "We'll escort you through." The colonel started to lead the way.

"Just a minute." Brownie was checking Petunia's load. She was skittish for a moment, but calmed to his touch. The burro had all the sleeping bags. There were three other small packs – lunch and jackets mostly. Harry, Meridell, and Jeff picked them up. Brownie tightened Petunia up a little. "Okay."

The colonel headed off. The two M.P.s with rifles – now more or less at rest – fell in behind. The civilian stayed with the major, who still sat on the ground. The other M.P. retrieved his sidearm and went off in another direction.

Harry had a pretty good idea they were skirting the area he and Brownie had been over, not far from the meadow. He was sure when Brownie said, "What's that truck doing in the Wilderness?" Harry looked but could not see it through the trees. He thought Brownie was pushing his luck being so aggressive.

"Classified. None of your business," was all the reply the colonel allowed.

The soldiers left them on the West Trail, well below the area of activity. They followed the trail about three quarters of a mile. Brownie had Suzie and Petunia go first and had everyone else make a point to scuff out the tracks. Then they cut off on the route Harry and Brownie had scouted.

"Wouldn't take much to trail us, but they probably won't bother. Pretty dumb anyhow."

"Why'd you say anything about the truck?" Harry asked. "You didn't really expect an answer."

"He acknowledged it's there. Now we got six witnesses to a motor vehicle in the Wilderness."

"So what? The Forest Service knows about it. They haven't stopped them."

"It's an election year."

There was just no end of surprises with Brownie, Harry thought. "Yeah. So?"

"So it's time to write your congressman. Congressmen like things to make a fuss about. It gets their names in the news."

"You really think it'll do any good?" Meridell asked. She nodded back up the hill and added: "The bastards."

"Can't hurt. Sometimes the best protection is to lay low and quiet. Sometimes the only safe way to go is to make a lot of noise."

"You don't think...?" Harry trailed off.

"They think we'll be missed's the best life insurance we can buy."

"They wouldn't." Meridell was visibly shocked.

"I heard things in California'd turn your stomach....Suzie, you were great....Boys, you were real brave. But look before you leap next time. Your lives are worth more than Petunia's."

"I thought he was gonna shoot my mom."

"I know you did. But he wasn't."

Where did Brownie get that poise? That power? Wherever it came from, Harry was thankful for it.

Brownie got out his pipe, filled it, lit up, and passed it to Harry. Harry's mouth fell open. He had forgotten all about it. Brownie had faced down those guys with the pipe and bag of bud right in his pouch. Harry took a toke. It was good bud, but the quality of the pot was not entirely responsible for the rush that tingled up his back and burst through his head.

Meridell took a little token puff too. Harry felt it was more a statement of solidarity than for the effect of the pot. She looked grim.

The boys looked elated. They were high on the adventure.

Suzie looked pensive. After a while she spoke. "I never saw the Indian Woman mad before."

"When'd you see her?" Brownie asked.

"When I closed my eyes. She didn't like that man grabbing my mother. She's the one that told Petunia to kick him."

Harry was not sure what to make of that. The support of the Indian Woman did reassure him somehow. He had seen a few funny things in his life; he had never taken Spirits very seriously before. He was glad to have this one around.

Harry realized he now had a new reason to call his folks. He was not sure how to mention what had happened to his dad. – The old man had just had a heart attack. But Harry knew what he had just seen was not the way his dad's version of the army worked. Like Brownie had said, the more people watching the better. What next, Harry thought.

What next was the scene that met them in town. Harry had seen Burl Trent twice in the three months he had been in Elk Stuck. He had never heard him speak.

Burl stood in front of the empty Overman house in the middle of the street shaking his fist. He was in his seventies, barrel chested, a little spindly in the arms and legs. "Ya bastard, I told you I'd outlast you. And I did. Son of a bitch!" He spat.

They were almost to him before he noticed them. Harry had no idea what the strange old hermit would do. To his amazement, Burl smiled. "Howdy, kids. Nice day, ain't it?"

Harry saw Meridell start in surprise. She recovered immediately, however. "Yes it is. How are you?

"Just fine." Burl shook his fist at the empty house again and growled. "Just fine."

Burl stayed where he was as they continued down the street.

They already had Petunia unloaded when Brownie said he was going back. Harry's first thought was of his legs. He could no more have climbed that hill again than he could fly to the moon. "You gotta be kidding."

"I want to find Johnny."

"Who?"

"Private Higgins."

"Alone?...You can't play ignorant again."

"Won't have to. No one's gonna know I'm there. Not even Johnny. I just what to make sure he's there."

"Be careful."

"I will." Leprechaun twinkle, and Brownie was off.

All three kids were brushing Petunia down and telling her how wonderful and heroic she was. Jim was not home. Harry thought they should tell Chuck and Louella what had happened. Meridell said she would come too. She wanted to wash up first. That sounded like a good idea to Harry.

It was the first time Harry had taken a shower with Meridell. She actually had an inside shower and a hot water heater. – There was no inside toilet though. She used an outhouse like everyone else in Elk Stuck. The only flush toilet in town was at the Overmans'. – And they were now gone. – The shower was a lot of fun.

Jim was at Chuck and Louella's. Cindy too. They were well into a bottle of Jack Daniels. There was no shortage of beer either.

"Hey there," Chuck bellowed.

Cindy turned around. She had been seated with her back to the door. "Bud or Stroh's?"

"Stroh's, thanks," Harry said.

"Meridell?"

"Could I split one? Either's okay."

"Don't worry," said Louella. "It won't go to waste."

"Okay. Stroh's."

Cindy passed them two brown bottles.

"Whadya know?" boomed Chuck.

Harry and Meridell told the tale of their encounter. Chuck, Louella and Cindy all made various small sounds of interest and outrage.

Jim just sat there and glared. Twice Harry watched him pick up the whiskey bottle in a death grip and guzzle down about half a cup. The story ended. Jim was the one to break the silence. "Fuckers. I fought for those pigs in Nam?"

There was a little discussion. No one really knew what to do. Then Louella remembered Harry had gotten a letter yesterday.

The letter had the return address of Harry's sister, Sally, in Little Rock, Arkansas. She was married to a surveyor there. She was two years younger than Harry. He had meant to visit her the whole time he lived at Strawberry, Oklahoma, but he had never gotten around to it. This was the first he had heard from her in four years. The letter had come the same route as the one from his mother. This time the original postmark was

Concord, Massachusetts. The date was ten days after the other one.

The news was much the same. Harry's dad was out of the hospital. He was doing pretty well. Sally was staying another week. She had Jennifer, who was just over a year, with her. Jeanne was in kindergarten and home with Bob. – Jeanne had been a baby the one time Harry had seen her. The main point of the letter was that Harry really ought to call.

Harry was glad his dad was better. Relieved too. Now he would not be so hesitant to tell him what had just happened. – Still, maybe not right off.

"Who's tending the shop?"

"No one. Town's been dead all weekend. Said the hell with it and came over here to get drunk," Chuck replied.

"Could I go over there and make a call collect?"

"Of course."

Meridell did not have her key with her. Louella got hers out. Harry headed across the street.

CHAPTER SIXTEEN

Sonofabitch.

Ivan Sonofabitch, with the accent on the "of," pronounced, "off." It took Harry two days to get the joke.

Harry was eight when the Soviets invaded Czechoslovakia. He was about to start third grade on the base at Wiesbaden, Germany. He remembered the tension, the threat. The: What if...?

Then there was Vietnam. Harry was in Hawaii. Honolulu was fun. So many kinds of people from all over. But his dad was away. Again, there was that ominous atmosphere.

Now the threat was his own army.

Harry jumped. Someone was at the door.

"Are you open?"

"No. But I can open up for you since I'm here."

"If it's not too much trouble."

Harry had just been sitting in the shop for at least fifteen minutes, thinking about his world. The couple who now entered looked about his own age. The woman was pretty, with wavy brown hair styled in layers. The man looked like he worked outdoors. The accent was familiar.

"Where you folks from?"

They were from Tulsa. The man was a baggage handler at the airport. The woman was a teller at a bank. They were on their honeymoon. They bought a little weaving and some turquoise. Friendly people.

When they left, Harry found himself thinking about his life back in Strawberry, Oklahoma. – It was about fifty miles from Tulsa, toward Arkansas.

In Strawberry, he had lived a life of leisure. Squalid leisure. But that was by choice. He worked enough to eat. The rest of the time he hung out. Played frisbee a lot. Fucked the landlady. – She was only two years older than him and divorced; had kids too, and worked her butt off to support them. Harry did not take any of it seriously.

Cut firewood when you ran out. If it was raining, you just might burn the furniture. That was the philosophy he had lived by.

Then there was Alamogordo. He did not know what to make of that. He had hitched out on a lark. A job offer he thought was a mistake. Turned out to be testing space equipment. Weird. Half the stuff blew up or was radioactive. – Sometimes he had to wear a radiation suit that weighed as much as he did. He got sucked right in too. Started out at a nice leisurely ten hours a week. By the time he got busted, he was going full time.

Jail was hot. The cops were not all that bad, and most of the other prisoners were okay. A weirdo once in a while. Mostly just boring and hot. He was grateful when they let him out to work on the dog pound.

And now...

Harry picked up the phone. His sister's letter with the number was spread out next to it on the counter. The operator had a standard nasal voice.

"Collect call from Harry Upton. Will you pay for the call?"

"Yes."

"Hi. Ma?"

"Harry. It's so good to hear your voice."

"Good to hear yours too. How's it going? How's Pa?"

"He's better. Just a second." He could hear her call out: "Earl, pick up the phone. It's Harry."

"Harry, how the hell are you? *Where* are you?"

Harry flashed on his father doing pushups before breakfast. Earl Upton was a man of iron self-discipline. Now Harry could feel it willing health back into his body.

Harry's family were not emotionally demonstrative, but they did care for one another. They exchanged news. – Harry did not mention jail and wondered what indignities were left out on the other end.

Both Harry's parents thought the mountains sounded beautiful. "You're still there after I retire, we'll come visit."

"Stay in touch, Harry. We miss you."

"I will, Ma."

He told them where he was calling from. They took the number and said they would call him in a couple weeks. Harry decided to let the situation with the army in the Wilderness wait till then. – Maybe he would know more anyhow.

They told him about Massachusetts. They were at Fort Devens, not far from Boston. "Worst drivers in the country. – Almost as bad as Belgians." Harry vaguely recalled jokes about Belgian drivers when he was in Germany.

"Oh, Harry, you should see the leaves. We drove up to New Hampshire yesterday. Just beautiful."

"Here too, Ma."

"Glad you called, Son."

"Me too, Pa."

"You take care, Harry. Remember we do love you."

"I love you too, Ma."

It was starting to get dark when Meridell came looking for him. He was still standing with his elbows on the counter.

"Everything okay?"

"What a trip." He had a far-away look. But he was smiling.

Meridell came in and put an arm around Harry's waist. "Your dad better?"

"Ready for bear."

Meridell smiled too and gave him a squeeze. "Let's go have dinner."

"Okay."

They brought the key back to Louella. The party was getting maudlin. Then they walked slowly up the street in the dusk.

The kids had already eaten. – They never did have lunch. Meridell fixed herself a sandwich and put on water for ramen. All Harry had had since breakfast was beer at Chuck and Louella's and he hadn't finished that; but he wasn't hungry. He picked at a bowl of ramen, left most of it. Then he got out a partly smoked joint and took a few tokes. Meridell didn't want any.

"Wonder how Brownie's doing."

"I hope he's okay," Meridell answered.

Suzie had come in too. They were listening to a quiet tape. "He is." No one asked how she knew.

The boys were at Jim's. Jim was spending a lot of nights at Cindy's. Jeff and Steve thought it was great having a house to themselves. Jim did not mind Jeff sleeping there, so Meridell didn't mind either, so long as she saw he ate right.

There was a knock.

Harry jumped and looked to be sure the joint was out of sight. No telling if you could still smell it.

Suzie went to the door. "Come on in, Jim."

Jim's cap and shoulders showed water drops. Harry had not noticed the clouds coming in, but it was sprinkling now. Jim did not look too drunk, but it was hard to tell. Jim looked around.

"Boys aren't here?"

"No," Meridell answered.

"That's funny. They're not at the house either."

"There's school tomorrow." Meridell looked more annoyed than concerned. It was about eight-thirty.

"They'll show up." Jim turned to Harry. "Hey, Sport, I forgot earlier....Wanta make some money?"

"Gonna rob a bank?"

Jim grinned. That was a relief. Jim's vibes could be awfully heavy at times. "Heard about a default on a contract. I'm gonna pick it up."

"Thought you didn't want to be in the woods in hunting season."

Jim shrugged. "Winter's coming. Money's money."

"Where is it?"

"Greer."

"Where's that?"

"North. Arizona side. White Mountains."

"How long?"

"Couple weeks. Month at the most. Can't let it go much longer than that. Days get too short. You end up eating your profits just to stay warm even if it don't snow. Good money if we get on it though."

Harry did not want to leave. He did not want to be away from Meridell. He wanted to know what Brownie was finding out.

"When?"

"Tuesday, I hope. Quick as I can get it together anyhow."

"Who else is coming?"

"Cindy some. That's it unless Brownie comes up."

"Let me think about it."

"I gotta know before I go to town tomorrow. You don't want it, I gotta get someone else. Don't want to be up there in ten feet of snow."

Harry got out the remains of his joint. He and Jim finished it off. Like Jim said, money's money.

"Okay."

"Good deal. You got long johns?"

"Yeah."

"Bring 'em."

They talked a little longer.

"I'm going to look for the boys," Meridell said.

Jim grunted and pulled his ratty levi jacket on. They all got up. Before they could get out the door, Jeff and Steve burst in.

"Guess what?" Jeff said.

"Where have you been? I was beginning to worry. It's a school night."

"Burl Trent's," answered Steve. He looked like the cat that ate the canary.

"Yer shittin' me."

"No, Dad. He invited us in."

"I been in Elk Stuck six years. Burl Trent ain't invited anyone in I know of."

Steve shrugged. "He's okay, Dad. He even gave us cookies."

"Probably poison. You'll both be dead before morning."

Harry looked to see if Jim was serious. He was beginning to feel like he did not know what to expect. Jim did not look serious.

"Burl remembers what it was like here way back when," Jeff said. "I invited him over. He's a good guy. You'll like him."

None of the adults knew what to think, but Suzie spoke with assurance. "He's been living with the mountain a long time. I think he's all right. I see the Spirits at his house. He was just hiding."

"From what, Suzie? What's different now?"

"A lot's different, Mom. I think he was hiding from Mr. Overman though. Now they're gone and Mr. Trent's come out of hiding."

Meridell shook her head. "Things sure are happening around here."

Jim stretched. "Think I'll go start getting my shit together and catch some Zs. See ya."

Steve left with him.

Jeff stayed. It was bedtime anyhow, and his school things were there.

Harry sat contemplating while Meridell saw Jeff settled. When she came back in he said, "If it's not too wet, how about we get another load of firewood tomorrow?"

"Don't you want to rest up?"

Harry shrugged. "It'll be a while before the next chance. We might as well use the damn permit while it's good."

Firewood permits were a fairly major bone of contention locally. The town of Elk Stuck was a small island of private land completely surrounded by the Gadsden National Forest. In the Southwest, trees grew in the mountains and in the few desert river valleys. Piñon, juniper, and oak, the most popular firewood species, grew at middle elevations, ponderosa pine somewhat higher. Douglas fir, spruce, and aspen grew only in the high country. Cottonwood grew where there was lots of water. It burned well but was not popular and was hard to split.

Much of the forested higher land in the Southwest was Public Land: National Forest or BLM. For people in a little town like Elk Stuck, the National Forest all around was the obvious place to get firewood. Wood was the only source of heat for most residents and a major means of cooking for many, as was still common in rural areas of the Southwest. The local Forest Service office was in Lariat.

Firewood permits were one of the many reasons the government in general and the Forest Service in particular were so unpopular. It was not many years since rural people just gathered firewood when they needed it. Now, not only were they required to obtain a permit first, but every year the restrictions became more complicated.

Permits were now only good for a month. You had to buy a minimum of two cords on a permit but a maximum of ten cords (in many districts six) all year. If a saw or a truck broke down or a good seasonal job came along and you could not get the full amount the permit was for by the time it expired, that was just tough luck. The woods were legally closed to firewood gathering altogether from Christmas to May. If you ran out or, God help you, moved in winter that was just too bad.

The purpose of all these restrictions, according to the Forest Service, was to stop commercial thieves from El Paso and Phoenix from stealing vast quantities of green trees. There actually was a problem with that sort of thing. However, these thieves hauled their wood late at night when the Forest Service officials were home in bed. It was local legitimate woodcutters who got checked. People locally generally believed the whole permit program was a conspiracy on the part of the government to drive them out of their homes so the government could take over the whole country.

What made it all especially offensive was the economics: Forest Service officials were forcing their neighbors, who generally had incomes a fraction of the federal tax-supported government Forest Service salaries, to burn gas and waste time driving to the Forest Service office at increasingly frequent and inconvenient intervals for permits.

To add insult to injury, the State of New Mexico had recently passed a law making it illegal to transport any wood anyplace without a permit or bill of sale. This meant that if a cottonwood tree fell down in someone's yard in Lariat or someone had some construction scrap and he felt like giving some of the wood to a friend in Elk Stuck, it was a crime for the person from Elk Stuck to take the wood home unless they drew up a bunch of legal papers first.

People from Elk Stuck generally managed to get to the Forest Service office in Lariat when it was open for a permit. They kept most of the firewood legal, but they resented the hell out of the nuisance and expense. If the restrictions got any tighter, being legal was going to become impossible. For now, Harry and Meridell had a current permit.

Meridell gave Harry a big kiss.

"We don't have to start first thing," Harry said.

Meridell kissed Harry again. The tension seemed a little relaxed for the first time all day.

Suzie very deliberately went in her room to read.

"She's something," Meridell said.

"Umm. So are you."

CHAPTER SEVENTEEN

Route Six Sixty-Six. Harry could hardly believe they had used that number.

"Smelter at Douglas is at one end. I don't know where the other end's at. Someplace in Utah, I think."

Jim, Cindy, and Harry all rode up together in Jim's truck. If Harry had realized how far it was, he might have hesitated.

The part of Route Six Sixty-Six they were on ran through about seventy-five miles of spectacularly beautiful high country — and no towns. They came out at Alpine. Alpine, at eight thousand feet, was as high as the Elk Stuck post office, but in a broad, open valley. Pretty country. A lot of aspen, a lot of color, though there were already bare patches here and there. Not at all what most people expect of Arizona.

It was the farthest Harry had been from Elk Stuck since he got there. He could feel the distance, but he was too busy at first to pay much attention.

All three of them worked their buns off a solid ten days. Except Saturday night they cleaned up and went into Alpine to the Sportsman. There was a television there. It seemed like an artifact from another planet. Jim and Cindy knew a few people. Just hearing local names from someplace else amazed Harry with how much he had gotten involved in one little scene. Alamogordo was never so real. He had done his best to keep jail from getting too real. Even Strawberry, Oklahoma, which he once really thought of as home, was nowhere near as intense as Elk Stuck.

The second weekend, Jim and Cindy made a run home. Jim asked Harry to stay and keep an eye on camp. Harry missed Meridell. He almost protested, but then the thought struck him that he had not just spent a couple days alone in a long, long time.

They worked a full day Friday. It was dark by the time Jim and Cindy got gone. Harry kept the campfire burning a while. Then he got in his bag to watch the stars. The moon was just past full – awesome, rising through the fir-covered slope across from camp. It had a ring around it.

Harry had in mind to put in a few hours Saturday, but when he got up, it was so quiet.

He sat by the fire drinking coffee till the sun rose. It was freezing at night pretty good, but the sun was bright and warm.

Harry shed his jacket and strolled up a ridge. By the time he got there, he had his shirt off too. How clean the air felt. Definitely time for a day off. He would wash up and put on clothes that did not smell like essence of chainsaw.

The ridge met the logging road farther up. Harry walked that far and then ran the half mile back down to camp, bounding exuberantly. His pants about stood up by themselves when he took them off.

"Wahoo!" You could not help but shout. The creek was a real waker-upper.

Clean pants. Clean socks. All the woodchips and most of the grease out of his beard. Harry felt like a new man.

He listened to the squirrels scold a few minutes. Then he decided to go get on top of something and see the view. He had not done that here yet.

One ridge led up to the next. After a couple hours, Harry was on a peak. He did not know what peak or how high. Whatever it was, it let him see a long way in every direction.

Though the peaks were about the same height, the White Mountains were a much broader range than the Thunders: forested ridges as far as Harry could see in every direction. There were a couple of cabins and a little bit of road visible to the north, some kind of cut to the southeast. Otherwise there was not a sign of human life.

Harry felt a little shiver of exhilaration run through him. There was something objective, more than human, about so much Nature.

It was different from Elk Stuck too, and not just because he was alone. Partly, it was being on a peak instead of in that tight canyon. There was an openness, calmer, not so urgent.

Harry felt, though, that the Spirits here really were less compelling. Something was happening on Thunder Mountain that was not happening here. Harry was not sure if it was the place and what was happening that he could feel so strongly about Elk Stuck or if it was just that it had become *his* place. He knew he had no choice, though. Whatever was happening there had him hooked.

It was the people. Meridell had come to mean too much to him not to see it through. The others too: the kids, Chuck and Louella, Brownie. They were his life now, like family.

Harry shivered again. This time there was a little puff of wind.

He looked up. The clouds to the west seemed to be getting thicker quickly. The sun was still bright but almost faded out in the haze. Harry did not even have a shirt with him.

His walk back to camp was brisk. When he got there, he decided to get a good pile of firewood and put everything up just in case.

Harry was glad he did. Inside of two hours, the first flakes were falling. Harry strung the biggest tarp by the fire and kept on with the firewood a while longer. By the time he quit, it was really coming down.

Harry sat on a cooler under the tarp and fired up a joint. He set the coffee pot on and a pan of Spam and watched the snow come down. It was still snowing when he went to bed.

When Harry got up, the snow was tapering off. It was fourteen inches deep on the level. He did not know when he had seen anything so magical. It never snowed like that in Alamogordo or Strawberry. It had been years.

Harry hated to mess it up. He was not about to let things get wet in this weather though. He brushed all the snow off and well away from the tent. It was light and fluffy. By the time coffee was ready, the job was done.

It seemed like a good day to cook beans. They took forever at this altitude, but he did not figure on going anywhere. Harry set a pot on the fire, seasoned it with garlic and chile, and sat on a cooler to drink coffee.

Snow still wisped down, but the sun was visible through the thinning clouds. Flakes sparkled as they fell. Trees seemed to be stretching their limbs, waking up in the lightening air. Every now and then a branch released a white cascade.

By noon the sky blazed scrubbed mountain blue, and the snow was melting. By evening, the snow was compacted to about four inches, and the beans were done.

A clear sky and snow made for a cold night. Harry went to bed early, resolved not even to think about getting up till sun hit the tent. That night, Harry dreamed:

He was in the army. Not the U. S. Army...but it was *his* army. It felt like his father's army, nothing like the sleazeballs he had met on the mountain. This was an army of strong men with a strong sense of honor. Harry felt the weight of responsibility – and proud to carry it.

Someone was approaching. Harry stood alert, waiting to see who it was. It was his commanding officer, come to take him to his post. Harry saluted smartly. "All ready, Sir."

"Good man."

As the officer returned the salute, Harry realized he had Brownie's face. It was Brownie just like Harry knew him, yet the officer also seemed older, experienced, reassuring.

The officer/Brownie smiled on Harry. There was a strength in that smile and an awareness of the officer's confidence in Harry to do his part. Harry knew his commander was the kind of chief who inspires men to give their all – by doing just that himself. Harry felt honored.

He felt a little scared too. There was a grimness to the officer/ Brownie's smile he made no attempt to conceal.

There was another soldier ahead, standing guard. Harry thought he looked tired. His salute was brisk and alert though as they approached.

"I've brought your relief."

"Thank you, Sir."

The soldier shook Harry's hand, saluted again, and left.

As Harry woke, he realized the other soldier was Burl Trent. All of itself, the thought popped into Harry's head: He's not going to live long.

Harry was glad he had a lot of firewood. Even with the sun up, it was cold. He made a roaring blaze and got comfortable. Eventually, the sun did manage to warm things up. By the time it set, bare patches were bigger than the white patches.

That night was not quite as cold. By afternoon the only snow left was a little pile here and there in the shade. The road was not too muddy. Harry was not surprised when he heard engines shortly before sunset. A few minutes later, two trucks rolled in. Cindy had brought hers too this time. Jim had Brownie along as well.

There were fresh groceries, fresh bud, and beer. All the noise and activity seemed strange to Harry. Cindy had a camper on her truck. She and Jim made their bed in there. Brownie set up in Jim's tent. The sunset colors were still in the sky when they all gathered round the fire.

"Learn anything?"

"Yes, I did."

Harry waited while Brownie collected his thoughts and passed the pipe.

"Nice."

"Most of it's drying now. I left a few plants. There's a little growing time left down where they are."

Harry looked around at the outlines of the fir trees in the last of the dusk. The air was already quite nippy. "Could of fooled me. What's happening with our military and mining buddies?"

"Whatever else they're doing, they are set up to mine down below. Up on the mountain, I don't think they're even going to pretend."

"Do you know what they are going to do?"

"Build something. Post people. I don't know what for yet."

"In the Wilderness?"

"Yep. Authorized too. Some congressional committee. I'm not sure even they know what it's for."

"How did you learn that?"

"It's amazing what a bored, lonely soldier'll say to a guy that's sympathetic but not too interested."

Something clenched in Harry's gut. His old man would be incensed. "How's Meridell?"

"Okay. She went to a craft fair up at San Lorenzo."

"Where's that?"

"Other side of Silver City."

"Thought she was sending everything to that agent."

"She hasn't gotten a check in a while. She figures the woman don't own her. She was kind of freaked for a couple days, but she's feeling solid again now. Didn't make much at the fair, but the trip paid for itself. I think she felt better being on her own again too."

Harry hoped she did not feel better being on her own from him, but he did not say anything.

"She says to tell you she misses you and hurry back. The kids miss you too."

Harry felt warm inside.

It was cold outside though. The next storm might not melt so quickly. They all wanted to get on with the job and gone, so they went to bed early.

Next morning, it was: Up well before the sun in the cold, coffee and a few pancakes for fortification. Then to work.

Brrowr. Brrowr. Chainsaws and little fir trees flying. Bar-oil-flavored sandwiches for lunch. Sweat all afternoon; smelly clothes; beer and pot over a short evening campfire; Jim and Cindy rocking the truck. Then up and at it again next day.

Friday afternoon, Jim figured they could be done by Monday if they worked straight through. A few clouds had drifted by that day. A few more came in Saturday. Sunday it flurried off and on, but then broke up. They pushed right on through.

Monday was clear. Jim drove in to a phone to get an inspector up. They spent the afternoon touching up here and there. Tuesday was the inspection and a little more touching up. That afternoon, they packed most everything but what they needed for the night. Jim and Cindy wanted to leave in daytime so they could hit the stores. They also wanted to go to town right now for the evening and hit the bar. Harry wanted to get back to Meridell.

"Why don't you guys go on in my truck. I'll ride with Cindy."

Harry grinned. "Thanks, Man." He thought a moment. "Could you do me a favor?"

"Sure. What's that?"

"See if you can get a call through and ask Meridell to meet me at the hot springs."

"You bet."

CHAPTER EIGHTEEN

Cocaine!

"Hey, Man, how's it goin'? How ya been? What's happenin'?"

Shit, thought Harry.

Harry and Brownie had packed up and headed out early. Jim and Cindy had gotten back to camp from the bar late. Harry had not woken them to ask if they had gotten through to Meridell. It looked like they had not. She was not at the hot springs. Wayne was.

In a way, Wayne looked good. His hangdog slouch was gone, and so was a good deal of paunch; but he looked off balance. Harry had tried coke. You couldn't help but like it. He did not like what it did to people. He avoided anyone using much of it.

Could be speed, Harry thought, but Wayne looked too happy for speed. Harry wondered how Wayne was affording enough coke to lose that much weight that fast.

"What'cha been doing?" Harry asked.

"Got a fencing job," Wayne answered.

"Makin' good bucks?"

"Shit, no."

Minimum wage, Harry would bet. Wayne must be spending damn near all of it on cocaine.

The bath felt good, but it was not exactly what Harry had in mind for a hot springs stop. He and Brownie did not stay very long.

They'd only gone a mile farther up the road when Brownie asked Harry to stop. "I still got plants in the ground. I been away long enough."

Harry let Brownie out. Brownie had put on his buckskins when he got out of the hot spring. He did not take anything with him but his knife and what fit in two small belt pouches.

"See you in a couple days."

"Take care."

Brownie was gone and out of sight in a flash. Harry was another mile up the road and getting into the pines when it occurred to him: Wayne never even said hello to Brownie. It was almost as if Brownie was invisible to Wayne.

The sun still shone on him as Harry came over Post Office Ridge. In the canyon, it was already gone. There was light at the store; Harry stopped.

"Mmmm. I missed you."

Harry fell in love all over again during that kiss. "I missed you too."

They closed up the shop together, and rode up to Meridell's in the truck. When they got there, they just sat for a while, holding hands, watching the quiet dusk, not saying much, being alone together.

"Hey! Harry's back!"

Jeff jumped up as Harry and Meridell came in the door, grabbed Harry's hand, then gave him a quick little hug. Steve got up and shook Harry's hand too.

"Remember me?"

"Oh, hi, Mom." Jeff and Steve were already back at their game.

Meridell shook her head. Harry gave her a little squeeze.

Suzie came in from the kitchen and threw her arms around them both.

"Whew! Feels like coming home."

It was. Harry just hung out the next few days. He shot the shit with Chuck and Louella, said hi to Jim and Cindy when they got in, wandered around town a little. Mostly he stuck pretty close to Meridell.

Saturday they made a firewood run, with the kids. Monday Harry made another, with Chuck. Wednesday, he got paid for the thinning contract.

That weekend, Meridell had a craft fair to go to in Tombstone. Harry went with her. When they got back Harry was driving a 1962 beige VW bug. It looked like it had leprosy, which made it nice and cheap. It ran perfectly.

When they got back from Tombstone, they learned Brownie had been and gone. They were sorry to miss him. Elk Stuck saw its first snow that week: about an inch. It melted as soon as it fell, but it was a sharp reminder that winter was not far away.

Chuck had not touched the water line while Harry was gone. A couple sunny afternoons, and Harry had it pretty well filled. Where the ground was wet, the north side of the dirt pile was frozen. A few times he had to take out what was loose on the south side and wait for the rest to thaw.

The next couple weeks, a lot of attention went to firewood.

"By God, if that ain't enough, the hell with it. I'm through."

Harry and Chuck had just finished unloading Chuck's truck. Harry had done most of it.

"Shit, all you do is drive the truck."

"Watch your tongue, Boy."

Chuck looked ferocious. Harry started feeling paranoid. He knew perfectly well Chuck was doing as much as his back ought to. Besides, Harry enjoyed the work, but where did Chuck get off bitching at him about it?

Chuck could not hold the thunderface pose any longer. "Come on in the house. I'm gonna wash your mouth out with beer."

November was also deer hunting month. Louella got one opening day. Jim never got around to going out in black powder season, so he went out in the regular season. He got one too. Chuck did not. Harry wished Brownie was around to give him advice on where to hunt, but he wasn't.

Harry's license was for the week before Thanksgiving. He hunted high enough that snow patches were not melting much. The first three mornings, he didn't even see fresh sign. The next two days were weekend, and the woods were wall to wall clowns in orange day-glo. Harry didn't even bother to go out. The day after that, it snowed about two inches.

The final day of deer hunting season dawned clear and quite cold. The high pressure woke Harry early and invigorated. What the hell, he thought.

Chuck's old thirty-thirty was parked by the door. He drove the VW to the top of the ridge and headed out. The sun rose, but it stayed cold. There were a lot of fresh tracks, but he didn't get near enough to anything even to tell if he saw a rack, let alone close enough for a shot.

I'm too close to the road, he thought. They're all spooked here.

Harry headed off across the slope toward a part of Upper Double Eagle Creek Canyon he had never been to before. The country got rough as it sloped down steeply to the creek. He began to wonder if this was a good idea.

As he got close to the bottom, he felt sure it was. There were several clear deer trails through the fresh snow.

There was not a bit of wind. Harry got above one of the most used-looking trails, behind some bushes, and waited.

A couple does came by and did not notice him at all. They drank, then continued on across the creek and back into the woods.

Harry waited some more. His feet started to get cold, but he stayed put. Morning was getting on, but the sun had not reached the canyon floor. He was not sure it ever would in winter. The slope was quite steep to the south.

After a while, Harry heard something coming. He clenched and unclenched his fists a few times silently to limber up his hands. Then he checked to be sure the safety was off, readied the rifle, and waited.

He raised it as the deer came in sight, but it was another doe.

He could hear another coming behind.

This time, it was a little spikehorn. Not very big, just enough antler to be legal, but young tender meat.

The deer were moving slowly, but they did not seem wary. Another doe and a last spring's fawn emerged from the woods.

Harry waited for the young buck to come closer. It did. When it was as close as it would get, Harry took a breath and held it, aimed for the base of the skull, and squeezed the trigger.

Kerblam! How loud the shot was in the still canyon.

The spikehorn dropped instantly. The other deer froze for a fraction of a second, then vanished. Harry set another bullet in the chamber and ran to the deer. His heart was racing. Killing was always a heavy thing. He did not do it often. When he did, he wanted to do it right.

The deer was dead. Harry slit its throat, then gutted it.

Harry was just as glad it was a small deer. He had quite a struggle getting it up the hill. At the top, he shouldered the deer and carried it to the road. He had to stop and rest several times along the way. By the time he got there, his hair and jacket were full of blood.

He had the meat all cut up and put away before Meridell got home. He really did not like to kill, but he sure did like seeing all that meat go into Meridell's freezer.

They had the heart and liver that evening for dinner, along with some of the backstrap. Real tasty. That night Harry dreamt of bears.

Jim and Cindy were taking Steve to his mother's for Thanksgiving. Steve threatened mass mayhem if the grownups failed to get along. Jim and Cindy picked Steve up at school at noon on Wednesday and left directly from there.

Meridell was having Thanksgiving at her house. Paul and Pat were coming down. Chuck and Louella would join them too.

The evening before, Brownie came in. He was done with his harvest. He had sold two pounds. He figured to sell two more later. That left four pounds to share with his friends. He gave Harry about an ounce and a half of some of the most beautiful bud Harry had ever seen.

"Don't keep this in the house. Things are gettin' weird."

"Sure, Man. Thank you."

Brownie also donated about half an ounce to a big batch of chocolate chip cookies Pat baked up Thanksgiving morning. He did not tell her he had grown it or how much he had. She also baked an even larger quantity of straight chocolate chip cookies for those who preferred them that way. It was Thanksgiving: the holiday devoted to the maximum possible celebration of food.

There was a store-bought turkey Paul and Pat brought and a wild one Brownie brought in. There was also a vension roast from Harry's deer. Louella brought sweet potato pie, pumpkin pie (her own pumpkin from the garden) and homemade cranberry relish. Meridell and Suzie cooked up a dozen different dishes from salad to strudel.

About noon, Jeff rushed in all upset. Hadn't anyone invited Burl? No one had thought of it, but of course, he was welcome.

Jeff tore over to Burl's house and almost dragged Burl back with him. Burl was fidgety at first, but he soon settled in and enjoyed himself.

Saturday, Harry's folks called. They were planning to spend Christmas at Sally and Bob's in Little Rock. They did not want to force anything on Harry, but if he wanted to join them, they would buy him a ticket.

Harry only had to think about it a few seconds. Meridell was already planning to take the kids out for Christmas with the grandparents in California. Brownie was going to ride along and see his mom. They would have to drain the water if no one was in the house.

"You don't have to give us an answer right now. If you decide to come, let us know, and we'll send you the fare."

"Gosh, Ma, it sounds great."

"We do love you, Son."

"I love you too, Ma."

"Bet you're getting pretty salty with a chainsaw. Maybe you can show me a few tricks."

"Sure thing."

Pa sounded almost like his old self. It would be good to see them, Sally and the girls too.

Jim and Cindy were staying. Meridell thought of asking them to take care of the house plants. Somewhat to her amazement, Burl volunteered.

Burl was out and about quite regularly now. He was a little socially awkward. What could you expect after all those years of solitude? He was friendly though and interested in people. Mrs. Martinez was the only person in Elk Stuck who had ever seen him sociable before, and that was a long time ago. No one could quite tell if Burl was aware just how long he had kept completely to himself.

Harry checked on airlines. There was no place reasonable to fly from. El Paso or Tucson were both two hundred miles away.

He tried calling the bus. It was long distance, and he got a recording telling him to hold – twice. He gave up in disgust, not sure what to do.

Harry was calling from the shop. Meridell was dismantling her loom to move it up to the house. It took up a large portion of the living room. But there was nowhere near enough business to justify heating the shop in winter.

"Try Amtrak."

There was a toll free number. Harry called it. He could get on in Lordsburg, get off right in Little Rock. The price sounded reasonable. Why not? A train would be fun.

Brownie made one more trip out between Thanksgiving and Christmas.

Private first class Johnny Higgins was pissed off. He was stuck at Fort Bliss for the holidays. The bars in El Paso or maybe Juarez were all the celebration he would get.

"No God damned reason for it either. I don't have a shittin' thing to do. Just regulations. Certain number of personnel got to stay. Fuckin' army."

Brownie was sympathetic. Johnny was grateful for someone to talk to.

Brownie told Johnny he had been over to Elk Stuck.

"Nice place. Good people. I might even stay on there."

"I don't know, Man. Way I hear, we're going to clear everyone out."

"What do you mean?"

"Classified project. Civilians are going to have to move."

"Most of the people own their homes. I don't think they will move."

"Quit shittin' me. The army says: 'Move,' you move."

"They won't like it."

"I don't like it either. Man, this ain't what I signed on for. I may not be the world's greatest patriot. I was just looking for a sure job. But this is the U. S. of A. I didn't join up to fuck my own people in the ass."

Harry had more sympathy for Johnny Higgins when Brownie told him that. The man was not just a slob with security. It was not like he was talking to the Soviets. He was warning his fellow Americans that their own government was screwing them. Even Harry's old man could understand the justification for that kind of divided loyalty – maybe. Harry hoped to find a way to bring it up over the holidays.

Harry did not know what the army or LemTron could do to force people to move. He did not like it though. He would fight for the people that had become the closest family he had. Except, so far, there was not really anything tangible to fight.

There was not any more by the time everyone started heading out for the holidays either. Snow was already accumulating up high. No construction appeared to be going on this year. No one had heard anything from anyone about their houses. Even Wayne, who wanted to sell, could not find anyone to talk to.

Of course, that did not prove much. Wayne was getting pretty flaky. Dumb shit coke head, Harry thought. Bad as a drunk. – Maybe worse. Jim and Cindy drank an awful lot, and Chuck probably never went a day without. They might get obnoxious once in a while, but they at least kept it together. Wayne was definitely slipping. Of course, you could not blame coke for all of that. Wayne was not all that together to begin with.

A steady job and Jesus to tell him when to wipe his nose, Harry thought, and Wayne could pass for a man. On his own, he was just another clown cruising for a crash.

Jesus was worried about him too, but Jesus was not in Elk Stuck much. There was plenty to do on the wrecker, and it was a lot warmer down by the Interstate. Jesus was pretty well moved down there for the winter. What he would do in spring, he would decide in spring.

Harry asked Jesus about Wayne on one occasion when Jesus was up getting some of his things.

"He don't have sense enough to slow down, all you can do is stay out of the way so he don't take you out too when he goes."

Not the nicest philosophy, but Harry had to admit it was the only realistic one he could see either.

One other sour note had to do with Meridell's weaving. There were several Christmas season craft fairs in warm places nearby, more in California; Meridell did not have much to sell. Aspasia Suny had it all.

Meridell called three times. Every time she got the answering machine. She never did get a call back. Perhaps Aspasia was selling all Meridell's work for fancy prices and Meridell would have a fat check waiting when she got home after New Year's. She tried not to get angry, but she was angry. Christmas sales could make the difference between a comfortable winter and a miserable one. There was nothing she could do. Even if she went to Santa Fe, which she was not really considering, she did not have a street address for Aspasia – just the phone and a post office box.

She finally forced herself to calm down. It was Christmas time. The kids were excited about the trip. She did have some money and some work to sell. Christmas preparations and Harry were what she wanted to focus on. So she did.

Harry was about moved in now. He had not exactly moved out of the shed at Chuck and Louella's, but he was staying with Meridell all the time. They had not exactly decided to do things that way. It just pleased both of them. Suzie and Jeff liked having Harry there too.

Harry's good-by to Meridell and the kids was more emotional than he expected. He had never been in love like this before. He sent Christmas presents along for all three of them. They did the same for him.

"Next trip, I want to make together."

"Me too," said Meridell.

Chuck and Louella dropped Harry at the station in Lordsburg about one in the afternoon on Monday, December twenty-second. A day and a half later, about one in the morning, after a change in San Antonio, Harry got off the train at Little Rock, Arkansas.

CHAPTER NINETEEN

"*PRAISE GOD!!!*"

It was easier to get into rapport with his parents than Harry thought it might be. All three of them were uncomfortable with Bob and Sally's religion.

Jennifer was too young to know the difference. Harry felt sorry for Jeanne. So did his folks. None of them wanted to say anything. It was Bob and Sally's house.

Harry's parents were more or less generic Protestants. They believed in God. They believed in Jesus. They taught their children Christian values, and they lived by them. They went to church once or twice a month. What one they went to depended more on what was handy or where they liked the minister and congregation than on denomination.

Sally and Bob were Born Again and on fire with it. They jumped on Harry within thirty seconds of getting off the train.

"Do you read the Bible?"

"Uh, sure."

"Do you read it *every day?*"

"Well, no."

"You better! You better read your Bible every day! You better *pray* to be saved!"

Bob was getting red in the face. Sally looked like she was in a trance. They were still on the train platform.

"*Hallelujah!*" Sally shouted.

"*Prraise the Lord!*" Bob replied.

It kept up all the way back to the house. Harry's parents were asleep. Harry was thankful it was late and he could soon do the same.

Christmas morning there was a tree and presents. Bob would not let Jeanne near them till after church. That was tolerable. What was not tolerable was that Bob and Sally seemed to be doing their best to keep Jeanne frightened and miserable.

Harry might not have dared, on his own, to refuse to go with Bob and Sally to church. His mother took the initiative.

"I'm old enough to worship my Maker as I see fit. I aim to enjoy the Lord's birthday. I'll stay here, thank you."

"We'll pray for you." Sally's expression looked more like a curse.

"You do that."

Bob and Sally strutted out, full of self-righteousness. Harry and his parents settled around the kitchen table with coffee. Their first real conversation was a strategy session: how they were all going to survive ten days of Bob and Sally.

"The hell with it," said Harry's dad. "I didn't come down here to satisfy the Inquisition. They can't act civilized, we'll go rent a damn motel room."

Inside of half an hour, Harry and his folks were laughing and having a fine time together.

Harry's dad looked a lot better than Harry was afraid he might.

"I've got to watch the cholesterol and the coffee, work up to any physical exertion gradually for a while. That's it for restrictions."

"Cover your ears, Earl."

Harry's dad smiled and did.

"He also had to quit smoking. – He doesn't like to be reminded."

Harry's dad uncovered his ears. Even if he had not heard, he knew perfectly well what his wife was saying, but he chose to pretend otherwise. If Sally and Bob would just get a little sense of humor, Harry thought, this could be a fun Christmas.

Earl Upton's heart was not seriously damaged. What had gotten him, really, was a severe preretirement attack of workaholism. A desk job, twenty cups of coffee a day, trying to save the taxpayers a buck.

"Like fighting the tide. Damned politicians and generals may have more education than me, but they never read history. I just hate to see a great country go down to moral laziness and waste."

Margaret Upton obviously agreed, but she wanted her husband healthy. She emphatically washed the coffee pot instead of making more when they emptied it. She also took the first opportunity to change the subject.

Enlisting his parents' sympathy, it appeared, for what was happening at Thunder Mountain, was not going to be difficult. Harry's only hesitation now was whether he wanted to wish it on them.

Harry's dad was due to retire in late February. Earl and Margaret had bought a small motor home. They planned to use Bob and Sally for a mailing address and spend at least six months on the road before making up their minds where to settle.

"Who knows?" said Harry's mom. Maybe we'll like it and turn into regular geriatric gypsies."

It seemed strange to Harry, his parents talking about being old. They were the same age as Chuck and Louella.

"One nice thing about the army," said Harry's dad: "A little trip to the hospital doesn't eat up your life savings."

Bob and Sally did not get back till after noon. They had not let Jeanne eat anything before church. Now she was so hungry she was not even interested in Christmas. Bob and Sally wanted to do the present ritual right away. Margaret put her foot down.

"The Lord's birthday is a day of joy. You have done everything in your power to ruin it for that child."

Harry held his breath. Bob and Sally held their tongues. Margaret fixed her granddaughter a bowl of Cheerios with banana, milk and sugar. Two minutes after she was done eating, Jeanne was asleep. The presents waited.

"Sally, I think we better have a little talk."

"Yes, Mother."

They all tramped into the living room, rather grimly. It seemed bizarre to Harry to watch the Christmas lights flashing on the tree while they all ignored it.

"Sally, this is you and Bob's home. I'm not going to tell you how to live. But the Jesus I know is a God of love and of life. I won't stay in this atmosphere, and I will not have your father subjected to it."

"Yes, Mother."

Harry could not figure out what was going on. Apparently his mother couldn't either.

"For Heaven's sake, Sally, what is it?"

Sally was too close to tears to talk. Bob answered.

"We spoke to Reverend Moore. He said, 'Honor thy father and thy mother.' We just want to bring you the Good News."

Harry's dad answered: "You might do a better job if you'd quit assuming you're the only ones that know it."

Sally was sobbing quietly. Her mother took her in her arms.

After that, things were not exactly comfortable, but they were better. Harry used his parents for a shield. When one of them was around, Bob and Sally kept the preaching toned down. Alone he was fair game. He would have stuck with his parents anyhow. They were certainly the better company.

Christmas was on a Thursday. Sunday morning, Harry and his parents did go to church with Bob and Sally. The sermon was appalling. Harry was not sure what the subject was supposed to be. He thought they had started with one of the usual Christmas texts. Most of the sermon, however, seemed to be on the theme of: Everyone else but us is damned. The words said to save them. Unspoken, seemed an attitude running through the whole congregation that everyone else deserved to be damned. Worst of all were Catholics and Mormons. As for Jews, God both loved and hated them more than anyone else. Moslems or other religions were not mentioned.

The singing at least was fun. A few of the songs had pretty morbid words, but the music was up-tempo. Everyone let themselves go. I guess they've got to have something to enjoy, Harry thought.

Harry was mightily relieved to get out of that church. He could see his parents were too. Bob and Sally were behaving themselves. Margaret and Earl did not say anything. They had lunch at a cafe. It seemed odd to Harry to see a menu with no Mexican food on it.

That afternoon, Harry called Meridell in California. He talked to Suzie and Jeff too. They were all having a good time. The weather was kind of rainy, but they'd had a couple sunny days. They had spent yesterday at the beach.

"I miss you."

"I miss you too."

Harry blew a kiss to the phone.

Margaret was delighted Harry had a girlfriend he really cared about, even if she was divorced with two children and five years older than he. She wanted to know everything about Meridell. Harry was sorry he did not have any weaving to show – or a picture.

The next day, Harry's parents came in with a package.

"Christmas present."

Harry opened it. Inside was a camera, two rolls of film, and a coupon to have them developed.

The weather was mostly clear and pleasant. Tuesday was the nicest day yet.

"Want to go for a ride?"

"Sure, Pa. Where to?"

"Your mother and I have been considering buying a place in the Ozarks when we do get ready to settle. We thought we'd go see what it looks like up there."

They took Jeanne with them. She was wild with excitement. They went for several short hikes. The rest of the day they spent driving, looking at scenery.

At six-thirty, Margaret called Sally to say they were having dinner at Mountain Home and they were staying the night so they could look at property in the morning.

That is just what they did too. First thing in the morning, Margaret called three real estate agencies. At the third one, she found a woman named Jessica Horton who had time to show them some places.

They spent most of the day. Jessica did not believe in the hard sell. Her idea of a real estate agent's job was having the information to get people who had a place to sell and people who wanted to buy together.

"'...Believe I'll have my turnips fried today.'"

"You ought to go on TV."

They were all roaring with laughter for at least the forty-fifth time. Jessica knew enough Ozark Mountain stories to keep going for hours. No one wanted her to stop. She was a great storyteller.

By four o'clock, it seemed like they had looked at half of northern Arkansas, and a fair portion of southern Missouri too. Reluctantly, Margaret and Earl said they had better head back so as not to be driving too late.

"It is New Year's Eve. Thank you for giving us so much of your time."

"It's a pleasure. I always figure it's a privilege having a job showing nice folks country I love." They could tell she meant it.

On the way back to Little Rock, Earl stopped and bought a bottle of champagne. He had never been much of a drinker. He and Harry had had one beer apiece in Mountain Home last night.

"If they won't let us toast the New Year in the house, we'll go out in the yard."

Bob and Sally obviouly did not like alcohol in their home. They insisted it was all right, however, and even joined the toast. Harry noticed they barely let it touch their lips, but no one said anything. They really did all want to get along.

"Stay in touch, Son."

"I will, Ma."

It was six o'clock Monday evening. Margaret noticed another family in the station with a camera. The young man looked about Harry's age. She walked over and said she would take a picture of them with their camera if they would take a picture of her and Earl and Harry with hers.

It was a warm good-by.

Harry rode with the other young man all the way to San Antonio. Turned out the Alamo was not far from the station. It was eleven at night. The train was not due to pull out till after four. Harry walked over to see the Alamo.

The folks were all right, Harry thought next day as West Texas rolled endlessly by. The two days driving in the mountains were great.

"Look, antelope!"

The couple in the seat just behind Harry looked like an ad for western clothes and turquoise jewelry. They had made it a point to tell the whole car they were Hoosiers and on their first trip west. They wanted to see White Sands, The Grand Canyon and Tombstone. They seemed to have no conception they were talking about places spread out over five hundred miles.

Harry never had mentioned the situation with LemTron and the army at Thunder Mountain. He could not figure out what to say. Why aggravate his folks unless there was something constructive to be accomplished?

It was a reassuring visit. Elk Stuck was awfully remote. The way of life there was not exactly American standard. Harry's parents lived in a far more conventional world. When it came to basic values, though, he could see they lived very much in the same world. That helped.

The train pulled into Lordsburg at six-thirty in the afternoon. Meridell and Chuck were waiting on the platform. Chuck's right arm was in a sling.

CHAPTER TWENTY

A biting wind blew across the platform.

Harry shivered.

There was a moment, as Harry stepped off the train, before Meridell or Chuck spotted him, when he saw something: Was Meridell just hunkered down to face the wind, or was some weight pressing on her?

The wind made Harry squint. He saw Chuck was doing the same as their eyes met. Mean little pig eyes!

Pop!

He was inside the aura, back with the people he knew. The strange view was gone.

"There he is," Chuck's bellow was hearty as ever.

Meridell saw him too and smiled like sunshine. Their embrace of greeting was long and vibrant.

Chuck pounded Harry's back.

"What'd you do, Chuck, tangle with a bear?"

"Had a wreck."

"Is Louella okay?"

"Sore from head to toe. Two cracked ribs. Real colorful bruises. Looks like hell."

There was something Chuck was not saying, but Harry did not know what to ask − or whether he should.

"I hope you won't mind..." Meridell sounded uncomfortable.

Chuck and Louella's truck was totalled. They needed groceries. Chuck needed to see the doctor. Meridell's truck was just a two seater. Ordinarily, Harry could drive and Meridell could sit in Chuck's lap. It had only been since Saturday after Christmas. Chuck's collarbone was not really set. Someone needed to ride in back.

"Of course....You should of brought the VW....In fact, why don't you and Louella use it till you can get something else together....I guess Louella'll have to drive till you can use that hand to shift."

Chuck's, "Thanks," was a growl.

It was quite a bit later before Meridell explained. Chuck had been in trouble for drunk driving before. The other driver was over the legal limit too, but barely. Chuck was obviously stinking drunk. The wreck was also obviously his fault; he had been belligerent to the police besides.

The other driver was not seriously hurt. His girlfriend was. She had a broken hip, a broken nose, and half her teeth knocked out. At twenty-nine, she could expect to walk again, but it would be a long, expensive recovery.

Chuck had been to court once. He had to go again. The best that could happen to him was a year's suspension of his license.

Several other things had happened while Harry was gone. One of them was pleasant: Burl Trent was teaching the boys to carve wood. He had a real genius for seeing the gnomes and elves hidden in the natural flow of the grain. He was a surprisingly good teacher too.

The most major event was that every property owner in Elk Stuck had received an offer from LemTron to buy them out. The prices offered were an insult. The only person even considering accepting was Wayne, and he couldn't: His mortgage had a penalty clause for early payment. LemTron was not offering enough to pay off the bank. The bank would not let Wayne sell.

Meridell was worried about her house. Her landlady was eighty-two. She had said no, but LemTron had made it clear they planned to get pushy. Meridell did not know Flora Quintana. She had only spoken to her on the phone once. She had connected to her through Mrs. Martinez. Flora was Mrs. Martinez's aunt. She was in good health, but at that age, how much pressure would a person be willing to take – over a house they did not need themselves.

"You don't know Flora," Mrs. Martinez said. "She's a fighter."

Still, Meridell was nervous.

Everyone else owned their homes. Jesus and Cindy thought they might sell if the price was right. No one else was willing to consider it at any price. There were also several small plots of private land, some vacant, some with houses in various states of disintegration, whose owners lived elsewhere. A couple of these people were negotiating with LemTron over price. A couple others were refusing to sell. Several no one in town knew about.

Mrs. Martinez was also upset about the mail. It was being opened. She had filed an official complaint and been told, pretty bluntly, to shut up and mind her own business if she wanted to keep a job.

"I look at the stamps. They still have little American flags on them. They still say U. S. A. I keep thinking it's going to be Paraguay or Bolivia."

Mrs. Martinez was scared. Everyone was. Opening people's mail! Louella had written their congressman, both senators, the president, and the governor. She had mailed the letters from Douglas. There had been no reply yet, but it had only been a few days.

The next few days were odd. Harry recognized the feeling. It was like when he got back from that last thinning contract. Only this time it took him by surprise because he had not paid attention to the place where he was while he was with his family. With them, he was in an atmosphere that meant something to him, personally; so he had not really noticed the lack of a focussed objective vibe of place.

It hit him as they topped Post Office Ridge. "The Thunders are strong," he said aloud. The feeling was ambiguous though. The place, itself, felt wonderfully good to Harry, but there was an ominous feel on the air too.

It also felt like things had changed in some way while Harry was gone. Not only was the aura at Elk Stuck focussed in a way it was not at Little Rock or Greer. It was now growing more intense. Maybe it's just winter, Harry thought: Cold. Snow. No traffic. Two or three days at a time when no one in their right mind would even want to try the road....He did not believe that.

The dream he had his second night back did not help: He thought the Indian Lady was in the dream somewhere, but he could not remember where. That was a lot of why the dream made him so uncomfortable. That was how the dream felt while it was going on too: He knew she was around somewhere, but he could not find her.

Why it mattered, he was not sure. Did she need him, or did he need her? Or was it the mountain that needed them to be in communication? Something was urgent, and there was some confusion interfering with whatever it was he was supposesd to be doing.

Then there were the...Harry was not sure what they were. Nothing he could think of to identify them after he woke quite adequately described them.

What they were, actually, was stones that came to life and attacked like a startled bear. Only they were not like a bear because they were cold blooded. It was like a bear, only more so: more objective Nature, less human.

Only...something cared, even in the stones. Not only were the stones that attacked him not themselves the evil. They were its realest victims. And they cared about him; not like a person; not even like a bear a person had made friends with.

The feeling was a resonance of life energy. Something so deep and honest it felt like Creation itself was in agreement between Harry and the stones. Something was in violent turmoil too. The dream was not a nightmare. It was also not a pleasant dream. Meridell was a help though. She seemed to know just how Harry felt.

It was noteworthy to Harry that he and Meridell were in clear agreement about who here was in tune with whatever he was feeling: all three kids, Mrs. Martinez, and Burl Trent.

Louella sort of was in tune, but she was as if behind a wall whose substance was Chuck and her loyalty to him. Something in Chuck was running, evading responsibility. Harry thought of a war story his old man had once told him whose essense was: Never trust a coward, even if he is a buddy.

Jim and Cindy seemed confused. Wayne was in a panic — though his everyday behavior was just slightly nervous. Wayne had never had a whole lot of personality. What he did have was bovine. Harry suspected immediately that Wayne was still doing coke – and wondered how he could get it. – Wayne was very broke; that is what he was panicking over. – Even a cow will get twitchy on cocaine, Harry thought.

Jesus stopped in once. He was quite clear: clear that he was glad to be living somewhere else.

"Man, my people been fightin' ghosts for a thousand years. You can have it."

Harry could not fault him. What Jesus said felt true. It was their turn. Jesus felt just the opposite of Chuck. This was not Jesus' war for some reason. He was making a way and a living in the Anglo world that had swallowed up the country of his ancestors, and justly proud of himself. That was Jesus' responsibility in this life. Chuck, Harry felt, had a responsibility to the mountain that had given him a home, and he was evading it.

Brownie was still in California. Harry sure wished he would get back.

It was a couple days after the dream when Chuck got Harry alone: "Harry, I hate to ask, but you know how lawyers are. I gotta be in court the thirteenth."

"How much do you need?"

"Could you manage eight hundred?"

Harry had that much money. He had more than that much. He was sure Chuck knew that. He also had little prospect of paying work anywhere near Elk Stuck till spring. He wondered if Chuck had any savings, but he could not bring himself to ask.

The thirteenth came and went. Chuck and Louella, Harry and Meridell all squeezed into the VW and rode to Apex, the county seat. Louella drove. Harry and Meridell rode in back. First time Harry ever saw Chuck in a jacket and tie.

Nothing happened. The lawyers performed their ritual for a few minutes. Then the case was continued till March second. Chuck acted like this was some sort of victory. The lawyer encouraged this attitude.

Sam Hoyt, Chuck's lawyer, was a big, hearty man. He seemed friendly and sympathetic. Harry did not like him. "Cancer of the soul," was how he found himself describing his feeling that night to Meridell.

Chuck wanted to eat in town. He did not offer to treat. Harry did not want to spend the money, but he did not say anything. The burritos were good and quite reasonable, but Harry still did not like it. He paid for his and Meridell's. He had the feeling Chuck wanted Harry to pay for them all, but Louella took care of his and her own. Was Harry imagining things, or did he see some little angry fire fly between Louella and Chuck?

Chuck also had them stop at a liquor store where he bought four cases of Coors and a half gallon of Jim Beam. Harry did not really want any, but he would have taken a couple sixpacks home – except he was feeling poor. Chuck's disability check usually came around the third of the month. He had not said anything about paying Harry back.

That night Harry let himself go enough to talk with Meridell about it.

"What! He hit me up for twelve hundred."

96

Harry's first reaction was just concern. That was that much less money any of them had to get through the winter.

CHAPTER TWENTY-ONE

Later Harry started to simmer.

It was winter. There was not that much to do and less to do for money. He had worked his tail off all fall. So had Meridell. There was no damned reason for them to be poor.

Louella was very closemouthed. Chuck spent most of his time drinking – and was manifestly drunk more than Harry had ever seen before.

Meridell and Jim both confirmed this was Chuck's usual way to get through the winter. Jim and Cindy had the same approach. They spent a lot of time together.

A year ago, Harry would have been right with them. Now, he couldn't. The party was not fun.

Things came to a head about mid-February. Suzie's boots were falling apart. There was snow and ice on the road. The VW was much better on snow and ice than Meridell's truck (which was acting tired anyhow) and got better mileage too. It also had room for four inside.

"Chuck, how about letting us have the car Saturday so we can take the kids into town."

It was Thursday morning. Chuck was not quite drunk yet. Harry really wanted to take the car back altogether. Chuck was out of the sling and was driving it himself – drunk and badly.

"You gonna leave us without?" Chuck's bellow was now peevish and intimidating rather than amusing.

"For Heaven's sake, Man, it's just one day."

"We need it."

"We can get by," Louella said, with a brief scowl at Chuck.

Harry was grateful. "We can leave the truck keys in case you have an emergency....But don't drive it unless you have to. It's not running too well....And, Chuck, how about a hundred back on that loan. Suzie needs boots. I want to get a carb kit for the truck...."

"Can't do it."

Chuck's expression was indignant. Harry thought about arguing, but then he wilted.

They bought Suzie boots that would get her through the winter. For twelve dollars more they could have bought her boots that would get her through three winters – and kept her a lot warmer doing it.

They also spent about half what they would have liked to spend on groceries. Not that they would be hungry. You can live just fine on beans and sprouts. – Meridell kept both alfalfa and mung beans going all the time by choice. But why the hell shouldn't he be able to add a can of black olives to liven things up?

Harry was pissed. He was doubly pissed because it was the kids' first trip to town since New Year's. The movie playing did not look very good, and they wanted to negotiate the road in daylight, but money was the real reason they did not watch it. They did eat in a cafe. Everyone liked bean burritos. Everyone also knew it was the cheapest way to get a good meal.

At least there was still plenty of venison. They had shut down the freezer to save electricity. It was a severe winter. The shadiest corner of the house was an unheated shed. Things did not stay totally frozen all the time, but they did stay cold enough to keep till they were used up.

"One less motor to listen to. I did it last year too."

Harry was not mad at Meridell. He did not want to rub salt into the situation by saying anything. He also knew that last winter Meridell was poor. This winter should have been different. Paul sent money for the kids, of course. But these days when it so often took two parents working outside the home to maintain one household for children, the divorce meant Meridell really needed her earnings.

When they got home, the truck was gone. Harry and Meridell were both concerned. Jim and Cindy were gone too, in Jim's truck.

No one had come back by the time they went to bed, but Harry slept poorly. He heard both trucks pull in and checked the time: Quarter to three. The bars closed at two.

"Son of a bitch." He barely spoke aloud so as not to wake Meridell.

Next day was clear and calm. By ten the sun was shining warmly. It would be gone from the canyon by three. Harry wanted to work on the truck.

About eleven, Harry walked down to Chuck and Louella's. There was no sign of life, but the key was in the ignition. So he drove the truck back up the street. It was missing horribly. Harry looked under the hood.

"What the hell?"

A spark plug wire had somehow come loose.

"They drive up the hill like that? Fuckin' drunk coulda' fried the bastard."

Mechanicking angry does not work. Harry forced himself to calm down. The weather stayed calm and not too cold, even after the early canyon sunset. By the time Harry quit, around five, the truck sounded much healthier.

Both vehicles stayed at Meridell's till Wednesday. That afternoon Louella came over. She was a little tense, but Harry and Meridell were both glad to see her.

She wanted to get groceries next day. – And she and Chuck wanted to look for a used truck while they were in town. Harry actually felt pleased for her to take the car.

Friday night, there was a dance in Lariat. Harry and Meridell had not been dancing since they got home from the holidays. The car was still at Chuck and Louella's. The truck had better heat, but the warm days had left icy spots all over the road. The car was really the vehicle to take.

Harry walked down to Chuck and Louella's determined not to be angry.

"Hell, why don't we all go. Me'n Louella need to get the old corpuskles circulatin' too."

"Long as I drive home." Harry tried to say it lightly, but he knew there was a bite to it.

"Sure." Chuck's joviality was only slightly forced.

They had found a truck. Put fifty dollars down on it. They had liability insurance on the old truck, what the law required. It did not cover a replacement.

"If the law leaves us anything from the next check, we can drive it home from court."

Harry knew that would mean no repayment for him or Meridell that month. But what the hell? Chuck and Louella needed a vehicle of their own.

They had fun at the dance.

Tuesday, after mail time, Burl Trent came over. He came by about once a week now. Someone stopped in on him nearly every day. The boys were there a lot.

Burl was interesting company, and knowledgeable too. He read news magazines. He used the State Library Books By Mail Program. He read a lot of historical novels. "Good way to learn. You don't die of boredom. – They cross-reference just as well as something dull."

Not everyone would think of that. Burl was surprisingly sane for someone who had been so isolated so long, but he had his own point of view:

"We're as well-informed here as anyplace. Maybe better. The same information is available and less activity to confuse it."

Burl was not impressed by the society in the world around him. Yet he was, by no means, opposed to modern technology and convenience.

"I'm getting old. I don't do a lot any more, and I don't want to. Glad I don't have to."

That was his view of technology. Since it benefitted him, he was tolerant of other people's use of it. As for the amazing amount of information now available to anyone who wanted it, Burl's sense of history gave him an awe for it. This awe often animated stories he told, both of incidents in his own life and general anecdotes he had picked up from a book or magazine.

"It makes him a wonderful teacher," Meridell commented one day. "I feel privileged he is available to my children."

Burl had worked, for many years, for a large architectural firm. His only degree was a B.S. in chemistry. Most of his career, he had spent doing the engineering of big commercial buildings. He had worked on projects in two dozen American cities and several foreign ones. When it came to how to do it and what it would cost, his opinion carried more weight for many years before he retired, than any of the vice presidents of the corporation.

Today, Burl had come by because of the mail. Burl sometimes got rhetorically irate when talking about the idiocy of the world. This was the first time Harry had seen him really angry.

"Like conquistadores: Indians won't move; give 'em blankets infested with smallpox....How dare they!"

The letter was from LemTron. It was a bit vague, but the point was clear enough: The army was behind them. The United States government had the legal power to condemn land and do what it pleased with it at whatever price it felt like paying the owners, if any. Mr. Trent and the other property owners of Elk Stuck really ought to start behaving reasonably while they still had a position to bargain from.

Mrs. Martinez felt the same way Burl did. She intended to stay and fight. She planned to call Flora Quintana, Meridell's landlady, that evening. Meridell and Harry did not know what they could do. This was their home but they did not own property.

This fact set Burl off on a round of philosophy. "I remember when kids grew up, the community set 'em up to farm: Tools, animals, a house to live in. Then it was their responsibility to carry their weight in the community and raise kids of their own.

"Now. I feel sorry for you young folks today. Same thing happened in the late Middle Ages — just before it crashed, and the Renaissance came out of that. It's just overpopulation. No one to blame, and not really all a bad thing. I still feel sorry for anyone's got to be young in times when there's no place for you."

Harry had felt just like that but had never articulated it. He did not see it in historical terms — just his own generation and his elders.

That lack of a place to sink his roots had once made Harry cynical. Now he found that he did have roots, however tenuous, here on Thunder Mountain. That realization made him feel ferocious. Harry also felt grateful to Burl for acknowledging his position in life so sympathetically. It made Harry want to do anything he could to see that Burl kept his house.

Harry and Meridell certainly did not want to move from Elk Stuck to anyplace else, but if they had to, they would survive. Burl had been there too long. He belonged to the mountain like an old fir tree on a high ridge.

Burl also had something concrete he wanted to do. He had been exchanging Christmas cards regularly with one of the old company lawyers. The man was eighty and mostly retired, but he still took a case now and then if he believed in it.

"Never trust a cop under forty or a lawyer under seventy," Burl said. "Joe Sartanian had principles all along. Now he can afford to live by them. — Old age is a pain in the neck...and every other joint in the body. It does have some advantages though."

Joseph Sartanian lived in Tucson. He planned to be up March fifth, weather permitting.

"Same week Chuck goes to court," Harry commented.

"Didn't realize that. Hope he's not allergic to lawyers."

Harry was confused momentarily.

Meridell chuckled and gave Burl a squeeze on the shoulder. Then she offered a pot of Almond Sunset tea all around. They all had a cup.

At daybreak on March second, there was another foot of fresh snow on the level. Chuck was supposed to be at court in Apex at ten. It was a mail day. The plow might make it through by noon. Could he come in the afternoon?

Chuck's lawyer, Sam Hoyt, called back from the courthouse in Apex at ten forty-five. Chuck's case was postponed till April seventh.

"I'd have asked for a postponement anyhow. The longer we string it out, the better our chances."

By one, Chuck was roaring. He passed out around seven. The plow did not make it through till nine-thirty the next morning, the mail right behind it. Not another vehicle came into town all day. Cindy went out right behind the plow.

At seven-thirty that evening, there was a knock on the door. Suzie opened it.

"Brownie!"

Everyone leapt to the door. It was a brilliant, clear, cold night.

"How'd you get here?"

"Walked."

"All the way up from the highway?"

"Sure."

Brownie looked it. His cheeks were fairly glowing.

He set down his pack and, after hugs all around, peeled down to his T shirt and hovered over the stove.

"Venison chile and cornbread sound good?"

"You bet."

"I'll warm them up."

"Mind if I wash up? I been on the road four days."

"Of course. Go ahead."

After eating, Brownie got out his little pipe and offered it around. Harry took it and realized he had barely smoked since before Christmas.

"Did you carry this on the road?"

"Sure."

"There's a witch hunt going on out there."

"They ain't burned me at the stake yet."

Next morning, Burl Trent showed up early. Joe Sartanian did not want to drive up the hill. His reflexes were not what they used to be, and there was still snow and ice on the road. Could they meet him in Lariat? Of course. Just a matter of sorting out riders.

There was smoke on the air when Burl came in. There was a moment of tension. Would he notice? Did he already know they smoked pot? Would it matter to him?

He did notice. He sniffed. Then he smiled.

"When I was a kid it was illegal to sell tobacco to anyone under eighteen. Marijuana was legal, so we'd smoke it instead. Of course, what we really wanted was cigarettes."

Chuck grumbled about having to go down the hill twice to make both the meeting and a connect for his new truck the next day.

You could be going to jail, Harry thought. But he did not say anything.

Everyone else was as co-operative as they could be. Burl came back to the house with Harry, Meridell and Brownie when they had it all arranged.

"You know, back in the thirteen hundreds, when the plague hit, people concluded the culprit was witchcraft. They probably did remove a few perfectly awful people the world was better off without, but mostly they killed innocents. Mostly women.

"They also took it into their heads that cats were the familiars of witches, so they killed every cat they could catch. When there was a rat population explosion and the plague got worse, they figured they better attack witches even harder."

Burl was talking about the self-destructiveness of a government that preyed on its own citizens, but a powerful rush surged through Harry when Brownie's response to Burl's comment was to pull out his pipe.

"Do you mind?"

"Not at all. You want to gum up your lungs, that's your privilege."

Not only was Burl remarkably sane for a man who had been so isolated so long. He was saner, Harry thought, than most people.

The meeting with Joe Sartanian was set for six o'clock, over dinner, at the State Line, on Burl.

CHAPTER TWENTY-TWO

Flora Quintana was a jewel. She was just five feet tall — with her shoes on. Her son, Manuel, drove her over from Hachita. Mrs. Martinez had mentioned that she could barely speak English when she was widowed at forty. Now, at eighty-two, she had more of a lilt than an accent.

"They called Pancho Villa a bandit, but I remember him. He used to come to the house and smoke and talk with my father. I sent two sons to the fight against Hitler. They were both wounded in action, but they both came back." (She crossed herself.) "My people always fought for justice."

The old people did most of the talking, except for Brownie. The meeting was mostly to exchange information. Brownie knew more about what the army was doing — or appeared to be doing — than anyone else. No one really knew who LemTron was.

How strange, Harry thought, looking around the table. Mrs. Martinez in her sixties, Burl Trent in his seventies, and the two octogenarians all seemed full of certainty and conviction. Brownie, the youngest person there, sounded clear-headed and competent. All the others, the ones in their prime adult years, just seemed impotent and ineffectual.

Everyone wanted to fight though, including Cindy, who was no longer considering selling her house. (Wayne and Jesus were not there. Jesus was busy and not really interested. Wayne was too scared to go.)

Later, Jim commented, "I thought I was fighting for my country in Vietnam and got fucked in the ass. Not again!"

Saturday, it clouded up. By evening, it was snowing. By morning, it was raining hard.

Double Eagle Creek was up a foot by noon.

The rain kept coming in sheets. By dark, the creek was spilling onto the road and roaring.

Harry had never seen anything like it. Whole trees fairly shot through town. Big ones. Huge boulders crashed in the water. A five foot culvert twenty feet long stood ponderously on end and hovered for several minutes before crashing down and lodging against the side of the canyon, which, in many places, was now the only bank the creek knew.

In the morning, the rain finally stopped. The creek settled back to three or four times its normal volume by afternoon.

The road was in fragments. Here a piece of it would be intact, but bow shaped, dropping off to a new level scoured eight feet deep. There it would be impossible to tell there ever was a road.

The Overmans' house was gone. So was a shed at Jim's.

They had barely saved Chuck and Louella's new tan '69 Chevy half ton. A thick rope held the right front corner to one tree. A come-a-long held the left front corner to a second tree. The rear wheels were suspended over space where the flood had washed the ground out from under it.

News crews came in — by helicopter — from Albuquerque, Tucson, ABC, and *Newsweek*. It was Brownie who recognized the opportunity. The first reporter ignored him. Then he hid his hair in a wool hat and got the attention of the others.

Only the flood made it on the tube, but *Newsweek* titled its article: "Double Trouble," and actually mentioned that the army wanted their homes. There was no suggestion that anything was improper about this, just unfortunate; but it was there. People knew about them, knew they were up against something, even if they did not know what.

"It was the Indian Woman," Suzie insisted. "I could hear her singing all through the flood. The mountain has to do something. It didn't hurt us."

The road was passable in a week. It was supposed to be all fixed up long before tourist time. There was little damage outside the canyon, and the rain had washed away every bit of snow.

March nineteenth was a balmy, sunny day without much wind. (Wind is often a prime feature of spring weather in the Southwest.) About two o'clock, Joseph Sartanian drove into town. He had wattles and a little bit of a paunch, but he had a full head of straight white hair, and his brown eyes were clear. He walked sturdily, if a little stiffly.

He stopped at the bottom of town, inspected the road and consulted a map, then drove straight to Burl Trent's house. Soon they both came down to Meridell's.

The kids were in school. Harry was reading a year-old *Asimov's* science fiction magazine. Meridell was weaving. Brownie was cleaning his ancient twenty-two. He never had taken that elk. Now he was talking about getting a deer. Harry's was gone. They could certainly use the meat. Brownie was staying with them. He liked it better than Jim's, and they were all pleased to have him though it was a little crowded.

Brownie had sold four pounds of pot, total, at six hundred dollars a pound. It was all prime bud. Bust stories in the papers always talked about "Street values" three and four times that high. The stories were all bullshit. The stories calculated prices on the basis of the smallest unit at the highest price. Brownie sold what he sold by the pound. — He also gave away as much bud as he sold at all — and all the leaf. That twenty-four hundred dollars was most of Brownie's income the past year. He was not broke, but venison was certainly the most affordable contribution he was equipped to provide the household.

Joe Sartanian looked a little out of his element in his dress slacks and city shoes, but he was genuinely friendly.

"Been wanting to see this place. It sure is beautiful. I didn't call ahead because the lines may well be tapped."

Brownie shot Harry a pointed look. If a lawyer talked about phone taps he probably knew what he was talking about.

"I've been tracking down LemTron. The address you got off the mining claim notices proved most useful. Thank you."

He nodded to Brownie.

"LemTron is a mineral exploration and refining company. They either set up where someone else is going to mine or contract the mining. They build their own plants. That turned out to be a key point.

"LemTron is a wholly-owned subsidiary of a corporation called Quadra Realty.

"Quadra Realty has a variety of holdings from a chicken processing facility in South Carolina to a tin importing business in Bolivia. Their biggest single asset is land and mineral rights. One of their major corporate assets, however, is a construction company called Vitor Construction.

"For many years, Vitor Construction built military housing. Eventually, they specialized in security systems. Recently, they have been building quite a lot of prisons."

"So what does it add up to?" Meridell asked.

"I don't know yet. I have got one other piece of information though. Back when the bill was up to create the Thunder Peak Wilderness there was considerable objection due to the high mineral concentrations. That is a lot of the reason the Wilderness is no bigger than it is.

"The whole south side of Thunder Mountain is full of copper, with a good deal of silver and gold mixed in and very little lead. There is also a big pocket of azurite and probably turquoise too, though not much has been found.

"The silver and gold are commercially recoverable only as a byproduct of the copper. There's no market for copper and plenty of operating mines if there was one. There is probably something worth mining on that site, but minerals are just no reason for going into the Wilderness at ten thousand feet."

"We figured that," Harry said. "What is the reason?"

"I don't know yet, but I will, if someone doesn't knock me off first."

"Are you serious?" Harry asked.

"Entirely. To quote the bard, 'Something is rotten in the state of Denmark.' The reference was to a corrupt king. Kings do not like their linen aired in public – especially if it is very dirty."

The next week, Meridell finally got a letter from Aspasia Suny. There was even a check for a hundred sixty-five dollars. The letter mostly gushed about Europe. It seemed Aspasia had spent the winter in Spain, Southern France, and Italy. It did not appear that she had been putting any significant effort into selling Meridell's weaving. She had great hopes for the coming summer in Santa Fe.

Meridell was unsure what to do. She tried calling, but once again, she got the machine and no return call.

Meridell wrote Aspasia a note saying she needed to talk if they were going to continue working together. In the meantime, she was glad she had a fair amount of her work to bring to craft fairs, which were going to be picking up again soon.

The last week in March, Louella planted peas and radishes. Chuck got a letter from Sam Hoyt. His case was postponed till May nineteenth. He spent the next three days even more drunk than he was most of the time. Harry could not see how he could tend the shop at all if he kept it up.

Jim had a tree planting contract coming up in April. He asked Harry if he wanted in on it. Harry had barely turned a dollar in four months. He certainly did. Brownie was planting.

Thanks to the flood, the winter snow was all gone. Spring snows melted quickly. It was a Saturday when the first Vitor Construction workers showed up, April eighteenth, Paul Revere Day.

CHAPTER TWENTY-THREE

"Could you tell me what elevation we'uh at?"

Harry had walked out to the road prepared to dislike anyone who spoke to him. Now he couldn't.

Whoever else LemTron might be, they were apparently an equal opportunity employer. Both men in the sturdy-looking four wheeler pickup were black. Both looked genuinely friendly.

The man in the passenger's seat who spoke was about Harry's age, with a forthright face and the same slim, muscular build as Harry.

"About seven thousand feet. Where you're going's ten thousand."

"Whoooee! We're going to need space suits." The accent was Deep South.

Harry grinned in spite of himself. "Where are you folks from?"

"Mississippi. Hattiesburg. My partner here's from Meridian."

Nearly sea level. They would be huffing and puffing for a while.

"You'll get used to the air. You might still get snowed on though."

"Damn! What a man's got to do to make a living." He held out his hand. "I'm Harry Smith."

"I'm Harry Upton."

They shook.

The driver shook hands too. "Buford Torley."

"Say, anyone here's looking for work ought to come up Monday. Vitor's real good about hiring locally. Might not be anything to do for a month, but the supervisor'll be up for a day or so. He'll talk to anyone that wants to work. Pay's union scale."

Harry's first thought was that it would be working for the enemy. Then it occurred to him there was no better way to learn what was going on. Harry Smith did not seem like an enemy anyhow. Get to know him, he might even be an ally.

"Why, thank you. I just might check it out myself."

"Ask for Lonnie Markham. Tell 'im Harry sent you."

Both Harrys grinned. The truck drove on.

The planting contract was due to start that week.

Harry spent the weekend talking to everyone in town about his taking a job on the construction. The only person who did not like the idea was Jim. Harry suspected he had ulterior motives:

Jim, himself, preferred working in the woods and odd jobs, especially welding jobs. He liked his independence, and he liked having time off between jobs. What many people would regard as financial insecurity, Jim enjoyed. Hustling work kept life interesting. Jim's jobs often required more than one person, especially the forest contracts. Harry was reliable and a hard worker. Jim did not want to lose him.

He finally came around to approving the idea, however. He compared it to the war.

"I'll miss you, buddy, but anyone can sling brush. A fellow volunteers for reconnaissance, I ought to be grateful."

Harry talked to Lonnie Markham eight o'clock Monday morning. The supervisor was about thirty-five, a little fleshy, with thinning sandy hair and neatly trimmed beard. Harry wondered what time he had gotten up to be on the site at eight. Harry had driven up in the VW. It took the rough road like nothing short of four wheel drive.

There was an application form. Harry filled it out on the hood of the car. Lonnie Markham was favorably impressed that Harry listed his father's occupation as, "Retired military."

"Which service?"

"Army. Master sergeant. Just retired a couple months ago. Thirty years."

The supervisor did not comment on the fact that Harry had never been in the service himself.

The application asked for felony convictions. Harry was glad he could leave out the misdemeanor he had pleaded to in Alamogordo. He hoped they would not check N.C.I.C. He did not want to have to explain an arrest for stealing government property on the job.

The form also wanted former employers for references and reasons for leaving previous jobs. Harry listed Jim and, "Contract work." He also listed Jason Sanders, his old boss from Alamogordo. He smiled as he, quite truthfully, wrote, "Company went out of business," as his reason for the end of that job.

Harry wrote, "No," where the form asked about medical problems or drug dependencies. He figured he better ask someone if they tested.

"We'll start you as a carpenter's assistant at eight dollars an hour. You show you can work on your own, you'll move up. Start up'll be about June first. We'll give you a week's notice."

The timing was perfect. The planting contract should take three weeks to a month.

Harry spent the rest of the morning walking around the site — where he now had a right to be. The main thing happening seemed to be clearing and breaking ground.

Harry Smith was running a D-9. They talked at his coffee break.

"By the time you get up here, there'll be a whole trailer park. Gonna be two hundred men on site."

It was going to be a very different sort of summer. – The bars in Lariat would be needing circus tents for additions.

Harry asked if his new employer tested for drugs.

"They might, but they give plenty of warning unless they're out to get you. You take a little risk with pot; it stays in your system so long. You flunk the first time, they give you a second chance though. Lots of guys stick to coke. Me, I don't plan to be an old man at forty. I take my chances with the weed. – They don't want to run off good workers anyhow."

Harry felt he could live with that. He agreed about cocaine too. Once in a while did not do any harm, but he had seen people that got into it all the time. It could mess a person up as badly as alcohol – and do it a *lot* quicker.

The tree planting job went well, if a little slowly. Harry got back May twenty-second.

Chuck's case had been postponed again, this time to July seventh. Nearly six months since the wreck, Chuck still did not know what he would be charged with.

The other driver had already pleaded guilty to driving while intoxicated, second offence, and done ten days in jail. His girlfriend was walking with a cane.

Meridell had moved her loom to the shop while Harry was gone. The shop was now open. There was not much business yet, but the weather was suitable, and they might as well be ready when things picked up at Memorial Day.

The second day Harry was home was a Sunday. Louella was tending the shop. Meridell and Suzie were working in the garden. The boys were off somewhere. Harry was just wandering, enjoying a beautiful spring day, when Chuck came up. It was about ten in the morning. Chuck was still remarkably sober.

The greeting was boisterous as ever but rang false. Chuck soon came to his point.

"I need another thousand."

Thanks to a month of tree planting, Harry had that much. He really did not feel like feeding any more of his hard-earned money to the bottomless maw of the law.

"Business'll pick up this next month, and hell, you'll be makin' a bundle."

That was not quite the point. Harry did not say anything.

"Dammit, Boy. Who took you in when you were homeless and just out of jail?"

He could not refuse. He did not feel right about it though.

Next day, the start-up call came from Vitor. It was for the following Monday, June first, right on schedule.

Harry soon saw that was probably the only thing that *would* be on schedule.

Vitor was running two crews, two shifts: Seven days a week, twelve hour shifts, thirty days on, thirty days off. The out-of-staters got flown home on their month off. The bars in Lariat were not all that busy after all. Vitor had its own on site. (It was Jim who wondered, when he heard about it, how they managed the liquor license.) No one had a lot of energy left over to drive down to Lariat. Efficiency was extremely low.

Turnover was fairly low too. Short of slitting a supervisor's throat, it was almost impossible to get fired. More than half of every week was at time-and-a-half. Pay added up fast – even if you did not do a thing the off month.

It was going to be a weird summer.

Sunday, the day before Harry was due to start work, looked to be a breathtakingly beautiful mountain day. Lilacs were in bloom in Elk Stuck. The sky was blue clear to Heaven.

Harry and Meridell made slow, relaxed love at dawn. Then they got up and watched the sun rise while the coffee brewed.

Harry took his steaming cup outside, wearing just his levis. There was a little dew on the grass, which felt nice on his bare feet. The air was slightly chilly, but perfectly calm. The sun, just now fully over the canyon wall, was a delight on his shoulders. Every cell felt alive, drinking it in.

Suzie was out in the yard, absorbed in breathing the air. She looked up at the sound of the door, smiled, then turned back to the sun. After a few minutes, she got up, gracefully, and said, "How about we all hike up to the meadow?"

None of them had been there since last summer except Brownie. A year ago, Harry would have wanted to spend the day alone with Meridell – or Brownie – or at a bar. Now he found the idea of a family outing highly appealing.

So did everyone else. Even Jeff and Steve came too. Brownie was back from his latest excursion. It was already hot and dry down at the lower elevations where Brownie had his crop, so he had to water frequently. He made the thirty-mile round trip hike several times a week. Harry found this amazing. He *was* glad Brownie was with them.

Suzie always had a poise and maturity to her. In the last year she had started to be a woman. As she and Brownie walked chastely side by side ahead of him, Harry realized, with some shock, that in only a few years they could be a couple.

They followed their old path up the ridge. There was no need to hide from the construction activity, but they preferred not to see it.

All of them felt a little ambivalent about the contruction people. They knew they did not want whatever was happening on their mountain. Yet they liked most of the workers they had met.

None of the workers had yet spent much time in Elk Stuck. There were no groceries, no restaurants, no bars, no entertainment; and the residents were a little stand-offish.

The workers did come around some though. It had meant a lot of early summer business for the shop. Western and ghost town trinkets were selling real well. Meridell had sold several small weavings too. Men wanted them for their girlfriends or wives.

Suzie was the one to comment on the lack of woman workers. It was noteworthy. Nowadays you were as likely to see a woman as a man driving some of the big machinery on a road crew. (There were two on the crew that repaired the flood damage.) Vitor was racially quite diverse – and apparently harmoniously so. There were hardly any women though, and the ones there were seemed to be just go-fers.

"It's the Spirit behind them," Brownie said. "The old dragon is building a castle here for his defense. Each Spirit attracts what it can understand."

The meadow was magic as ever. If another human soul had been there, they had left no sign of it. Yet it was different. Because of the intervening ridges you could not quite hear the construction, but you could feel it.

Something else was changed too. It took Harry a few minutes to figure out what. Then he realized: The animals had moved.

He was not sure how he could tell. It was late morning. You would not expect to see elk or deer out and about. You could never expect to see a mountain lion. He could tell they were gone though.

Steve confirmed Harry's feeling with something concrete: "Hey, there's no elk tracks."

Something was wounded in the mountain. The meadow, itself, was still pristine, but it wept in the beauty of the day.

There was a wild call overhead. Harry thought of eagles and hawks. He looked up. It was just a Stellar's jay. Still, it was a magnificent big blue bird.

Only the big animals were gone. Squirrels chattered here and there. Birds flew about. Butterflies landed on early summer flowers.

Thanks to the flood, the winter snow was all gone early and the ground thawed. Spring snows had melted rapidly in the sun and wind. There had been quite a bit of rain in May – something that did not happen every year, even this high.

The meadow was almost incredibly lush and fragrant. It fairly ached with bursting life.

They wandered, silently, for some time. Harry and Meridell held hands. The others each walked alone.

Brownie disappeared around the corner of the rocky canyon mouth to look in at the cave. The boys explored this and that in different directions.

Suzie eventually found her way to the middle of the meadow, then sat abruptly on a rock overlooking the little lake.

Harry and Meridell stood a while over the mouth of the valley, surveying the scene. Then they walked slowly down.

A little breeze came up. It was gentle, but it whispered sad secrets in the rocks. Up here, it had a bit of a chill to it, even in the midday sun.

Suzie was the magnet of the company. She sat, face down – a child-madonna, dressed in levis and soft red-checked flannel, in meditation.

One by one, the others came to stand around her. Brownie was the last.

At the very same moment, Brownie and Jeff each reached out a hand and rested it gently on one of Suzie's shoulders.

Suzie looked up slowly, a little bit bedazzled. There were tears rolling down her cheeks.

"Can't you hear her?"

"Who, dear?" Meridell knew, though she did not hear, but she asked anyhow to give her daughter the opportunity to reply.

"The Indian Woman. She weeps on the wind. Her animals are frightened. Her mountain is hurt."

Brownie put a comforting arm around Suzie's shoulder. He was wearing his old, stained buckskin leggings and loincloth. He had removed his shirt.

Harry thought of the Garden of Eden, but that was not quite right. These two were innocent, but they were not ignorant.

"You look like Indians, yourselves," said Steve.

"Indians that just met the white man," Brownie said, his face an old man, "and wonder how anyone got so insane."

CHAPTER TWENTY-FOUR

Vitor Construction certainly seemed insane.

Harry reported for work at seven o'clock Monday morning. No one who knew anything showed up till eight. That was okay with Harry. He shot the shit with Harry Smith and met some of the other guys.

"Man, it's cold here."

That was the consensus. Most of the men were from Mississippi, Louisiana, and East Texas. It had been hot there for a month. For that matter, it was hot at Lariat, but not at ten thousand feet.

About a third of the crew were black. There were several Vietnamese and Filipinos and two Indians.

The Indians turned out to be Cherokee-Creek from eastern Oklahoma. They knew where Strawberry was, the little town up the road from Muskogee where Harry used to live. Harry found himself talking about his old hangout, the Panther Bar.

"Got the oldest working pay phone in the United States."

"Any stills in that country?" asked the taller Indian, Johnny Sixkiller.

"None working I know of. Lot of ruins."

"I know an old man in North Carolina still makes whiskey. White man, but his old lady's Cherokee. Old man wanted to teach his boy the family trade. He just wanted to grow weed in among the corn."

The little knot of men all laughed.

The majority of the men had been working for Vitor for some time. This was the first day for most of them on the Thunder Mountain job. Harry Smith was one of only a few who had been there for the the ground breaking six weeks ago. The men that had worked the last month, who went off duty when Harry's crew came on, all left immediately. No one had any idea what was happening till the supervisors showed up.

The supervisors worked a regular forty hour week. There were four assigned to the day crew, only one for the night crew. If anything productive happend during the day, it was usually completely confused again by the next morning.

"What happens if a crew starts on a weekend?" Harry asked.

"Nothin'," said Jim George, the other Indian. "We just report in and wait for Monday."

Since Harry had seen the construction site a small city had been created.

There were a hundred forty residential trailers. There was a big rec hall – sheet metal on posts. Harry's first thought when he saw it was: Man, that'll cost a mint to heat if this job goes on till winter.

Inside were pool tables and games, three restaurants – each with its own bar, a laundry, and a store. The store was well stocked with shaving cream, candy, and biker, trucker, and girlie magazines.

Harry noted that the only booze available was in the bars. Someone's cleaning up on that one, he thought.

Harry also soon realized there was only one kitchen for the three restaurants and asked Harry Smith about it one day on break.

"They split it up to prevent race problems."

Harry looked around the room. The races certainly did not seem to be feeling any need to keep separate that he could see.

"Us country boys have learned to get along," said Johnny Sixkiller. "They get a crew from Chicago, it's another story."

"It was a lot worse ten years ago," added Harry Smith. "But everyone likes this set-up better'n a big mess hall, so they keep it."

This was one of the few pieces of Vitor policy Harry saw that made sense.

When Harry finally did get to work, he was setting forms for footers – dozens of them. Quite a few of the buildings were to be housing for somebody.

What the rest were remained obscure. They had names like: Office Complex C and Security Complex H. All Harry knew so far about the former was that it was big. All he knew about the latter was that it was considerably bigger – and that they were burying a reinforced stemwall twelve feet in the ground below the basement.

Harry could not see how this architecture could possibly add strength to the building. That much disturbed dirt was bound to leave huge air pockets.

The ground was stable anyhow. It was mostly solid rock from a few feet down clear through to the middle of the Earth. At least the rock had been solid till last month's crew blasted it all to bits. – That was what all the "Whumps" had been Harry recalled hearing last week.

The attitude of the workers was familiar enough to Harry. It was the atmosphere of the world he had lived in before he came to Elk Stuck. – Or rather before his relationship to Thunder Mountain and to Meridell had changed him. – He could no more say which came first than the chicken or the egg.

Harry wondered if he had come to see more clearly in the last eleven
months or if things really were so much clearer here: The Vitor workers'
view of their position, all but stated, was that they were either bandits or
slaves. They were not sure which but they were sure it was one or the other
and nothing else.

Harry largely knew before he started work why they felt that way.
It soon became clear as the mountain sky.

You worked six months a year. Pay was excellent. Physical
accomodations were a little rough, but certainly ample. The level of
productivity required was minimal. You had to be able to produce quality
work about three hours a day. — Most of the rest of the time went to fixing
mistakes.

That was where things got crazy. You did not have to accomplish
much, but you had to look busy twelve hours a day, thirty days straight. By
the middle of the second week, most of the men were completely nuts.

Coffee was consumed by the tanker. Cocaine use was commonplace.
So was crank. Most of the men drank themselves to sleep. The rec hall was
a sea of cigarette smoke twenty-four hours a day.

Every day, at seven and seven, over a hundred men had to look
alive. Few men on the day shift knew anyone on the night shift. The other
monthly crews might as well have been on another planet.

There was light everywhere. A huge diesel generator ran continually
day and night.

Trucks roared in and out constantly. The road was worn down a foot
in places. Harry wondered what it would be like when it started to rain.

The craziest thing of all was that no one seemed to know what they
were building.

There were three men from Lariat and one other from Elk Stuck:
Wayne. All the locals were on the same crew. Harry could not tell if this
meant anything or not.

Wayne told Harry Jesus was selling his house. "Getting a fair price
too."

"How about you?"

"Yeah, I guess I'll sell. No hurry now I got this job. The bank's
working it out. I might just stay on with this company. This is the best job I
ever had."

Many of the men felt that way. Few could make anywhere near as
much working twelve months a year back where they called home.

"I got a girlfriend at Safford now. Maybe I'll settle there," Wayne
volunteered.

Wayne had lost weight. It made him better looking. He seemed more
self-confident too. — Or maybe it was just cocky. — Or coky, thought Harry.
With an income, Wayne's cocaine use appeared to be skyrocketting.

Confusion was rampant. Mistakes were the norm. By the middle of
the second week, there were beginning to be a lot of injuries. This was
apparently the norm too.

That Sunday, Harry Smith warned Harry the company was going to do a drug check.

Harry quit smoking completely, of course. He was nervous all week. He had heard that marijuana lodges in the fatty tissues and stays detectable for months.

Thursday, four men were called for a test. All of them were flagrant cocaine abusers and a menace to their co-workers. All four tested positive. Two were just told to cool it. One was recommended to take a break, and some couselling. One was fired.

That was the end of the drug testing. Harry was not called at all. Neither was Wayne.

Wayne was a little upset anyhow. The man sent off for counselling was his favorite supplier.

Harry was too tired for much socializing, but he did go home every night. Naturally everyone wanted to know what was happening.

"Where's the fuckin' Forest Circus?" Jim asked.

"Hasn't been a sign of them."

"Sheeit. You'r me wanted to build a corral up there for Petunia they'd be all over us. Those jokers are buildin' a fuckin' city, and the Freddies don't even check 'em over?"

"I haven't seen any."

Burl Trent found this dereliction of duty particularly offensive too. So Louella said she would see what she could find out. It was not long before she and Chuck ran into Ray Morse at the Chiricahua.

"Ray said everyone in his office is asking about it. His boss asked the Forest Supervisor and didn't like the answer he got, so he wrote his congressman and some Department bigwigs in Washington. A week later he got visited by an F.B.I. man.

"The F.B.I. agent said the Thunder Mountain Project is a National Security matter and Forest Service personnel should not stick their noses where they don't belong."

"Whew!" said Harry.

Everyone agreed.

Brownie was mostly gone. It was hot and dry. His crop needed watering frequently. He also was scouting. Toward the end of the month, he showed up with some new information.

"They're gearing up for something at the LemTron plant down there. I'm going to go see if I can find Johnny Higgins."

Next day he was off.

The farthest down the hill Harry had been all month was the hot springs. El Paso sounded like Australia.

As the month progressed, Harry realized Meridell was unhappy about something. At first he did not focus on it. None of them liked what was happening on their mountain. None of them liked the constant truck traffic through town. (The road was not at all built for that kind of use; even the new flood repairs were one long, nasty pothole now from end to end.)

As well, Meridell was still distressed over the Aspasia Suny situation. The agent was selling some of her work in Santa Fe again and wanted more for July and August. Meridell was selling it nearly as fast as she could make it though right in Elk Stuck.

Tourists were down a little, but the construction workers made up for them. The construction work would not last forever, but Aspasia had left her hanging all winter. Meridell was not sure what to do.

Gradually, however, Harry realized there was something else wrong. One night, in bed, he asked her about it.

"Oh, Harry, you're giving so much."

"And?..."

Meridell burst into tears.

Harry held her. She was stiff with tension.

"Every night you come in tired and overwound and smelling like a truck stop. It's like a poison. I'm afraid it's going to eat you up."

Harry felt a quick flash of anger, followed by shame. Meridell was concerned for him. She was not criticizing him.

He caressed her hair and cheek.

"We'll make it."

She hugged him tighter and continued crying.

Next morning Suzie joined them at Harry's quick breakfast before he headed up the hill.

"I had a dream."

Harry looked up from the scrambled eggs he was wolfing down.

"The Indian Woman came to me with a basket of grease and sage mixed together. It smelled real strong from the sage. She said we should all rub it on our bodies and in our hair so the mountain would recognize us as its own."

Harry thought of the Bible and the blood of the lamb.

By the last week of Harry's month on the job, nothing made any sense at all to him. They were pouring concrete now. He figured the pours would probably be solid enough, but none of them were even close to level.

About half the houses were to be frame. Most everything else was block. Poorly packed dirt around footers was making for lots of four inch slabs that were really ten inches thick. No one seemed to mind the waste. Harry knew of dozens of places where wiring and plumbing was laid in wrong or missing altogether. – Gonna be lots of fun drilling though all the concrete to fix that, he thought.

The slab at the Security Complex was meant to be ten inches thick. Many places it was more than double that. Just as well, Harry thought. It would be hanging in space all around the edge where the loose dirt and stemwall were going to settle. It was the size of a football field and varied in level by over a foot from one end to the other.

"Damned thing'll make a man seasick," said a worker from the East Texas coast.

"Gonna be a bitch going up too," Harry replied. "But what is it?"

"Prison, I expect. Damned if I know who for though."

No one else knew either. Everyone in town was concerned when he reported the conversation.

There were not all that many people in town.

114

Cindy was away fighting fires. Jim was working in the woods. Steve was with his mother. Jeff was with Paul, and Suzie would soon be joining him for the rest of the summer. Paul was still with Pat. Suzie was predicting they would get married.

Jesus was gone. His house was empty and boarded up with a big "No Trespassing" sign on the front gate. Word was that several of the nonresident property owners had sold out too or were about to.

Harry's last few days of work, he felt like a marathon runner just trying to complete the ordeal. He had to respect guys that did this all the time – especially coming up from sea level. His only plan for when he got off was to sleep for a week.

Two days before Harry was due to lay off for the month, he came home to find Louella visiting with Meridell. Harry could feel something was not right, but they just seemed to be making small talk till Louella left an hour later. Harry asked right away what was going on.

"It's Chuck. His lawyer says the case is going to come up this time. Says he thinks everything's going to be okay, but he's not promising anything. Chuck's worried 'cause the lawyer acted like they should really put it off at least a year. He could go to prison."

"That's a rough one, but he did hurt that woman pretty bad."

"Yeah. That's not all though."

"Oh?"

"Louella didn't quite say it, but I think Chuck has been getting pretty abusive to her."

Harry chilled. "That son of a bitch."

Next day, when Harry got home, Brownie was there.

"Army's due up here on the ninth."

That was just two days after Chuck went to court.

The next day was Harry's last day of work till July thirty-first.

CHAPTER TWENTY-FIVE

"Smack."

"Yer shittin' me," said Harry.

"No, Man," said Jim. "I saw enough in Nam to know. Them dudes'r junkies."

Harry's first day off, he just lay around in a near stupor, savoring being clean. Next day, he wanted to get away from the noise of all the trucks coming through town.

"This weekend's the Fourth. Next week, things'r happening. Let's go somewhere right now."

Meridell liked that idea, but needed to check with Louella about the shop. – Hours were a little irregular, but they were long. Between tourists and catching both construction crews, the shop was usually open by seven-fifteen in the morning and often stayed open till nine-thirty or ten at night. Nearly all of it fell on Meridell and Louella. Chuck was mostly drunk and obnoxious.

Louella said she would watch the shop. "Or maybe I'll just shut down. Being closed a day won't break us."

Harry and Meridell stuck their sleeping bags in the back of the VW and headed out the back way. Harry was shocked to see there were nearly as many trucks coming in from the Arizona side as there were rattling through town. Even the main road was not designed for such heavy use. The back road was really not made for that sort of thing at all.

It was nearly five in the afternoon when they set out, but the valley was still hot. It had not rained down there since April and did not look like it would anytime soon. There were a few clouds beginning to build over Thunder Peak, but they did not amount to anything yet. Harry had heard barely a rumble of thunder. – He wondered if he would even have noticed, though, with all the construction noise.

They stopped at Rodeo for gas and also bought some honey. Then they headed into Arizona through Portal and back uphill into the Chiricahuas.

They drove through Paradise and on up away from everyone. Then they parked the car in a quiet spot behind some bushes and walked over a ridge away from the road.

It was getting on to dusk. The evening was warm and clear. They just took their sleeping bags, some chips and dip for supper and a water bottle. They kept their eyes peeled for rattlesnakes and walked carefully but did not see any.

"We may be too high for them," Meridell said.

Harry shrugged. "I dunno."

The forest was tinder dry. They did not make a fire. They just found a comfortable spot to settle and watched the night come on. There was a crescent moon in the west. The stars were so peaceful. The loudest sound was a whip-poor-will.

Harry lit a joint of Brownie's good bud. Meridell accepted a token puff – mostly to share Harry's communion. Harry took four tokes and then put it out. Brownie had kept him better supplied than he had ever been. Four hits was enough though. More than enough, really. Brownie grew some good smoke.

K'blam! K'blam!

Whirr; crankety; whirr.

Pocketa, pocketa, pocketa, pocketa.

Construction noises rolled through Harry's head. He felt like there was a whole layer of his brain he just wanted to peel off and wring out.

A pack of coyotes began to sing.

"Ahh."

Harry unthinkingly began to massage his head.

"Com'ere. Let me do that."

Harry looked to Meridell, then moved in front of her and lay down with his head in her lap. She massaged his head and neck and shoulders. Her weaver's fingers were strong, sensitive, and soothing.

An owl whooed. Another answered. There was a moment of total silence. Then the cricket chorus picked up its song.

Harry could feel Meridell and the quiet mountain night working the

116

tension out of his body, out of his soul. The sense of release and fulfillment was more passionate than sex. Harry almost started to cry.

They did have sex later, toward morning, after they slept some. That was good too.

Harry did not even mind not having any coffee in the morning. He gave Meridell a massage as she lay on her belly naked in the rising sun. Her shoulders were tight too, and not just from weaving.

Harry worked the tension out of his lover. Then they changed places.

When they were both thoroughly molten they lay down together. Eventually they made love again.

The sun was getting high and warm.

"We're going to burn our butts," Meridell said.

They both laughed. Slowly, they got up and put on some clothing.

There was a patch of lighter green across a wooded valley in front of them. Harry pointed to it.

"Let's go see if there's a creek."

"Okay."

It turned out to be farther than they realized. They walked a couple miles without getting anywhere near the place they had headed for. So they decided to go back. The woods were mostly ponderosa. The air was filled with pine fragrance.

They were about halfway back to their camp, walking hand in hand, when Harry caught something out of the corner of his eye. At the same moment, Meridell squeezed his hand hard.

They both stopped and looked. A great big, sleek, fat, black bear strolled regally past, not fifty yards off to their left.

They could not even tell if the bear noticed them. It was headed the other way on some business of its own and was soon out of sight.

"Wow!" said Harry, long drawn and low, when he could breathe again.

They both looked at one another, their eyes wide.

After they got back to camp, they rolled up their sleeping bags and walked on up to the car to make peanut butter and honey sandwiches for breakfast. From there they could see where it looked like there was a creek only a couple hundred yards across the road.

After a while, they walked on over. Sure enough, there was a clear little stream running through. Most of it was just a few inches of water, but there were pools two or three feet deep.

"Must be year round," said Meridell, pointing. "There'r fish."

They spent most of the day near the stream. This time just before the summer rains started was the hottest time of the year. Down in the desert, it was staggering. Even here in the mountains you could feel it.

They got in the water several times. It was a clean refreshing delight.

Harry smoked a little. Meridell passed.

The area right by the creek was brilliantly green. Elsewhere the land looked thirsty.

"Bet Cindy's keeping busy," Harry commented once.

"She is," Meridell replied. "She's on a big fire in the Gila right now, near Beaverhead."

"I'm ready for another swim."

"Me too."

They walked down the creek a ways to a good sized pool. It was not really big enough to swim and actually too cold to stay in long anyhow, but they did get wet and cooled off.

"What's that?" Meridell asked.

They were walking back up the creek. Something had ducked into a shaded pool.

"Why, it's a turtle." She answered her own question. "I don't think I've ever seen a turtle before in a stream in the Southwest."

They both watched the long-necked turtle swim across the bottom of the clear, foot-deep pool. Then it lay still, perhaps its idea of hiding; but it was in clear sight. They watched for two or three minutes, then walked on.

About six-thirty, they packed up and drove slowly back down to the valley. They ate dinner at a cafe in Rodeo. They did not hurry. It was still hot.

The sun had finished setting, but it was not yet fully dark when they started up the back road into the Thunders.

Harry had just switched on the headlights when they saw the flashing red ahead.

A large Vitor truck sat broken down by the side of the road. Two men guided traffic around it. There was plenty of room for the VW. Another big truck would be a tight squeeze.

Both men looked grey and nondescript, faces expressionless. They moved woodenly. Harry could not tell if they were twenty or forty. Both wore levis, colorless long sleeved shirts and shades, though it was about dark.

"Need a hand?" Harry asked as they pulled up.

"We got help coming."

"Okay." He drove on. A couple minutes later he asked, "Meridell, did they seem weird to you?"

"Like zombies."

Jim was home the next day. Harry mentioned the incident to him.

"I can smell it, Man. These ain't the same dudes that were here a month ago."

Harry didn't know. He had never been around people using heroin – and did not want to be. He knew something felt wrong though. He decided to go up to the job site and see what was happening.

He drove up to the turnoff and started in. A man in some sort of police uniform stepped into the road and halted him.

"I.D., please."

"What's going on?"

"I need an I.D., or I can't let you in."

"I work here. There was nothing like this going on before."

"Look, chum, this is a security area. If you don't have a valid Vitor

118

I.D., A or B crew, then turn around and quit blocking traffic."

"I...I'm C crew."

"Then you don't belong here this month. So scat."

He could hear a truck pulling up the road behind him. He thought about making a scene but quickly decided that would do more harm than good. He turned around and drove back down to town.

Harry shut off the car at the house and sat pondering.

Pop! Poppetty pop, pop, pop!

Harry jumped.

Some tourist's kid had set off a string of little fire crackers in the street.

It was the Fourth of July.

It was also a Saturday. There was a dance down at Lariat. Harry was not sure he wanted to go, but he could tell Meridell wanted to dance. He decided he did too.

The dance was crowded, but fun. As the evening wore on and people got drunker, however, the atmosphere became sullen.

Near the last, Chuck got in a fight with his old buddy, Tony Firenzie. Everyone knew they fought for fun like a couple of overgrown kids. This time, though, they had to be pulled apart. Someone was going to get hurt.

"Snap out of it, Man," Harry said to Chuck.

The look that came out of Chuck's eyes was not even human. Harry did not think Chuck knew who he was.

Luckily, he soon passed out. Harry and Jim helped Louella lug Chuck out to the truck and pour him in.

Jim had been drinking whiskey all evening. He was steady and coherent, but something about him was so black and cold it made Harry shiver.

Next day, no one bothered to open the shop till noon. Meridell finally did open up. Harry walked down with her. The phone began to ring just as they got there. Meridell opened the padlock as quickly as possible and rushed in.

"Elk Stuck Emporium."

"Hello, Mama?"

Harry could hear the voice clearly on the other end of the line.

"Suzie?"

"Mama, I've got to come home, right now."

CHAPTER TWENTY-SIX

The demon was blind.

But it was awake.

Shlurp. Suck. Gobble.

It drew toward itself like a vacuum cleaner, like a black hole.

Its hunger was insatiable.

It had no purpose, no goal. It just consumed because that was its nature.

Tinker toys.

No; a post and beam frame.

Steel I-beams and inch-thick rivets.

Up and out, broader and wider the structure went. Was it going to fight the demon?

Not at all.

A trough was laid over the frame.

Men and women began shoveling pig-slop onto the trough.

A great motor started.

The pig-slop slid up and over the frame and poured in a gushing, slimy cataract into the gaping maw of the demon.

The demon grew bigger.

Stronger.

Hungrier.

The slaves shoveled faster.

More joined them.

They began throwing one another into the trough.

The little bodies floundered about, terrified in the ooze. The viscous flood carried them with it into the demon's mouth.

There were screams.

The screams ended abruptly in a crunch of pulverized bones.

The demon grew bigger.

Still it was blind.

And yet —

As the demon digested the human intelligence it murdered, stealthy little glimpses of cunning popped briefly into its awareness.

The slaves were afraid.

The demon liked that. Their fear was wine to wash down the demon's hideous feast of shattered, liquified life.

The demon gibbered with delight.

The slaves built ever more frantically. — A bulwark, an ark, a shield.

Fear drove them.

At last it drove them insane.

"The end! The end is upon us. We must leave someone to carry on."

They turned to one another for children to outlive their deaths.

They clung to one another for love, for the touch of life.

More and more slaves were born. The faster they were born, the more the demon could slurp up.

The demon grew fat.

The bigger it got, the hungrier it got.

The food was not enough. The slaves were not enough.

The demon began eating the buildings of the great city the slaves had built to house themselves while they fed the demon.

Swwsshh.

The demon's paw flew through the air.

Crrunnch.

The steel bucket lifted another load of rubble.

The rust-tinged teeth were four inches thick.

120

Fourteen cubic yards of dirt and stone lifted into the air as the steel cables hummed.

The black-painted metal shined above the dirt. The steel forearm was one hundred thirty feet long.

It rose skyward, to an elbow with gear and cable drive, then descended to the body.

The yellow crane swiveled on its track.

Whirr. Rrr. Rrr. Rrr.

Hmm. Mmm. Mmm.

"Harry!"

"Mmm. Mmm! Mmm!"

"Harry! Wake up! You're having a nightmare."

"Mmm."

"Harry!"

Meridell was shaking him.

Harry was stiff, paralysed.

"Mmm!"

He felt clammy.

"Ohhh."

Suddenly, Harry was limp – and soaking wet. His nose came alive first. Something stank. It was his own sweat.

"Meridell?"

"Harry, are you okay?"

He could not focus his eyes yet, but he could hear the shaking in her voice.

"I...I'm not sure."

It was mostly light.

They got up and made coffee.

It was time to get up anyhow. They had to get ready for town. Chuck was due in court in Apex at ten. Suzie would be coming into Lordsburg on the bus at four. Paul wanted to drive her home on the weekend. She was not willing to wait that long.

Both sides of the street got plenty of sunshine at this time of year. Because the sun set down the canyon, evenings were long, but it rose over a steep bluff in summer, slow to reach the house.

Harry shivered. Was this the place he loved so well?

The nightmare atmosphere did not really leave him till they met the sun part way up Post Office Ridge. On top it had been up for over an hour. Mrs. Martinez was just opening up. She waved and smiled. That helped.

Every few miles, they would pass a Vitor truck, or several, till they passed the turnoff to the LemTron plant. Harry had not been down this way since before he started work. He had not realized so much of the truck traffic came from the LemTron facility.

"They must have a hell of a stockpile in there."

"How's that?"

"They're bringing all their materials from there."

Meridell looked. You could see across the dusty open country to the huge fenced enclosure several miles away.

"Harry, I think that's new. I don't think all those trucks were coming from LemTron when you were working."

"I sure would like to know what they're hauling."

He looked back over his shoulder to the turnoff receding behind them. Another truck slowed for the turn. It was impossible to tell what the load might be. All the trailers were either fully enclosed or covered by tarps.

The VW putted on. It was only nine, but it was already getting hot.

Chuck and Louella roared past them doing about eighty. Chuck was at the wheel.

The air in the courthouse smelled faintly stagnant.

Court was in session. A young woman was being arraigned for shoplifting.

Harry and Meridell waited in the lobby while Chuck and Louella went with Sam Hoyt in a closed side room.

A large, multi-generational Spanish family gathered around a lawyer on the other side of the lobby. Harry watched the interaction:

A woman of about seventy asked a plump woman of forty-five something in Spanish. The younger woman translated the question to the lawyer, who replied, in English, directly to the older woman. She did not wait for a translation, but began berating a man in his twenties. Harry could hear the rhythm enough to tell who spoke which language but could not make out the words.

The old lady spoke quietly in Spanish. The young man nodded a meek affirmation several times.

I wonder what that's all about, Harry thought.

Sam Hoyt came out of the conference with Chuck and Louella and went into an office.

After a while, the judge took a break and went into the same part of the building. Sam Hoyt eventually reappeared with a sheaf of papers, while the judge went back into the courtroom.

Shortly thereafter, Chuck came out and beckoned to Harry to come over to him.

"I need another five hundred."

"What the hell? You bribing the judge?"

"No, Man. This is all legit. It's administrative fees. Besides, you can't buy a judge for five hundred bucks."

"I wouldn't know."

They stood there silently.

"I gotta have it, Harry."

"Dammit, Man. I busted ass all fall to make a nice winter for Meridell and the kids. I busted ass again this spring. Why don't we just throw it down the outhouse and shit on it?"

Chuck did not say anything.

Harry shuffled back and forth a little.

"All right, dammit, you've got it."

"Thanks, Harry. You're a real friend in need."

Ten minutes later, Chuck and Louella and Sam emerged from their room again. Sam went into the office briefly with his papers and returned without them. They all shook hands, and Sam left. Chuck and Louella came over to Harry and Meridell. Chuck was smiling.

"All charges dismissed."

"Just like that? No hearing or nothin'?"

"All done."

"Son of a bitch." Harry shook his head.

He thought of his own experience with the law as he and Meridell walked up the hot street. He had come away without a felony record, but he had had to go to court. He had spent more than three months in jail too. — And he had not hurt anyone.

Harry told Meridell about the five hundred dollars.

"I wonder what that woman's medical bills were." — A broken hip could cost more than Chuck's insurance covered.

They wandered about a bit. Despite the heat, Harry was restless. It would be hotter later too, and Meridell had a good number of errands she figured she might as well do while they waited for Suzie's bus.

It was not noon yet. It was not quite one when they parked at a cafe in Lordsburg. They ate a slow, somber meal. The rolled enchiladas were not bad, but the grease the sopapillas were cooked in was rancid. They left most of them.

The day got hotter and hotter. Meridell did not want to buy groceries till after they picked Suzie up in case the bus was late. The food would be out in the heat long enough just from the ride home.

They finished all they really needed to do, then killed time looking at this and that in the stores.

At last the bus arrived, only twenty minutes late. Harry saw Suzie at the door. He wondered if they looked as tired and frazzled as she did. He suspected they did.

"Oh, Mama!"

Suzie threw her arms around Meridell and hung on tight.

They got Suzie's bag and walked slowly to the car. Then they drove to the supermarket. Suzie still had an arm tightly around her mother's waist as they walked across the parking lot.

"You're sure there wasn't a problem with your dad?"

"He doesn't understand, but he's okay. Pat too. He just thinks I'm having growing pains."

"And?"

"Mama, this isn't me. It's the mountain. The mountain needs me.... Needs us all."

Suzie looked up briefly to her mother. Then she looked to Harry.

Harry was walking alone a few feet from Suzie and Meridell. He was feeling hot and generally freaked out. His eyes were to the ground.

Harry felt something warm and comforting. He looked up. Both Suzie and Meridell were looking his way. They still had their arms around one another.

Suzie held out her other hand.

Harry took it.

The three of them walked into the grocery store together.

CHAPTER TWENTY-SEVEN

"Paul, you are not a failure. It's not even me they're interested in. It's just...This is their home."

"Let me talk to him, Mama."

Meridell handed Suzie the phone.

It was seven o'clock Thursday evening. They were in the shop. Harry was there too, waiting on some customers.

The man was balding. The woman wheezed. She was not grossly obese, but she was flabby. At first glance, Meridell would have guessed them at forty. When she looked a little closer, she realized they were probably not thirty yet.

Meridell went over to see if there was anything she should help with. She felt embarrassed that strangers were hearing the conversation with Paul.

"Daddy, we love you just as much as Mama. It's the mountain. Thunder Mountain needs us."

Paul had planned to call anyhow to be sure Suzie got there all right. Now Jeff wanted to go too.

Jeff did not talk about the mountain like Suzie did. He just said he was bored. Paul said didn't he like being where there were other kids to play with? Jeff only squirmed and looked unhappy.

Paul had made plans for the weekend. It would have to be next week. Jeff did not act so urgent as Suzie had. He just glumly conceded he could survive that long in Colorado. − He had been planning to stay another month.

"Daddy," Suzie was saying, "don't you let it get to you. It's not your fault. You really are a good father."

Meridell left the customers to Harry. She was sure her face must be red as a beet.

"Hey, I talked to kids in your class while I was there. You're one of the most popular teachers in the school. You're good with kids."

Paul must have answered: "But not with my own," as Suzie replied:

"We're not trying to get away from you. We just belong *here.*"

Meridell indicated to Suzie to give her back the phone.

"I love you, Daddy. Here's Mama."

Eventually, Paul's insecurities were soothed and plans made for the following weekend. The customers left, and Suzie went on up to the house. Harry and Meridell stood in the doorway watching the slanted evening sunshine on the street.

The couple who had been in the store drove past, headed back out of town. Their car looked new. California tag.

"You know, I thought at first they were forty years old. I wonder what ages them like that."

"Paying for the wheels."

Harry had a mischievous little grin.

Meridell looked at him, then laughed. It felt good. There had been far too little laughter lately.

An hour later, Suzie brought them down supper: miso soup and chicken salad sandwiches. No one had come in in the meantime. "I'm not sure there's any point to staying open late," Meridell said between bites.

They stood in the doorway watching the sunset as they ate. Suzie watched with them.

"Last month, when you were working, the shop was full every night at this hour. They bought; they were good guys too. I enjoyed meeting them."

A truck came over the top of Post Office Ridge. Meridell looked the other way, up the road toward the construction site.

"Now nothing. – And the few that have come in are so morose they make Jim look like the original good-time Charlie."

Another truck followed the first, and another. Harry looked with a little more attention.

"Hey, Brownie was right. That's troop carriers....I sure wish he'd show up. He's been gone all week."

Kablam!

Smack!

"What the?..."

Harry and Meridell ran across the road.

Chuck stood outside the back door, a hand to his cheek. He looked surprised.

Louella was holding the twelve gauge shotgun just above the trigger, pointed straight up. She looked ferocious as she turned, briefly, to see who was coming.

"Damned fool's gonna fight the army now. I actually had to slug him."

"You pack a wallop too, Woman."

Harry could not help himself. He broke up.

"Well, shit," said Chuck, still feeling his jaw to be sure it was all there. "Come on in the house and have a beer."

"We better tell Suzie everything's okay first," Meridell replied, "and close up the shop."

Kablam!

"Holy shit," said Harry.

"Not again," said Louella.

Gunfire was actually not all that unusual in Elk Stuck – or anyplace in the rural West. Sighting in on beer cans. Varmints in the garden. Showing a friend a gun. Guns were part of life. Jim once shot at a mouse on a bookshelf with a twenty-gauge shotgun. He missed the mouse, but Steve complained for months about having to shake shot out of the books.

It was not the sound of the gun that drew Harry and Meridell to Chuck and Louella's. It was the sound of Louella's fist on Chuck's jaw. This time, though, it was the gun that told them all something was wrong. None of them had ever heard a gun fired inside Burl Trent's house before.

They all headed up the street at varying rates. The troop carriers were passing through town now.

Harry was the first to arrive – followed almost immediately by Jim coming from the opposite direction.

The front door was open. They both dashed right in.

"Oh my God!"

Most of the head was gone.

It had to be Burl though.

He lay in the middle of the living room floor, his finger still on the trigger of his old single shot twelve gauge.

The others soon joined them: Meridell, Suzie, Louella, and eventually Chuck.

They stood silently. There was nothing else to do.

The sound of the troop carriers disappeared over the ridge beyond town.

The evening sounds outside smoothed out to their customary rhythm. The only sound inside was Louella crying.

"We better call the sheriff," Jim said eventually.

People began to move after that. Suzie was the one to notice the note.

"Look."

They did.

Written in bright red felt-tip across the whole top page was: "READ."

They all went over to the table.

In normal sized writing on the same page it said: "Neighbors, read this when I'm gone."

Jim turned the page. The one under it read:

> My life is over anyhow. I've called congressmen. I've called newspapers. What has happened to our country? This is supposed to be America. If my death can accomplish something, use it. It's the last shot I've got.

"Gawd," said Harry.

"I'll go call," said Louella.

"I guess I should close the shop," said Meridell.

"I'll take care of it," Louella replied.

Chuck suddenly bolted for the door. The others all looked. Then they turned back as they heard him outside throwing up.

Three quarters of an hour later, Pete Wiggins, the local deputy, was up looking things over and taking statements.

"Just a damned shame." Pete shook his head. "Was he sick?"

"Not that any of us know," Jim answered.

"Withdrawn?"

"More sociable than he'd been in twenty years," said Louella.

"He was so good with the kids." Meridell was teary now. "Just...He was just so upset about what's happening on the mountain."

By ten-thirty, Burl's body was gone and his house sealed. No one knew if he had any family or, if so, where. No one knew if he had left a will either.

"Somebody ought to call Joe Sartanian," Jim said.

"Think we should wait till morning?"

"It's only nine-thirty in Arizona."

Jim went over to Chuck and Louella's. They plugged in the phone at the house, and Jim made the call. Harry went along too, then joined Meridell and Suzie at home.

"He was sorry, but wasn't even all that surprised. Told Jim he'd seen suicide in Burl thirty years ago. He's coming up tomorrow."

No one felt able to sleep.

Meridell put a quiet tape on and made a pot of herbal tea. The three of them sat, listening to the music, not speaking.

Harry jumped up. Someone was coming to the door.

It was past eleven-thirty.

The door opened, and in came Brownie, followed by a young man in a U. S. Army uniform.

"Glad you're still up. This is Corporal Johnny Higgins."

"Brownie, Burl's dead."

Meridell told Brownie what had happened. Brownie was shocked. So was Corporal Higgins. (The promotion was just a week old.) Johnny Higgins was twenty-three, with a strong chin and clear grey eyes. Harry was pleasantly surprised. He had half-visualized Higgins as a moral wimp. Now, on the contrary, he saw, the soldier was there as a matter of principle – and taking a big risk to be there. As it was, he did not dare stay more than an hour.

"I joined up for a job. But I believe in my country, and this ain't it."

Johnny told them what he knew. It seemed there was a fight going on in the government between Wilderness advocates and people who wanted access to all public lands.

"The 'Use it All boys' scored one somewhere. Thunder Mountain's the prize. I'm still not sure what it's for."

"Does it have to be for anything?" said Suzie.

"What do you mean, dear?" Meridell asked.

"Like in history." (Suzie read a lot of history, both straight and fiction, and liked the subject in school.)

"Like the Christians and the Moslems in Spain, or Napoleon. They didn't really conquer places *for* anything. They just conquered to conquer. Then they used it for whatever they felt like."

Harry thought of his dream and shivered. He had tried to explain it to Meridell. He had not mentioned it to Suzie.

"Maybe you're right. Sure seems like a catchall project for anything the brass and their buddies can think of."

"How's that?" Harry asked.

"We got a Security Complex big enough for a city. It could be used to evacuate Tucson. Could just as well be a concentration camp. – Or the last-ditch defense for a command bunker.

"We got that too. You could monitor a hundred miles of Border

Patrol — or SAC."

Brownie filled his pipe, lit it, and passed it. Johnny started to refuse. "I better not." Then he thought about it. "What the hell. They catch me coming back, it's an excuse."

He took the pipe and commented between tokes: "What I really don't like is there's something funny going on with drugs."

"What do you mean?" Meridell asked.

"I don't know. Supposed to be helping keep 'em out. But I don't believe it. They're down on weed all right. Lot of weed's still independent. But coke and heroin...There's a lot of noise, but I think we're importing the stuff. I don't think the U. S. government is trying to stop it at all — just control the market."

"Wouldn't surprise me," Brownie said. "That's how it worked in Viet Nam."

"Yeah, I guess I heard about that," Corporal Higgins replied.

"I haven't," said Meridell.

Suzie was looking with the eye of historical interest.

Harry did not say anything. He was thinking of his father, of the U. S. Army Earl Upton had just retired from. He had heard stories too, but always at a distance. Things were picking up too fast. He thought of Burl Trent's buckshot bouncing off the inside of his own skull. He wondered why his head did not explode too.

So far as Harry knew, Brownie had quit school at about fifteen. He was certainly too young to remember the Vietnam War. He had picked up a very definite sense of history somewhere though.

"When the Communists won in China, a bunch of Nationalist War Lords retreated to the Golden Triangle. They forced the locals to grow opium for them and sold heroin. The C.I.A. ran the system. The U. S. armed forces provided the transportation. Same thing's going on now all over Latin America."

"But the U. S. government is pressing for more drug enforcement," said Meridell. "They're insulting allies doing it."

"Don't believe it," Brownie answered. "Those Latin countries mean it when they complain about America interfering with their independence. But we're not doing a thing to stop the drug trade. Our government controls it."

"What about the people that get caught?" Harry asked.

"Mafiosi shoot each other," Brownie replied. "And they have more honor. They back their own. U. S. government'll throw *anyone's* not an American citizen to the sharks no matter what 'e's done for them. — Maybe even if he is a citizen."

None of them knew enough to affirm or to refute Brownie's version of the situation. Johnny thought it as plausible an explanation as any for whatever was going on.

"What about minerals?" Harry asked.

"I can't tell," Johnny replied. "But if they want 'em, there is enough equipment going in up there to mine and refine right through a siege....Or do anything else. Hell, there's enough shit going into this mountain to rebuild civilization a week after Armageddon."

"And what are you doing here," Harry asked, "and for how long?"

"Playing soldier. War games. Battle techniques in the Mountains. How to guard a vital industrial complex, or Command Central, or fifty thousand civilians, or fifty thousand prisoners."

That was how Corporal Higgins had extrapolated his view of the Thunder Mountain Project: From what he was here for.

"We're here for three weeks."

"Just?" Harry asked.

"To the day."

"You leave with this crew. I go back to work the next day."

They all looked at one another.

"Brownie, I don't know how you got me through the woods so fast coming down but we better do it. I don't want to be missed."

"I'll try to be back in time to see Joe Sartanian."

Harry saw Brownie and Johnny Higgins to the door. There was a little bit of a rumble over Thunder Peak. He looked and saw a brief lightning flash. The thunder was barely audible.

The soldier and his guide were quickly out of sight. Harry came back in.

Meridell had heard the thunder too.

"Rains are a little late starting this year," she said. "I don't think there's even been any on the Peak yet."

"You know," Harry said, "I think it's just about exactly a year I've been here."

It was still quite a while before any of them were able to go to sleep.

CHAPTER TWENTY-EIGHT

"How do the dogs know?"

Harry and Meridell were lying on their backs, next to each other, in bed. Harry had an arm around Meridell's shoulders. It was just first light. Speed Bump and Imogene were both howling as Harry had never heard them howl before.

"He talked to them when he wouldn't talk to anyone else."

The dogs' song for the dead was the only sound. There was a profound stillness over Elk Stuck.

When Death comes to a family or a community, it rends the fabric of life. Everyone close to the hole feels the deep, cool air of the Great Beyond.

It is an awesome sensation. Some are afraid in its presence. Some feel the presence of a loving God.

It is also dangerous. Those too close to the hole can fall in. Death can be contagious.

That is why there are wakes. The people in *this* world need to remind themselves, make life solid again.

Harry and Meridell got up as if in a dream. Suzie joined them, like one of the Mountain Spirits, as they sat by the table sipping their coffee.

Brownie arrived before the sun.

"It is intense up there. I *think* Johnny made it back in okay. I decided to get off the mountain while it was still dark."

Chuck arrived a few minutes later.

"Sartanian called. He's leaving in an hour. Figures to take a break at Douglas. We can expect him about two, two-thirty, our time. I'm putting a sign on the shop. You can open if you want to."

"Thanks, Chuck," Meridell said.

"Sure. Guess you heard."

"Yeah," Brownie replied.

"Brownie's got some news too," said Harry.

Brownie kicked Harry pretty hard under the table. Harry jumped. Brownie broke in at the same moment:

"We still don't really know what's going on up the mountain, but I've been able to talk to people a little closer to whatever it is. Let me just tell it once, when everyone's together."

"Oh, okay. When the lawyer's here's the time....Burl did leave some kind of papers too. Sartanian's got them. Says he'll tell us all about it when he gets here."

"Where shall we meet?" Meridell asked.

"Here or our place is fine. He said he'd come here 'cause he knows it."

"Why not here then. Save him the climb up the hill to your house." Chuck left.

Meridell scrambled some eggs.

A Vitor truck finally broke the atmosphere.

"They don't even know what they've done," Meridell said.

"They better watch out," Brownie answered, gesturing toward the passing truck with his toast. "When you're blind to the Spirits, they'll bite you, just like a snake. Snake don't want to bite, but you step in his face, he will."

Harry just felt angry, the more so as a whiff of diesel fumes floated through the house. Yet, at the same time, there was a sense of relief as the world reasserted itself.

"Guess maybe I ought to catch up on my sleep," Brownie said. He set his plate on the pile by the sink.

"Use our room if you like," said Meridell. "It's quietest."

"Thanks."

Joe Sartanian showed up a little early. Brownie was still washing up. Chuck and Louella saw Joe pull in and came on up the street. Harry went to get Jim. Even Mrs. Martinez came down. She had never been in Meridell's home before. — She remembered the house though, from fifty years ago, when it was her Aunt Flora's family home.

"Who are Steven Barnes and Jeffry Devore?"

Meridell and Jim explained who they were.

Burl Trent did not have any close living relatives. The nearest he did have was a second cousin in Topeka. She had been informed. She said she would sign any releases needed for the body so long as she did not have to pay for anything. She barely remembered who Burl was and was not especially interested.

Burl *had* left a will.

"Maybe I should have been suspicious when he had me draw this up. He didn't have a will before. I just thought he wanted to do what he could for the people and place that meant the most to him. You get to our age, you don't expect to live forever."

Burl had left his house to Steve and Jeff. He had left them each five thousand dollars too. He left Suzie twenty thousand, "For education or dire need. To be released to the beneficiary at age twenty-one if anything is left." Meridell and Jim were named trustees.

Burl had also left twenty thousand dollars to his cousin.

"I don't think she'll contest the will," Joe said. "It's all legal. She could use up that twenty thousand dollars in a court fight and still lose. It can't go through till she signs a release though. It'll take a while even then. No one should touch his things in the meantime."

"Shouldn't we at least get any perishable food out of there?" Jim asked.

"Let me get in touch with the judge first. He'll probably send the deputy up. May need to check a little more anyhow."

"What for?" asked Harry. "They don't think someone murdered him, do they?"

"No. But they do make an investigation any time there's a violent death. There'll be an autopsy too."

"Did he say what he wanted for a funeral?" asked Louella.

"Nothing official, except he wants his body donated to the medical school at UNM. He wasn't a member of any church that I know of."

"No, I don't think so," said Meridell. "One time he said to me, 'I don't want any damned preacher telling a bunch of lies over me when I'm gone.' I'd like to do something though."

There was a general murmur of agreement.

"Of course. That's up to you."

Burl had almost two hundred thousand dollars in various accounts. He had been getting a good pension, had savings when he retired, never spent anything. Other than the personal bequests, he wanted the rest used, "For the preservation of the town of Elk Stuck and the way of life that has been customary there." He wanted a trust fund created and named Joe, Flora Quintana, Mrs. Martinez, Meridell and Harry to administer it.

"As a lawyer, that made me uncomfortable. I'm in favor in principle though. I'll do what I can, though I'm not sure any of that money will be available in time to do any good."

That led them to their other business. They made the psychic move slowly. Everyone could feel the pull of the vortex that leads to the next world. Coming back was fighting the current. They did though. They had to. Life's demands were too urgent to ignore.

Brownie told what he had learned. He did not mention Corporal Higgins. He left it slightly obscure just how he knew what he did, just said he had talked to some soldiers.

Joe thanked him for the information. He had some too.

Joe Sartanian was old pals with a recently-retired former state attorney general. The man was a major figure in state party politics. He had a lot to do with how one of the current congressmen got elected. The Representative was on a subcommittee that reviewed military appropriations.

"He couldn't get too detailed. There *is* classified information involved. It *is* a National Security Facility they're building here. Geography is really the determining factor: mountains and the border. The official title of the project is: 'Primary National Security Contingeny Unit, Thunder Mountain Military Operations Area.'"

"They just want to be ready," said Jim, "Ready for whatever. I don't like it, but it shows more military sense than the bozos that gave the orders in Nam. If you're gonna get your ass in a war, at least you can make a real attempt to win."

"So where does that leave us," asked Louella.

"I'm not sure," Joe replied.

"Well, I'm sure of one thing," said Mrs. Martinez. "If this is my country, I'll stand up for it, and it should do the same for me. There's no war now. There's no excuse to squeeze us out of our homes. What is this, the Soviet Union, where the government has to hide from its own people?"

Harry felt a jolt — like a boat, he thought; like a boat that was drifting loose, and someone managed to set the anchor.

There was a metallic taste in Harry's mouth. He did not want to fight. He certainly did not want to fight his own government. And yet...you could feel what was real, even if, rationally, it seemed contrary. Harry felt a weight he wished he could evade. At the same time, he felt a sense of relief to hear someone else acknowledge where he knew he stood.

"I am doubtful, at this point, that you can stop the construction. They have congressional authorization. We could file a lawsuit, but it would probably be a waste of time and money."

"What about our homes?" said Louella.

"Don't sign anything. They may back off. If they try to condemn them, demand a jury trial. A jury is always a gamble, but it is one of the strongest protections the Constitution gives us. The government might decide you're not worth the cost — or the risk of setting a legal precedent — and drop the matter. If we go to court, we have twelve independent citizens to hear our case — maybe six times that many if we can keep the cases separate.

"One other thing that might help a little. Burl's house is the oldest structure in Elk Stuck still in use. It is over a hundred years old. He got it listed with the National Historic Register years ago. They might help too. A lot of those folks are the kind of conservative that believe the value of the individual is what America is all about."

Joe had slept poorly last night and was tired from his drive. They all asked him to stay the night, and he accepted. Mrs. Martinez had the most comfortable house, so he stayed there. They also had a pot luck supper there. It was the first time Harry or Meridell had been in her house.

Harry saw a light at Wayne's and stopped to say hello. He cautiously mentioned a little of what was happening.

Wayne was shocked and sorry to hear about Burl Trent – mostly shocked. He really did not know Burl. Wayne was not interested in fighting the government though. He was selling for the best price he could get and thought the others were foolish not to do the same. Harry did not mention Joe or supper.

"Let me know if you get a service together," Wayne said as Harry was leaving.

"I'll do that."

Joe Sartanian was going to see Flora Quintana on his way out next morning. Since it was Meridell's house, she and Harry rode down too. It was the first time Harry had been to Hachita. The valley was hot.

Saturday was a mail day, so Mrs. Martinez could not go. She did call her Aunt Flora, and talked to her at great and expressive length in Spanish. Harry and Meridell heard the end of the conversation as they came to meet Joe. They would follow him down the hill.

"You know," said Harry, "I haven't seen anyone Spanish on the construction crews this month. There weren't a lot on my crew, and some of those were Cubans – from Florida. But there were a few Chicanos. I don't think there are any this month."

"Are you sure?"

"No, but I bet I'm right....It's like, the Soviets send Russian soldiers to Afganistan. They don't send Moslems from Turkestan. My old man told me that."

Harry found himself thinking about his parents a good deal as they drove across the parched valley.

Flora Quintana had not known Burl Trent well. She had met him a few times when he first settled in Elk Stuck. – She used to come up every so often back then. The meeting they had all had was the only time Flora had seen Burl in over ten years.

Flora reacted to Burl's death with tremendous passion all the same. It spilled over onto her feelings about Meridell's house.

Though Meridell barely knew her either, Flora hugged her and kissed her and made a fiercely emotional speech about how she would never let those murderers and thieves take the roof from over Meridell's children's head – nor the house Flora had been raised in.

It was a Saturday in July. Chuck and Louella could not keep the shop closed. Harry and Meridell stopped in when they got back.

There was a message for Harry. His parents had called. They were leaving Little Rock today. He could expect them Monday or Tuesday.

Somehow Harry was not surprised.

CHAPTER TWENTY-NINE

"I volunteered for the draft."

Earl Upton, Harry, and Jim sat under a tree in Meridell's yard. Margaret was with Meridell at the shop. The motor home was parked next to the house. It was Thursday afternoon. Clouds were really beginning to build over Thunder Peak at last, though it was still sunny in town.

"I'd been 1-A for three years. Couldn't get a decent job. No one wanted to put a lot into a guy that was liable to be drafted any time. Figured I'd get it over with and get some security. By the end of a year, I felt like I'd found a home."

"I had in mind to get it over with too when I joined up," Jim said. "Sure never felt like home to me though."

"I only really thought about getting out for one reason." Earl turned to Harry. "That was a long time before Women's Liberation. I was ashamed to have your mother work. I felt like I wasn't providing right for my family, but on what they paid an enlisted man in those days there was no other choice."

Harry vaguely recalled the tension in his childhood, the seemingly senseless fights over his mother's jobs. She worked as a cashier mostly. Managed to stay with Woolworth's through two moves.

I was ready to quit in '65," Earl continued, "but then Vietnam came along."

"And?" There was a hard edge to Jim's voice and a far-away look in his eyes.

"I missed Korea. I'd have felt like a shirker − and a coward − to leave. And the guys coming in were so young. Even the officers. Especially the officers. We used up second lieutenants faster than anything. They didn't know what they were doing. Someone had to look out for the men. I knew how."

Harry watched Jim melt. For a minute, Harry thought Jim was going to burst into tears.

"Stay alive. That was the best we could hope for. Why'd you stay in after?"

"How old were you?"

"Eighteen. I was a pretty good high school track man June first. July first, I was a soldier. I was still eighteen when I got to Nam."

"How'd you feel when you got home?"

"Like a leper − at first."

"Then?"

"Then I got into Vietnam Veterans Against The War."

Now it was Earl's turn to look hard and far away.

"It was 1971," Earl continued, an ominous tone to his voice that had not been there before. "I'd been back Stateside about a week. First time in four years."

"You were in Nam four years?"

"Two. I went from Germany."

"Hmh."

"Went to a shopping center one day in uniform. I wanted cigarettes. Margaret wanted celery. Funny the things you remember. Here you'd call it humid, but I remember how light the air felt after Nam.

"I was walking across the parking lot when I saw this kid coming toward me. Probably no younger than half the men I'd seen fighting and dying the past two years, but he was a kid. You could tell from the way he walked. He had on a blue work shirt. I remember noticing how it wasn't

134

tucked in on one side and thinking it looked sloppy.

"Next thing I know, he's right in front of me and shouts: 'Murderer!' Then he ran away. I was too shocked to even move for a second. Lucky for him. I'd have broke him in two if I'd caught him."

Harry remembered that day. He had flunked a math test in school. He was relieved when his parents were too preoccupied to ask him how his day had been. The reason why only sank in later.

"By the time passions cooled, they were paying a living wage. I didn't know anything else. And, dammit, I still believed in this country. Still do."

"I wish I did."

"You're not a damn Commie, are you?"

"Shit, no. I'll turn down a good job just so I can work for myself. I don't like *anyone* telling me what to do."

Jim thought of tree planting and thinning as working for himself because he had to bid a contract and was paid only for production, rather than getting a salary whether he did anything useful or not like a regular government employee. The fact that the source of his contracts and his pay was tax money bothered him far less than the bureaucratic restrictions and the economic inequities he had to live with.

To Jim, as to so many Americans, Freedom and Communism were opposites. Being free was an individual matter. Being controlled by someone else, especially a big, bureaucratic someone else was Communism to him, regardless of whether that someone else was the government or a big corporation. He trusted neither one, though he distrusted government most.

"I fought the Communists in Nam," Jim continued, "and I would again. But we *gave* them Vietnam by supporting the only people we could find that were worse."

"Maybe."

"And how about you and me? I watched my buddies die taking the same hill three times in three months. Every time we won it, we abandoned it, and Charlie took it back.

"Another time, I watched six tons of sugar dumped in the ocean. What for? The red tape to move it was too complicated to bother with. I checked on that one later. Found out who had the sugar contracts. People that made big contributions to political campaigns, that's who. You know what got the Vets Against the War?"

Harry was uncomfortable, but there was no stopping Jim now.

"Heroin. Pushed by the United States government."

"I never did believe that."

"I did. Even us vets were still naive kids. Our friends that didn't go were worse. Just the opposite from that snot that called you a murderer. Too timid and respectful us vets thought. Too full of guilt 'cause we went and got shot at and they didn't.

"I remember a girlfriend I had. Scrubbed clean, wholesome Midwestern type, but she was against the war early. She went to a demonstration one time. It was '67 I think. I'd been back Stateside a couple months, but I was still in the army, so I didn't go. Maybe a month before I was discharged. Peaceful demonstration. Most of them were then. Just carrying placards and singing.

"She left for the demonstration bright-eyed and full of ideals, wearing a clean, pretty dress. She came home in tears and all dirty. Some wino was throwing garbage at the demonstrators and hollering, 'Take a bath.' A cop was encouraging him. The peace people took a hell of a lot more abuse than they ever gave. They believed in peace though. I know I did — for a while.

"Peace and love was the word then, and we meant it. We smoked pot, and we took acid too. Made everyone mellow and gentle. Then the acid all started coming laced with speed.

"After a while, we couldn't get acid any more, but there was lots of speed around. Everyone got real wired. We were going to make things right, by God, *now!*

"People got strung out. When heroin showed up on the scene, it seemed like just what the doctor ordered.

"The war ended anyhow. We were going to change the country. Not a Communist revolution. The second *American* revolution. What a crock. Bunch of fucked up junkies.

"I was lucky — or maybe just not quite as dumb as some of my buddies. I never got hooked. I got out. Came here.

"Maybe I wasn't so smart though. I been working the woods ever since. You take a beating working that hard. I'm not forty yet, and I'm gettin' old."

They sat in strained silence a few minutes. A Vitor truck came down from the construction site, rumbled through town and on up Post Office Ridge.

"Only thing I've managed to get in this life's that house up the street. Now the government wants to take that away from me."

The truck disappeared over the top. Jim opened another beer.

The mountain grumbled. Harry looked up. "Clouds are getting thicker. We could sure use a rain."

It was a relief to all of them to change the subject. Earl had watched the weather patterns a lot of different places in his many moves. He was interested to learn what the seasons were like in this area.

"Climate's basically vertical here," Jim explained, getting into the subject with some enthusiasm. "We're at seven thousand feet. Valley's about four. Peak's nearly eleven. Mountains catch weather systems. We're twelve miles from Lariat by road, a lot less as the crow flies. They get ten inches of moisture a year. Peak's only a few miles the other way. It gets about forty."

"And we're overdue now," Harry added, thankful for the lighter subject.

"Not for long, by the looks of things," said Earl.

He was right. By five o'clock, there were squalls passing through town, and it was really storming on the mountain.

Harry and his father went on in the house. Jim drove up the hill to get the mail. A little later, Margaret and Suzie came in, between showers, talking animatedly about gardens. They soon went back out to pick snow peas for supper.

"That's probably the biggest reason for us to settle," said Earl: "So your mother can have a garden. She didn't mind *too* much moving away from her friends every few years. But she sure hated leaving so many gardens."

Meridell was tending the shop. Suzie took dinner to her and stayed. Harry helped Margaret with the dishes.

"You were awful wild for a while, Son. I wondered sometimes if you ever would find yourself. Raising someone else's children is not an easy row to hoe. But your Meridell is a fine woman. And Suzie is delightful."

Harry blushed.

"Suzie said her brother and father are coming down this weekend. I'd like to meet Jeff, but will we be in the way?"

"Not as far as I'm concerned," Harry answered. "I'll ask Meridell; it shouldn't be any problem. We all get along. Just a full house."

Harry did talk to Meridell later.

"They're welcome, but Paul's still feeling insecure about the kids not wanting to stay with him. We need to be sensitive to his feelings...."

Harry explained the situation to his parents the next day.

"Why don't we go to the Chiricahuas for the weekend, or Mexico, and come back next week for a few more days," Margaret said.

That was what they decided to do, but when they told Meridell, she insisted there was no need for them to get out of the way.

"You're family. I just want you to know the situation."

They stayed.

That afternoon, Brownie came in. It had rained on his crop in the night, so he didn't need to water. He wanted to check things out on the mountain.

Brownie immediately saw that it would be too crowded at Meridell's, so he went on up to Jim's. An hour later, he was back.

"Harry, do you think Chuck and Louella would let me stay in your old place for a night or two?"

"What's up?"

"Jennifer showed up with Steve."

"Oh?"

"Her first line, right as she got out of the car was: 'You turned my son against me. You can God damn well keep him.' I decided: Elsewhere!"

Harry couldn't help but smile. "We'll go talk to them. I'm sure they won't mind. Seems like everyone's coming back."

"Oh, that's another thing."

"What's that?"

"Jim got a letter yesterday." Cindy ate a little too much smoke on a fire in Idaho."

"Is she gonna be all right?"

"Yeah, she's okay, but she's on indefinite leave. Should be home in a few days."

"I'll be damned."

On the way down the street, Harry asked Brownie how his crop was doing.

"I'm glad it's finally starting to rain. Plants may be a little small, but the heat makes strong smoke. Won't know till I see how many are female, but there might be as much as last year. More if we're real lucky on the mix. Nothing at all if we're unlucky."

Harry chilled. It was not like Brownie even to mention being unlucky.

Chuck had stayed sober for three days after Burl Trent shot himself. He was roaring now. Louella was pretty loose too.

"Sure," Chuck bellowed. "Stay as long as you want. Have a beer."

"Out of the frying pan, into the fire," Harry said, barely audibly, to Brownie.

Brownie shrugged and grinned a little sheepishly. Then he accepted the can of Coors Chuck offered. Harry had one too. Brownie's was less than half gone when Harry refused a third and went back up the street.

Chuck was ranting about how he had, "Beat the God damned stinking law."

Harry would not want to see Chuck go to jail. He would not want to see anyone go to jail. However, he was not at all sure it was a good thing for Chuck to have gotten away with that wreck. Chuck seemed to have forgotten entirely that he had hurt someone quite seriously.

Paul, Pat, and Jeff got in about one-thirty, said a quick, sleepy hello; then Jeff went to bed, and Paul and Pat made camp on the living room floor.

Next day, Louella ran the shop, and Meridell stayed home.

Far from making Paul uncomfortable, Margaret and Earl made him more comfortable, Margaret intentionally, Earl inadvertently.

This visit and Christmas was the first time Earl Upton had really gotten to be with his son as a grown man standing on his own feet in the world. Earl's retirement was also recent enough to have him reminiscing a lot.

At one point, Earl spoke about his own insecurities as a father. "You get so caught in the moment. Worry about things that aren't even real." It was healing balm to Paul.

Paul and Pat both had to be back at work Monday. They left five o'clock Sunday afternoon. By the time they went, everyone really did feel like family.

Earl and Margaret left Wednesday, for the Grand Canyon and the California coast. Next day, Cindy got home. Suddenly all the residents of Elk Stuck were there, and no one extra.

"Let's do the service for Burl this weekend," Meridell said.

"Yeah, let's," said Harry. "I got to go back to work the end of next week."

They talked to everyone the next day, even Wayne. All agreed on Sunday morning. Brownie wanted to make a quick trip down to check his crop.

"It's raining every day in the high country now, but there's no tellin' if that little piece of desert's gettin' any."

He promised to be back for the service. He wanted to be there as much as anyone.

They called Joe Sartanian and Flora Quintana too. Both of them planned to come. It would be the first time Flora had been up to Elk Stuck in twelve years.

Meridell was a little nervous. Flora was her landlady; the house had once been her home. But Flora put Meridell at ease:

"I hope you will show me some of that wonderful weaving I've been hearing about."

Brownie planned to see what he could learn on the mountain right after the service.

"Safer to look up Johnny someplace else, but I want to check things out once more while they're still here."

"Want company?" Harry asked.

"I do. They don't though. You're welcome, but it could be risky."

CHAPTER THIRTY

"Am I dead?"

"Yes you are."

"I thought so, but I wasn't sure."

Burl was in a sort of grey, formless place. He was bemused at first, distracted. When Harry confirmed that he was dead, Burl focussed.

"I always loved mathematics," Burl said: "It's the music of God. I can get lost in it. So clean. So balanced. X equals plus or minus seven or plus or minus the square root of minus twenty-one. The amazing thing is that all those answers are true, but only one tells you how to space the I-beams so the building will stand. That's why I could do the engineering so well. It was a sacrament to me."

Burl now seemed clear, but Harry was a little confused. Burl was talking about a piece of his life Harry had never seen. Or was he?

Maybe Burl was talking about his present circumstances. He now was in a place where time was plastic. Forty years ago and last week were equally current. The question for him was not which was true, but which was the active truth in a world of time and space to which he no longer had a bodily anchor.

Suddenly, Burl became very strongly present. Harry started to feel dizzy.

"Well, young man, we've got a job to finish. Are you ready?"

The place where Burl was started to shift, like a TV image coming into focus.

Harry saw Thunder Mountain now, as if through mist or rain.

K A B L O O M !

Harry leapt up – and almost fell on his face.

"Watch it!"

Jeff and Steve were showing each other various treasures they had brought back on the living room floor. Harry teetered over them. They seemed far away.

"I...I must have fallen asleep."

"You did," answered Jeff. "You been snorin' away for half an hour."

Harry sat back down in the dilapidated, faded red easy chair.

Lightning flashed outside, followed quickly by another boomer, almost as loud as the one that had woken Harry.

It was Saturday afternoon. The memorial service was set for noon the next day.

"Where's your mother?"

"At the shop."

"I thought she wasn't going down there today."

"Someone wanted to see her about her weaving."

Harry wanted to tell Meridell his dream. He also wanted to learn what was happening. – A good sale for Meridell, he hoped. – He washed his face, neatened his shirt, and walked down the street.

The storm was building fast. Lightning flashing furiously. Thunder was a constant rumble, punctuated by frequent loud crashes. Looks to be a humdinger, Harry thought.

The weather was making up for lost time, raining both long and hard nearly every day now.

"I have to make a living."

"You're just like the rest. Want to have your cake and eat it too."

"I cannot tie up my work all year to sell for two months."

Harry realized, before he entered the shop, that this must be Aspasia Suny. With Chuck all but worthless, the shop fell almost entirely on Meridell and Louella. An unannounced call on a day off was irritating, worth it for a good sale, but...

Harry wanted to say to Aspasia: "You're the one that wants to have her cake and eat it too." One look, however, told him to keep his mouth strictly shut unless Meridell asked him to open it.

Perhaps he should turn right around and get out of there, Harry thought. Meridell's eyes told him a witness would be welcome, so he stayed.

"A little success, and you want to do whatever you please."

"You have gotten a good price for my work, and I appreciate it. I will not give it to you exclusively, when you don't even answer a letter or a phone call for six months."

"It takes time in this business. You don't build a reputation overnight."

"My children have to eat every day. If I can make three hundred dollars at a craft fair, I will. If you want to handle my weaving, good. I am not going to give up all other sales for you."

"Miss Devore, if you want to peddle your wares for pennies to a lot of riffraff, that is your privilege. You will not contaminate *my* professional standing."

"Then send back my work that's probably been sitting in your closet for the last year."

Aspasia gasped, furiously. "I certainly will." She stalked out.

"Well, so much for the great artiste."

Meridell was too angry to cry. She did let Harry take her in his arms and soothe some of the tension out of her shoulders.

Louella stopped pretending not to be there and put a comforting hand on Meridell's shoulder too. After a while, Meridell took them each by the hand and squeezed. "At least I've got my family. Thank you for being here."

KABLOOM!

It started to rain.

BLAM! Bangety, bangety, bangety. BLAM! BLAM!

"Hail," said Harry.

"I hope it doesn't tear up the garden," said Louella.

Meridell squeezed Louella's hand a little desperately.

"Honey, it's not the end of the world."

"I know. It just feels like it."

The hail did not last. The downpour did. There was no point trying to go anywhere till it quit. Harry told his dream to both Meridell and Louella.

"I had a dream a little like that once," Louella responded. "When my mother died. – She went real sudden. Tried to do too many errands one day when it was a hundred and ten. Had a heart attack in the Safeway parking lot.

"A few weeks later, I had a dream where she was confused. I told her she was dead. She felt much better after that."

The rain slacked off after a while, but did not stop. Meridell and Harry eventually went back to the house. Suzie was reading. Jeff and Steve were still there too.

Harry and Meridell went in the kitchen, where Meridell fixed herself tea and toast. Harry heated a cup of coffee. After a bit, Meridell put her finger to her lips and nodded toward the rest of the house. They both listened.

"I tried to tell my mom about the Indian Lady. She just got mad."

"My dad thought it was a game. He even wanted to join in. I couldn't make him understand it's real."

Meridell and Harry looked to one another pointedly.

"Boy, I'm glad I'm not your sister."

"Why not?"

"At least we've got each other. She doesn't have anyone."

"Yeah....The kids in Colorado were just like the grownups. They didn't none of 'em know anything 'less it came off the tube."

"Show Low too."

Everyone went to bed sort of early. About eleven, a very wet Brownie came in.

"Sorry to wake you. Just didn't see any point in staying out. I sure don't need to water. It's raining everywhere."

That night, Harry dreamt again.

"A yodel-a-dee, yodel-a-dee, yodel-a-dee-oh, a-yodel-a-dee-oh, a-yodel-a-dee-oh..."

The old cowboy rode through the high desert at a slow clip-clop. He barely held a hand on the reins. Knees and voice were plenty to

141

communicate between man and horse.

Desert sparkled in new-risen sun, last night's rain not yet dry on prickly pear or juniper. Here and there towered yellow-blossomed agave flower stalks and white yucca blooms. Cactus bloomed too: yellow and royal scarlet.

Thanks to the rain, the land, pale brown ten months of the year, was now carpeted with purple, yellow, white and red wildflowers. Sage was fragrant on clear, moist morning air.

The horse whinneyed.

"I agree."

The cowboy guided the horse to a lush patch of grass, briefly sprung to tender luxuriousness in the wet season.

"Here you go."

The cowboy dropped the reins on the saddle horn. They were long enough to let the horse eat, which it did contentedly. The cowboy surveyed the horizon.

Harry did not know where Brownie's crop was, but he knew the general direction. It was a view he had never seen, but this must be what Thunder Mountain looked liked from there.

The cowboy watched the mountain, which shimmered in the morning sun.

"She's a-gonna blow. Yessir, she shorely is."

He scratched the horse's shoulder affectionately.

"You know, some folks don't like Apaches. That's their business. But a man's a fool not to listen when someone's learned something through hard experience and wants to tell you."

The horse took a step every so often as it munched. The cowboy's only response was to shift his weight slightly and scratch the horse's neck. He watched the mountain for a while.

Once he reached down and picked a particularly long, new green grass stem to nibble. Harry could taste the slight moist sweetness.

The sun rose higher.

"Well, we best go get you a drink before it gets hot."

The horse whinneyed.

Harry started to wake.

It was dawn.

The horse whinneyed again. Then the sound turned to a donkey's bray.

"What the...?"

"Petunia! Bad girl!"

Suzie, in nightgown and bare feet, rushed out the door.

By the time she came back in, everyone was up, except Jeff, who looked out the window, then lay back down to finish sleeping.

The burro did not do much damage to the garden. When she brayed, she was looking in the living room window at Brownie, who was sleeping under a blanket on the couch.

When Suzie ran out, Petunia trotted right up to her and let her hitch a rope to the halter and tie her to a cottonwood tree out of harm's way.

Brownie sat up and stretched. Then he slipped on his pants and went out to say hello to the burro and the day. It occurred to Harry that Brownie wore pants a lot now and buckskin leggings and loincloth a lot less this year than last.

Harry gave Meridell a good-morning hug. Then he got up and put on the coffee. Meridell got up too and made a fire. The rain had cooled things off considerably.

Soon they were all seated at the kitchen table over coffee: Harry's and Brownie's black, Meridell's quite light. Suzie had a cup of warm milk with honey and just enough coffee for some color and flavor.

They had all dreamt. Meridell told hers first:

"There was fire in the air over the mountain. Not a forest fire though. Like fireworks – or bombs. Music kept passing through my head: The chorus of 'Fire On The Mountain.' – That song always makes me think of beauty – tragic beauty – and violence. – And the line from 'The Star Spangled Banner.' You know: 'Bombs bursting in air.' A band was playing. I listened to the tuba oompah like I used to back in high school. – I played glockenspiel in the band." (She blushed at that.) – "That song's got a wonderful bass line. – Then Petunia hollered, and I woke up."

Suzie went next:

"I was with the Indian Lady. – I'm with her a lot at night. – We went over the top of a ridge to a place where the ground was mostly bare and rocky. We came to a sandy spot with a sun temple..."

Harry was not sure what that was. He barely cocked his head, but Suzie responded as if he had asked aloud. –

"...Red ant hill....We stopped and watched. The ants were carrying their eggs up and taking them away somewhere in a steady stream."

Brownie told his dream:

"There were colors. Colors like sunflowers and fall leaves and rainbows. Colors on the trees and the sky and on people. I've seen auras before. This was more. Everything was just half-material. The other half was colored light."

Harry chilled. He was not sure why. Brownie continued.

"I was an Irish minstrel, walking down the road from one little village to the next. I had a little harp slung over my shoulder. I reached back for it. Then, suddenly, I was an Indian. The harp was a bow. I nocked an arrow. My family was in danger. The Bluecoats were invading my homeland. I had a burro behind some mesquite. He brayed. I looked around. I didn't want anyone knowing I was there. Then I woke."

"Me too."

They all jumped. No one had noticed Jeff, who was now standing at the kitchen door.

"I dreamt of rats. There were rats trying to get into the walls of the house. We were fighting them off. All of us. Burl was there too. Steve and me were chasing the rats. Burl handed us both sticks."

They held the memorial service in Burl's front yard.

"It may not be strictly legal for us even to be on this property," the lawyer said. "But no judge would accept charges."

There was no problem. Joe Sartanian said a little about Burl's life: "He was a man of clear vision and strong principle. Not a conventional man, but a deeply committed man."

Steve had a little bit to say too: "He was the best teacher I ever had. I just want to say thank you."

They all prayed silently for a while. Louella recited the Twenty-Third Psalm. Then they all recited the Lord's Prayer. There was another brief silence.

Flora crossed herself and said, "Amen," aloud. Mrs. Martinez did the same. The others echoed the, "Amen."

Then they broke and went back down to Meridell's for a pot luck meal. It was the first time Wayne and Jim had been in the same house since last fall.

"A suicide goes to Hell, but a martyr goes to the right hand of God," Mrs. Martinez said. "I don't know why he had to do it, but Mr. Trent gave his life for us and this mountain. May he rest in peace."

The others all agreed with the sentiment, but Flora had something to add. "A martyr he may have been, but I'm not sure he's resting yet. He has work to do on the other side first."

Joe had one piece of news – about Burl. The autopsy had been done. No one had expected to find any indication his death was anything but the suicide it appeared, and none had been found. Something else was discovered, however.

"His liver and kidneys were riddled with cancer. Maybe he even knew it. He wouldn't have lived another year. Probably not six months."

It rained again that afternoon, but cleared in time for a rainbow and a sunset.

Brownie woke Harry in the middle of the night. The moon was well past full and rising late, but it cast a little light.

"Let's go."

"Now?"

"Right now."

"What shall I take?"

"Nothin'. What we don't have stashed we'll do without."

"Okay."

Harry slipped on levis, a green T-shirt, and a brown checked flannel shirt, tennis shoes, and a plastic ball cap. Brownie already had on his buckskins and moccasins.

"Be careful," Meridell said, sleepily but earnestly.

"You better believe it," Brownie replied.

And they were off.

CHAPTER THIRTY-ONE

Brownie moved like magic. It was quite an effort for Harry even to keep up. He ran into a lot of branches. Brownie flowed right past them – or through them, Harry thought: like he's made of light.

Harry was getting frazzled and irritable, wondering why he had come.

"Shh!"

Harry froze. He was sure his heart was audible half a mile away. He looked and listened. Nothing.

Brownie touched Harry and pointed. Harry had to jog his head back and forth before he could see through the trees. There was light. Once he had the direction, he heard sound too. Nothing distinguishable, just sound he knew did not belong to the mountain.

They had climbed the ridge behind the house to the East Fork Trail. Then they had circled above the meadow and the upper trail to the construction site. They had moved very fast. The construction site was still behind several ridges and a couple of miles away, but they were headed toward it now rather than circling away from it.

They started again. Harry was not able to maintain anywhere near the quiet Brownie could. Harry constantly broke sticks and bumped into things. Brownie seemed not too concerned at first.

"We better be quiet now. Security's not very tight. – They're not looking for anyone like us anyhow, but we're getting close. They do have guards posted."

Harry did his best. He still broke sticks, and grimaced every time.

Brownie led them right to the cave through the woods. Harry had no idea how Brownie found it. It was the one farthest from the trail and closest to the construction. It was just first light.

"Skraw. K'skraw."

"That'll do."

Brownie had a tree picked out. It gave an excellent view of the entire construction site – but not such a good view of the ground below it. There was a hillside across from the tree where Harry could keep watch at ground level. If either of them needed to signal the other, he could call like a raven.

Harry watched Brownie climb the tree and settle. If he did not know Brownie was there, he could never have spotted him. Brownie got out a little pair of binoculars and studied the construction site and adjoining encampment. He stayed there a long time, nothing moving but his head and that just barely.

"K'skraw! K'skraw!"

Harry chilled. It sounded just like a real raven, but the sound came right from Brownie's perch.

Brownie was down the tree so fast Harry thought for a moment he had fallen.

"Back to the cave. Now!"

It was the longest sprint Harry ever ran. By the time they got there, he could hear the plane too.

"Couldn't we have just got under some bushes?"

"They might have infrared."

Harry wondered if even the cave was sufficient to hide them from heat-sensitive equipment. He did feel more secure, though, with several hundred feet of rock and dirt between him and the eye in the sky.

"Might not even matter. Could just be some private guy flying past, but better safe than sorry."

Whatever it was, it did not just fly past. It circled the construction half a dozen times, passing almost directly over them each time. It made Harry very nervous.

"I think we're okay," Brownie said when the plane finally went away. "It didn't act interested here at all."

They stayed in or close to the cave for several hours. The plane, or another one, came by twice more. It did not show any sign of being aware of them.

Brownie climbed his lookout tree again in early afternoon. By then it was clouding up. It was the last chance he got in daylight. It rained all the rest of the afternoon.

Rain quit about dark. A couple hours after full dark, there were stars. Brownie climbed his tree one more time. He was far more relaxed when he came down this time than he had been in daylight. An old-time Apache might have been able to sneak up on them. The people they were concerned about, however, would advertise themselves a long way off.

Brownie fired up a bowl at the base of the tree. They passed it in silence a couple of times. When it was empty, Brownie tapped out the ash and put the pipe back in his pouch.

"Well, we've learned what we can. Let's get out of here."

There was no moon yet. They moved more slowly than the previous night. As it was, Harry had no idea how Brownie found the way.

The moon rose on them as they came out on the East Fork Trail. They lost it again going down into the canyon.

It was still the middle of the night when they got to the house, but they were both too keyed up to sleep. They were into their second pot of coffee by the time Meridell joined them.

"The original crispy critters," said Suzie, as she came in. "You look crazed."

Harry and Meridell had finished a rather impassioned hello. Now they were both staring intently at Brownie, who was describing what he had seen. He started over for Suzie.

"Most of what's going on is underground, between the Security Complex and the Office Complex. No telling how big it is or where it goes down in there."

"What about the army?" Meridell asked.

"I don't know. Some of them were on guard duty. A lot of them were indoors. I didn't see anything that looked like war exercises this time. Last time they ran around in the woods some. The construction's the interesting part. Everything I've seen's going into that underground dude – whatever it is."

"I ought to be able to tell when I go back."

"Then what?" asked Suzie. "What do we know, and what do we do?"

No one had an answer.

They kept getting more information, but it never added up to anything. It certainly never added up to anything they could get a handle on.

"Sometimes I wonder if it even matters," Meridell said. "So the government's doing something on Thunder Mountain. So life goes on."

"Do you believe that, Mama?"

"No. I know how I feel. But I'm tired of worrying – and not even knowing what it is I'm worrying about."

"You're worrying about evil," said Suzie. "Maybe they don't even know what they're doing themselves. Don't they call the Devil the Prince of Darkness?"

Harry shivered. He thought of the demon he had dreamt of. Then he was overcome by paranoia. He felt surrounded – and incompetent. How come Suzie, at thirteen, could make so much more sense of things than he could?

"I don't know what to do about it either though," Suzie concluded. Bwown'nwown'nwown'n.

Waves of energy oscillated through Harry's body and shivered out his fingertips and the top of his head.

Brownie passed the pipe. Harry took a toke – and immediately regretted it.

"I think I better lie down."

Harry stood up – and crumpled.

He did not quite pass out. He was aware of his body dropping and even managed to avoid hitting his head on the back of the chair. Then he was lying on the floor, a whirlpool spiraling above him.

...Laughter. Nasty, brutish laughter.

The men had heavy features and dull eyes. They had the animals surrounded – deer, elk, bear, rabbits, everything.

The men threw rocks. Some of the rocks exploded. Some just cut or bruised. They could hardly miss. All the animals crowded together. Many bled or limped on three legs. Every now and then one went down.

Something caught Harry's eye off to one side. He looked. It was Burl Trent. Burl was building something out of metal. Something like a big shield.

Something warm and wet was on his face.

"Harry, are you all right?"

Meridell wiped Harry's forehead with a warm washcloth.

Harry sat up, slowly. Meridell and Brownie helped him to the couch. He was soaking wet with sweat.

That day, a lot happened, none of it good.

Every property owner in town received notice that unless they began negotiations for sale, condemnation proceedings would be initiated against them. The only exception was Wayne as he was negotiating to sell.

In the same mail was notice that the Elk Stuck Post Office would be closed September fifteenth. Mrs. Martinez was told to begin preparing her final records and to fill out the necessary forms for retirement.

There was also a notice to Chuck and Louella that the shop was to close permanently and forthwith.

Meridell tried to call Flora Quintana. There was no answer. They also tried to call Joe Sartanian. There was no answer there either. They kept trying till well into evening. Nothing at either number.

In the morning they tried again. Still nothing. Louella finally tried the number on the notice they had received about the shop. She got a recording:

"The Southwest Regional Bureau Citizens' Liason Office is open from ten AM to noon on the first and third Thursday of every month. If you need earlier assistance, please leave your name and daytime telephone number when you hear the tone."

Louella hung up, enraged.

There still was no answer at either Joe's or Flora's number. Meridell decided to drive down to Hachita. Harry went with her. They took the VW. Harry wanted to gas up before he started back to work anyhow.

It was only eleven in the morning, but clouds were already thick. It had poured yesterday. Harry was glad. It eliminated any tracks he and Brownie might have left. It looked like it would soon be pouring again. It was already starting to sprinkle when they set out.

"You a U.S. citizen?"

"Yes, of course."

Border Patrol roadblocks were fairly commonplace, but they still made Harry nervous. He had never heard of one on the Elk Stuck road since he had been there.

"May I see your driver's license please."

Harry got it out. The Border Patrol had never checked his I.D. before.

"Thank you." The man wrote something on his clipboard and handed the license back. "Yours too, Ma'am."

Meridell gave him hers. Then he wrote again and gave it back.

"Thank you. You can go now."

They went on. Both of them were shaking.

Even in the valley, the rain had cooled things down considerably, though it was rather sticky. The desert was very green.

There was no response at Flora's. They did not know what to do. They stood around wondering. Then Harry noticed a man sitting on the porch of a house down the street. They walked over. The man was rather fat, seventyish, wearing slacks and an undershirt.

"Excuse me, Sir."

"Eh?"

"We were looking for Mrs. Quintana." Meridell pointed back to the house.

"Oh, have you not heard? It is so sad."

"What? No! Has something happened to her?"

"The ambulance came the day before yesterday. She fell down. It's not good for an old lady to fall."

"Do you know where she is?...She's my landlady — and a friend."

The man called back into the house. A woman answered in Spanish.

"Maybe Silver City."

They thanked him and started to leave.

"You know her son, Manuel?"

"We've met him once."

"He lives right over there." The man pointed.

They went over. Manuel was not home. A woman who might have been his daughter was. They explained why they were there. She burst into tears. Manuel had gone to the hospital. Something had happened. She did not know what.

They thanked her and said they were sorry and left Chuck and Louella's number.

"Let's go to Silver City."

They were ten miles up the road.

"I don't know. I feel uncomfortable being away from the kids with all that's happening. Let's call."

So they found a bar with a pay phone.

"I'm so sorry. Mrs. Quintana passed away this morning."

The roadblock was still there when they got back. There was a state cop now along with the Border Patrol officer. It was the same officer, but they had to get out their licenses again and the proof of insurance on the car as well.

The state police officer radioed the information somewhere. They had to wait till he got an answer to go on. Both officers were polite.

"Sorry for the delay. Thank you."

Another shower was starting, but it went by quickly.

"I need to unwind. Let's stop."

"Okay."

Harry pulled into the hot springs turnoff. There was a chain across the road and a big, new sign. "Closed to the public. No trespassing." As if to make the point, a whole pile of smashed beer bottles rested around the base of the sign.

They went on up the road. Louella answered the door. They told her about Flora. She told them she had continued trying to call Joe Sartanian. The last time she got a recording that said his phone was not in service.

The shop was open, but there had not been a tourist in town all day. The only traffic to come through was Vitor trucks.

That evening, they gathered at Chuck and Louella's: Meridell, Harry, Suzie, Jeff, Steve, Jim, Cindy, Brownie, and Mrs. Martinez. Chuck was drunk and disruptive. Louella eventually told him to shut up or she would club him with a frying pan.

Manuel Quintana called soon after Harry and Meridell arrived. His mother had broken her hip in a fall. She died of a stroke. The funeral was the day after tomorrow. He did not say anything about the house. Meridell did not feel it was the time to mention it but felt she had to.

"I know she didn't want to sell it. I want to respect her wishes."

That was not exactly an answer, but Meridell did not feel she could push Manuel any further right then. She let the matter drop.

Jim and Steve picked up what was obviously an ongoing argument.

"I know when I'm licked."

"We gotta stay."

"We gotta cut our losses while we can. That's one thing I learned in the war. That's how I stayed alive."

"But it's wrong."

"I don't like it any better than you do."

Cindy wanted to sell too. Meridell's house was out of their hands. Chuck was too incoherent to know what he wanted. That left Louella, Mrs. Martinez — and Burl Trent's house.

All three children were sure they wanted to stay. Meridell said she would back them — and fight to keep Burl's house for Jeff. Steve wanted to fight too.

"It's fuckin' suicide, Man," Jim said. "Fuckin' suicide." He had to pause before going on.

"I came home from Nam, I came home to America. A shitty America, an America that didn't give a hoot in hell what I'd done for my country or what I'd been through. But it was still America. This ain't America. It's fight for nothing or survival just like Nam."

"At least they're not shooting at you," Cindy said.

"No," said Jim, shaking his copy of the notice each property owner had received. "A knife in the back instead."

Next day Jim was cold as ice. "Piss on the government," he said over coffee at Meridell's. "I fought for my country. I'll fight for my son's home."

He had decided to drive to Tucson and try to find Joe Sartanian. Cindy was going with him. Brownie would stay at Jim's house and keep an eye on the animals and Steve.

Afternoon showers had spread out till it was now cloudy day and night. It was raining more than not. The creek was muddy and high, though nothing like the time it flooded.

The troop carriers passed through town that afternoon, headed down the hill. That evening, shortly after shift change, a fleet of cars and trucks passed through. Again, there was not a tourist in town all day.

About ten, there was a crash from down the street. Harry and Meridell looked at one another. Then Harry went down to investigate. Someone had thrown a beer bottle through the big front window of the shop.

Harry helped Louella clean up and nail up a sheet of plywood to keep rain out. Chuck wanted Harry to come up to the house for a drink.

"Man, I got to be at work seven o'clock in the morning."

Harry went back up the street. It was after eleven and starting to rain again. Meridell was waiting up for him. Soon they went to bed. Neither of them could sleep.

Harry and Meridell lay in bed listening to the rain. After a while, they made love. Harry felt like a soldier on his last night before going into battle. At last they slept.

CHAPTER THIRTY-TWO

"Joe's dead."

Harry sat bolt upright. It was dawn. His statement had Meridell

150

fully awake too.

"How do you know?"

"I saw him with Burl."

"Oh." — A small, round sound surrounded by silence.

"They were working on the shield. — To protect town. — To protect us. It was taking a beating, I don't know from what."

The last few days were not the best preparation to start back to work twelve hours a day. A short night and a disquieting dream did not help. Harry got up and started getting ready anyhow. Meridell got up too and fixed breakfast.

"I don't want you going up there."

"I don't want to go, but..."

They both were tight-lipped and grim. Suzie came in but did not say anything.

"You know," Harry said, "I always felt a little guilty not going in the service. I got a lot of respect for my old man. But...I could never see what it was for. Now I feel like I am in the army, but I still don't see what it's for."

Suzie got up silently. Harry and Meridell watched her go in the living room and return with a book. She opened it, quickly found the page she was looking for, and began to read aloud. Her voice was clear and strong, though not loud. More than once, it trembled with emotion:

> We hold these truths to be self-evident, that all men are created equal, that they are endowed by their Creator with certain unalienable rights, that among these are life, liberty and the pursuit of happiness. That to secure these rights, governments are instituted among men, deriving their just powers from the consent of the governed; that whenever any form of government becomes destructive of these ends, it is the right of the people to alter or abolish it, and to institute new government, laying its foundation on such principles, and organizing its powers in such form as to them shall seem most likely to effect their safety and happiness. Prudence, indeed, will dictate that governments long established should not be changed for light and transient causes; and accordingly all experience hath shown that mankind are more disposed to suffer, while evils are sufferable, than to right themselves by abolishing the forms to which they are accustomed. But when a long train of abuses and usurpations, pursuing invariably the same object, evinces a design to reduce them under absolute despotism, it is their right, it is their duty, to throw off such government, and to provide new guards for their future security.

There was a long silence when she finished. Meridell was crying softly.

"You're not supposed to be thinking about things like that — not at your age — not in America."

"Yes I am — especially in America."

Meridell cried harder.

"If only..." Harry began. "It's all so damned murky. Ghosts and feelings and...I don't know what I'm fighting. I don't even know what I'm fighting for."

"Remember what the high meadow was like last summer?..." Suzie said.

Harry drained his coffee, squared his shoulders, and went on out.

"I.D., please."

Harry got out his driver's license and showed it to the guard.

"Sorry. I need a Vitor I.D. or you can't come in."

"I don't know anything about that. I'm supposesd to be at work in ten minutes."

"Just a minute."

Two pickup trucks lined up behind Harry. Most of the men must have come in during the night as there was not a big line.

The guard went into his booth, checked a list, then made a call.

"Pull over there out of the way, please. Someone will be down."

Harry pulled around off the road. The guard checked the other men's I.D.s and let them in.

Wayne drove up. He apparently had his I.D. as the guard let him pass. He waved to Harry but did not stop.

Another truck went through. Then the men from Lariat pulled up, all three riding together. The guard stopped them too and had them park next to Harry.

"What the hell?" said one.

"Why didn't they tell us ahead?" said a second.

"They damn well better let us in. I turned down another job just last week."

Harry did not say anything.

Two more trucks went through. That was the end of it. They waited. Fifteen minutes went by, twenty. It was getting close to seven-thirty when, finally, a truck came down from the site. Harry noticed that the sign on it said LemTron rather than Vitor. Not that it mattered.

"Sorry for the holdup. If you'll follow me, we'll get you set up."

The three Lariat men got back in their truck, obviously relieved. Harry was not so sure, but he did follow.

He was still less sure when they took his fingerprints, but he did not think it prudent to object. At least they did not want a urine sample, he thought.

It was a few minutes after eight by the time they were all done and had their new plastic Vitor I.D. cards.

"Go on up to the rec hall. They're just starting." The man sounded friendly enough.

Harry and the others went on. Men were still going in. Just like last month, not a thing had happened the first hour of the shift.

Back in Crazyland, Harry thought.

Most of the men Harry had met last month were there again. He saw Harry Smith and the two Indians from Oklahoma. There were a lot of new men too though. In fact, the crew looked about twice as big as a month ago. – Must be sleeping them four to a trailer, Harry thought.

It took most of the morning to get everyone organized. Harry began tying rod about ten-thirty. It was nearly lunch time before the last of the men came out to their jobs.

Very little had changed visibly since Harry went off thirty days ago. The main difference Harry could see was a tunnel entrance off one side of the basement wall of the Security Complex headed toward the Office Complex.

The tunnel was big enough to drive a semi in. There was a locked gate in front of it now.

"Must be deep," Harry commented to Johnny Sixkiller at lunch. They did all the digging from down under."

"Wonder what they did with all the dirt," said Johnny. "That's a lot of dirt."

"Compacted it," said Harry Smith.

"What?"

"Yeah, Man. Do it right, it's a better fortification than concrete. More flexible, 'specially with 'jello.'"

"What's that," Harry asked.

"I don't know what it is. Don't even know its real name, but it's amazing stuff. Bonding agent. Most of the time it's solid, but in an earthquake – or an explosion – it goes liquid – and real sticky.

"I saw a demonstration once. They set off a hell of a charge between two buildings. Concrete block was a mess. This stuff was just a little crooked. Didn't even have cracks. Make you sick to watch it though. Nothin' that big should wiggle like that."

"That's still a lot of dirt," said Johnny.

Harry was curious. On his way back out, he looked and, sure enough: There was a pile of dirt behind the Office Complex – and a big machine of some sort. The dirt was half hidden behind sand and gravel piles, bins of cement and stacks of concrete blocks.

Harry worked on the Security Complex, setting rebar for poured concrete walls. The rebar was two inch, and they were putting in a lot of it. A small mobile crane held the twenty foot lengths while men wired and then welded it in place.

"How thick's the wall?" Harry asked the man he was working with at the moment.

He did not know, but another man overheard who did:

"Forty-two inches."

"Man, they're gonna be ready to stop a tank."

"Gonna be ready, all right," said Harry. "Ready for what?" he did not say.

About four, Harry Smith came looking for him.

"Who do I talk to to cut you loose?"

"What's up?"

"I need someone to follow me down in a truck."

"Oh?"

153

"Yeah. I gotta bring a cat down to town."

"What for? It need repairs?"

"No, to your town. Elk Stuck. I got a house to knock down."

"What?!"

"Company owns it. Used to belong to a guy name of Lucero."

"Jesus...He sold....They're gonna bulldoze it down?!"

"Uh, yeah. I don't like being the one to tell you, but...way I hear it, there's not gonna be any town of Elk Stuck when the company gets done."

"Not if we can help it," Harry said, grimly.

"I'm with you, Man, but don't get squashed. Man's got to stay loose on his feet to survive."

"How about kids?"

"That's rough, but you gotta roll with the punches. Best you can do for them's just the best you can do."

Harry had not explained that the kids in question were not his own. Harry Smith assumed they were. Harry did not feel like a father, but he realized he felt something just as strong.

Harry found himself slightly paranoid about Harry Smith. He was also very reluctant to be the one to accompany a demolition crew into Elk Stuck. The warrior in him, however, told him this was a good opportunity to learn more from Harry Smith away from the other men. Something in him also said Harry Smith wanted to get off to talk to him.

Harry pointed out the rebar crew foreman. Harry Smith spoke to him briefly, then came back.

"Let's go."

Harry's intuition was right. The dozer was slow. Harry drove ahead of it in a Vitor pickup with his lights flashing to warn oncoming traffic. Oncoming traffic consisted exclusively of Vitor vehicles. Though it was Friday afternoon in peak season, there was not a single tourist.

When they were about halfway down and well out of sight of both construction and town, Harry Smith signaled for a stop. Harry pulled over and walked back to the dozer.

"Something wrong?"

"Piss break." He nodded at the machine, which he left running. "Like to vibrate my balls off."

Harry Smith went behind some bushes. Harry got off a little too to be away from the noise and exhaust. When Harry Smith came back, he walked in a direction that met Harry well away from both vehicles. He beckoned him a little farther away.

"Probably no one listening, but what the hell?...I want to talk to you where no one up there's gonna get suspicious. If anyone you know comes along, be real cool. Okay?"

"Sure."

They went back to their vehicles. What could he know, Harry wondered, to be that cautious about?

It was six before they got to town and parked the dozer by the house where Jesus used to live. They spent the next hour walking around, figuring out how to do the job.

Naturally, everyone came to see what was happening. Everyone was not a whole lot of people. There were Chuck and Louella, Meridell and the kids. – Meridell was still dressed in the clothes she had worn to Flora's funeral. Mrs. Martinez did not know they were there. Jim and Cindy were still away. Harry was sure Brownie was watching too, though he did not see him. Harry did most of the explaining.

"How about coming up to the house before I drive you back."

"Sure. Only, we talk outside."

"I'd trust everyone there with my life. Only one's not together's Chuck."

"The drunk?"

"Yeah."

"He's in a bad way."

"I know it."

"Reason I want to talk outside's in case the house is bugged."

"You shittin' me?"

"No. These boys play nasty. They pay good, and they treat you equal. But you stand in their way, they'll mash you like a mosquito. They'll do anything it takes to get you too."

CHAPTER THIRTY-THREE

"If you love me, you will keep my commandments. And I will pray the Father, and he will give you another Counselor, to be with you for ever, even the Spirit of truth whom the world cannot receive, because it neither sees him nor knows him; you know him, for he dwells with you, and will be in you.

"I will not leave you desolate; I will come to you. Yet a little while, and the world will see me no more, but you will see me; because I live, you will live also. In that day you will know that I am in my Father, and you in me, and I in you. He who has my commandments and keeps them, he it is who loves me; and he who loves me will be loved by my Father, and I will love him and manifest myself to him." Judas (not Iscariot) said to him, "Lord, how is it that you will manifest yourself to us, and not to the world?" Jesus answered him, "If a man loves me, he will keep my word, and my Father will love him, and we will come to him and make our home with him. He who does not love me does not keep my words; and the word which you hear is not mine but the Father's who sent me.

"These things I have spoken to you, while I am still with you. But the Counselor, the Holy Spirit, whom the Father will send in my name, he will teach you all things, and bring to your remembrance all that I have said to you. Peace I leave with you; my peace I give to

you; not as the world gives do I give to you. Let not your
hearts be troubled, neither let them be afraid.
John 14:15-27.

Suzie looked up when Harry and Harry entered but continued
reading to her mother till she finished the passage.

"May I?"

Suzie handed the Bible to Harry Smith. He quickly found what he
was looking for:

Hear the word which the Lord speaks to you, O
    house of Israel. Thus says the Lord:
"Learn not the way of the nations,
    nor be dismayed at the signs of the heavens
    because the nations are dismayed at them,
for the customs of the peoples are false.
A tree from the forest is cut down,
    and worked with an axe by the hands of a craftsman.
Men deck it with silver and gold;
    they fasten it with hammer and nails
    so that it cannot move.
Their idols are like scarecrows in a cucumber field
    and they cannot walk.
Be not afraid of them,
    for they cannot do evil,
neither is it in them to do good."

There is none like thee, O Lord;
    thou art great, and thy name is great in might.
Who would not fear thee, O King of the nations?
    For this is thy due;
for among all the wise ones of the nations
    and in all their kingdoms
    there is none like thee.
They are both stupid and foolish;
    the instruction of idols is but wood!
Beaten silver is brought from Tarshish,
    and gold from Uphaz
They are the work of the craftsman and of the hands
        of the goldsmith;
    their clothing is violet and purple;
    they are all the work of skilled men.
But the Lord is the true God;
    he is the living God and the everlasting King.
At his wrath the earth quakes,
    and the nations cannot endure his indignation.
Jeremiah 10:1-10

Harry Smith flipped a few pages and read again:

"Hear the word of the Lord, O nations,
    and declare it in the coastlands afar off;
say, 'He who scattered Israel will gather him,
    and will keep him as a shepherd keeps his flock.'
For the Lord has ransomed Jacob,
    and has redeemed him from hands too strong for him.
They shall come and sing aloud on the height of Zion,
    and they shall be radiant over the goodness of the Lord,
over the grain, the wine, and the oil,
    and over the young of the flock and the herd;
their life shall be like a watered garden,
    and they shall languish no more.
Then shall the maidens rejoice in the dance,
    and the young men and the old shall be merry.
I will turn their mourning into joy,
    I will comfort them, and give them gladness
        for sorrow.
I will feast the soul of the priests with abundance,
    and my people shall be satisfied with my goodness,
                        says the Lord."
                    Jeremiah 31: 10-14

Quiet filled the house. How different, Harry thought: How different from Bob and Sally's strident self-righteousness. Just troubled people turning their hearts to the Word of God for comfort.

Meridell and Suzie had met Harry Smith before, but this was the first time he had been in the house. Meridell invited him to stay for dinner. He hesitated, then accepted.

"What the hell. Those bastards don't own me."

A few minutes later, when things were about ready, Meridell asked Harry to call Jeff.

"He's up the street, I expect. Tell Steve and Brownie there's plenty if they want to come too."

Harry and Harry walked up the quiet street in the dusk. It had barely sprinkled this afternoon, the least it had rained in over two weeks. Now the heartbroken sunset colors were just fading from deep orange to purple on the bottoms of the scattered clouds. Lightning flashed occasionally over toward the Chiricahuas, barely visible and silent. The air was as humid as it gets in Elk Stuck, New Mexico.

Harry Smith breathed deeply: "Almost like home. I feel safer when the air's thick like this. Feel like it hides me from the eyes of evil."

It was the opportunity Harry Smith was waiting for to talk.

"I talked with men back home, men that've worked on other Vitor jobs. It's not healthy to get in their way. People that get in Vitor's way get hurt."

"Why do you work for them?"

157

"Big companys are like that. Some are worse. Some hit out of pure meanness. This one only hits for a reason, even if it is a bad one. At least with Vitor I know if you play by their rules you can come out okay. I want to go to college, become an engineer. I got a good enough record to get some scholarship money. – Being black don't hurt a bit on that. – But I still gotta eat while I study. Operating heavy equipment for Vitor, I make fifteen bucks an hour. – That's before overtime. My other alternative is to stay home and shovel shit for minimum wage – if I'm lucky."

"Yeah." Harry felt a terrible weight. The air did not feel protective to him. He felt like he was suffocating.

Brownie and the boys were playing with the animals. Brownie and Steve had not done anything about dinner.

"You're sure it's no trouble? We got bread and peanut butter and jerky."

"I'm sure."

"Well, okay. Thanks."

Jeff and Steve raced down to Meridell's. Harry and Harry and Brownie walked more slowly, watching the evening drink up the last of the daylight. Stars were beginning to appear through spaces in the clouds.

"They could even have the street bugged," Harry Smith said, "but they probably don't figure you're worth the bother. Watch what you say in the house though."

"I just listen, listen to the air," Brownie said.

Harry had learned in the last year. He did not have Brownie's calm, but he no longer felt like a barbarian outsider. He heard now, too, and had learned to let honor and the Spirit guide him, rather than fear.

Brownie got out his pipe, lit up, and passed it to Harry Smith.

"Sure, Man. Thanks." Harry Smith took a puff and passed the pipe to Harry.

He had a toke and passed it back to Brownie, who had another, refilled it, and passed it around again.

"You don't worry this could cost you your job?"

"Not a whole lot. They usually just give you a warning the first time or two, and I ain't been caught yet. – And if they really want to bust me, I'd rather it be for pot than to have them sneak up on me with something worse."

"Stop it!"

All three men ran for Chuck and Louella's. Meridell was not far behind.

"Stop it! Enough!"

"I'm a rinkadandy. Whoo! Whoo!"

Chuck was hopping around the house, naked except for an old T shirt. He had a twenty-five pound bag of flour with about five pounds left in it, which he was scattering in great puffs.

Louella was dodging through the house, simultaneously trying to grab the flour sack out of Chuck's hand and avoid his reach. Her blouse was torn in several places.

Chuck grabbed for Louella's breast. Louella socked him hard in the jaw. Chuck fell to the floor, clutching the side of his face and laughing insanely. Louella snatched the sack of flour and set it to the back of the counter. Then she picked up a heavy cast iron frying pan and held it over her shoulder with both hands like a baseball bat.

Chuck looked up, almost focussed, then lay flat on his back, put his thumbs to his nose, and wiggled his fingers.

"Wabbly, wabbly, wabbly. Quack! Quack! Quack! Quack!"

"Are you all right?"

Louella glanced over to Harry, at the doorway, with the others behind him.

"So far. I may have to brain my husband."

The phone rang.

"Would you get it." Louella nodded to Meridell.

Meridell went to the phone. Harry went with her. Louella stood over Chuck, her feet planted apart, the frying pan poised.

"Hello."

"Please deposit a dollar eighty."

Coins clicked.

"Louella?"

"No, this is Meridell. That you, Cindy."

"Joe's been murd..."

Click.

The line was not just disconnected. It was dead.

"Wheeee." Chuck rolled over and grabbed for Louella's skirt. Louella kicked Chuck hard in the shoulder. This finally brought him back, at least some.

"Oh!" said Chuck.

"Oh my God," said Meridell.

Chuck crawled outside to puke and pass out. Louella and Meridell went over to the shop. The phone line was dead there too. The only other phone in Elk Stuck any more was at Mrs. Martinez's.

"Why don't you go on back to the house and start dinner. No reason to go to the apocalypse on an empty stomach."

Harry wanted to be with Meridell, but he felt an obligation to act as host.

"Well, okay. Louella, you think you'll be okay?"

"I think so. He's not likely to come to till morning now. Just a damned mess to clean up."

"Has he done that before?"

"It's gotten worse."

"It's getting demonic," said Brownie. "There is something eating Chuck up. I don't know how it got in, but I don't like what it's doing to my friend. Not one bit."

Brownie's whole demeanor was philosophical, but he seldom talked about it. Harry looked pointedly.

"Think we ought to carry him in?" Harry Smith asked.

"Thank you. I think not. He won't freeze tonight. I'll throw an old tarp over him. Maybe when he wakes up on the ground in his vomit he'll learn something. Lord knows nothing else has worked."

"I didn't realize..." said Harry.

"None of us did," said Louella. "It's been slipping up on him, on us all."

Harry suddenly realized Louella and Harry Smith had not really met, though they had seen each other this afternoon.

"Oh, excuse me....This is a friend of mine from the job, Harry Smith. Louella Randell."

"Pleased to meet you." She smiled tiredly. "I usually keep a tidier house."

Suzie and the boys were already working on seconds when the men got back to the house. There was meatloaf and mashed potatoes, baked zucchini with bread crumbs and cheese, and a big garden salad.

Harry looked at the time. It was quarter to ten. He had to be at work at seven in the morning, and he still had Harry Smith to drop off tonight. Just as well to eat now.

Meridell came in a few minutes later. Mrs. Martinez's phone was dead too.

Even at Bob and Sally's, Harry could not remember a more tense meal.

"Um, I better be gettin' back," said Harry Smith with a nod toward the clock.

Outside, Harry asked: "Think we ought to cut and run?"

"You've probably got more time to talk. If not, you're probably too late anyhow."

Something was very, very wrong, but it was hard to believe it was real. This was their home. This was America. You don't just run off into the night....What would you run to? Harry felt like that was exactly what they should do, but what seemed substantial was dinner, work, the Vitor truck he needed to bring back. To let go of everything and just run did not feel real. It gave nothing to focus on.

The guard gave Harry and Harry a hard time over being out late in a company truck.

"Check the mileage," said Harry. "We didn't go anywhere in it."

Almost anything ordinary and everyday was a relief, even being hasseled over bullshit.

Harry drove the VW home and went pretty much straight to bed. It took him a while to get to sleep, but he had to; eventually, he did.

In the morning, everything had the appearance of normal: coffee, wash up, breakfast and off to work. The sunrise was beautiful and fresh. Something screamed in Harry's belly: "Do something! Do something! Do something!" He had no idea what to do. All he could do was keep on and keep his eyes and ears open.

Harry drove Harry Smith back down in the Vitor truck and watched Jesus' house turn into a pile of trash. Two dump trucks drove to the demolition. Harry Smith loaded debris into the dump trucks, and they drove off. Then he smoothed out the yard and started back up the hill. Harry followed, lights flashing once again.

They checked in the truck and bulldozer. It was eleven-thirty.

"You missed coffee break. Might as well make it an early lunch."

With just a few insomniac night shift men at the tables, the rec hall rattled emptily. The kitchen crew was busy preparing for the noon rush. Air smelled of stale cigarette smoke.

Harry and Harry got coffee and took a table. After a while, Johnny Sixkiller and some other men joined them.

"Drilling crew started up this morning," said Johnny.

"What's that?" Harry asked.

"Power plant."

Harry had heard the project was going to have its own power, but not what kind. "Oh?"

"Geothermal....Pump water down to where it's hot. Get back steam — and a hell of a punch. Way I hear, they hardly have to drill at all here. There's cracks a mile deep under this mountain. They got fourteen hundred feet last month already."

Harry visualized a torrent of cold water splashing on white hot rock a mile and a half beneath Thunder Mountain. A humming started up in his ears. He started to feel dizzy and to sweat. Harry shook his head. He did not want to trip out here.

Harry looked around the table. If anyone noticed his momentary slide toward the world of vision they did not let on. Most were eating. One man was reading the paper.

"Shit, listen to this; this is just the next county."

He read a story about a pot patch being raided. The story concluded: "'An authoritative source says, on condition of anonymity, that the marijuana would have had a street value of eighty thousand dollars at maturity.' You know how they calculate that," said the man reading the article.

"How's that?"

"They figure every plant for a pound, which it wouldn't be. They figure every plant for female, which it wouldn't be. Then they break it up into ounces at two hundred dollars an ounce or whatever it goes for to rich people in Los Angeles. And they never heard of giving anything away."

"Mmpgh."

Harry did some arithmetic. He did not know how many plants Brownie had last year, but he knew the half or whatever that were female had produced eight pounds. Counting the imaginary bud from the male plants, that would have given Brownie's pot a "street value" of just about sixty-four thousand dollars. Brownie's actual pot sales had amounted to twenty-four hundred.

Johnny sang a line from a song:

> Never make a deal with the Devil,
> 'Cause the Devil always cheats.

Harry walked back out with Harry Smith. They both needed to find out what to do next. Harry was back on rebar. Harry Smith was supposed to dig something with a small four-wheel-drive backhoe, with a gasoline engine, that could get in and out of anyplace. It was parked on the way to the Security Complex. They walked that far together.

"Check you later," said Harry Smith, as he climbed on.

"See you." Harry continued.

"Look out!"

Harry jumped around.

When Harry Smith turned on the backhoe, the arm was engaged and would not let go. When nothing else worked, he tried to shut the machine off, but too late. The bucket chewed into the earth and caught.

The backhoe bucked. Harry Smith grabbed for *anything* to hang onto now. The tread started rolling. Tread and arm pulled against one another momentarily. The powerful machine shook like an aspen leaf in a high wind. The backhoe bucked again. Smoke poured out of the engine. Flame flashed down the fuel line.

K A W H O O S H !

The gas tank erupted. A tower of flame shot up. The heat and concussion knocked Harry back, like a blow.

"Ah, ha, ha, ha, ha."

Was he hallucinating? Was it just the fire seething? Or was there really something demonic laughing in a high-pitched wheeze?

CHAPTER THIRTY-FOUR

"That witch!"

The last thing Harry needed was to come home to more trouble.

"Look at this." Meridell handed Harry the letter. It was from the I.R.S.

"What the hell?"

"That lying, cheating, stealing, backstabbing Aspasia Suny, may she burn in Hell forever."

"I don't get it."

"She told the I.R.S. she paid me thirty-five thousand dollars last year. Deducted it as a business expense. Now they want to know why I haven't paid taxes on it."

Harry was speechless. In fact, he was about numb. He plodded to the couch and plunked down.

"You're getting the couch wet."

"Harry Smith's dead."

It was Meridell's turn to be speechless.

There was nothing Harry could do for Harry Smith. He had not been allowed to stand around. He had tied rebar all afternoon in the rain. Now he was tired, wet, and sick at heart. He had no idea what to do about this latest disaster.

Harry and Meridell faced each other like two former people some sorcery had turned to stone.

"Ow!" Clunk.

"Oh!" Meridell jumped. Mother instinct broke the spell.

"It's okay," Suzie called from the kitchen. "I just should of used a potholder."

The tension relaxed in Meridell's eyes and shoulders, but not much.

"Jim and Cindy get back?" Harry asked.

"No."

Brownie and the boys came in shortly. They had been feeding Jim's animals. They walked down the street when they saw Harry drive up.

"Mom, can we go for a hike with Brownie tomorrow?"

Jeff and Steve both looked up at Meridell very earnestly.

"What have you got in mind?" Meridell asked suspiciously.

"Patricio told Mrs. Martinez there's an outrageous roadblock on the Elk Stuck Road when he brought in the mail. We want to go scouting."

Meridell turned to Brownie with a hard look in her eyes.

"I want to get close enough to hear. I want someone watching me in case I get caught."

"Why didn't you ask me? They're children."

"That's just why I asked them instead of you, Meridell. No one's going to pay any attention to a couple of kids half a mile away even if they do see them."

"Let me think about it."

"Soup's on!" Suzie called from the kitchen.

After a while, Harry asked Meridell how Chuck was.

"Too sick to be much trouble, but paranoid — crazy paranoid."

"DTs."

"Yeah, I suppose. Louella says if it keeps up she's going to hospitalize him at Fort Bayard. She'd like to take him to the V.A., but that's all the way to Albuquerque, and they don't pay transportation expenses any more."

"I didn't know he was a vet."

"He was in Vietnam in the early sixties. '61; '62 maybe. He doesn't talk about it. I think there's something he's ashamed of."

"Mphh," said Harry.

Harry scooped in another spoonful of tuna casserole. He had no idea what the food tasted like. He was too exhausted in his soul.

"Louella told me he was in something called the Phoenix Program — whatever that was."

"Murder and kidnapping," said Brownie. "Run by the C.I.A."

No one asked how he knew. No one asked anything.

It did not really clear at all that night. There were only a few holes in the clouds when Harry left for work in the morning. Brownie, Jeff and Steve headed out cross country about the same time.

Harry and Harry Smith's other friends got off an extra half hour at lunch to hold a service. The body was covered up. It was not recognizable. It would be shipped home to Mississippi that night. Otherwise, Harry tied rebar in intermittent rain all day.

Machinery roared. The generator pounded. The drilling rig snarled. Harry did not talk to anyone. All the men were quiet. Everyone had seen the fire. All minds were on Harry Smith's accident, even those who did not know him.

Brownie and the boys got in shortly before Harry. Mrs. Martinez and Louella were already there. Chuck was not. He had been feeling well enough to be obnoxious today. Louella said he did not make any sense at all any more. She hated to think what he was liable to be doing to the house.

"I can't watch him like a baby though." She was on the verge of tears.

There was still no sign at all of Jim and Cindy.

"Roadblock's being run by the army," Brownie told them. "Only if you didn't know, you might think it was Border Patrol. They're using Border Patrol vehicles. Puke green trucks parked all over the place."

"What are they doing?" Harry asked.

"Keeping people out. They didn't let anything but Vitor vehicles through. I saw them turn Pete Wiggins away."

"They wouldn't let a deputy sheriff through?!" Mrs. Martinez was truly shocked.

"Nope. And, Harry, I think maybe your folks tried to come in earlier."

"Oh?"

"I did get close enough to listen. — Heard Pete Wiggins give them quite an argument, but they still wouldn't let him in.

"After he went, I heard them joking about the one other person who had really tried to bull his way past. They said he was a retired master sergeant with his wife in a motor home and that he talked about having a son in Elk Stuck."

"Tomorrow," said Louella, "I am going to town. I need to shop. And I need to do something about Chuck."

"Let us get down there again first to watch — just in case," Brownie said.

Louella only thought for a second before answering. "All right."

It was not thunderstorming any more. It was just cloudy and cold all the time. Meridell had the fire going most of the time. Harry left for work next day in the rain. It rained off and on all day, mostly on. Harry felt like he weighed a thousand pounds by the time he got home. What a contrast, he thought, to how light and bouncy he had been swinging a pick on Chuck and Louella's water line this time last year.

Harry knew it was time to do something — long past time. Gravity had gotten so thick though. Inertia was a leaden weight, making it difficult to move in any way but routine. Harry felt too worn out even to think about what to do.

Everyone was at the house again when Harry got there, even Chuck. Chuck seemed to relate to the conversation, but his eyes were crazy. Harry thought he was really elsewhere. Not a nice elsewhere either.

Louella had tried to drive out, with Chuck, that day. They were stopped at the roadblock. The soldiers had made insulting jokes to Louella about Indians and Mexicans and to Chuck about fat old men with beards. Chuck had been completely cowed. Louella wanted to tear them limb from limb, but restrained herself and went home. While she was turning around,

164

she heard one of the soldiers start to tell another a disgusting story about an Apache whore. She was sure he was talking loud enough for her to hear on purpose.

Mrs. Martinez thought someone – i.e. Brownie – should walk out for help. Louella thought they should all walk out. Suzie thought they should stay:

"If they wouldn't let in the sheriff they won't let anyone in. The mountain's the best protection we've got...and it wants us here."

"What can we do for the mountain, dear?" Meridell asked.

"Witness. Witness the truth," Suzie replied without a moment's hesitation.

Mrs. Martinez did not like it but had to admit Suzie was probably right about going for help. This left Louella's proposal the most rational. However, to run meant abandoning their homes. Then what? It was the same question that had paralyzed Harry just a few nights earlier, when he and Harry Smith talked.

The rain was steady, cold, and heavy. The dark, when it came, was impenetrable.

"I don't believe I could walk out tonight," Louella said at last. "If they don't shoot us in our sleep, I'll see how I feel in the morning. This can't go on much longer though."

Everyone agreed. No one knew what to do. Not even Suzie, though she seemed the most self-assured of any of them. Jeff and Steve had no idea what to do either, but they were enjoying the adventure too much to be very worried. Everyone else was plenty worried.

Steve was getting quite concerned about his father and Cindy though. They all were. If Brownie and the boys could spy on the roadblock twice without incident, Jim and Cindy should have been able to get back to Elk Stuck somehow. Both of them were in good shape and knew the country. There were a hundred places they should have been able to walk from in less than a day.

That night Harry dreamt:

First he was on top of the ridge behind the house in the area where he and Brownie had once tested the air the day Vitor – no, LemTron, and the army first came through town.

As on that day, the air changed as Harry moved up the ridge. Suddenly, the flavor was of Thunder Mountain. Harry looked up. The Indian Lady was walking toward him, hand in hand with Brownie and Suzie.

The scene changed. Harry was in town. Imogene and Speed Bump, Jim's dogs, were frantic. They're not howling, Harry thought. He can't be dead. The dogs were listening now. Petunia snuffled nervously. Her long, delicate ears swiveled in the same direction.

Harry looked. Whatever the animals were listening to was coming from the direction of the construction site. Harry listened too.

All he could hear was water, but why should that disturb the animals? With all the rain, you could always hear water.

The scene shifted again. It was a little vague now. Harry was rapidly returning from the dreamworld.

Burl and Joe and Flora were working as fast as they could on the shield. Chuck was around somewhere. He was causing trouble. Brownie was around somewhere too. Harry was grateful he was.

The alarm went off. Harry came to, disoriented. He found himself with a thought: Jim and Cindy can't be dead. They were not there. Only later did it occur to him to wonder what Chuck or Brownie were doing in the dream with Burl, Flora and Joe. When this did occur to Harry, he shivered.

It was five-thirty, Tuesday, August fourth. A couple weeks ago, it had been light by now. Today, with the rain, it was still night. Harry wondered if he should go to work. He had just an hour to decide.

Meridell did not know what he should do. Brownie had ideas, but they contradicted themselves:

"If you don't go, they'll notice. Cuts our options. If you do go, you might not be able to get out."

"Thanks. You're a big help."

Brownie shrugged. "I'd like to try to get word to someone before we do anything — if we've got time."

"What have you got in mind?" Meridell asked.

"I don't think I better try Lariat, but I can walk to Rodeo in a day. Only thing is who to call."

Jennifer did not seem like a good idea. Neither did Bob and Sally. Calling friends in Lariat might not do any good. They settled on Paul and Pat — with Chuck and Louella's son, Jerry, as a backup.

Harry, Meridell, Brownie and Suzie discussed it. The three adults agreed they thought someone somewhere else should be aware of their situation before they made any rash moves. Suzie remained convinced the mountain would tell them if they should move at all, but she, too, thought it was just as well for someone to know what was happening to them.

No one was comfortable with the alternatives available to them. No one was comfortable with Brownie going off alone either with no sign of Jim and Cindy. However, anyone who went with him, even Harry or Suzie, would make the trip take twice as long and would get back too exhausted to do anything.

Brownie went to ask Louella and Mrs. Martinez's opinion. Harry went to work.

Work was weird, weird because it was so ordinary. He might be on any construction job anywhere. Men talked about sex and beer and stupid supervisors.

"Man, if they'd pay me one percent of what they waste on a job like this, I'd be a rich motherfucker."

It was still raining most of the time. Harry was still tying rebar. The construction site was a swamp. Everything was covered with mud.

It was mid-morning when Harry realized the three men from Lariat had not been on the job the past two days. Wayne was still there though. Harry asked him about it at lunch.

"Beats me, Man," Wayne said.

Something about Wayne was off, Harry felt. Something about Wayne had been off for a long time, but it was more so now: a qualitative change more than a quantitative one. Something about Wayne felt alien – not related to the mountain, not human either.

And not nice, Harry thought, as he walked away; but he could not put a finger on what it was.

That night, Mrs. Martinez was wildly upset. There had been no mail delivery. She had agreed that morning to postpone any decision till Brownie had time to get back. Now she wanted to leave right away.

When the mail did not come, she drove down to the roadblock and told the men there about it. They had firmly, and not altogether politely, told her no one could come in and no she could not go out to do anything about it.

They had not exactly said so, but Mrs. Martinez had the impression they might let her pass so long as she did not try to come back. Now that was exactly what she wanted to do. No one liked the idea. No one quite had the heart to talk her out of it either.

She finally said, "I'll wait till daylight. But in the morning, I'm going."

Not even Suzie tried to convince her otherwise.

In the morning, Harry saw Mrs. Martinez's car head up the ridge as if she were going to open the post office early. It did not stop at the top.

One more day, Harry thought. His whole being resisted going back to the job. Brownie should be home by tonight. Harry forced himself to get ready.

Jeff and Steve wanted to see what they could see.

Meridell did not like it, but she did not forbid it either. She just told them: "For God's sake, be careful. This is no game."

Once again, work was ordinary – banal. Harry tied rebar in the rain. He was so tense his teeth hurt. He ate lunch with Johnny Sixkiller and some of the other men he was friendly with but did not dare say anything.

Nothing happened all day. Harry was on his way home when it occurred to him he had not seen Wayne all afternoon. That was odd – but did not really prove anything. He had seen Wayne that morning.

When Harry got home, Brownie was back. He had gotten through to Paul and Pat. They were very concerned. They would see what they could do. That was all he knew.

Jeff and Steve had news too. Mrs. Martinez's house had been ransacked. She had not come back.

Jeff went to get Louella and Chuck. Steve went to tend to the animals. It seemed they had better think about hiking out. Saving their homes was no longer a consideration. Saving their lives, or at least their freedom, was. The only question left was when to go: Now or morning?

"Run!"

Jeff burst in the door, followed almost immediately by Louella, Chuck, and Steve.

It was raining, not terribly hard, but enough to deaden sound. It was also dark. There was no question, though, when they stepped out the door. The trucks coming over Post Office Ridge, standing out in each other's headlights, were troop carriers. The vehicles parked on top – and on top of the other ridge, facing down into town, were tanks.

CHAPTER THIRTY-FIVE

"I'll catch up with you on the ridge."

"Harry, no!" said Meridell.

"We should know what we can."

Brownie looked at him hard a couple seconds. "He's right. We can't wait though. Can you fnd the scout cave?"

"I think so."

"Okay."

Brownie and Louella herded Chuck toward the hillside behind the house. Everyone else scrambled in the same direction, except Harry.

Harry ran across the street and leapt the swollen creek – somewhat amazed that he could jump that far. The troop carriers were coming as fast as they could, but that was not very fast on the steep road with its four abrupt switchbacks. Harry thanked God for the mountain road. He thanked God for the rain, deadening the sound of his friends' escape and eliminating any sign.

Harry slipped behind a thick patch of little junipers on the hillside and waited. Lights were on at Chuck and Louella's, Meridell's, and Jim's. He could see the first two houses clearly, the third just barely, from where he stood.

The troop carriers speeded up when they got to the comparatively straight and level street through town. Harry noted that none turned off on the South Fork Road, where Wayne's and Mrs. Martinez's houses were.

There were five trucks. One stopped at Chuck and Louella's, one at Meridell's, and one where Harry figured Cindy's house must be in the dark. Two went around the bend toward Jim's.

Harry heard barking, then a gunshot, a horrible sound, then two more shots.

He dashed across the side of the steep bluff like a deer, avoiding prickly pears, sharp tree branches, and loose rocks as if by magic. He came out behind some boulders on the hillside above Jim's.

Headlights illuminated the yard. Speed Bump lay inert on the ground. Petunia lay twitching spasmodically. The gentle burro moved one more time, then lay still. Imogene was not to be seen. Both the front and back doors of the house were smashed.

Stupid shits, Harry thought: I know it wasn't locked. The back door doesn't even have a lock.

Several soldiers looked warily around, assault rifles at ready. More were inside, apparently tearing the place apart. They made a lot of noise.

Harry watched in rage, completely at a loss what to do. Then he noticed a big handgun silhouetted in the front doorway. It caught his attention because the hand holding it waved it to gesture some direction.

"Watch it, ya dumb fuck."

Harry knew that voice. He waited. After a timeless eternity, a face leaned out the door above the hand holding the pistol. The face belonged to Wayne.

The face disappeared back into the house. Harry melted across the face of the bluff, climbed a little higher and continued diagonally at a level across the side of the steep, rocky hill that was the wall of the canyon he had come to call home.

Above the next bend in the road, out of sight of Jim's house, Harry ran back down. He was vaguely aware that under ordinary circumstances he would have considered it impossible for anything short of a mountain goat to run ten feet on such terrain.

As Harry's foot touched the road, a sensation rushed through him as if he had stepped on a bed of coals. It was not the people of Elk Stuck that were under attack. It was the mountain.

Thunder Mountain, itself, was under assault. And the road, a tool which might be used for good as well as evil was now possessed by the demon.

Harry was running far too fast to stop even had he wanted to. Something caused him to turn his head and cock it forward to look down the road just as his feet left the ground to fly back across the creek.

Harry could never be absolutely sure in the dark and rain, but he felt sure that flash could only come from a big handgun. A rifle would look different – and sound different. Harry had seen only one handgun.

What he *was* sure of was that the inspiration to turn his head saved his life. As it was, the bullet just creased his scalp, slightly above his right ear.

Harry felt like a high speed skilsaw had zipped across the side of his head. He had no idea how badly he was hurt. All he knew was that it did not slow him down.

He raced diagonally across the side of the hill: up but back toward town rather than toward the mountain. Even in the wet, he was making a good deal of noise. Two more shots sounded but did not come close.

Harry was nearly to the East Fork Trail when he reached the top of the ridge. He had never run so fast in his life. He would not have believed a human being could climb such a steep hill so fast.

He stood panting and listening for several minutes. Nothing. He was pretty sure there was no way to follow but by sound – or maybe infrared. His breathing gradually slowed to almost normal.

He felt the side of his head. There was a lot of blood. He was not sure what to do. The only thing he could think of for a bandage was his T shirt. It was the same dirty shirt full of dank sweat he had worked in all day. His levis and boots were fairly sopping too. At least the levi jacket he had changed into to drive home was dry from being in the car, though it was dirty too.

He slipped out of the jacket, pulled the T shirt off, and put the jacket back on. It actually felt better than the shirt, being drier. Then he tied the T shirt around his head to stop the bleeding. It was the best he could do. With the emotions that ran through him, he had no idea how much of what he felt was the wound or loss of blood.

He was still on his feet anyhow. Now he had to make a decision. Should he risk leading their enemies to his friends?

The mountain was big. If they did not know where he was now, they were no more likely to find him than the others. If he joined them, he could warn them. And yet...

...Was he spacing out? He felt the bandage. It felt wet, hardly surprising, but not sticky. He held his hand in front of his face, but could not see enough to tell. It just felt like rain and sweat though, no blood soaking through.

Harry took a few steps. His body felt strong and steady – and somehow light. This was how he used to feel; all the weight of working at Vitor was gone. And yet, this was not quite how he used to feel.

Harry felt light because he was riding with the flow of life again. It was not the same as winterizing a friend's water line. Now, light as he might feel, the stream of Harry's life was boxed into the canyon of a war.

Harry felt rage: No fucking fair. What did I do to deserve this?

There was no answer, but his next thought was of Meridell and the rest of his friends – his family. His feet began to move of their own accord.

Harry could feel it clearly now. He was not spacing out. Just like on that day he and Brownie had stood on this ridge, there were two Spirits alive on Thunder Mountain. One belonged there and drew Harry, filled him with life, filled his heart and guided him. The other was an invader, both alien and malicious, and it repelled him.

Harry's feet moved of themselves. All Harry's will did was listen to his heart and choose not to interfere.

Harry was not surprised, though he was amazed, when he all but ran smack into Meridell.

As ridges came together, there were broad flat areas with no distinguishing features. Going up, even in the dark, was not difficult. Everything went to the same place. It was impossible to be lost.

Coming down was another story. If you did not know what you were doing, you could come out at the bottom twenty miles from where you meant to be.

While it was impossible to get lost going up, there was no particular reason to be able to find another person. Little ridges were everywhere. The forest was dense. The little troop of Harry's family had already started across the side of the mountain. They might have been anywhere. Harry went right to them.

"Oh!" Meridell kept her exclamation low.

"It's me, Harry."

"Thank God! I heard shots."

Harry did not reply. He was uncertain whether to tell her he was hit or wait till they could stop. He was still more uncertain what to say about the murder of the animals. Before he could make up his mind, Chuck burst out:

"I'm going to break every bone in your body, Woman, bringing me

170

out in this rain."

"Hush," Louella replied.

Chuck was out of breath, but he was still loud. "Where the fuck are we?"

Whack. Harry and Meridell both gasped, then sighed with relief when Chuck's voice whimpered the next line:

"Don't hurt me."

"I said hush, damn you. Now hush."

They were all holding hands. Meridell was in the rear, then Steve, then Jeff. That was as far as Harry could see. Brownie was leading, followed by the unwilling Chuck, Louella, and Suzie in the middle. Louella was setting the pace. It was not slow.

"I was seen," Harry stage whispered, hoping all the right people would hear and none of the wrong ones. "I don't think I was followed though. – Or if they did, they lost me."

Someone grunted acknowledgement. Harry thought it was Suzie.

Brownie led them unerringly through the woods. It still took a long time. It was not raining very hard, and the trees – fir, spruce, patches of aspen – caught a lot of that. The trees were drenched themselves though, and dripping. Everyone was sopping wet long before they reached the cave they had stocked just a few months earlier...in what seemed another life.

The cave was pretty full with eight people. They huddled together and wrapped the two wool blankets that were there around all of them. Brownie passed around some jerky.

"Help keep you warm. Everyone okay?"

Everyone said, "Yeah," except Chuck.

Louella swatted him.

"Leave me alone."

"Uh, I probably ought to tell you I was hit."

"Harry!"

"Side of my head. I think I'm okay. There sure was a lot of blood though."

"Lot of blood vessels in the scalp," Brownie said. "Lot of scalp wounds look worse than they are. No concussion?"

"I don't think so. It sure didn't slow me down any. I got my T shirt wrapped around it. I think the bleeding's stopped."

"Let's see."

Brownie came over. Harry guided his hands. There was not any seeing to it.

"I don't feel any fresh blood. You want I'll light a lighter. I'd rather not, at least for a while."

"I haven't dropped dead yet. Let's wait."

They did check it with the lighter about an hour later. The wound did not look serious. There was a lot of dried blood in Harry's beard and on the shoulder of his jacket – especially when you considered that most of blood had probably washed off from the rain.

"You let us know if you get lightheaded."

"Man, I get lightheaded when I'm not shot."

171

"That's okay. You trip out and have a vision, we'll want to know about that too."

As the night wore on, the rain thinned out and eventually stopped. No one could really get comfortable enough to sleep; most managed to doze some.

The air was washed clean by all the rain. As it stopped and the moisture cleared, the ominous rumble of the construction site gradually became audible. At one point, the sound changed. Some major piece of the machinery was doing something different. There was a: "Kerwhump!" they felt as well as heard.

Brownie stepped outside to see if he could see anything.

"Well?" Harry asked when Brownie came back.

"Nothin'. Just the floodlights reflecting off the clouds."

"Floodlights?" said Chuck. "Where?"

"At the construction site, of course," Harry replied.

"Oh."

There was a moment of silence. Then Chuck spoke again:

"I'm going to get warm."

He started out.

"You're going to stay right here," Louella said quietly.

"Lemme go, Woman," Chuck bellowed.

Meridell gasped at the noise.

Chuck broke free and lumbered out of the cave.

"Holy shit," said Harry.

"Bastard," said Louella.

Brownie dashed after Chuck. Harry started to go too.

"No!" Brownie snapped. "Run. Suzie, you know where."

There was brief confusion.

"Do it!" Brownie called back.

Harry was amazed how far away Brownie was already. Getting out of the blankets and standing up in front of the cave could not have taken more than a few seconds.

Brownie was already so far away Harry was not sure he could find him. Chuck was even farther, rolling toward the construction site like an avalanche.

Harry still hesitated. Louella grabbed him.

"No damned point getting lost."

Another cloud blew in so fast Harry was not aware it was there till he felt the rain. It instantly drowned out the sound of Chuck and Brownie.

There was no choice.

Suzie led the way as surely as Brownie had earlier. Harry knew where they were going, though he was quite sure he could not have found the way with such certainty.

First light hinted at a blur through the rain as they reached the meadow. Suzie led them straight around to the side canyon and into the cave. Harry wondered if they should crawl into the inner cave, but did not say anything.

Once again, they wrapped up in two wool blankets and tried to get comfortable.

Harry found he felt faint. He touched his cheek. His hand came away sticky.

"Uh, I think this last hike set my head bleeding again."

Harry felt a little dizzy.

A whirlpool suddenly spun above his head.

A tornado.

Harry was falling.

No. He was rising.

Harry saw some people in a cave. His friends. A man collapsed in their midst. Arms caught the falling body. That was him!

CHAPTER THIRTY-SIX

Mmmmmmmmmmmm.

Harry had heard that sound once, an aeon ago, in Chuck and Louella's well. The mountain resonated in its own hollow innards. How different the mountain hum of life was from the angry buzz of Vitor's machinery. The sound felt warm and reassuring. Harry realized he was very glad Thunder Mountain was his friend. The sound was *big* and though it reassured him, Harry knew the mountain was angry too. Harry would not want to be the object of that anger.

The spinning sensation continued. Then Harry found himself looking at town from the air. Burl and Flora and Joe worked frantically on the shield. It was *not* finished. It was *not* enough. It *was* under attack.

Brownie appeared. "Let's put it all on my house. We can guard that better than the whole town."

The three old people, who moved with the strength and agility of the young *and* the certainty of their years of experience, all concentrated on one section of the shield.

But Brownie doesn't have a house, Harry thought. Then he saw it was the cave they now protected. He felt a moment of relief. His friends were safe — as safe as they could be.

Burl caught Harry's eye. It was the first time, Harry realized, that the dead had acknowledged him in this vision. He wondered if he was dead too, or dying.

"Good man," Burl said. "You're on the job."

Harry did not exactly articulate his question in words, nor did Burl exactly speak again in reply.

"What's the job? What am I doing?" something in Harry asked.

"You're here to report, to report back to the world of the living what you see, to maintain the link," Burl answered, more a physical sensation than ephemeral words.

The work on the shield was done. Their friends were protected now in the bosom of Thunder Mountain, itself. The strength of the shield was the strength of the Spirit of Thunder Mountain. Even that carried no guarantee. The Spirit of Thunder Mountain was at war with an adversary of its own kind, of its own magnitude....That shield was as much as Harry could hope for.

Harry's heart filled to overflowing. Would the people he loved be all right? The children? What about Brownie? Was he here like Harry, to report back? Or was Brownie now one of the dead?

These questions barely formed in Harry when the whirling energy caught him up once again. A comment his father had made once about journalists in Vietnam flowed through Harry's mind:

"Reporters are noncombatants, but they are not necessarily neutral. And they are not immune."

Chuck was running like a madman. Harry gasped. Chuck *was* a madman. Chuck's soul was gone, Harry did not know where. The body of his friend was now a possessed thing, possessed by the demon that was devouring him.

Fear gripped Harry. Was Chuck going to betray their companions?

He couldn't. He did not know where they were. Something else was happening.

The demon's maw hung open, slobbering with greed, just waiting to eat Chuck up.

Stupid demon, Harry thought, then was surprised at the thought. But he found it reassured him, chased away his own panic. Now he could look with a clear eye.

When he did look, he realized what it was that made him think the demon stupid. The demon was so possessed by its own insatiable greed that it had no strategy at all: Just take everything right now and consume it immediately. Power, itself, and fear, were its only weapons.

The demon was not to be underestimated. It was very, very powerful. But it was also blind, even more blind than the people who were lost in the darkness of their own terror.

Snap.

Something indescribable happened in Harry: Pain and loss and anger and hope.

Harry had a brief flash of a skinny, broken body in long hair and buckskins lying on the wet ground. A dark, mindless shape separated from it, moved toward...

...The demon!

Harry saw it now. My God it was big! He had no idea. It was far bigger than Thunder Mountain. Could anything stand against such a monster?

A point of light flashed past. Harry looked: Brownie, like a tiny diamond sword flashing in the dark, ominous sky.

Three more points of light joined him: Burl, Flora, Joe.

Then the Indian Lady was there.

Suddenly they were all lined up, like segments of a bridge.

Harry gasped. He was no longer just a reporter. He was part of the bridge. He was the piece anchoring it to this world. The Indian Lady was the piece at the other end. The four beings of light were the bridge itself.

Never had Harry felt such peace, such awe, such terror, as what flowed through him now.

174

The Spirit of Thunder Mountain was never blind like the demon. But it was not of the human world. It had its own priorities. Of itself, it might or might not even notice human beings.

The Spirit of Thunder Mountain was under attack. It was moving to protect itself. The frail little bridge of souls between this world and the next gave it human eyes.

The Spirit of Thunder Mountain still was not human. It was a Spirit, however, in full accord with the God Who created human beings. Because the six human souls were there at the occasion of its battle, the Spirit of Thunder Mountain included the humans among the created beings for whom it fought.

Harry thought briefly of Jim and Cindy, Mrs. Martinez's flight, letters to congressmen, the call to Paul and Pat. He knew now, all that was futile. The battle was being waged by forces so much bigger than any human being.

Yet, if their efforts were futile, they were still significant, even necessary. They might be too puny to have any effect on the outcome of the battle, but it was the quality and intent of their efforts which told the Spirit of Thunder Mountain which side they were on. Because they cared and had acted accordingly, Thunder Mountain now cared about them right along with the elk and the wild flowers.

The town of Elk Stuck that was Harry's home and the home of the people he loved, Vitor which had been his employer and his enemy, the United States Army which had somehow been vampirized by the opponents of everything his father had taught him to respect: All these Harry now saw as so many trees and rocks on the mountainside. They might be healthy or rotten. The rocks might be flung as a weapon or used as the foundation of a house – or left to sit in peace and beauty. But they were just little objects on the surface.

Mmmmmmmm.

Thunder Mountain was awake.

Thunder Mountain was beginning to move.

The demon had lulled itself into oblivion through its greed. It had thought it could consume indefinitely, eat up the trees and the rocks and the animals and the people.

Life and death were part of the cycle of the mountain. The Spirit of Thunder Mountain would not intervene to stop a man from felling a tree any more than it would stop a beaver. There was balance, however.

The demon, in its greed, had gone too far. Now a being of its own scale was awake, acting, prepared to stop it.

The Spirit of Thunder Mountain began to take on form. It was not at all like the demon. It was not bloated or gross or blind.

The Spirit of Thunder Mountain was made of light: light in the shape of a sword – of a tooth....The Mountain could consume too – not out of greed – not to get fat. The Mountain could cleanse, could consume like fire, like a whirlpool of wind and water and fire. The Mountain *would* cleanse.

...If it could.

Harry felt like a man caught on an electric line. A billion billion

175

volts of current roared through him. The bridge of souls, of which he was one end, was the line. He could not let go to save his life. He did not want to let go though he was terrified. He was sure the thundering power pouring through him would kill him. He did not care. All Harry cared about was the safety of his friends and the outcome of the battle. Thunder Mountain had to win. That was the only acceptable resolution to Harry's soul.

However, the battle was not over. Victory was not certain. It was only now that Thunder Mountain had decided anything needed doing at all. Only now had Thunder Mountain chosen to rise to do battle with the demon that had planted its noxious tentacle in the sweet soil of the mountainside.

Mmmmmmmmm.

The Indian Woman was sweeping her hearth. Her ankle-length, full cotton skirt swished back and forth as she swung her broom.

The skirt was an undyed natural off-white. The many decorations sewn on it were of every color.

The decorations were shapes, forms of people and things. They were the scenes of daily life, of everyone's life in the world. There was himself and Meridell and a family of squirrels and a pine cone....And...

Her body was warm with life. It hummed.

The sound was the reality of which OM is a feeble approximation.

> In the beginning was the Word, and the Word
> was with God, and the Word was God. He was in the
> beginning with God; all things were made through
> him, and without him was not anything made that
> was made. In him was life, and the life was the
> light of men. The light shines in the darkness,
> and the darkness has not overcome it.
>
> John 1:1-5

The sound was the Word. It was the Word God speaks in all Creation.

The hearth the Indian Woman swept was a small crystal dome, with a gentle curve like the lense of a bright, healthy eye.

The hearth, the dome, the eye radiated light. It was filled with light, filled with light like the rising sun.

Like the sun, the light that shone from the hearth in the heart of Thunder Mountain was a piercing light. The light penetrated the darkness, broke it up, dissipated it, drove it away.

Something nasty approached, something filled with slime that exuded foul odors.

The repulsive something dared not come too close to the blazing hearth. It did not like light.

The nasty thing liked to eat though. It liked to eat the life the light made possible.

The light nourished a world. All manner of beings grew there.

The nasty thing was not one of the creatures the light nourished. It did not live from the light. It was a parasite, a vampire. It lived by stealing the life out of the creatures the light sustained.

The creatures took the life the light gave, and they lived. And in their living they gave life to one another and back to the Source from which it came.

The nasty thing only took. It gave nothing in return.

It was not good for the nasty thing to come so close. It took too much. It obscured the light because it did not like light. It must be stopped.

Life, itself, was not in danger because the Source of life, itself, was of another magnitude entirely than the hearth-eye-sun in the heart of Thunder Mountain or the parasitical being that attacked it.

That portion of life, however, was in danger. The nasty thing must be driven off, or *that eye* would die and those creatures that depended on it would all die with it.

The nasty thing was already too big. It had already consumed too much of God's good Creation. It ought to be destroyed. But whether that was yet ordained or not, it had to be stopped. Enough was enough. The vicious all-consuming, parasitic vileness must be stopped — *right here* — *right now.*

The Indian Woman set aside her round, straw, homemade broom and picked up a little sparkling amethystine violet vial. The vial was about as long as two joints of a woman's little finger. The vial contained clear, pure rainwater.

The woman poured the vial of water on the face of the sun which was her hearth.

The eye blinked.

Never had Harry felt such an instant of pure terror in all his life. Now he knew what it felt like inside the abyss of Unbeing.

A little puff of steam rose above the blazing hearth.

Mmmmmmmmmm.

Harry was in the whirlpool again. Only this time it was carrying him down. Down the tornado, back to someplace, someplace familiar — his friends. Ground. Rock around it. Light in front.

The cave.

It was daytime.

All the others were standing outside looking at something.

Harry sat up slowly. He was still dizzy, but he felt all right.

He touched the side of his head. No more fresh blood.

He got to his feet. Still okay. He walked outside and joined the others. Meridell took his hand and squeezed it.

Overhead, the clouds were breaking up. Morning sun was even shining through a little. The warmth felt good.

Toward the construction site, which was straight out beyond the mouth of the canyon the cave was in, however, an incredibly dense black cloud roiled full of lightning and thunder. Under that cloud they could all see a torrent of rain pouring down such as none of them had ever seen before.

The rain stopped as abruptly as the end of the flow from an empty cup. Within seconds, the black cloud had faded to just one more rolling mass of grey. In a few more seconds, it blew apart to pieces indistinguishable from any other patch in the remains of the overcast that now really did seem to be thinning away.

Where the rain had fallen, they could hear water rushing.

"What's that?"

They all looked harder where Jeff pointed.

A little white column of vapor was rising into the air above the construction site.

The ground began to rumble beneath their feet.

W H S S H H H H H !

It was a sight so powerful it carried a sound whether ears heard anything or not.

Over the construction site, a geyser of steaming boiling rainwater now rose higher than the point where they stood. The meadow was fully seven hundred feet above the construction site. The geyser rose at least half again as high.

Soon the view was full of mist. They were several miles from the construction site. Even at this distance the mist was warm.

"No point getting wet all over again," said Louella.

She started for the cave.

"Think it's safe?" asked Meridell. "There could be earthquakes."

"It's all right," said Suzie.

Harry thought of the shield and knew she was right.

They went back in the cave.

CHAPTER THIRTY-SEVEN

"Now what?" said Louella.

It was midafternoon. The steam cloud had lasted several hours but finally cleared. There had been an hour of warming sunshine. Now it was overcast again, though not so thick. Perhaps the heaviest of the monsoon was over.

Everyone had gotten at least a little sleep. Meridell had washed Harry's head and found a cleaner piece of cloth than his T shirt among the supplies in the cave for a bandage. The wound still appeared superficial in daylight. He felt okay – or as okay as he could feel under the circumstances.

There was enough food to last a couple of days. There had not been enough sun for anyone to get completely dry. They did not dare make a fire. There were five or six more hours of daylight. If it was clear, there would be a moon, but there was no certainty about the weather. At this elevation, it would be chilly in any case. They had to decide what to do.

There had been several planes and helicopters, but they were uncertain whether to let themselves be seen. There had been no sign of Brownie or Chuck. Harry had told his vision as best he could. They all believed Brownie was dead, perhaps Chuck too.

"We've got to check," said Suzie. "What if he's just hurt?"

Painfully, they agreed. The next question was who should go.

Suzie's sense of direction was best. Someone needed to be able to carry a stretcher. Harry was strongest, but he was hurt.

"Maybe we should all go – not let ourselves get separated," Meridell said.

"We may have to walk over the mountain," said Louella. "I'm not sure how much of this hiking my old legs are good for."

At last, it was decided: Meridell, Suzie, Jeff and Steve would go. Harry felt wrong, unmanly, to stay behind.

Steve pulled himself up straight as an arrow: "Boy," he said, "you're on the disabled list."

Harry gasped. Master Sergeant Earl Upton could not have spoken the line better.

Jeff giggled.

So did Meridell.

Inside of four seconds they were all rolling on the ground, laughing like their hearts would break. God, it felt good to laugh again. How long had it been?

There was still plenty of serious business to be done though, and done soon.

"Maybe you ought to take this," said Harry, finding Brownie's old twenty-two single shot by feel.

"What for? They've got tanks for God's sake," said Meridell. "They've got the U. S. Army down there."

"That's not the U. S. Army. That can't be my country's army."

"No. Nor mine. But it's the U. S. Army's trained men and fancy equipment."

"A twenty-two'll still stop a man if you shoot first."

Meridell looked uncomfortable.

"He's right, Honey," said Louella.

It was Steve who took the gun.

Time passed.

Harry was getting nervous. It was getting late.

"What the...?" said Harry.

"Why that's..."

Louella got up and went out to the front of the cave to look through the bushes down the canyon. She could see feet before she could see faces because of the protruding rock wall which helped hide the cave. She stood peering intently. Harry joined her.

"It is," said Louella. "That's Imogene."

The dog's tail wagged as she made the half-whine that was her, "Hello," and trotted right to the cave.

Jeff and Steve appeared around the corner, each carrying the end of a pole. Meridell and Suzie walked beside the stretcher. Jim held the other end.

Brownie lay on the stretcher. His face had no color at all. The skin lay flat against the bone. There was nothing to hold it out.

"Poor bastard was still breathing when Imogene led me to him."

"How'd she do that? All the rain..." Harry trailed off.

"He opened his eyes when she nuzzled his face. Didn't move. I think his back's broke or his neck. Then he said something, but I couldn't hear it. So I got right down on my knees and put my ear to his mouth. You know what he said?...He said, 'Thank you.' Then he just let out his breath....And it was the last one."

Jim was crying. So was Louella. So was Harry.

"Imogene got us too," said Suzie. "We were wandering around below the cave, just starting to look."

"She nuzzled my hand, and I looked up," said Jim. "There you were. I don't even know how long I was there."

"What happened to you?" Louella asked.

"Bastards," said Jim. "Joe was dead. Clubbed on the head with his own kitchen chair. Supposed to been a simple robbery. I don't believe it.

"When the phone went dead, we went looking for another one. Half a block down the street, three cop cars boxed us in and pulled us over. Searched the truck; busted us for cocaine."

"I didn't think you or Cindy did coke," said Harry.

"We don't. They brought their own....Fuckers.

"Cindy made bail yesterday morning. Got me out late afternoon. The truck was impounded. By the time we found it, the lot was closed for the day. We finally got it eight o'clock this morning. Son of a bitch charged for the extra day too."

"Where's Cindy?" Louella asked.

"Probably up in a helicopter. You know what we found at the house. Pete Wiggins was there. He told her the Forest Service firefighting crew was helping with the rescue....There's scalded men all over the woods. It was still foggy in town."

"What happened?" Harry asked.

"That's right; you don't know," said Meridell. "It was all the rain."

"The geothermal hole collapsed," said Jim. "They'd cut through to a natural fault. A big one. When all that water hit bottom...You saw it go off."

"Man!" said Harry.

"There was a mudslide too. You know Ray Morse?"

"Sure," said Louella.

"A little," said Harry.

"He was in town. He told us most of the construction is gone. Where the ground was torn up it just flowed like a river. Scoured the whole place twenty or thirty feet deep. Some of it piled up against the woods and the next ridge. A lot of it went down the hole. Chewed it back up to where you can't even tell where it was."

"And now?..." Harry said.

"I'm going to make a fire," said Louella. "Then I'm going to say good-by to as fine a young man as I ever met....What about Chuck?"

There was a hardness when Louella said her husband's name.

"I don't know," said Jim.

No one else knew either.

There was dry wood in the cave. Louella built a fire and lit it. Jeff and Steve went to gather more wood where it had gotten at least some sun.

They brought the stretcher with Brownie's body into the cave and sat vigil over it. Everyone got dry too. Jerky and raisins made the rounds. No one spoke much.

It was too late to get down in daylight. The clouds had come back in, obscuring the sun. It showered a little again toward dark.

"Brownie told me once what he wanted done when he died," said Jeff. "He just wanted to be buried in a blanket. He wanted his body to go back to the Earth."

"Is it all right?" said Meridell. "Can we just do that?"

"Who else?" said Louella.

They did not have anything to dig with. They looked around, though, and found a cut where the rain had washed a hole toward the upper end of the meadow.

They wrapped Brownie's body in the brown wool army blanket that had been used for the stretcher. They laid him reverently in the hole. Then they piled rocks. They spent most of the morning at it.

The sky had really cleared in the night. Now there were only a few scattered clouds. The sun was bright. Birds sang. The air was clean. There were butterflies and bright summer flowers.

Toward noon, they said their final good-by and headed back down the hill to town.

Pete Wiggins and Cindy were waiting for them. Pete was just shaking his head at what had been done to their houses.

Jim's, Cindy's, Meridell's, Chuck and Louella's, the shop, Mrs. Martinez's and Burl Trent's houses had all been torn to pieces. Burl's belongings were scattered everywhere, indoors and out. The dead dog and burro had been removed from Jim's yard, but Pete knew about them. Jim's house was also partially burnt. The kitchen was destroyed. Most of the house was full of soot.

"Rain's all that saved it," said Pete. "Know any reason they might have had it especially in for you?"

"Wayne was here," said Harry.

Jim shook his head. "He never did forgive me for firing him."

It was Pete's turn to shake his head.

About forty bodies were found. Chuck's was one of them. It was hard to tell who died of scalded lungs and who drowned in mud. Not that it mattered.

"Maybe it's just as well," Louella said. "I don't think I could have stood a murder trial."

Harry gasped. It was true though. It was almost surely Chuck that killed Brownie.

Another hundred men were never found. Over a hundred fifty were injured seriously enough to need medical attention – mostly from breathing superhot steam. Quite a few of them died.

Buford Torley, Harry Smith's friend, was one to the men who died in the hospital. Jim George, one of the Indians from Oklahoma, was one who was never found. His partner, Johnny Sixkiller, was one of the survivors.

"'Why don't you go out for a real sport, like football,' they used to say when I was in high school. Guess being a track man paid off."

The troop carriers and the men in them and the tanks had apparently gone in the night before the blowout. The roadblock had disappeared within an hour afterwards. Plenty of people had seen the men there though and knew they were the army.

Paul and Pat showed up that night. Earl and Margaret showed up the next day.

"Always were a few generals that thought they were God," Earl said.

Something in Harry's heart rose. His father's faith was not broken. Earl did not know anything about Spirits. Harry did not try to tell him his visions. Earl *did* know the difference between the country he loved and had served all his adult life and some travesty that perverted it.

It was another day before Mrs. Martinez came back. When she did, she brought twenty relatives with her. All of them exclaimed long and loud to everyone who would listen at the outrages to her person and her home:

When Mrs. Martinez had gotten to the roadblock, she was first told she could not go through. When she insisted and would not be turned back, a man finally said he would escort her.

Two men went with her. When she tried to turn off, they would not let her. They eventually forced her to drive to a motel in Lordsburg. They told her she was being held in, "Protective custody." They would not let her speak to anyone or use the phone. They kept her in a cabin and guarded the door. Suddenly, what turned out to be a couple hours after the blowout, they simply went away.

Mrs. Martinez had waited, afraid to do anything for several more hours. No one brought her supper or appeared to be paying any attention to her. About midnight, she just walked out the door, got in her car, and drove to a cousin's house.

Perhaps as important as anything, a number of reporters were there, including the one from *Newsweek* who had covered the flood. *Newsweek* did not give very clear coverage to what had been done to the residents of Elk Stuck and to their homes. If you did not know what had really happened, you might pass over what was printed without having any idea. The article did imply, however, that something about the Thunder Mountain construction had been grossly improper.

Among the things that did make the news several places was the roadblock – too many people had been stopped to ignore it – and the lack of acceptable procedures before the construction began.

Newsweek pointed out how unnecessary, as well as illegal, it was to build in a designated Wilderness. The *Albuquerque Journal* editorialized on the obvious safety hazards that had been overlooked in undertaking the project without an Environmental Impact Study.

The Silver City Enterprise picked up on the safety point and expanded on it...but in a quite-different tone:

"Many people think environmental issues are just frills. They have been used too often as an excuse for ever-more government. Failure to respect the real environment is not only ugly and stupid. It can also kill."

That column got reprinted all over the country – mostly in small newspapers in conservative rural areas.

The man from *Newsweek* wrote a lot more than *Newsweek* printed. He sold more-detailed articles to several smaller magazines. *Mother Jones* printed a real strong story. *Utne Reader* picked up most of it. The reporter eventually got a contract to write a book and came back to do in-depth interviews.

CHAPTER THIRTY-EIGHT

Liberty

America, how quickly you have grown decadent.
The life of a nation is long,
And you can hardly claim to have reached maturity.
Yet already you look down your nose
At the way of life of the people
You depend on for all your necessities
And trample them or toss them aside altogether,
In a manner any feudal lord
Would recognize as immoral and irresponsible.
Are you determined to demand only luxury and subservience
Till you cut your own throat
Like the emperors of Rome
Or the Czar or the French king?
Have you forgotten that it was your revolution
(For all the abominations of racism it tolerated)
Which long inspired the whole world?
Do you think, misguided nation,
That it was the battle-cry of the conqueror,
The lust for power and plunder,
Which made you great in the eyes of humanity?
Do you actually believe that endless greed
And an infinite proliferation of cops
– Or a society requiring them –
Can or ever could fool all mankind?

Take up the torch again, oh America,
Which you so valiantly earned.
Liberty! That was your cry.
And, for all the foibles of your youth,
You came close enough to embodying that shining ideal
That you were the example and the beacon
To the aspirations of all who love freedom.
You call the Russians enemies
Because their rulers threaten yours.
You should pity them instead;
Their revolution was inspired by yours.
They fell into the grips of tyrants.

But they fought, as we did, for freedom.
And now we are told we should fight them
To increase the power of our own tyrants.
Are we so morally exhausted
As to believe such claptrap?

When twin monsters arose half a century ago
In economic collapse and in Hitler,
We still had the spiritual strength
To respond to the reminder
That our only fear was fear itself.
What now? Will we cower in dread
Of the sacrifices our ancestors did not hesitate to make
In Boston Harbor and at Valley Forge
And all the other places and times
Both we and our true brothers and sisters around the world
Have stood up and stood their ground
And even, when evil necessity demanded, fought
For the ideal upon which our nation was founded?
Arise again American people;
Be again a light to the world.
Remember your reason for being here,
And begin, whatever it takes,
Once again to live as you deserve.
As children, we were taught to pledge allegiance
To the banner of liberty and justice for all.
Did we learn nothing more than to obey authority
When it issues hypocritical orders?
Are we slaves who must mouth praise to our oppressors?
Arise again American people,
And let our cry, battle cry if need be,
Be once again what it ever was.
Let us stand together in honor, in justice, and in love.
And let what we stand for be
As it was to our nation's founders:
Let us claim our birthright once again.
Give us liberty; it is rightfully ours.

"Whew!" said Meridell, when Harry was done reading the poem his mother had included with her letter. "Where'd she find that?"

Harry looked back at the letter. "Local paper, I guess."

It was spring. Earl and Margaret Upton had gone back to Arkansas and bought a house in the Ozarks from Jessica Horton.

"Close enough to see the grandkids often, but not too close," Margaret said. "Sally and Bob do mean well, but they're as overbearing as ever. Maybe it's just as well. – We've each got our own lives to live."

Elk Stuck was quiet. Sun was getting into the canyon as the days lengthened.

Jim had never really lived in his house again. For a while, he stayed with Cindy and did not do anything about fixing up the house.

Jim and Cindy had to go to court in Tucson the last week in August on the planted cocaine possession charge. They were pretty concerned. When they got there, they learned the charges against them were dismissed. The evidence had disappeared. Everyone was mightily relieved. Of course, they were still out several thousand dollars to a bail bondsman, lawyers, and impoundment fees on the truck.

Of all the attackers on their lives, the most intractable was the I.R.S. *Nothing* but their own procedures mattered to them. Even when Aspasia Suny's former (and vindictive) boyfriend testified about a whole bunch of her shady dealings, the I.R.S. still kept after Meridell to prove she had not made more than the forty-two hundred dollars she had declared.

"Damned bureaucrats live so fat at the taxpayers' expense," she said, "they can't believe anyone could survive on so little."

Meridell finally wrote them a very blunt letter saying she had no records of money she did not have. She wrote that she did not make it a habit to record things that did not exist. She added that if she got any more threatening nonsensical correspondence from them she was going to sue them for harrassment.

"Not that I could afford it, nor would bother, but they can understand a threat like that."

"You're looking for trouble," Cindy said. "They don't like the peons getting uppity." But for whatever reason, Meridell's letter worked. It turned out that even the I.R.S. understood you can't get blood from a turnip.

Labor Day weekend, a couple in their early thirties from Boulder showed up, by the names of Andrew and Priscilla Hennicker. They had heard the news stories. They oohed and ahed over Elk Stuck and Thunder Mountain.

The shop was open. The news had brought in quite a lot of sightseers. There was enough of Meridell's work undamaged – and no shortage of trinkets in the dumps of the last hundred years for souveniers. It was the only immediate source of income for either Meridell or Louella. They needed it – both materially and spiritually:

"I've got to feel like my life's going on," Louella said. "Seeing the shop in business is balm to my wounds." She had replaced the window glass on the very first trip to town.

"She cleaned up the garden before the house too," Meridell commented to Harry a few days later.

Meridell was tending the shop the day the Hennickers showed up. They asked her a lot of questions. All polite and caring, but Meridell found herself irritated.

These damn yuppies, Meridell thought: They live in a powderpuff world. You'd think the worst thing they'd ever known was skinning a knee when they were kids.

"Has it affected your work?" Priscilla asked.

"What do you mean?"

"Your weaving. Do you find yourself weaving different patterns or colors?"

"I don't know. I haven't been able to afford the parts for the loom."

It was Priscilla's turn to ask what Meridell meant. Meridell explained that when the invaders – whoever they really were – tore up the shop and houses, they smashed her loom.

All of a sudden, it got real for the Hennickers. He turned green as a frog and sat down abruptly. She turned purple. Meridell thought to check the ears for smoke. She found herself liking Priscilla and Andrew Hennicker a whole lot better.

They bought one of Meridell's larger, more expensive weavings. They also asked about property in Elk Stuck.

"I'm not sure," Meridell replied.

She explained about the way LemTron had tried to force them to sell. Now the "offers" to buy were all cancelled. The notices had come just the past week. LemTron was no longer interested in Thunder Mountain.

"The geological structures are too unstable, and the mineral deposits have insufficiently profitable potential," the letters said.

No apology. No explanation. Strictly business. The LemTron operation down by the highway appeared to be closing too, soon to be just another skeleton in the desert.

Jeff and Steve were in the shop and heard the conversation.

"Um, you in a hurry?" Steve said.

"No," Andrew replied, somewhat mystified.

"Lemme go talk to someone."

"Is it all right to walk around town?" Andrew asked.

"Sure. I'll meet you at our house. It's the last one – the one with the room burned off of it."

Andrew and Priscilla went for a walk. Steve and Jim met them at the house half an hour later.

The Hennickers wanted a place to get away. Priscilla was in the health food supply business. Andrew designed and built computer systems for small to medium-sized businesses. What they wanted more than anything was someplace quiet and slow and nowhere near anywhere to spend a month a year and long weekends when they could. By Boulder standards, Elk Stuck looked the quintessential ghost town even on a holiday weekend and with extra gawkers news stories brought.

Andrew and Priscilla were both pilots and owned a small plane. Steve knew there was a landing strip at the LemTron plant. He reminded his father.

"You might be able to lease that," Jim said. "There's one over by Lariat too."

They wrote up a draft of a contract on the spot. Two weeks later, they were sending each other signed copies.

Harry was amazed that Jim would sell his house. Meridell was not.

"It would never be home to him again, not after they killed Petunia and Speed Bump. I hope he'll be all right."

Jim wanted to go to Alaska and weld. He did not know if there were any jobs but thought he would go anyhow.

"Bet I can get work repairing chainsaws if nothing else," he said.

The only complication was Steve. Steve did not want to go wandering off with Jim. He also did not want to go live with his mother in Show Low. He wanted to stay in Elk Stuck. Jim did not feel right about it.

"Dad, you weren't around much when you did live here."

This comment did not help Jim's self-esteem. It was true though.

Jim wrestled with himself a few days. Steve used the time to negotiate with Meridell and conspire with Cindy. Meridell explained the situation to Harry; he let her know right off that she had his full support.

A letter from the probate court helped swing the balance. It appeared Burl Trent's will would go through. Steve was going to be half-owner of his own house in Elk Stuck. The letter also gave permission to clean up at Burl's and get things out of the weather. They had not waited. Pete Wiggins had let them know he would not file a complaint even if anyone made one. No one made one.

Steve, and usually Jeff with him, had spent the rest of the summer sleeping all over town. Sometimes they stayed at Meridell's or at Cindy's with Jim. Often, they stayed in Steve's room at Jim's, which he had cleaned up himself. Imogene liked that best.

Cindy did not want to sell her house, but she was thinking about heading out too. — By New Year's, she would be in Oregon and showing signs of staying there. She and Jim would keep in touch, but they had never meant to be a couple.

Came firewood time, Steve and Jeff very earnestly came to Harry and asked him to do as much firewood hauling as he could on weekends.

"We want to be able to stay at Jim's all winter, so we want to do our share," Jeff was the one to say.

It turned out not to be Jim's. The Hennickers were agreeable but Burl's house became available, and the boys decided they would rather set up in their own house.

"I wonder what they'll do when they get old enough for girlfriends," Harry said.

"Impress the hell out of them having their own house," said Meridell. "They've got more privacy there than they'd have here. I wonder what they'll do when they get old enough for their own families."

Jim stuck around long enough to help Steve set up for the winter. — One of the last things he did was to move the woodpile from his house — now the Hennickers' — to Burl's — now Steve and Jeff's. He left in mid November. Cindy visited him on her way north, in Reno. He was welding for a big truck repair outfit. He still planned to continue to Alaska in the spring. He said he would call Steve every week, but it was actually more like every three weeks. He sent money more regularly than he called.

It was October when it occurred to Harry no one had harvested Brownie's crop, and no one knew where it was. He had smoked only a couple of times since the blowup — mostly when Jim offered a joint. He enjoyed it when he smoked, did not miss it the rest of the time.

Andrew Hennicker wanted to know if Harry could read a blueprint and do wiring.

"Long as you specify what you want for wiring. I can put it in safe and clean, but I might not know what to get."

No problem. Harry would have paying work right in town for the winter fixing up Jim's house for Andrew and Priscilla. Ten dollars an hour. Straight time. Work when you want. No records. The wages felt high to Harry, though he knew that they were not by Boulder standards.

The post office did close. Mrs. Martinez was retired and spent most of the winter fussing over her house. It took her a long time to feel right after the way her home had been violated. Louella might have been able to get widow's benefits from Chuck's disability. She did not even check on it. There was a small paid-up insurance policy. Louella used the money to buy the post office building for a cafe.

"I'm going to hire someone to fix it up," she told Harry. "I can't pay no ten dollars an hour, but the job's yours if you want it."

Harry said he would be glad to do the work for free. Louella would not hear of such a thing. They settled on six dollars an hour. As soon as the papers went through, Harry put the Hennickers on the back burner and concentrated on getting the cafe ready to open for Louella. – The Hennickers' house was livable by then anyhow.

Louella planned to advertise the Post Office Cafe as the southernmost restaurant in the United States over eight thousand feet.

One evening in February, Johnny Higgins showed up. He was riding with a friend from South Texas who thought the road was terrifying.

Ex-corporal Higgins had had troubles of his own since they saw him last. Without explanation, he had suddenly lost his security clearance. Then he flunked a urine test, was busted back to private, and transferred to a post cleaning runways in North Dakota.

"Windiest damned place I ever saw," he said.

His enlistment was up in December. He had once thought to make a career of the army. Now he was thankful to be out.

Johnny had heard a little of what had happened on Thunder Mountain. He was sufficiently nervous coming there that he actually hid under a blanket and waited till well after dark to have his friend drive him up. He was shocked and very sorry to hear about Brownie. He said he was not sure where he was going next. Harry had the impression he would not say if he did know.

Now it was spring. Harry and Louella had the cafe nearly ready to open. Andrew and Priscilla planned to come down for the party.

They had been down about once every six weeks. They were real pleased with Harry's work on the house. Some of their concerns seemed silly to people in Elk Stuck. There were some realities that having money had protected them from ever having to recognize. But everyone in town was getting to like them.

Meridell's loom was fixed – at least partly thanks to the Hennickers' purchase, and she was weaving again. She and Priscilla talked about ways in which the past year's experience *had* changed her work. Priscilla and Andrew also got Meridell's weaving into several nice shops in Boulder. They wanted her to come up for a visit. She politely let them know she was not interested.

Amazingly, but not surprisingly, Harry and Meridell were talking more and more seriously about getting married and even about having a baby. When he arrived in Elk Stuck, nothing could have been further from Harry's expectations. Now it seemed likely they would do it, and probably soon.

Jeff and Steve wanted to do a memorial for Brownie when the snow melted in the high country.

And Suzie was dreaming.

It was the day after the letter from Earl and Margaret. They all had RFD boxes now. Patricio Vasquez still drove the mail route Tuesdays, Thursdays, and Saturdays. He now came all the way into town.

"Bet the plow never did such a good job through town before," Patricio said. It was true.

The school bus still only came to the top of the ridge.

The weather had been clear. Days were pleasant, nights still freezing. So far this spring had not been too windy. It was a Sunday now, so Suzie did not have to rush off to catch the bus. She told Harry and Meridell she'd had a dream over morning coffee, but she waited to tell the dream till the boys came in to join them later for sausage and pancakes:

"Burl and Flora and Joe were in my dream. The Indian Woman came from another direction and joined them. They'd come to say good bye.

"'I guess you have earned your rest,' I said. But that wasn't quite it. They'd finished *something*. They were going farther from this life, but not all finished. Just farther away.

"'Who's going to protect Thunder Mountain?' I asked.

"'You are,' said Joe.

"They were gone, but where the Indian Woman had been, all of a sudden, Brownie was there, smokey old buckskins and all.

"'Hi, kid,' he said. 'I'm stickin' around awhile.'

"He smiled then, like he used to – just like a leprechaun."

They knew Brownie's mother lived in California and his father in Ohio. They did not know if he had any other family. They had tried to find addresses for his parents but had been completely unable to do so. Brownie had never received a single letter or phone call in Elk Stuck. None of them even knew if his name really was Brownie McGee.

"You know, Mom," said Suzie, "the snow's pretty well gone on the ridgetop. I wonder if we could get up to the meadow."

Meridell looked out the window at the bright morning sunshine, then glanced to Harry, whose smile readily agreed.

"It does look like a nice day for a walk...however far we get."